This Side of Hades

The Story of Medea of Colchis

by
Horatia Thomas

B

εἰπέ τις τεὸν μόρον

They called me a witch. They called me a murderer. They called me a harlot. *They* were men. They didn't understand. And instead of trying to learn the unsettling truth, they dismissed me as just some woman from Colchis – a foreigner to be despised as a barbarian; a priestess to be shunned as a witch; a princess to be called a whore. They never stopped to think what *I* made of them. No, your true Greek never does – they are so full of their own superiority, their smugness, their arrogance that it never occurs to them that others might despise them. Naturally, a Greek should be proud of his country and ready to die for it, but did I find Greece a cradle of free thought and enlightenment as I was told I should? Of course not. I found it full of smug men who preened themselves before the mirror of their supposed cleverness. And the worst of all of them was the man who brought me there – Jason.

PART ONE: COLCHIS

I

It has taken a long time for me to reach the point when I finally feel able to state what happened. But now that I am ready to speak, I ask you, my readers, to forget everything you have heard about Jason and to ignore the slanders which were written about me. For this is the true history of Medea, princess of Colchis.

Aeetes, my father, was the king of Colchis, near the Black Sea. Indeed, Colchis could rightly have been called the Black Kingdom. The soil is rich and black, not like the thin scraping which covers the steep Greek hillsides. Our soil grew innumerable crops: the fat ears of grain, the long whiskers of barley waving in the gentle wind. Then there were the luscious cherries ripening under the life-giving sun, their scarlet globes a promise of succulent flesh to come. Or the tall cypress trees which whisper mysteriously at night, their dark green branches sooty against a black sky. And finally, the delicate purple crocus, so prized in Greece for its saffron. So many flowers to be plucked, their stamens plundered of their secret gold before the resultant dust is packaged, exported and traded for real gold and silver.

Perhaps I was a crocus.

Greeks sneer at Colchis, but they fear it too. They scare each other with tales of many-headed monsters which, they claim, infest the region. Greek traders who have come to buy amber or wheat tread warily lest they be snatched by burly cannibals or ensnared by a witch. They find the silence oppressive and the mountains, so much more thickly forested than their own bare peaks, menacing. I thought it beautiful.

Somehow, I find it easier to write about my homeland than my home. I grieve for Colchis – the lush fields, the mist rising from the lakes in the morning, the sacred groves of trees. I grieve for Theonoe, the slave who nursed me, and Phrixus, my father's seer. But I do not grieve for my family. My mother I hardly knew and my father was disappointed at my birth. He wanted a son and never forgot his disappointment, even when he got his precious heir five years later. I should have liked to have loved my father, but I rarely saw him. When he did appear, he was busy with his nobles and had no time for me. But most of the time he spent long hours immured in his private rooms in the palace or making secretive journeys to a gloomy grove of trees which was approached through hostile thickets of bushes which never bore fruit. Eventually, he would emerge, re-invigorated and powerful. It was only later that I learned of what he kept hidden there.

I suppose if I believed in the new study of the soul I might begin to consider that Aeetes did me grievous damage by his mode of life. But I can see little difference between how my father behaved and how other men behave. Certainly, Jason only showed any interest in his children when it looked like someone else wanted them.

As for my mother, she disappeared every time her stomach began to bulge – she had lost one child the year before I was born and my father had decreed that she was to rest when pregnant, in the hope of carrying his heir to term. Naturally, the presence of a mere daughter was deemed a nuisance by him, although I have no idea what my mother's feelings were on the subject. Since there were several miscarriages before my brother Apsyrtus arrived, I was banished at regular intervals and once the long-for heir appeared I was still less important. Probably after this great event a female child would never have been sufficiently important to be allowed to pester her mother. However, except for occasional fleeting glimpses, I never had the chance to find out. After she had fulfilled her purpose in life, my mother lingered for a few months, before slipping quietly away to the underworld.

That was the moment when I realised that my father had little respect for women. As I sat, hidden amongst the hangings of my mother's room, trying to understand what death meant, my father invaded her last retreat. It is the custom in Colchis to bury the dead in their finest clothes and jewels. When my father lifted up the casket of jewels which lay by my mother's still-warm corpse, I assumed that he meant to add more necklaces and brooches to her lifeless body. Instead, he stripped off what little she had worn in her final illness.

"There are plenty who will enjoy these bits of finery," he declared to his steward. "The gods know that any female can be bought with a trumpery piece of gold. And whilst the women enjoy these jewels, I shall enjoy the women."

With the death of my mother, things changed in the palace. Instead of a bewildering variety of serving-women, I was turned over to an old slave-woman who belonged to an up-country farm. Theonoe tried to tell me that my mother was happy where she now lived, and, in my innocence, I thought that Theonoe could not know that my mother had been buried bereft of jewels and her honour as a queen. It did not occur to me that slaves gossip, and that my father's treatment of the queen had been whispered about ever since my mother's body was laid out for its final journey.

Theonoe tried to distract me from my uncomprehending first encounter with death by telling me that it would please my mother's shade if I looked after the son she had left behind. Since there was no-one else to advise me, I tried to do as she said. Indeed, even without

Theonoe's words, I think I would have been drawn to the fascinating tiny creature which was my brother. I knew that his birth had led to my mother's death, but when I heard his happy gurgle of laughter, or felt his enchanting minute hand clutching my finger, I found it hard to convict him of destroying her. Perhaps this fascination might have lasted. Perhaps it might even have grown into love, just as Theonoe was teaching me to respond to her swift comfort and all-encompassing embrace. Perhaps. Instead, Aeetes intervened. Catching me tickling Apsyrtus with one hand whilst I wiped my dribbling nose with the other, he bellowed in wrath at the tire-woman for letting me into the room.

"Keep that girl away. She's not wanted here."

I suppose that Aeetes must have feared that I would infect his heir with my sniffling cold and that Apsyrtus would sicken and die. However, at the time, all I felt was the pain of rejection. When I still persisted in sneaking in to play with Apsyrtus another pain followed, that of actual physical hurt. Aeetes was filled with wrath at my presence and he shook me so hard that I reeled into a wall when he released me. Later, I listened to him beating Theonoe; heard him threatening to hurt her still worse unless she kept me away from Apsyrtus. I began to sense that Apsyrtus was a menace to Theonoe. So together we shunned my father and brother – Theonoe because she wanted to protect me, and I because I wanted to protect Theonoe.

As I grew older, Theonoe told me things I had never known. And with that new knowledge came questions and anger. I was a princess. I was the daughter of the king. I, should my brother die, would become the ruler of Colchis after my father. Why was my brother given a suite of rooms, suitable for a prince and his retinue, whilst I was thrust away in a shabby, battered shell? He had furniture of ebony and lacquered oak; my quarters (if I may dignify the dirty, dull, poky room with that name) boasted peeling plaster and a worm-eaten door. Absyrtus slept next to my father's rooms, but I resided perilously close to where the slaves bedded down. Why? What did my brother have which I lacked? Was I not older? Could I not already talk? So why was I to be shunned and driven away?

Despite my anger at my situation, there were certain compensations. My new nurse was, as I say, from up-country Colchis – the area reputed by Greeks to offer sanctuary to werewolves and cannibals. Poor Theonoe dreaded the night and, as a slave, rarely tasted meat of any sort, let alone human flesh. Instead, she carried the lore of the country down to the palace with her. From her I learned the power of roots and herbs in medicine; I learned how to propitiate evil spirits; I learned to interpret the flights of birds and the way water flows. I even learned love. By the time I was eight I could use rue and anemone, and knew of the secret cures of saffron. While my brother played knucklebones with his father, I learned to cast amber beads and predict the future. And as the priests carried out their sacrifices, there was always a girl watching somewhere – concealed, but learning.

A year later, I shocked Theonoe by asking to have my hair cut short.

"But why, when it's as pretty as the corn in the fields?"

I shrugged and looked mutinous. Theonoe looked upset. "If only I could dress you in the pretty fabrics which you deserve. A princess should wear silk and jewels. Then you would see how beautiful you are and there would be no more talk of losing your lovely hair."

"I want to look like a boy."

"What do you want to look like one of them for? Nasty little ragamuffins, always running around screaming and teasing people for the fun of it. You're a lady, Medea, and don't you forget it."

I giggled. "That's not what you called me when you caught me at the honeycomb."

Theonoe tried to look stern. "Ladies don't steal sweetmeats. And don't you go thinking that if you were a boy you'd be allowed to steal, either."

"I don't want to be a boy; I need to look like one. Then I could get the priests to teach me things."

There was a catch in Theonoe's voice as she replied. "Am I not able to teach you?"

I bit my lip, aware that I had hurt her feelings. This was certainly not the moment to explain the excitement I felt as I observed my father's seer inspecting sacrifices or chanting out the thoughts of the gods. Instead, I cast around for some excuse to salve her pride. "You have taught me lots, but I take up too much of your time. I don't want you to get into trouble."

Theonoe shot me a sharp look, but she seemed to accept my excuse. "You never take up too much of my time, Medea. Now give me a hug and tell me that you don't despise old Theonoe."

I thought that I had fooled Theonoe, but she must have seen straight through me. A few days later, as I slipped into my favourite hiding-place near the shrine of Artemis, an old priest made a beckoning gesture in my direction. I stayed motionless, hoping that he had not seen me. He came closer. I wondered if he was furious with me for spying on the gods. I wondered if my father would punish Theonoe for not keeping me under closer guard. I wondered if I should flee.

"It's Princess Medea, is it not?"

The voice did not sound angry. In any case, I had already been spotted, so there was no point continuing to hide. I cautiously uncurled myself and emerged, attempting to look unconcerned.

"Greetings, o seer."

"Greetings, Princess."

There was a pause as we inspected each other. He must have seen a thin little girl with sharp eyes and a mass of golden hair coiled in plaits round her head. I saw an old man with a gentle expression, but sad eyes.

"Well, my lady, are you interested in the words of the gods?"

I nodded dumbly, suddenly aware that most people would think that it was very wrong of a nine-year-old to pry upon priests.

"Do you know how to make an offering?"

I nodded again.

"Shall we make one together?"

Slowly, reverently, we made the preparations. Once the seer had offered me a handful of whiskered ears of barley, he watched me out of the corner of his eye. I selected the best of the ears and laid them down carefully on the altar as I had been taught – three twisting to the west, three to the east, and three twined together to point to the underworld. Then we lifted a heavy jug of wine and poured libations, first upon the parched earth and then on the altar itself. We bowed and made our silent prayers, before retreating.

After our offering was over, the priest began to ask me questions. At first, they were easy, such as what roles each of the gods performs. Then they became harder, and finally I had to admit ignorance.

"It is good to acknowledge what you do not know," commented the seer mildly. "And it is good that you already have learned much."

"Theonoe taught me," I stated, determined to give her credit for my knowledge.

"Then Theonoe must be a good teacher and you must

respect her knowledge. But there are many forms of knowledge. Would you like to know more?"

"Yes. I want to know *everything*."

"Then let us start with who I am. My name is Phrixus and I am a Greek."

The next twelve months were wonderful. Theonoe had always done her best to teach me the ways of the immortals, but I had never dreamed that there was so much knowledge in the world. One fact led to another and each day brought new paths to follow, new discoveries to be made. Moreover, not only was Phrixus learned, he treated me with respect. He never once laughed at me or suggested that it was odd that a scrawny little girl who lived next to the kitchens wanted to learn the wisdom of seers and prophets. Nor did he restrict himself to temple matters; he also taught me Greek, devoting as much care and attention to my accent and choice of words as he did to preparing a sacrifice.

Looking back, I can see how generous Theonoe was. A lesser woman would have kept me away from Phrixus, but Theonoe took the risk that I might transfer my respect – and my love – from her to Phrixus. Of course, some might say that I was a nuisance and she was glad to get rid of me for part of the day, or that she was a slave and, as such, was incapable of generosity or love. It would be easy to say, but it would be totally untrue. Apart from anything else, Theonoe must have been terrified in case Phrixus complained that a slave had had the unparalleled effrontery to approach him with a request to teach her nursling. I doubt that my father would have been kind to her had he known what she had done. He certainly was displeased when he discovered that Phrixus was teaching me.

It was one of the scorching days which we get in Colchis, where the air hangs motionless and it seems blasphemy to break the silence with the crunch of pebbles underfoot. Phrixus had pointed out a solitary eagle, soaring far to the east, a speck of black against the intense blue sky. I was watching it avidly, trying to decipher the gods' will in its wheeling flight; so avidly, in fact, that I failed to hear any sound behind me. The voice came as much as a shock to me as it did to Phrixus, who was beginning to grow a little deaf.

"Well, Phrixus, is this how you watch over the fortunes of Colchis?"

Phrixus rose from his kneeling position beside me. "My lord?"

My father stood dark against the sun. "I need you to perform a sacrifice."

"Then I shall do so when I have purified myself."

This suggestion that the king of Colchis might have to wait for his will to be enacted appeared to anger Aeetes.

"I pay you to be ready when I need you. I don't pay you to waste your time on a girl."

"She is your daughter, my lord."

"Yes. And I have a son. If you have anything worthy to teach, then you can teach him."

I had just enough sense not to say anything in front of my father or Phrixus, but when I reached Theonoe she could see that I was upset. Eventually, she coaxed me into telling her what was wrong.

"Phrixus won't teach me any more."

"There, there, lovey, don't you cry. If you've annoyed him I'm sure he'll forgive you."

"You don't understand. Aeetes won't let him teach me. He says he has to teach Apsyrtus instead."

Theonoe frowned. "Maybe Phrixus will be able to persuade the King."

I sensed her lack of conviction. "You're only saying that to cheer me up. You know that Phrixus will have to obey my father. Why does Aeetes forbid me from doing what I want? Why does it matter that I'm a girl?"

II

The next day, Phrixus confirmed that the King had ordered him to begin to teach Apsyrtus.

"I am sorry, Medea, but your father has forbidden me from instructing you any longer."

"He is no father to me. I hate him."

"You must not talk of hate. Moreover, he may relent. In the meantime, you must keep practising what I have taught you."

"And who," I demanded, "is to teach me Greek?"

I think Phrixus must have heard the tremor in my voice because he did not take offence at my imperious words.

"Talk to the gods and the birds and the land."

"But I want to talk to you."

Phrixus put his arm round my shoulder to comfort me. "We are not forbidden from talking or smiling at each other. I merely cannot teach you. And since you are a princess you will be brave and not let anyone see that you mind." He sighed momentarily. "Priests are meant to be brave, too."

It soon became apparent that my father had no intention of changing his mind. I fretted and fumed with frustration as the days turned into months. I saw Phrixus occasionally, but I did little more than exchange greetings with him. In desperation, I even tried to teach Theonoe Greek, but she did not want to learn and I lacked Phrixus's patience. Finally, I decided to accost Aeetes directly. After all, I was now ten. I was nearly a woman. I could not keep wasting time, forgetting what I had learned. And I missed Phrixus.

I waylaid my father one morning. He had just

dismissed his companions and was laughing at some jest one of them had made. I hoped that this meant that he was in a good mood. All the same, his brow contracted when I greeted him.

"What do you want, girl? Can't you see that I'm busy?"

My carefully prepared speech evaporated from my memory. "I want to keep learning."

"Learning what?"

"All the things a priest knows."

"What good will that do you? When I come to marry you off, your husband won't be looking for a priestess. He'll want a good, obedient wife who does as she's told."

Since this statement suggested that I was bad and disobedient, continuing to argue was easier than I had expected. "But I can do lots of things already. It is a waste not to improve my knowledge."

"Is that some Greek idea or your own? And what can you do already?"

I reeled off a list of accomplishments. Aeetes seized upon the least impressive of them. "Perform a prayer to avert blight? Pah, Apsyrtus can do that already and he's far younger than you." He caught sight of Apsyrtus cavorting with a hunting-dog and snapped his fingers. When Apsyrtus ran up, he repeated my claim. "You can recite that prayer, can't you, my boy?"

Apsyrtus's face turned sulky. "I don't *like* learning prayers. Can't we go hunting instead? You promised."

Aeetes's voice hardened. "Recite the prayer."

"O Demeter, mother of crops, you who... who..."

As Apsyrtus faltered, it was my father's turn to scowl. "Phrixus doesn't appear to teach you very well, my son."

Eager to defend Phrixus from calumny, I leapt in. "You should say 'mother of crops, protector of the land'." Having corrected my brother's original mistake, I proceeded to rattle off the entire prayer. However, if I expected either of my relatives to be pleased, I was mistaken. Apsyrtus was clearly furious, whilst my father did not commend Phrixus's teaching, as I had hoped. He looked at me thoughtfully. "I might find a use for you, after all. You can attend Apsyrtus's lessons to make sure that he's paying attention to what he's being taught."

I was somewhat insulted at this new role, but not as insulted as Apsyrtus, if his wail of protest was any indication of his feelings.

"I don't need a nursemaid! I'm a man."

Aeetes bent down and stared into his son's eyes. "You will learn what I order you to learn or it will go very much the worse with you."

So we began to have lessons together. Whereas I was delighted to regain Phrixus's presence, Apsyrtus hated Phrixus's lessons. He turned up late, he invented excuses for why he could not remember anything he was meant to have learned, and he fidgeted all through the lessons. When they finished, he raced off as quickly as possible. I was offended on Phrixus's behalf and I also resented having to share Phrixus with Apsyrtus. After all, my princeling brother had everything which I did not: status, honour and my father's love. Why could I not be allowed to enjoy Phrixus's company on my own? Apsyrtus didn't want it. Phrixus must have realised what I thought because he warned me not to show any resentment to my father.

"Be thankful that I can again teach you, even if it is only before and after Apsyrtus's lessons. Don't forget that the King can forbid me from talking to you."

"He is wrong and unjust. Why should I be kept apart from you?"

Phrixus sighed. "A king can order even husbands and wives apart if he wishes it."

"It is wrong." I repeated flatly. "What harm am I

doing?"

"None, Medea, but try to look kindly upon your brother. I know that he is bored by what I try to teach him, but he is very young."

Since Phrixus was generous enough not to resent Apsyrtus's yawns and sighs, I decided that I must do the same. Indeed, I wondered if I could do something more, which would protect Phrixus should my father choose to check how well Apsyrtus was learning his lessons. The next day, rather than staying with Phrixus, I walked back to the palace with my brother. He was surprised and not very pleased.

"What do you want?"

"I'm worried that our father may ask you what you have learned. I thought that I could help you to learn what Phrixus teaches you."

"You mean you want to show off. You're always showing off to Phrixus." A frown descended over Apsyrtus's face as he remembered old grievances. "And you got me into trouble with my father by showing off."

"I didn't mean to."

Apsyrtus kept on grumbling. "But you did. It's your fault that he expects me to learn things. He never did before. And Phrixus ought to spend all his time on me, not you. Why can't you weave cloth and show off at that, instead of pretending to be a prince?"

I tried to remain calm. "I don't show off, Apsyrtus. At least, I don't mean to. I just enjoy learning things from Phrixus. And I do want to help you."

"Why should you? I don't want to help you."

"I used to come and play with you when you were a baby."

"So did my slaves. Do you think that I want them in my lessons? I am a prince."

Forgetting Phrixus's admonition that my brother was

very young, I retorted, "And I'm a princess. That gives me just as much right to learn as you have."

"No, it doesn't. A prince is a boy. You're a girl, a weevil-brained girl! Phrixus must be so bored having to talk to a girl."

As Apsyrtus ran off, I gazed after him angrily. He seemed to have forgotten all memory of the smiles with which he used to greet my surreptitious visits. A girl was good enough then.

Phrixus soon realised that I was unhappy. Nor was he distracted by my admission that Apsyrtus had rejected my offer of help.

"That is not the only thing which is worrying you, Medea. You must tell me what it is."

I hunched my back and refused to speak.

"Have you being trying to cast harmful spells?"

I remained silent. Better that Phrixus thought that I had disobeyed his instructions than have him learn that I feared he found me a nuisance.

"Has the King forbidden your lessons?"

I shook my head.

"Do you no longer want to continue them?"

This was so far from the truth that I burst into speech. "No, but what if you want to stop them?"

"I? Where did you pick up that silly idea? Don't you realise that I will soon be able to teach you sorcery proper? Not only will I have the enjoyment of doing that, but your own standing in Colchis will grow as you become more knowledgeable."

This vision tempted me, but Apsyrtus's mockery had left me doubting myself. "Why have I not started learning sorcery already? Am I not clever enough to understand it?"

"You are too young now. Theonoe will explain."

Theonoe did indeed explain. At Athens, they are so backward that they send little girls of seven to a sanctuary to learn the goddess Artemis's secrets. Naturally, they don't succeed. At Colchis, we wait until a girl is on the threshold of womanhood before she learns the deeper arts. And she will only succeed if the first fruits of her adult body are dedicated according to special rites. This gift of blood binds her to the goddess and the goddess, in turn, will impart understanding which is denied to others. Such it was with me. Theonoe taught me the ritual and the secret words, and I obeyed her instructions. Ever since that first gift of blood, my knowledge has grown and increased in power.

To begin with, my new arts were concealed, but soon it became impossible to disguise my talent. When it became apparent that I was more skilled at sorcery than he was, my father re-admitted me to the palace proper. He seemed to think that I was a possession to be brought out when needed and cast aside when not. He treated his hounds better, lavishing affection upon them, calling them by pet names and never failing to praise them when they brought him a hare or helped him to bring down the ferocious boars which lurk in the depths of our forests, all rolling red eyes and lashing tusks. It never occurred to him that my eyes might flash and my hands could lash and that no hound would have the power to bring me down.

Nonetheless, whilst my father had no suspicion that I might ultimately become a threat to him, Apsyrtus continued to resent my very presence. He had never forgiven me for first condemning him to lessons with Phrixus and then showing him up for not learning them properly. At five he had kicked me and jabbed me with his elbows. By the time that he was nine, Apsyrtus ignored me wherever possible. If he was forced to speak to me, he never failed to emphasise his superiority over me, since he was a man and I a mere girl, there to do as I was bid.

Oddly enough, it was Apsyrtus's very contempt for my sex which led him to betray his father's greatest secret. For several years I had increasingly helped Phrixus in all the many tasks that fall upon the seer to a great palace. It was little enough recompense for all he had taught me. I wept as Phrixus grew old and ill, and I wept when we buried him. Since I was already carrying out many of Phrixus's duties, it seemed natural to continue to do so even when he was gone forever. Certainly, my father showed no desire to have to pay for a new seer when he had a young and competent underling who undertook the same duties more quickly and without charge.

Perhaps I hoped that my new position would lead to closer intimacy and affection from Aeetes; after all, had I not learned more than sorcery from gentle Phrixus? However, if I had thought that my priestly duties would re-establish me as a favoured daughter then I was soon disabused. My father treated me precisely as if I were a replacement seer; there was never any hint that he was proud of my abilities or that he held me in any honour for them. As for Apsyrtus, he despised me. At least, I think he did. On reflection, I sometimes wonder if my ability, coupled with the fact that I was the elder, made Apsyrtus feel inferior. Did he turn to derision to bolster his confidence? Whatever the cause, we were certainly too close in age for me to understand that he mimicked my father's attitude to women, and for him to understand that I was not a threat. Nonetheless, at the time, I was consumed by the anger which afflicts those who do not understand why their world rejects them. Once, when I lost my temper and threatened to curse him, he merely laughed.

"My father would kill you if you did."

"Aeetes would not; he needs me and he needs my

powers."

"Your powers? How stupid you are, Medea. Don't you know that my father has greater power than you?"

I was somewhat surprised by this comment, since it was an open secret that Aeetes lacked the truly great skills of his sister Circe. I had no intention of revealing my hopes that I, too, might have some of Circe's ability, but I wished to understand Apsyrtus's claims.

"What powers? He is descended from Helios, but so am I. Why has he made me his seer if he is a better sorcerer than I am?"

Apsyrtus shrugged. "It keeps you busy. And you're ugly. None of the men about the court want to marry you."

Given that Apsyrtus was far too young to make meaningful assessments of female beauty, I could only assume that he was repeating the views of Aeetes. Unwilling to appear upset by such a betrayal, I returned to the attack. "What is this special power which Aeetes has and no-one else has ever heard of?"

"He's got it; don't doubt that. And what is more, I shall have it too. He showed me it on my birthday, but he's never shown you it. Women aren't allowed in the grove. No-one is, apart from the ruler and his heir. And I'm the heir, not you!"

With that, Apsyrtus left, secure in the knowledge that he was loved and wanted. Ignoring him, I thought carefully about what he had said. For a long time I had suspected that Aeetes cherished some sort of spiritual connection with the gods, but it came as a shock to me that he possessed an actual physical object which was directly linked to his rule. Growing up practically in the slaves' quarters, I had been aware of hidden talk as to why their master regularly visited the silent, eerie copse which lay in a hollow some way from the palace. However, such talk was both rare and hastily hushed up for fear of Aeetes's wrath if anyone were caught whispering about what must never be mentioned. Hence I had assumed that what little I had heard belonged to the realm of fantasy. All the same, Apsyrtus had quite definitely stated that there was something secreted away from prying eyes – and Apsyrtus lacked the imagination to invent such a tale. What he did not lack was the malice to use any special powers to my disadvantage. Young though I was, I knew Apsyrtus might decide to act against me without waiting for the formality of inheriting his throne from Aeetes – particularly if he thought that my own powers of sorcery were growing dangerously strong. It was imperative that I discover exactly what was contained within the grove.

III

Since I have resolved to tell this tale with all honesty, I am forced to admit that I did not display the courage that I should have liked on this occasion. I could have marched off boldly to the grove, daring the Fates to produce whatever Aeetes had hidden away there. Instead, I retreated to a wayside altar to Artemis where I mechanically wove a chaplet of millet and barley stalks before offering up fresh figs to the archer-goddess.

"Lady, send me boldness and audacity. I, who belong to you, who tend your altars and interpret your word, I seek your aid. Lady, send me courage."

Why was I in need of such support? The obvious reason – that I was frightened of what my father might do to me if he discovered that I had visited the grove – was not the cause of my fear. Nor was I excessively shaken at the thought that my brother would try to harm me when he had the chance. No, the real reason for my apprehension was the grove itself. It sounds silly to admit to being frightened of a clump of trees, but remember that I had grown up in an atmosphere of hidden whisperings and warnings. A man who worshipped rational thought might have bade me ignore old Theonoe's advice since she was a mass of superstition. However, such a man would have been wrong – it was just as rational to argue that, since Theonoe could cast charms and interpret the cries of the soaring eagle, I should trust her judgement that there was something evil about the grove.

Whether rational or irrational, I had another reason to fear approaching the copse. I never knew whether my father had intended me to become coarsened and vulgarised when he consigned me to live amongst the slaves. If so, he had failed. Theonoe had told me again and again that I was a princess of Colchis and that the blood of Helios coursed through my veins. Nor had I not lost my sensitivity to atmosphere. On the few times that I had been near the grove I had intensely disliked the malignant aura which appeared to overlie the place. There was something curiously repulsive about the mists which curled round the tops of the glaucous foliage like the trace of some great animal which had gone to ground as it waited for its prey to approach. However, I could not flee merely because the sun never appeared to strike the hollow. If I did, I would never unravel the riddle which Apsyrtus had unknowingly posed.

By the time that I had reached the barren field of stones which abutted the hollow, I felt sick with a fear all the more substantial for being unformed. I did not know what awaited me in that sinister grove of trees but, all the same, I feared whatever it was. Calling upon the shade of Phrixus to protect me, I whispered a wordless prayer to the gods and walked across the stones. The sunlight blazed down pitilessly, exposing my small figure for all to see and throwing an enormous, distorted shadow of myself in front of me. Every step which I took appeared to be devoured by that lurking black shape, as if I were walking into the cavernous jaws of a deadly monster. Praying that this was not a hideous omen, I forced myself to continue, arguing that when I reached the trees at least my shadow would no longer threaten me. This was certainly true, but the ashen dark which engulfed me when I stepped out of the reach of the sun made me doubt my own wisdom in continuing my quest.

Pausing to scatter golden sesame and bright scarlet muscaria, the one a gift from vibrant life, the other a peace-offering to Death, I listened to the bleak silence. Somehow, we become so used to the incessant buzzing of insects, the soft susurration of the wind, and the slow rustles of tortoises making their secret way through stalks of barley that we no longer consider such whisperings to be noise. It is the everyday background to our conversations and music and song. But what lay in the grove was not the silence which falls when people are no longer talking aimlessly. This was complete and absolute silence: no bird song; no crisp crackle in the undergrowth to suggest an animal's secret foraging; not even a leaf moving. I was, quite frankly, overcome with terror.

Crouching only a few feet inside the grove, I flogged myself onwards with harsh words. "No true descendent of Helios shows fear; no princess of Colchis opens herself to mockery as a coward. Shall I spend the rest of my life in fear? Shall I wait for Apsyrtus to choose when to remove me? Shall I cower and tremble before him, despised and despicable? No, I act to protect myself, and to protect my own name and status. I am Medea; Medea of Colchis."

With such arguments, I forced myself to move away from the last comforting rays of the sun and to plunge boldly into the grove. The undergrowth was tangled. Snaky tendrils stretched out to trip me up and trap me. Thorns tugged and pulled at my body as if to ensnare me in a grip which would never let me go. I fought my way forward for what felt like hours. Finally, I struck a path. My immediate reaction was one of relief that I could now progress with less difficulty. Then caution urged me to beware. Since my father was the only person to visit regularly, presumably this path had been made by him. Not only must I be on watch in case he chose to visit that day, but it seemed obvious that the path must lead to whatever object was the guarantor of his – and, ultimately, Apsyrtus's – rule over Colchis. The gods do not relish investigation into their affairs and I knew that I had to take care lest I trespassed upon ground forbidden to me by those mightier than Aeetes.

As it turned out, I was wise to take the precaution of edging forward slowly and stopping regularly to check that I could hear no sound of anyone following me – or lying in wait. After some time it seemed to me that the deep shadows of the trees were not quite as dark as before. It became easier to pick my way between the boles of the trees and it was possible to discern that the leaves were actually a deep green rather than the sooty, charcoal black which they had appeared to be before. Unexpectedly, the path kinked and appeared to come to a dead end where two impenetrable bushes met. I stopped, unable to go forward. Could I have mistaken the purpose of the path? Why did it exist unless someone regularly used it? But why should anyone waste their time following a meandering trail which merely led to a pair of prickly thorn bushes? The expectations of Apsyrtus could surely not be represented by those, however much they may have summed up his prickly heart.

In the midst of these speculations, it suddenly struck me that I could see the silhouettes of the bushes – indeed, of some of the individual leaves – rather better than would be expected given the general gloom I had previously endured. If there was more light than before then surely that was a sign that I, the granddaughter of Helios, ought to continue forward. Did I not belong where the sun struck, rather than in the dismal murk? Encouraging myself with these thoughts, I stared in fearful irritation at the bushes, wondering how to proceed into the light. It occurred to me that, if I could see the light glimmering at the bottom of the bushes, there was perhaps a route below the branches rather than through them. And, if one were about to approach an object sanctified by the gods, perhaps it was not inappropriate to reach it on hands and knees.

Scrabbling under the branches and biting back a cry of

fear as a twig snatched at my braided hair, I saw that I was correct. There was indeed more light shining beyond the bushes. Moreover, now that I had ducked down, I easily discerned a distinct trail which led towards the clearing in front of me. Reciting the hidden names of Artemis to give me strength, I crawled under the thick black branch and stepped forward onto the threshold of light. At first, I was almost blinded after the dim gloom under the trees, but gradually I began to make out shapes and then details. It seemed to me that one part of the clearing shone with more vibrant radiance than the rest. Despite the light, my sense of foreboding and menace grew. Remaining motionless, I stared across the clearing, wondering what was the source of the glittering brilliance. Was it one of Zeus's thunderbolts, crafted by the Cyclopes? Was it an ivory statue of Selene, reflecting the goddess's silvery rays? Or was it some strange magical beast, charged with the light which comes from contact with the immortals?

Reassuring myself that at least I was not dealing with the fiery power of the Chimera, I stared closely at the dazzling orb. It appeared to hang from a branch, a mass of silver and gold. However, as I inspected it, I thought I could make out two protruding growths. These curved round in gnarled spirals, at once familiar and alien. Suddenly I realised that they were the horns of an animal – a ram, to judge from the shape, even although I had never encountered a ram which could produce horns of such magnitude. With this discovery as a guide, the nebulous mass beneath the horns resolved into a giant sheepskin. I breathed a sigh of relief. True, this was a creature of unheard-of size and its fleece did gleam in a most unnatural manner, but at least it was a creature which I could recognise, not some utterly outlandish monster.

In my thankfulness at having recognised what lay ahead of me, I almost forgot the precautions which I had been observing. However, a sibilant hissing recalled me to the fact that I might still be in danger. Pressing backwards into the thorny bushes, but otherwise too scared to risk a more obvious movement, I waited, eyes swivelling to discover the source of the menacing sound. A thick, slate-grey head appeared, swaying from side to side, whilst a thin black tongue licked the air as if trying to sense the presence of an intruder. Slowly, the rest of the beast emerged, sinuous curve following sinuous curve, until the entire creature lay coiled beneath the shimmering fleece like a grim sentinel. I gazed in horror at its great length and the thickness of its pulsing body. The light radiating from the fleece illuminated the scene around the serpent, but seemed in some strange way to fail when it fell upon the snake itself. There the golden light changed into thick, matt black, and only dirty, dark-green lines served to show the outlines of the many scales which covered the serpent's evil skin.

Some snakes are sacred, worshipped in temples and fed on tempting pieces of honeycomb. Other snakes lick the ears of the sick and heal them. But I had little doubt that this serpent represented the dark arts of Hades. Above all, I knew that behind the flickering tongue were sacs of venom. If this serpent sensed my presence and struck, I should be left writhing in agony upon the ground, my disappearance unsolved until the next time that Aeetes chose to visit his source of power and authority. My only hope seemed to be that the snake did not spend every second lurking beneath the ram's fleece. Logic argued that, if it had emerged from the thick undergrowth, it would perhaps return, at which point I could attempt to escape. Logic, however, is all very well when you are sitting in an Athenian house, surrounded by friends and amphoras of wine. In a forbidding, eerie place such as this, instinct is a far stronger force. And instinct urged me to flee, to dash under my thorny bushes, to clamber up the highest tree which I could climb and get well out of reach of the hideous creature which threatened me.

Fortunately for me, fear froze my steps so successfully that I could not even retreat the few paces which would have melded me entirely with my protecting bush. Instead, I recited soundlessly again and again a fervent prayer; "O Helios, god of the sun, father of my father, save me. O Helios, light of life, begetter of our race, preserve me. O Helios, defender of earth, protect me."

Glued as I was in the shadows, I did not at first notice how the fleece glowed more and more brightly. However, it began to be borne upon me that the serpent was growing uncomfortable. Naturally, I feared that it had somehow sensed my presence and was girding itself to investigate. Nevertheless, terror kept me where I was. Almost unconsciously, I perceived that the dim, gloomy area beneath the ram's carcase was shrinking, but it took me some time to realise that, as the sun moved across the heavens, Helios's rays were no longer striking from directly overhead. The more oblique angle now at work exposed the whole of the serpent's side of the clearing to life-giving light. The primeval creature grew restless under the rays. I do not know whether it wished to flee the heat or whether it disliked the light which picked out each scale in such detail that I could see the traces of slime upon its back. Whatever the cause, I watched with unparalleled relief as eventually it unfurled its full length, before hauling its monstrous coils back into the undergrowth to mount sentry from the other side. Mouthing a silent verse of gratitude to the all-powerful sun, I dragged myself under the thorn bushes before retreating, shaking, along the narrow pathway as quickly as I could.

IV

Once safely back at the palace, my first concern was to make a thanks-offering to Helios for preserving me. Indeed, such was my gratitude that I made many. Moreover, I kept a tiny oil-lamp burning in my bed-chamber to ensure that I still had a hint of the sun to protect me throughout the hours of dark. All the same, despite my fears, I was determined to find out exactly what the strange fleece was which lay in the grove. If I did not, I would be unable to safeguard myself against a future in which Apsyrtus ruled as king.

To begin with, I kept a discreet watch over my father's movements. I was rewarded after some ten days when he strode out of the palace, unaccompanied by any of his men or hounds. Normally, I should have assumed that his somewhat subdued mien meant that he was suffering from the after-effects of a more-than-ordinary bout of heavy drinking. Instead, remembering the sinister serpent with an inward shudder, I admitted that even a king of Colchis might have good reason for looking serious and restrained. I tracked Aeetes at a careful distance and, when I had observed him set off across the barren field of stones, I retreated. I could not follow him across a wide expanse of open countryside, nor did I want to be caught lingering suspiciously near the grove. I could not rule out the possibility that some page-boy had been instructed to meet him several hours later, bearing the strong brew of honeyed wine which we ferment at Colchis.

However, although I was pleased to have confirmed that Aeetes did indeed resort to the ram's fleece and the serpent's lair, I knew that the greater part of the mystery remained. Moreover, I felt frustrated as to who could elucidate the puzzle for me. Clearly I could not ask my father or brother, whilst none of the men at court could be trusted not to betray me, Even if I made only the vaguest of enquiries about rams, one of them might have casually referred to my query in Aeetes's presence. If Phrixus had still lived I should have asked him, because of all the men I knew at that time – or since – he was the only one who did not wish to take advantage of me in some manner or other. In his calm, measured way I believe that the old seer felt for me what my father never did – love. However, whilst casting a tear for Phrixus's shade, thought of love propelled me towards one who definitely did love me: Theonoe. She would never chatter carelessly of my doings and, as one who was versed in magic lore, she was more likely to know of any hidden history of sorcery at the palace than anyone apart from Aeetes himself.

Waiting until the sun had reached its zenith and the palace was settling into afternoon slumber, I slipped into the kitchen courtyard where Theonoe was wont to rest under a great overhanging vine. Thick black grapes were already bursting forth and I could see splashes like blood on the flagstones where a hasty foot had crushed the burgeoning fruit. Motioning Theonoe to follow me, I led her quietly towards a little-used side door.

"I wish to make a special offering to Helios. Will you accompany me?"

"Of course, my lady. It is correct that you remember to honour your ancestors."

I hid a smile at this remark. Theonoe had drummed into me from a little girl that I was descended from Helios and that, whatever my current circumstances, I was born the legitimate daughter of Aeetes, and thus a princess in my own right.

"Let me slip into the kitchen to bring my own offering."

"Not today, Theonoe," I cajoled. "Choose some ears

of barley and grapes ripened by the sun. They will be more acceptable to Helios than a gift baked by one of the kitchen-slaves."

Theonoe seemed ready to accept this argument although, as I listened to her wheezing alongside me, I wondered whether she merely lacked the breath to argue with her nursling. For, although I was by now fourteen and of marriageable age, Theonoe still regarded me as the child whom she had done her best to protect against a cruel world.

"You are good to me, Theonoe," I said once our simple ceremony was over and we were sitting in the shade of a gnarled olive tree.

Tears crept into her eyes. "I would lay down my life for you, my lady."

The harshness of the sunlight beyond our refuge somehow made my eyes blink. "I know you would, but I do not ask it of you." I paused, suddenly reluctant to ask what I did want to raise. "Theonoe, have you ever heard tell of some magical ram?"

A shudder ran through her frame. "Medea, never speak of it."

"Whatever do you mean?"

"Child, it means death to those who speak of it."

In the arrogance of youth, I scoffed at this claim. "Don't be silly, Theonoe. Isn't there a secret thing which the kitchen slaves whisper about furtively? Don't they talk about a ram's fleece which hangs in a grove in a hollow near the palace?"

"Hardly ever," she protested. "It is too dangerous."

"But they *have* talked about it and so have you!"

Theonoe trembled, but made no comment.

"Well then, they're alive and so are you, so it can't mean death to speak of it!"

Theonoe grasped my hand in her wrinkled, withered

ones before peering up at my face. "Medea, my child, my nursling, I beg of you, do not seek to understand that which is not right for you to understand. The ram's fleece is a matter for kings and immortals, not for you."

"Am I not the daughter of a king and granddaughter to an immortal?" I demanded proudly. "Have I no better right to hear of this than a kitchen-slave?"

"It brings death in its wake."

"Theonoe, I *command* you to speak."

At first, the only response was a whispered, supplicatory, "Oh, my lady, I beg you." Then, when Theonoe realised that I was resolved upon an answer, she drew a deep breath and began to tell what I had never dreamed of suspecting.

"We must never seek to judge the gods, my lady, nor the nymphs and dryads. Sometimes they have quarrels. Such a quarrel arose when Athamas left his first wife Nephele and took Ino as his wife instead of her. Nephele wanted revenge and, since she was the goddess of the clouds, she had an easy method of exacting her revenge."

I gazed round our parched landscape, noting the friable earth baked hard after months of torrid heat. "Do you mean that she refused to send the rain-bearing clouds, gentle daughters of the heavens?"

"Precisely. Ino was furious at this attempt of the rejected first wife to force Athamas to return to her. In her ire, she looked round for a way to make Nephele suffer for interfering in Athamas's new marriage. The way was obvious: Athamas and Nephele had had two children; a boy and a girl. Naturally, Athamas had kept the children when he drove Nephele off, and it struck Ino that she could make use of them to exact revenge. Her first thought was to kill the pair, but then it occurred to her that it would hurt Nephale even more if Athamas was the one to slay them. So she told Athamas that he could end the drought if he sacrificed the boy to the gods."

I bit my lip to prevent myself exclaiming at such malevolent cruelty. "What happened?"

"Somehow Nephele learned what was planned and she sent a great ram to rescue the two children. The boy mounted its back first and grasped its curling horns whilst his sister clambered up behind him and held on to its great, shaggy, golden fleece."

"Were they saved?"

Theonoe shook her head sadly. "The little girl did not have the strength to hold on during the long journey over the sea. The boy urged his sister to put her arms round his waist and he took one hand off the horns to try to cling on to her. But she fell asleep, or grew too tired to keep hanging on to him, and she slipped off as they approached the coast. In his anguish, the boy wanted to throw himself off after her, but the ram spoke to him and urged him to think of his mother's grief if she were to lose both her children. Even then, the boy wanted to die, but the ram foretold his future: 'If you remain on my back you will keep the story of your stepmother's treachery alive and you will preserve your sister's name forever. But if you die, there will be none who know that she perished in that stretch of sea, and none to set up offerings in her name.' And, of course, the ram was quite correct. Why else would we wrap our tongues around a name like the Hellespont unless it were called after Helle?"

I frowned momentarily as an elusive chord of memory struck. "What was boy called?"

"Phrixus."

"Phrixus?" I repeated in shock. "Do you mean…?"

"Yes, my child. Our seer Phrixus was the boy who was saved from his stepmother's wicked hatred. The ram brought him here and he chose to remain, rather than to return to Greece."

"And the ram?"

"It was honoured by Phrixus as his saviour. Then, when it grew old, he sacrificed it to Poseidon."

I winced at such lack of gratitude. How could kindly Phrixus have done such a thing? Theonoe noticed my reaction. "Do not grieve, Medea. The ram asked Phrixus to carry out the action whilst it was still in its glory. It did not want to depart this earth an old, hobbling creature with no memory of its splendid deeds. It wanted to return to its father Poseidon, still able to be honoured for its great strength and beauty. Phrixus was a good man. He wept as he killed the ram, but he did what it asked because he, too, honoured it."

I had more questions to ask. "Who was the ram's mother? And is the fact that Poseidon was its father the reason why my father worships it?"

Theonoe looked rather uncomfortable at my first question and chose to concentrate on the second. "Phrixus once said that the fleece represented concentrated divine power. I didn't really understand what he meant."

Unlike Theonoe, I was fairly certain that I did understand Phrixus's words. Any child of Poseidon – in whatever shape it occurred – would preserve some of the awesome majesty of its father. Thus it became even more important to discover the ram's mother. If she were merely a mortal woman (and, as we all know, the Olympians have notched up many a wretched female to their tally) then Poseidon's power would have been dimmed somewhat in the mixing. However, if it were a dryad or a sorceress then the fleece would represent much of Poseidon's undiluted power. No wonder my father was subdued when approaching the grove.

"Who was the mother?"

"The nymph Theophane."

"Theophane?"

Theonoe merely bowed her head in agreement. I stared at her aghast. Theonoe had taught me my family tree and she had always taken particular care to ensure that I knew all the intricate details of my heavenly family. Hence I was well aware that Theophane – just like me – was the granddaughter of Helios. Phrixus must have known it too.

"But why didn't Phrixus tell me? I thought he told me everything."

"Phrixus always tried to protect you. He must have feared that you would try to find the fleece."

I sat very still. I knew that Phrixus had tried to protect me, and I had always assumed that he did so because he cared for me. Now I was suddenly presented with an alternative reason – he had only acted out of gratitude to the ram. I was Theophane's cousin. Phrixus could thank Theophane for her son's help by looking after me. That meant he hadn't cared about me at all.

V

It took me some time to persuade myself that Phrixus's concern for me had come arisen from love. In the end, logic, rather than memories of his constant patience and generosity convinced me. After all, if my fears were correct and Phrixus had only looked after me because I was Theophane's cousin, why had he not spent more time guiding Apsyrtus? Apsyrtus constantly pointed out the superiority of the male and Phrixus, as a man, might have shared that view. Moreover, it was Theophane's son who had saved Phrixus, so it would make sense to nurture a male child in return. But whilst Phrixus had always been polite and patient with Apsyrtus, it had become increasingly obvious to me that he was as bored teaching the heir to Colchis as the prince was in being taught. Surely that meant that the hours which Phrixus had devoted to me had been directed by a desire for my company? If nothing else, it was I who had cradled his dying head, trying desperately to interpret his last wishes.

In the midst of these worries, I knew that I had to return to the grove to make offerings to all that remained of the sacred ram which had saved Phrixus. However, I could not summon the courage to do so. It was not that I did not want to carry out the appropriate sacrifices. Rather, I could not think how to distract the serpent for long enough to enable me to perform the simple ceremony. Nonetheless, I did not wholly waste my time. By keeping a discreet, but careful, watch on my father I discovered that he visited the grove every month at the time of the full moon. Once, when there was talk of a threat to Colchis's borders, he went three times within the month.

Slowly, I began to realise that the fleece was in some way a talisman for my father. Certainly, he always returned from any visit reinvigorated – both in terms of his energy and in his lusts. Theonoe told me that, even when my mother was alive, if Aeetes spent a day in the grove he would spend the evening – and night – in celebration of his power. My father's choice of celebration lay in feasting – rich chunks of skewered flesh dripping oil and fat upon the paving-slabs, to be torn at by sharp teeth or tossed to the louring hounds circling the room. The thin discs of bread and saffron cakes which accompanied this butchery were tolerated, but the real attraction of the feast was meat, washed down by great draughts of resin-scented wine. Servants would scurry in and out bringing their lord's every desire. By the end of an evening, their lord's desire generally included pulling the maidservants around; fondling their breasts and bedding the prettiest who caught his eye.

Theonoe reassured me that my mother was never present at such exclusively male gatherings, although she had remonstrated about the dishonour shown to her by such a blatant exhibition of Aeetes's seigneurial rights. Naturally, Aeetes greeted such complaints with nothing more than contemptuous laughter. After my mother died, there had been no-one even to attempt to restrain Aeetes's lusts. It angered me to learn that she had been dishonoured whilst alive and that her memory was still dishonoured by Aeetes, but I knew that my father would greet with scornful disbelief any request that I might make that he temper his sexual predations.

However, something more immediate than my father's conduct was soon to strike at my heart. Theonoe had been nearly forty when I was placed in her care and she had wheezed and puffed for years. I was used to that and had thought little of it, but suddenly she grew tired and sick before my eyes. Sitting by her bedside, coaxing her to drink a herbal remedy which she had taught me how to make, I gazed at her familiar lined face and the unfamiliar grey tinge which now streaked at it.

"Theonoe, you must rest. I have given orders that you are to do no work."

"Medea... my child...," she whispered, each word and breath coming with laboured intensity. "I am... not long... for this world."

I cried out at this prediction, but Theonoe waved away my protests with a feeble hand.

"Listen... to me. Phrixus... told me. The serpent... never... sleeps."

"Never mind the serpent. I want to make you well. Rest, Theonoe, and don't waste your energies on what my father does."

She shook her head. "Phrixus... thought... you would... try. He told... me... a spell." Then, tortured word by tortured word, she gasped out the last piece of her knowledge of sorcery: the secret of how to send anyone into a sleep so deep that it was like the final sleep of death. She made me repeat her words so that she could be sure that I had understood correctly what herbs to use and in what proportions. When she was certain that I had grasped her secret, she warned me not to use it except in emergencies.

"It is not... safe. It brings... danger. You... may... suffer."

More to reassure Theonoe than because I had, at that moment, any interest in sending anyone to sleep, I promised her that I would never use her secret for trivial ends. She seemed content at this and closed her eyes. I stroked her hair back off her forehead, willing her to recover, although I realised with terrified apprehension that she was approaching her own final sleep. After an hour or so, she opened her eyes and smiled at me.

"Are you feeling any better?"

"It is easier… to talk. Medea, make the correct… sacrifices… to Artemis. Bring offerings… to my grave."

"Don't talk of death, Theonoe. Stay with me."

"We cannot… prevent the gods' will."

I clutched at her hand, unable to speak. Theonoe's effort appeared to have tired her and her eyes wandered away from mine as she began mumbling to herself. There was one last rally and then she died, clasping my hand and begging the gods to keep her nursling safe.

I did what I could. She had a good burial. The best wine was poured as libations to the gods; the largest cockerel and a pure-white chicken had their throats slit and the blood offered at her grave. Pure locks of wool woven with saffron-yellow ribbons hung upon her grave and I heaped rue and antimony upon the ground. But still I grieved. Then Aeetes and Apsyrtus discovered what I was doing and then the raw, wailing misery of my grief turned to raging fury. Apsyrtus was incredulous at the idea of grieving for a broken-down old slave-woman and attempted to find a reason for it.

"I suppose that you feel quite at home amongst the slaves, Medea. After all you grew up amongst them." He preened himself. "*I* didn't, but that's because I'm the heir. You think that you're important because Phrixus liked you and let you play around in the shrines. You think that you're cleverer than me because you crouch on the ground mumbling prayers. But no-one who's important or clever would cry over some stupid, ugly old slave. She probably didn't even like you – nobody does."

If I could have killed Apsyrtus at that moment, I would have. It wasn't just that he was mocking me – after all, I had grown to expect nothing else from him – it was that he was mocking Theonoe, who had cared for me and taught me everything she knew. Now Apsyrtus was sneering at her. How could he know what Theonoe felt for me? Theonoe had died with my name upon her lips. Theonoe had died holding my hand. Theonoe had died asking the gods to protect me. Was that not proof that she felt far more than mere liking for me? Was it not clear from the evidence that she loved me? As for me, people might consider it strange – or even demeaning – that I, a princess of the blood of Colchis, felt such grief for a mere slave. But I am not ashamed of my feelings. Yes, I was a princess, but it was Theonoe who instilled that sense of status in me. It was she who explained that my special powers arose from my kinship with the gods. It was she who told me tales of Circe, my father's sister, and of Circe's wondrous achievements in the magic arts. Who else had shown love to me? Certainly not my father or brother. My mother I remember as a sad, faded ghost, but Theonoe had nursed and guided me until my fourteenth year. Little wonder that I grieved over her memory.

Aeetes's response was more twisted. Although he had not seen my body arching with intolerable anguish as Theonoe took her last breath, he needed no oracular powers to interpret my red eyes and unhappy bearing.

"Weeping for old Theonoe? What a fine daughter I have bred! Don't you know that neither a ruler nor his family can afford to show their emotions? I cannot imagine why I brought you back out of the kitchen quarters if you are going to carry on like this over a mere slave."

Aeetes's tone of lofty contempt infuriated me. "Theonoe showed me more care than you have ever done, for all that she was a slave and you the king."

Aeetes yawned. "Did you see her as some sort of mother? Dear gods, at least my son respects his status as a prince." He shrugged. "Mind you, you did have some sort of link to Theonoe."

Since my father was clearly waiting for me to ask him

to explain this mysterious link, I remained resolutely silent, whilst inwardly casting maledictions against this most unnatural of parents.

"Zeus and Ares, you're a stubborn little bitch. Before I send you to fetch more wine, I'll explain exactly what I mean and then, perhaps, you won't stare at me like that."

Ignoring the suggestion that I was some common servant-girl, I waited.

"My wife, the late, lamented queen, was dull in bed at the best of times, but whenever she suspected that she was pregnant she used to object to me sleeping with her. I did insist the first time she expecting, but she lost the child and, in any case, she grew so fat that there wasn't much fun to be had copulating with a mound of blubber." His gaze wandered round the room, although I doubted that he was seeking to recall memories of what my mother looked like. "A man needs some outlet for his appetites and slave-girls have more uses than merely serving at table or scrubbing my clothes. Theonoe caught my eye about the time that your mother conceived you. And, being a slave, she couldn't object to what I did to her."

I stared at Aeetes in revulsion. He drained his wine-cup. "I slept with Theonoe right up until her ninth month. She fell pregnant at practically the same time as your mother."

"Ninth month?" I repeated in horror.

"Why not? Mind you," he added reflectively, "it was damned inconvenient having two lots of bawling and screaming going on when the births happened. I can't see why you women make such a fuss – it's not as if you're fighting on the front line of battle. All you have to do is push a lump out of your body – that's no harder than a man pushing his sword into you."

"You are disgusting," I hissed, unable to contain my abhorrence any longer.

Aeetes merely laughed in the face of my anger. "But you'll still carry out my sacrifices for me and read the signs of the birds for me. And, when I'm ready, you'll marry the man I choose for you."

"Not if he's like you."

Aeetes was growing tired of my objections. "Don't be ridiculous, Medea. All men are like me. We do what we like with our property, and the sooner you learn that the better. And if you keep arguing with me, I may decide to return you to the kitchens for good. After all, now that Theonoe is dead, there is no proper witness to what really happened at your birth. Perhaps it wasn't Theonoe's child that died. Perhaps it was the queen's. Perhaps she and Theonoe swapped the children – the queen could please me by having finally produced an heir and Theonoe could watch her child being brought up in luxury."

"Luxury? You call a revolting room which isn't fit for stabling a donkey luxury?"

"It would represent luxury compared to the lot of some slaves. And you would soon long for it if I decided that Theonoe had made a death-bed confession and revealed that you were slave's spawn rather than a princess." He snapped his fingers at a passing slave to fetch more wine. "Currently, I think that you have more use as my daughter. But don't forget that if you annoy me too much I can trade you as bridal-goods to the leader of our barbaric neighbours. It would improve my diplomatic efforts no end, but I don't think that you would like it very much, my dear."

Determined to show no fear, I fought back. "Nor would you, father dear. Remember that I have skills of sorcery. I am no stranger to henbane and monkshood, and I know the rites and words to accompany powerful spells."

"Think yourself a second Circe, do you? Don't forget that interfering in what the gods decree is not always safe;

why do you think that my dear – my so very dear – sister is spending her life marooned on an island? She may behave like a queen there, but she has no subjects over whom she rules. If you poke and pry too much then you will discover that the gods are swift to punish you."

As Aeetes spoke, I was visited by a sudden hideous fear. Theonoe had begged me not to ask about the fleece. She had talked of death coming to those who spoke of it, but I had laughed at her fears. Was Aeetes correct? Had I meddled in what was dangerous? Had I been too sure of myself, too certain that I was right and that Theonoe was wrong. Had the gods punished not me, but her?

Aeetes must have noticed that I was feeling sick to my guts, but fortunately he attributed it to fear of his threats, rather than guessing its true cause. Telling me that he had not yet decided whether to marry me off, he ordered me to leave him alone with his son and true-born heir. I was delighted to do so.

VI

Grief is hard enough to bear, but when grief is allied to guilt the feeling of impotent misery becomes overwhelming. Although I tried to convince myself otherwise, I could not shift a strange and terrible sense of guilt over Theonoe's death. I went over again and again the conversations which I had had with her about sorcery. Again and again I returned to the one which we had had about the fleece. She had said that it was dangerous to discuss, but I had ignored her. She had said it brought death in its wake, and she now lay dead in her grave. My father had assaulted her. Had I killed her? Had I practically thrust her into the underworld by making her speak of what she was afraid and had begged me not to ask?

Kneeling by her grave, I spoke to her shade. "You said that you would gladly lay down your life for me. O Theonoe, if I have, in any way, brought the curses of heaven upon you, then I shall rue it for the rest of time. I pray by your grave that Hades will be kind to you." I paused, unsure whether to speak of what my father had done to her. Only I cared enough about her to want to apologise, but would Theonoe's shade be ashamed that I knew that my father had raped her? In the end, I attempted to approach the matter obliquely. "You could have hated me, Theonoe. You could have made my life miserable and no-one would have stopped you. My family harmed you. You could have sought revenge, but you repaid violence with love."

Suddenly, I burst into a torrent of weeping and lost all of the formality which is appropriate when addressing the dead. "Theonoe, I am so sorry. I never wanted to harm you. I would have saved you if I could. I never meant to take your life from you – I said that I did not want you to lay down your life. I said so. You know I did. Please, Theonoe, forgive me." Dragging my hand across my eyes and trying to pull myself together, I attempted a coaxing tone. "See, I have brought your favourite honey-cakes and a libation of rich, blood-red wine. And I have perfume, too." Then a shuddering sob wracked my body and I wailed out in keening anguish, "Theonoe, I miss you so much. Please come back. Please, Theonoe."

The rest of what I said lies between me and her shade. Even in this history, some things must remain private.

Some might feel that giving way to grief in the way I did was undignified, even unbalanced. My own view is that I was fourteen years old, balanced between girlhood and womanhood, and thus enduring the time when a female learns with particular vividness how cruel the world can be. My father had raped Theonoe, while I was her murderess – an assassin, a slaughterer. Nor were the altars of the gods as open as usual to provide me comfort, since I was unsure whether I was fit to approach them, despite my desperate attempts to purify my vile body. However, since I could not pray for Theonoe without resorting to the gods, I was prepared to risk heaven-sent wrath if my purifications had been insufficient.

I do not know whether my father sensed how insecure I felt, but he seemed to take an unholy delight in doing everything he could to make me feel even more isolated and alone than I already did. I kept telling myself that he would not suddenly claim that his acknowledged daughter by the late queen was, in reality, a slave's bastard. To do so would undermine his position at Colchis and, if nothing else, my father was politically very astute. However, I could not quite shake off the fear that he might follow such a course. And since the alternative of being married off to some barbarian was almost as unappealing as being turned into a slave, I realised that it was much safer to haunt the shrines and to avoid further confrontation with Aeetes whenever possible. In retrospect, I wonder whether Aeetes's threats were caused by fear of my growing powers. Perhaps his references to Circe, contemptuous though they had been, had reminded him that she – a mere woman – far outstripped him in matters of sorcery. Or perhaps his threats were an easy method of keeping me quiet and outwardly compliant. Whatever the reason, from this point Aeetes deliberately set out to hurt me. There was, for example, the question of my mother's jewels.

Since he had first summoned me back into his life, it had become my father's custom to divide the evening feast into two sections. The first was devoted to eating and drinking, whilst the second was solely devoted to drinking. Naturally, I was only present during the first part and, similarly, I dined elsewhere if Aeetes intended to dedicate his meal to drunken carousings throughout. Nevertheless, one evening shortly after Theonoe's death, Aeetes bid me remain for the entire feast, although he dismissed Apsyrtus.

I was wearing a dress which had once belonged to my mother. That would have made it dear to me, but it was still dearer because one of Theonoe's last acts had been to clean it and add some new embroidery to it. I did not want to dwell upon this fact, since I had no desire to weep in front of my father. Hence I was concentrating with fierce determination upon the rather uninteresting description of the day's hunt with which Aeetes was entertaining his company. As the narrative drew to its dreary close, I became aware that Mala, Aeetes's mistress, was staring at me. Aeetes always had a succession of women in tow, but Mala had lasted longer than most of them and the amount of jewellery which she wore suggested that she currently stood high in royal favour. Perhaps this was what gave her – the bastard offspring of a minor aristocrat and a slave –

the temerity to look at me with an air of mocking condescension. I put up my chin and glared at her.

"Well, Mala, have you never seen a princess before?"

She laughed. "Of course I have: princesses and queens. I can remember your mother wearing that precise dress." She shrugged delicately. "It looked rather better on Eidyia, if you don't mind my saying so. But, then, you don't have her colouring. And she had jewels to bring out the sheen of the fabric." She laughed again and ran her fingers arrogantly over the strings of amber beads draped negligently around her neck. Then she pushed back her golden oak-leaf diadem, causing the acorns to dance in their gnarled cups and the gleaming foliage to shiver as if the wind was passing through it. "Still, you're rather young for this sort of thing, aren't you?"

Only the knowledge that a princess does not demean herself by appearing to care about the insults of the spawn of slaves prevented me from slapping Mala's face. Naturally, I had realised that my father pressed his wealth into the bosoms of the women he slept with. That is the way of men. But the realisation that Aeetes had given away – thrown away – my mother's possessions on a meretricious slut filled me with such deep fury that I could hardly restrain myself from spitting on her and stalking out of the feasting-chamber. I looked her over, enumerating her jewels. First, a heavy golden bracelet of winding, twisting coils which ended in two great rams' heads. Next, an ankle-bracelet of amber strung on golden wire, to match the necklace about her neck. A pair of finely-wrought droplets of gold in the shape of writhing snakes hung from her ears. Then there were four oak-leaf brooches pinning together the diaphanous robe which revealed every line of her body. Finally, there was that glory of the jeweller's craft, the oak-leaf diadem, so cunningly made as to appear as if someone had merely painted gold over Nature's own design. And each one of those pieces of jewellery should have been part of my regalia by virtue of my birth. Instead, they decorated the body of a painted whore.

Mala tittered. "Oh dear, Aeetes, I'm afraid I've shocked Medea. I thought that she was old enough to know that men like to give a pretty woman pretty things. She must be a real baby. Maybe you ought to marry her off so that she can learn a few things."

It was at that moment that I decided to punish Mala. Her possession of the jewels was my father's fault, but her mockery of me was entirely her own choice. That it might not have been a wise choice was something which I needed to make clear or I should face unending insults in future.

Considering what has been said about me, it may come as some surprise that this was the first time that I had used my powers to exact revenge. Both Theonoe and, later, Phrixus had taught me the dangers of deliberately setting out to harm another. But they were both dead. Moreover, since I had unintentionally harmed Theonoe, it struck me that I might balance the scales with some intentional malice. My preparations were careful and precise. I checked and rechecked my ingredients, before going to a wayside shrine of Hera where I was unlikely to be disturbed. Indeed, the gods themselves seemed to approve of my plans – high above the cypress-covered slopes of the craggy hills, I saw an eagle drive off a vulture which had dared to enter its territory. How else could this be interpreted other than that royal blood was dealing with a usurper?

The Greeks, who fear the skills of Colchian sorcerers, seem to believe that we practise our arts with snakes wrapped round our heads. The truth is nothing of the sort. We braid our hair with flexible willow, the sign of regrowth, and certain plants which are appropriate to our spells. I shall not give all the details lest someone be foolish enough to experiment with the information which I write, but it is sufficient to state that I bound my forehead with the furry leaves of hemlock and the gleaming bright red of muscaria. Praying to the great goddess, I carried out my sacrifice and wove my incantations over the ointment which I had prepared so diligently. This pot appeared to contain nothing more than a beauty potion, but when Mala applied the unguent she would soon discover that it was rather more dangerous than her normal paints and salves. In fact, the balm was precisely like me – apparently safe to be mocked or ignored, but full of spirit and power.

After I returned to the palace, I turned my mind to more important matters. Theonoe's last counsel to me had been to explain how to send any creature to sleep. She had clearly intended this as advice for tackling the serpent in the grove, but I had been too concerned with burying her and observing the correct rituals for the newly-dead to pay much attention to snakes, however menacing they might be. Now it occurred to me that I might use her information to help her. Originally, I had intended to re-visit the copse to perform a sacrifice in honour of the ram. I still wanted to undertake this task, not least because the ram was a kinsman. Nonetheless, there was no reason why I could not combine two activities: thank the ram for having saved Phrixus, but also sacrifice to Phrixus to enlist his help for Theonoe. Even at fourteen I was enough of a realist to know that, however dear Theonoe might be to me, the ghost of a mere slave would not rank high amongst the guardians of the underworld. Phrixus was a seer. Perhaps he had not joined the great mass of grey shades, flitting about aimlessly in the Asphodel Fields. Perhaps he had some limited power granted to him. And if I sacrificed to him in a peculiarly magical place, heavily imbued with a sense of awe and mystery, then my sacrifice would be more weighty. That, in turn, would encourage Phrixus to look after Theonoe's shade. It was little enough to offer her, but it was worth attempting. It was certainly more likely to help Theonoe than my despairing, unlikely hope that if I cried a myriad of tears the gods might take pity on me and send her back.

Looking back at my younger self with the benefit of hindsight, it occurs to me that I probably did not much care if I failed to lull the serpent's watchfulness. I did wish to do some small thing to improve Theonoe's lot, in addition to the regular libations of thick red wine which I poured to provide her shade with life-blood for a brief moment. All the same, if the serpent woke up in the midst of my sacrifice to Phrixus at least I should be reunited with Theonoe, even if only for a flickering instant of love before Death conquered us both for all time.

As had happened on my previous quest into the grove, the incessant music of the cicadas ceased when I crossed into the barren stony field surrounding the hollow. Only the sharp cry of a hawk provided any sense that I might succeed. Reminding myself that the gods scorned cowards, I set out with a sham façade of boldness. Whether my dissimulation would have convinced any close watcher, I do not know, but I strode across the sharp flints as upright as a heroic soldier marching into war, a long, thin stick serving as my spear. Once amongst the grove, my pace slowed somewhat, not least because it was difficult not to entangle my long stick amongst the branches which did belong there. The hardest part was to crawl between the two final trees without ruining my careful preparations.

When I entered the well-lit empty centre of the copse, my sense of revulsion was as great as it had been previously. However, this time I did not shrink back fearfully into the protective darkness of the gnarled bushes, desperate to remain unseen. Instead, I advanced unflinchingly, the slender stick my sole protection and shield. An ominous hissing presaged the appearance of the serpent, larger and more monstrous than before. It halted for an instant when it saw me. Then, sinuously swaying its head as if in disbelief that its pray was offering itself up with no attempt to flee, it slithered towards me, fangs dripping poison as the mouth of a hungry hound drips drool before savaging flesh from bone. All depended now upon the efficacy of Theonoe's charms.

I clutched the end of the rod and waved it in front of the serpent, shaking and scattering the potion which was concealed in two hollow tubes bound onto the forked twigs at the end of the stick. As the droplets struck it, the serpent reared upwards, hissing still more furiously. I continued to brandish the stick above its hideous, misshapen head and saw short puffs of smoke arise wherever the potion touched the creature. Suddenly, it collapsed upon the ground. Advancing with great caution, I observed that the lids of its vile eyes had closed, concealing its menacing glare. I had a momentary hope that it was dead, but the slow heaving of its scaly plates revealed that it still breathed. Dashing some more of the potion upon its evil mouth, I made swift preparations for sacrifice.

Although I have carried out many offerings, this was perhaps the hardest one I ever had to make. No ritual succeeds unless the suppliant has their full mind upon their entreaty to the gods. I had to restart my sacrifice to the ram twice, and only the thought of how important my supplication might be for Theonoe made it possible for me to carry out my planned petition of Phrixus. It is no exaggeration to say that I was left shaking with exhaustion after the effort to concentrate on the ceremonies. And lest my younger self be thought feeble, I defy anyone to have found it easy to focus upon the demands of correct observance when a fiend lay only inches away and might have awoken at any moment.

When the rites were completed, I bowed thrice in the direction of the fleece, before whispering more informal thanks to the strange creature which had saved Phrixus's life so many years before. Then, casting a look of shivering terror at the primeval, snaky form slumped upon the ground, I retreated rapidly.

VII

That evening, I forced myself to appear natural in front of others. I was worn out, but my attempt to disguise my state of mind was made significantly easier by the fact that most of the men wanted to discuss Mala's state of body. Many had witnessed her being ejected by Aeetes from the palace at about the time when I must have been in the grove. Apparently, when loathsome pustules broke out upon her flesh, Mala had had no more sense than to run screaming around the women's quarters, begging all to advise her what to do. The uproar had reached Aeetes and he had taken one look at her scabrous state before sending her away from him, spurning her as if she were contaminated with Death itself.

"All her clothing is to be burned," murmured Kartvelia, who had been Aeetes's favourite before his eyes were drawn to Mala's heaving bosoms. She appeared to be enjoying her successor's downfall and I saw with some disgust that she had no objection to the groping hand of Tarsuros, who was conveniently seated between her and me.

Manly Tarsuros cast a hasty glance in Aeetes's direction in case he could be overheard. Reassured that the king was busily cursing a slave for not bringing the correct wine, he smirked gleefully. "Aeetes knows what's wrong with Mala. That's why he won't give you any of her gowns, my pretty. He wouldn't want you getting infected – you might give it to him, if he hasn't got it already."

Kartvelia drew back in shock. "Do you mean plague?" she whispered fearfully.

Tarsuros bellowed with laughter. "Of course not. If plague were loose in the palace, I'd have fled up-country by now without even stopping to sacrifice to Apollo

Smintheus. No, no, Aeetes thinks Mala's got a sexual disease. He'll be inspecting his own privates for the next few weeks in case she's passed it on to him." He paused to gulp down another mouthful of rich red wine. "I'll wager he wishes he hadn't got rid of old Phrixus now."

I gaped at him, wondering whether I had misheard him. "Got rid of Phrixus?" I repeated.

The huntsman turned round in shock. "Bless you, Medea, you were so quiet that I hadn't noticed that you were there. I wouldn't have made that silly remark about Mala and your father if I'd known that you were listening."

"Never mind that. What did you mean about Phrixus?"

Tarsuros looked very uncomfortable, but I pushed him relentlessly until he reluctantly disclosed the truth. "Well, Medea, they do say that your father had an oracle that he would lose his throne because of a stranger. To start with he never thought that it could mean Phrixus, and you know how he careful he is about letting people stray over his borders. He kept searching for more clues and eventually he decided that the oracle meant Phrixus. So he killed him. They say that he used ground-up yew berries which he bought from a travelling pedlar years ago and kept in case he might need them."

Trying to control my shaking hands, I ran my tongue over my lips, much as the serpent had done. I had a sudden fear that my heart was black as the serpent's. Phrixus had foresworn the use of magic for cruel ends. But, in the midst of my triumphant revenge over Mala, I had suddenly learned this vile, hateful news. Could, somehow, Phrixus's natural death have metamorphosed into something dreadful and wicked because I had used my powers for the sake of vengeance? Was that why I had been told the truth now? Was it a warning to me?

Naturally, from the standpoint of my current old age, I can dismiss these fears as the warped superstition of a young woman, but at the time I was terribly shocked. Moreover, I felt appallingly guilty that I had not noticed that something was badly wrong with Phrixus. If only I had, then I could have acted sooner. I had tried to calm his symptoms – the racking convulsive spasms, the vomiting and the slow, laboured breathing. But I had failed. I had stood by and watched the visitation of the cold hand of Death. If I had known that he was suffering from deliberate poisoning, perhaps I could have found a cure. Perhaps I could have saved him. It is easier to beseech the gods' help if you are specific than if you mouth vague prayers for aid. With knowledge, I might have been able to direct Apollo's intervention more effectively. Above all, if I had watched Phrixus more carefully, I should have had more time. More time to save him and more time to be with him, to listen to his dear voice, to reassure him that I loved him.

Tarsuros tried to speak to me, but I slipped out of the room, wishing that yew trees grew in Colchis.

VIII

Over the next few months, I found it difficult to concentrate on anything. Even the weather seemed to range itself upon me – howling gales drove pelting sleet across the face of the sun, and day by day the light surrendered more and more territory to icy winter. Certainly, I had no interest in returning to the grove. What was the point in lulling snakes to sleep if I was so blind that I could not notice when a man was poisoned before my very eyes? Eventually, my father noticed that I was less responsive than before and that I was disinclined to take part in prophecy. At first he commanded me irritably to get on with my tasks. Then, one day, an explanation of my grim mien and general air of sullen hatred presented itself to him. And, since he was a man, that explanation was neither flattering nor true. To make matters worse, he chose to reveal his thinking in front of Apsyrtus.

"Well, Medea, I've thought of a cure for your sulkiness and your rudeness. What you need is a man to master you."

I glared at him, but he was unfinished.

"A man and a man's ways will give you something to think about, especially if he's not as patient with you as I am. You'll soon have a good few children to keep you busy, too, unless you prove to be as bad a breeder as your mother was."

My brother now chose to add his contribution to the discussion. "But, Father, men want a pretty woman and Medea's so ugly. You'd have to provide an enormous dowry to tempt anyone to take her on. Is it really a good use of our treasury to give away so much gold?" He frowned in thought. "Wouldn't you be better just banishing her to a shrine somewhere off the coast? That would cost hardly anything and she'd be quite happy reciting prayers to the gods."

Aeetes was deeply amused with this concern for the finances of Colchis. "Spoken like a man and a prince, my son! Perhaps I should take your advice. But there would be no-one to tame your sister's sulky temper on a barren island. I don't imagine that the sea-birds would teach her to mend her ways."

Although my father seemed to have reluctantly decided against exile as a means of disposing of me, he did not progress far in his attempts to find a man to master me. Perhaps Apsyrtus's words about the cost of a dowry had struck home. Whilst I was grateful for this caution, there was a bitter irony in watching a man who happily squandered his patrimony on whores jib at providing his daughter with the finery suitable to her position. Admittedly, I may have done Aeetes an injustice. Perhaps what motivated him was fear, rather than greed or parsimony. Since he could hardly marry me off to a mere nobody without causing the most egregious gossip, Aeetes would have to select one of the nobles at court. However, that carried the danger that I might give all my loyalty to my new husband. In turn, he might pose a threat to Aeetes's throne – there are plenty of examples of thrusting young men who overturn kings and seize power for themselves. Such upstarts often choose to marry some beleaguered remnant of the royal family to provide legitimacy to their rule. Aeetes was quite crafty enough to fear that, if he did not chose the candidate for my hand extremely carefully, mere marriage to me might give my new groom ideas beyond the norm.

In retrospect, I think my wits must have been dulled by the dark winter days. It never occurred to me that there was a third possibility, which also involved exile, but not to an island. As shivering winter turned to spring and then summer, still my father taunted me with the threat that he intended to marry me off. I ignored him. However, beneath my carapace of contemptuous calm, a thread of worry wormed its way through me. I should be sixteen in the winter. If Aeetes did not arrange a marriage soon, people would begin to question why. Despite Apsyrtus's taunts about my appearance, I knew that I was not actively ugly. My skin was better than most girls' and when I smiled (which was rare enough these days) my face lit up with laughter. True, no man had deliberately sought me out to make better acquaintance of me. However, that was partly because of my position as princess. Although Aeetes enjoyed the appearance of being an approachable ruler who liked nothing better than to relax in the company of his hunting cronies, he had a strong autocratic streak to him. I strongly doubted whether any of the men at court would have the temerity to approach the king to ask for his daughter's hand in marriage. To do so would have been tantamount to admitting that they had aspirations to royal status themselves. We Colchians are brave, but not rashly foolhardy. Thus no suitor to my hand appeared.

But I was still busy. Every day I experimented and learned from my experiments. Common ears of barley were as useful as the spices and brilliant lapis which had travelled slowly down the Oxus. Fungus garnered before dawn produced results as interesting as those achieved with the strange mulberries, twisted and bleeding, traded from the innermost regions of Persia. Even the gnarled whorls of tortoises began to reveal the secrets of their patterns, although chelonemancy is an art so esoteric that it is hardly whispered of amongst seers.

Part of my work was driven by fear. I did not trust Aeetes and I dreaded Apsyrtus's malice should he become king. The greater my knowledge of hidden lore, the greater my chance of protecting myself against my male kinsmen.

However, I was also motivated by the sheer joy of discovery. Understanding the words of the stork as he clapped his beak at his mate might not prevent my father from marrying me off against my will, but such knowledge had an excitement all of its own. The only sadness that came from such discoveries was the awareness that I could no longer share them with Theonoe or Phrixus. I still grieved for both of them, particularly Theonoe. That wound remained raw, and the slightest breath stung and burnt. Only the lumbering tortoises and the cicadas heard my woe, for they could be trusted not to sneer or taunt me.

All too soon, the dark winter days returned, consuming the light and driving the sun to the far reaches of the sky. I could no longer flee my father and brother by devoting myself to research beneath the cerulean sky. Instead, I copied the sun, spending the daylight in far-off shrines and the dark immured in the palace store-rooms. Unfortunately, I could not always avoid the doubtful joys of Aeetes's feasts. In recognition of Apsyrtus's exalted status, he dined at my father's right hand every night. One night, when the stars were glittering with a bright magnificence, Apsyrtus celebrated the fact that he had killed his first boar. Naturally, he had been on hunting expeditions before, but then he had been helping his father. That day he had been treated as a man and allowed to act on his own. Now he was reliving the excitement of the hunt by retelling his tale to Tarsuros. For his part, Tarsuros listened with all the amused patience of a man who has no intention of offending the heir to the throne by pointing out that he had been ready to take action if Apsyrtus's aim – or nerve – had faltered.

"You should have seen the boar's expression when it charged, Tarsuros. Its eyes were rolling and I could see that it intended to gouge me with its tusks. That's when I threw my first spear. It hit the boar on the flank, but the brute still kept coming at me. I wasn't afraid, despite its size."

"Indeed not, you stood up to it as straight as any soldier."

Apsyrtus looked pleased. "Well, I'm a man now, so it's my duty to be brave."

I suppose that I ought to have scoffed at the idea of an eleven-year-old counting as a fully-grown man. Instead, watching his face, flushed with pride, and hearing his excited chatter, I wished that Apsyrtus was my brother in more than name. If we had ever been allowed to become close, I would have been praising him and exclaiming at his bravery, not Tarsuros. Apsyrtus might even have offered me the tusks as a souvenir. So compelling was the picture of what might have been that I leaned over towards him.

"You have shown yourself to be a true prince of Colchis, Apsyrtus."

He turned cold, expressionless eyes upon me. "I'm talking to the men. You don't have a place in this conversation."

I sat as still as if I had been transfixed by one of his spears. I tried to convince myself that Tarsuros had given Apsyrtus too much wine with which to celebrate his triumph, but I knew that my brother was correct. I didn't have a place. I didn't belong.

I am still unsure as to how I would have responded to Apsyrtus, but I was not forced to. At the precise moment that he had finished brushing me aside, a trumpet blared and the great bronze doors at the end of the hall were opened ceremoniously. Everyone turned to stare. Even Aeetes stopped eating, his hand half-way to his mouth. Clearly he was not expecting any visitor of consequence. Our steward entered, bowed low in the direction of my father and announced loudly,

"A noble stranger begs leave to enter and speak with you, my lord."

"Bring him in."

Like the others, I watched to see who would enter. The stranger could not be a mere trader or he would not have been announced with such ceremony. Moreover, the sea-lanes were still too dangerous for trading-vessels to risk the storms which ravaged the Black Sea without warning at this time of year. The dangers of sea-travel made it equally unlikely that the visitor was a pirate pretending to be an innocent man whilst he spied out the prospects for loot. I could not believe that some chance buccaneer would have been fool enough to challenge Aeetes when there was easier prey elsewhere. Aeetes kept a close guard on his coastal borders and pirates had never evaded his observation yet. Perhaps the traveller was a wandering seer from Persia. I rather hoped so, since then I might have a chance to talk to someone who shared my interests.

The stranger advanced, bathed in a pool of light shed by the torch which flamed and danced in the hands of our steward.

"Greetings, o noble king. I am Jason, son of Aeson, of Iolcos."

IX

Looking back, I really cannot imagine why I married Jason. But when he advanced in that pool of light, a sudden rush of interest surged through me. He looked different; he sounded different; he even strode forward in a way quite unlike the men I was used to seeing around the palace. His hair was crisply curled; his cloak was decorated with unusual embroidery; even his voice was a different pitch to my father's. He was, in short, foreign and exotic. I found that exciting. Exciting, too, were the adventures of which he spoke – strange beasts which he had destroyed, hideous tribes which he had conquered, a ship which could speak. Even my father was impressed, whilst Apsyrtus gawped at him as if he were a god come down to earth.

"A ship which can speak?" he repeated.

Jason nodded. "A section of oak in the prow came from a sacred tree in the sanctuary of Zeus at Dodona. There is an oracle at Dodona and the tree has acquired the power of speech from being surrounded by the presence of Zeus."

Although I should have liked to hear more about an oracular shrine, Apsyrtus's mind was running upon adventures. "Did you kill any men on the way here?"

Jason paused, as if wondering which of many tales to tell. "One of the most violent men we met was Amycus, the King of the Bebryces. He prided himself on being a splendid boxer and he constantly challenged his neighbours to fight with him. We had scarcely stepped onto the shore when he appeared and demanded that one of us box with him."

"An unusual display of hospitality," commented my father dryly.

"Indeed, sir. I need hardly say that I knew that I would

meet a different reception here in Colchis."

Apsyrtus was uninterested in this discussion about the correct method by which to entertain strangers. "Did you fight him? What happened to him?"

"Our best boxer was Polydeuces and he immediately stepped forward before anyone else had a chance to volunteer. He didn't know that Amycus had killed several men in similar fights, but it would not have stopped him even if he had. His muscles rippled in the sun as he stripped, and he looked as strong as the gods could wish a man to be. I glanced at Amycus, wondering whether he was regretting his insolent challenge, but he tied on his raw-hide gloves eagerly enough."

As Jason leaned forward to raise his wine-cup, I noticed how tanned and powerful his arms appeared to be. Months of rowing must have made him very fit. I dragged my mind back from such speculation and tried to concentrate on his tale. I disliked descriptions of fights, but if the quality of hospitality on offer at Colchis was on trial, it would not do for my interest to wander.

"The two combatants had scarcely held up their gloves when Amycus hurled himself forward, the weight of his body behind his charge. Polydeuces feinted to his left, but Amycus followed up every move, constantly upon the attack. So savage were his punches that I momentarily feared that Polydeuces must be defeated, but he stood up to Amycus and returned blow for blow. Blood was pouring from Polydeuces's cheekbones, but I could see that he had also gouged Amycus's face. The blows were incessant, but eventually the two drew apart, panting like horses which have been pushed almost to their limit."

"Was that the end of it?" demanded Apsyrtus, in disappointed tones.

"No, no. They fell upon each other again. Amycus rose to his full height and struck out at Polydeuces. It was like a man hammering an anvil, and, if the blow had gone home, I think that Polydeuces would have been felled to the ground. But he dodged to one side, so the blow only struck his forearm, not his head. Then Polydeuces landed a blow on Amycus's ear – one so heavy that it smashed the bones inside. Amycus collapsed to the ground in his death agony. That was when the Bebryces seized their clubs and charged forward to save their king."

"Presumably you intervened at that moment," commented my father, in a tone I did not understand.

Jason bowed in his direction. "Indeed we did, O Aeetes. We seized our swords and ran forward to meet them, striking many deadly blows. We were like a pack of grey wolves attacking a flock of sheep. They scattered in confusion and fled inland, so we rounded up a fine selection of cattle and held a great feast to celebrate our victory."

Apsyrtus listened enthralled to this account, but I have to admit that I winced inwardly at some of the more violent aspects. Jason's description of how he passed between the Clashing Rocks was more to my taste, since it showed real thought. Instead of dashing wildly at the rocks in the hope of making passage between them, he sent a bird ahead of the *Argo*. It flew straight between the rocks, losing only its tail-feathers. That indicated that the *Argo* would be safe, and so it proved to be when the Argonauts rowed through. Even more to my taste was Jason's readiness to ascribe his success to the gods. "I am fortunate that both Hera and Athena have helped me on my journeys. I never forget what I owe to the gods."

Jason's tales were certainly impressive and I listened with as much interest as the rest. One of them, however, came as a great shock to me. My father had just asked Jason how he managed to reach the palace, despite the fact that dreadful storms had been blowing.

"I came by an overland route, sir. Chalciope advised me not to risk sailing further south."

It seemed to me that my father's smile froze momentarily on the name. I wondered idly if Chalciope was some cast-off mistress – Aeetes had so many.

"She is in good health and sends you greetings, sir," persevered Jason, "but she asked me to tell you that she is lonely."

Aeetes frowned. "What does she mean by that?"

"She told me that her greatest dream would be to return to the palace and be by your side, as daughter and father ought to be."

If Jason had let loose his Harpies in the middle of the hall he could hardly have caused greater consternation. My father was clearly annoyed, whilst, for once, Apsyrtus and I were united in shock at this revelation of an unknown sister. Fortunately, I had sufficient sense not to ask the questions which Apsyrtus blurted out without thinking.

"Who is Chalciope? Who was her mother?"

Aeetes scowled him into silence, not wishing to have a son's odd ignorance of a family member displayed in front of a stranger. Instead, he turned back to Jason, addressing him in a less friendly tone than he had used previously.

"How did you meet my daughter? She ought not to be entertaining strange men in her house."

Jason gave a brief bow of his head in recognition of this universal truth. "Forgive me, o king, but I had good reason to seek her out. Naturally, I should have preferred to have spoken to her in your presence, but she lives in an isolated spot and I did not wish to delay the joy I knew she would feel at having her sons returned to her."

Now it was Aeetes's turn to display ignorance. "Why in Hades had they ever left her?"

"I gather," explained Jason cautiously, "that they had wished to make the acquaintance of their grandfather. They set off at the tail end of the sailing season. Chalciope had begged them to wait until spring, but you know how eager young men are when they get an idea into their heads."

I could not prevent myself from snatching a quick look at Apsyrtus to discover how he was responding to the fact that the unknown Chalciope had bred sons older than he. Judging by the black frown which had settled on his face, he was equally alive to the fact that these unknown brats represented a threat to his position as sole male heir to the throne of Colchis. Naturally, he had the advantage that he was a legitimate son, whilst Chalciope must have been born to one of Aeetes's many mistresses, but a grown-up bastard can often seize power from a younger, legitimate product of a king's loins. For his part, Aeetes seemed to be torn between annoyance that his grandchildren had set off without his authority and pleasure that they had the guts to tackle a potentially dangerous voyage.

"How did you encounter them?"

"They had run into difficulties at Dia."

"Difficulties?"

"Their ship had been driven aground. Since I could not guarantee when I might return to Dia, I offered to bring them back to Colchis."

Aeetes's face took on a saturnine expression. "Good, good. I am very much in your debt for your endeavours."

Watching Aeetes, I wondered exactly what he meant. In fact, I wondered rather a lot. Who was Chalciope's husband? Why had her sons chosen to leave Colchis at a most unsuitable time for travelling? What plans did Aeetes have for his grandchildren? Despite my own predicaments, I found myself sympathising with my new relations. If Aeetes had murdered his seer, would he have much compunction in polishing off a few unwanted grandchildren whom he must hardly know?

Since it would be regarded as poor manners to enquire too closely into the details of a guest's visit until he had been properly welcomed and wined, my father spent the night of Jason's arrival in a demonstration of lavish hospitality designed to impress. Flagons of honeyed wine were brought by panting slaves, whilst dish after dish of succulent meats accompanied by every variety of bread known to the palace was set before Jason. I rather suspected that part of this outburst of culinary accomplishment was intended to display quite how much gold and silverware my father possessed, but, certainly, Jason seemed to enjoy tasting some of our Colchian specialities. Moreover, since Apsyrtus's many talents did not yet encompass diplomatic interchanges with high-status foreigners, my father was forced to introduce me with considerably more respect than he usually displayed towards me.

"Here in Colchis we are accustomed to recognise the talents of the gods wherever they are found. My daughter Medea serves as my seer and chief priest."

Jason looked impressed and bowed low over my hand. "Colchis is fortunate in having such a talented princess."

Anxious to give credit where it was due, I attempted to explain my knowledge. "I learned my craft from my father's seer."

"Then you must be very knowledgeable indeed, Lady Medea."

Although Jason's foreign accent made my name sound rather strange, I was charmed at his method of addressing me. Involuntarily, I leant forward. "Do you practise any arts yourself, Jason, son of Aeson?"

Jason shrugged modestly. "I am fortunate that the gods have normally instructed me quite clearly. It must be much harder to learn their wishes from the flight of birds or the entrails of animals."

I was trying to suppress my admiration that the gods spoke openly to Jason when he added. "I should very much enjoy discussing your craft with you, Lady Medea. As a woman, a priestess has extra opportunities which are not open to a man."

"It is good to exchange knowledge of the will of the gods," I agreed, unable to believe that I had just heard this stranger recognise that a woman was not a contemptible object. That he had acknowledged that fact in full hearing of both my father and my brother was an added – if secret – joy.

"I gather," interrupted Aeetes rather heavily, "that in Greece you seek knowledge in strange ways."

"Not strange," Jason chided gently. "We seek knowledge wherever it may be found. For if the gods have provided the possibility of learning new skills or understanding, then surely it is right to pursue that understanding wherever – and by whomever – it can be discovered."

Apsyrtus had grown bored with such philosophical by-ways. "Do you hunt?" he asked abruptly.

"Of course," agreed Jason. "I hunt all sorts of animals. The harder they are to catch, the more exciting the hunt."

X

The next day I woke up conscious of a difference in the air. The weather was still dreary and sullen, but I was not. True, I was still concerned about the revelation of my unknown sister and her sons, but as I surveyed my face in my hand-mirror, I could see my eyes sparkling.

"Jason finds you interesting," I told my reflection. "Jason wants to talk to you." My reflection eyed me back, asking me what I thought about Jason. I blushed. I could hardly deny to myself that it was more than Jason's interest in prophecy which had caught my attention. "He's handsome," I whispered. My blush deepened. "He's *very* handsome. No-one has such black eyes as he does. And no-one else calls me Lady Medea as he does." I mimicked him saying it, before giggling. "I don't sound foreign enough. He has the most tantalising accent."

I walked over to the window, wishing that I could see Jason go past. But at this hour in the morning he was most likely to be inside and I could hardly hang round the corridors of the palace in the hope of accidentally encountering him.

I spent much of the morning unable to think of anything except Jason and when I would meet him again. I worried that my father might decide that it was inappropriate for me to be present in Jason's company again – after all, it was not normal for unmarried women to dine with strangers. I was deeply relieved when a message came to order me to attend another feast that night. I would be able to see Jason again; if the gods were generous, I would be able to exchange a few words with him.

I dressed with particular care that night, rearranging my hair at least five times until I was satisfied with the result.

My slave placed a chaplet of gold upon my head and I twined amber beads around my throat, hoping that Jason would admire the contrast between their throbbing honey-gold and my white neck. My appearance seemed attractive in the mirror, but how was I to know how pretty Greek girls might be?

In retrospect, I wonder whether my father really wanted my presence that night. However, he was given no alternative since Jason requested that he might have the pleasure of my company at the feast. Whatever my father's manners towards his family in private, in public he was suavity personified. Moreover, he had established that Jason was the current heir to the throne of Iolcos. True, there appeared to be an unspoken difficulty between Jason and his uncle Pelias who currently reigned in Iolcos, but my father had built up a network of high-status contacts within and without Colchis, and he appeared to have no objection to adding Jason to his list. Hence I assumed that, as far as Aeetes was concerned, my role was merely that which my mother would have played had she still been alive. I doubted very much whether my father would have encouraged my attendance had he known how eager I was to talk to Jason again. All the same, I was not so distracted that I forgot about my unknown sister.

On the second morning after Jason's arrival, I was repeating to myself the conversation which I had had with Jason the previous night when Aeetes sought me out. "Our guest wishes to make a sacrifice to Ares the Victorious. I want you to take him to the shrine."

I waited for more information. Certainly, sending me to escort Jason was more courteous than sending our herald – or a mere kitchen-slave. But Ares the Victorious was a man's god and my father's or my brother's presence would be more appropriate.

My father's habitual secretiveness appeared to be

waging war with the necessity of explaining to me exactly what he wanted me to achieve. Necessity won. "Find out why Jason is really here. I don't believe in this talk of restoring Chalciope's brats to her bosom. Even if it were true, why has he spent three days here? One evening would have been enough." Aeetes gave a short laugh. "If he hadn't shown up at the palace I might have suspected that Chalciope had been aiding potential enemies to sneak into my territory unannounced, in which case one hundred sacrifices to Ares the Victorious wouldn't have saved her from my justifiable wrath." He shrugged. "Not that I suppose that Jason would have cared particularly about Chalciope, but even if he had, he's stayed quite long enough to make it clear that he is not an anonymous infiltrator. So what *does* he want?"

My father's ready acceptance that Chalciope might wish to harm him struck me. Whatever his faults, Aeetes was not a fearful or timorous man. If he had suspicions they were unlikely to be the product of an over-fertile imagination – or, indeed, conscience. Ever since Jason had first mentioned Chalciope I had been impatiently waiting for an opportunity to learn more about my mysterious half-sister. Now it appeared that my opportunity had arrived.

"Can you provide me with more background information?"

"What do you mean?" Aeetes growled suspiciously. "I've told you why I'm unsure of Jason's intentions."

I looked innocently confused. "But, Father, it's not Jason who worries me. After all, why should a stranger wish to harm you? I agree that a Colchian, or one of our neighbours might have acquisitive eyes upon your territory, but this man is from Greece."

"Then why do you want to know more about him, if you don't think that he's a threat?"

"Not about Jason; about Chalciope."

My father's eyes narrowed, then he unexpectedly laughed. "Gods, how like a woman! I suspect a plot against me and all you can do is worry about a sister you've never met. You'll do as you are told, Medea, and no nonsense about the wishes of Artemis, either!"

"No, Father."

"I should damn well think not."

Realising that Aeetes had misunderstood me, I set my chin more firmly. "When I said 'no' I meant 'no, I shan't help you' – not unless you tell me what I want to know about Chalciope." I shrugged nonchalantly. "It would be unfortunate if I were unable to carry out the spring ceremony for the protection of the new crops." Watching my father's annoyance with grim relish, I thought of an additional argument to force him to speak. "Of course, you could command Apsyrtus to try to weasel out from Jason what you want to know, but how do you know that he won't let slip precisely all those things which you don't want Jason to learn? After all, he's bound to quiz Jason about Chalciope."

Hunting had trained my father to make up his mind quickly, and a lifetime of keeping our barbarian neighbours at bay had taught him when to give way whilst pretending that he had yielded nothing. "I suppose I should have known by now that feminine curiosity is incapable of waiting for a more suitable moment when I am not busy entertaining important guests."

I waited, resisting the temptation to point out that, far from entertaining his important guest, he was currently busy trying to get me to spy upon that guest.

Aeetes shrugged dismissively. "Both you and Apsyrtus would have learned everything about your older sister once Jason leaves. Even had Jason not come, I had always intended to invite Chalciope to the celebrations for Apsyrtus's twelfth birthday."

Since this revelation of my unimportance in comparison to Apsyrtus seemed not to wound me, Aeetes added rather unpleasantly, "Chalciope certainly knows about you two. After all, half the reason for marrying her off was to get rid of her whilst my new wife bred me sons. Not," he added reflectively, "that Eidyia was much use at that."

Ignoring the sneer at my mother's memory, I focussed instead on the previous sentence. Aeetes had referred to his new wife. Did that meant that Chalciope's mother had actually been married to my father? Aeetes appeared to read my thoughts.

"Oh yes, Medea, Chalciope is legitimate. She wasn't a boy, and her mother never did manage to produce a live boy-child, but she's as legitimate as you and Apsyrtus. And she was properly married off to Phrixus which makes her four boys my lawful and legitimate grandsons. If Apsyrtus were to die, she might well live to see her sons ruling in my stead."

I struggled to maintain my composure at the shock of this pronouncement. How could Phrixus have been Chalciope's husband? He had never even hinted that he was married, let alone possessed four sons. Again, I suddenly found myself wondering if Phrixus had cared for me. Or had I merely been a burden and an obligation? At that thought, I nearly burst into tears. I had believed that Phrixus had liked me for myself, not because I was some duty or the closest reminder he had of his absent wife. Perhaps I had been a burden to Theonoe, too.

Unable to bear the thought, I forced myself to consider the political angle to Aeetes's revelations. Whenever my father or brother had sneered at my insignificance, I had buoyed myself up with the reminder that I was important, that I was second-in-line to the throne, that I might one day rule Colchis. Now that hope had been destroyed. I should never rule Colchis whilst there were four male grandsons, ready to take Apsyrtus's place. I should never be judged important and worthy of respect. I should never have a role in life apart from that of some man's wife.

Moreover, I could not believe how stupid I had been. Whenever I had wondered why Aeetes had never married again and bred more sons, I had always assumed that he had not contemplated the possibility of Apsyrtus dying without issue. But such a conclusion had completely failed to consider the fact that my father was intensely proud of his bloodline. Such a man would clearly not risk his land falling out of the hands of his direct descendents. I had considered – and dismissed – the possibility that there might be illegitimate sons tucked away on some isolated farm. My father had never been shy about his sexual conquests and it was common knowledge that several girl-children had been born out of wedlock to him. Admittedly, the girls had soon died, but there had been no mention of sons. Nevertheless, in the midst of my speculations why had I not thought of a previous marriage? I must have been blind. Desperate for further information, I attacked my father where it hurt most: his pride.

"You must have been dreadfully ashamed of Chalciope if you hid her away from the palace. Was it the fact that your first child was a girl which made you react like that or is there something strange about her?"

"Gods, Medea, there was nothing strange about her or my getting rid of her. I don't have time to waste on female children. And I didn't want her mother wasting time on her either, so, after the naming ceremony, I packed her off with a wet-nurse. I suppose most people have completely forgotten about her by now."

I was stung by Aeetes's dismissive attitude towards his first-born, resembling as it did his own treatment of me. "If she was so irrelevant, why did you marry her off to

Phrixus? He was your soothsayer and an important man."

My father sighed impatiently. "Women *never* understand politics. I didn't want one of the court to marry Chalciope because, if one of them had, he might then have started plotting against me to seize the throne. Phrixus was a convenient alternative. He was foreign, and he was utterly dependent upon me. Without my patronage, he could not have practised as a seer. Indeed, without my approval, he had nowhere to live – he was an exile from Greece and if I expelled him, where could he flee to?"

Although Aeetes's explanation of why Chalciope had not been married to a Colchian noble exactly matched my own calculation as to why he was in no hurry to marry me off, my ire rose so much that I could feel my heart thudding against my breast. How could my father boast of using Phrixus for his own ends? Had he no conscience? Did he feel no guilt at having killed Phrixus? I wanted to shout out that he had murdered the man he had chosen to marry his daughter but something – perhaps Phrixus's shade – restrained me.

"Why haven't you ever mentioned her children to Apsyrtus?" I demanded. "It was unsafe to leave him unaware of these male relations."

Aeetes was amused. "A cunning attempt to disguise your own curiosity, Medea, but I hardly find it convincing. Apsyrtus would be most surprised to hear such sisterly concern – you've always given the impression that you hate him."

I scowled angrily, ready to point out that my father had happily encouraged my brother in his hatred and derision towards me. However, Aeetes was not finished. "You find out from Jason what I want to know and I shall tell you all about Chalciope's sons – and my plans for your future." He shrugged his shoulders. "Mind you, I suppose Jason may not find you particularly interesting to talk to, in which case neither of us will find out what we want to know."

XI

Whilst I was doubtful whether my father did actually have any solid plans for my future, I was suddenly conscious that I had allowed matters to drift. The discovery of the existence of my half-sister and her brood of sons now shocked me into action: if I had felt an irrelevance before when there was only Apsyrtus to consider, how much more did my insignificance apply when an entire family of grandsons was available to replace Apsyrtus? Hence the tempting bait which Aeetes had dangled hooked me. I needed to know what was to happen to me, so I would try to get Jason to speak. True, I might learn nothing, but the effort was worth making. Moreover, I had no intention of naively revealing whatever I discovered to Aeetes merely because Aeetes was my father. Nor was I foolish enough not to consider the possibility that my father might lie to me. The arrangement was – in my view – to be regarded as a business transaction: any intelligence which I might glean from Jason would be sold to my father, chunk by careful chunk, but only in return for similar information from him about his plans for me. Finally (if rather less admirably), the scarcely-concealed suggestion that I was insufficiently attractive to encourage Jason to speak had stirred my desire to prove Aeetes wrong.

Minutes later, I laid myself out to intercept Jason. He seemed pleased that it was I, and not my father, who was to lead him to the shrine of Ares the Victorious. We made our way through the fields which, at this time of the year, were barren apart from twisting weeds and the multitudinous stones which appeared to grow up from the earth in winter. However, Jason smiled happily, apparently not noticing his somewhat unpropitious surroundings.

"I do enjoy your company, Princess Medea."

Wishing that I could enjoy Jason's without having to worry about my father's plans, I murmured something pleasant. Half of me hoped that Jason would expand his flattering theme, while the other half urged me to discover what my father wanted to know. That might not make my heart race, but it would enable me to learn more about Chalciope.

"It's so nice to have someone I can talk to properly." He waved his hands around rather excitedly. "I mean, the men in the *Argo* are good fellows, but all they ever want to talk about is what battles we've fought and the great challenges which lie ahead of us."

"War is important for men," I commented diplomatically, wondering whether Jason was about to let slip some grand plan for the conquest of Colchis.

"Yes, but it is not the only thing which is important. Surely we ought to also consider matters of the mind? Hardly any of them would be interested in what you told me about the medicinal use of hellebore. Why don't they want to learn more about the world around them?"

"Perhaps hellebore is not a good example," I suggested tentatively. "I'm sure that Greek women would be interested to learn that it can drive out worms in children – that is, if they did not know about it already. Men are probably more concerned with averting blight on crops or charms to keep storms at bay."

Jason shook his head violently. "No, no. That is not what I mean at all. And as for women, Greek girls are brought up very differently. They learn different things and they conduct themselves differently." He suddenly sounded rather embarrassed. "I've never met a woman like you. You know so much; you are so different." He paused, wrinkling his brows as he tried to find the correct words. "I can respect you."

Whatever else I had expected to hear, it was not that.

Somewhere in my body a bird began to sing. I shut my mouth hastily in case the carolling grew so loud that it burst out of my mouth, leaving any passing stranger to wonder why the wintry fields resounded with throbbing song.

"I mean what I say, Lady Medea," continued Jason. "I have never met a girl like you. I never realised that women could be like you – so knowledgeable, so clever, and so free in spirit."

Although one part of me wanted to protest that I was chained by the twin fetters of my father and my brother, another part recognised that there was some truth in Jason's statement. I was free in spirit in the sense that I still retained sufficient independence of mind to loathe Aeetes's control over me. I hated the fact that he dismissed me as of no importance because I was a woman; I despised the fact that he encouraged all of Apsyrtus's worst traits; and ultimately, I suppose, I resented the fact that my own father had rejected me at birth.

"Have I upset you?" enquired Jason anxiously.

Realising that my face must have revealed some of what I was thinking, I shook my head. It was simply not safe to bare my soul to anyone, even someone as understanding as Jason. He could not possibly realise the necessity of preventing my father from gaining any additional control over me – my thoughts were all that were left to me. If they were made public, I should truly be a captive without hope of rescue. "You are very generous," I commented swiftly, "but you are wrong to praise me for my knowledge. If I appear clever, then that is because I was carefully taught."

"By whom?"

"Phrixus and Theonoe, who brought me up."

"Phrixus? Do you mean Chalciope's husband?"

"Yes."

"How strange," mused Jason, "that I should have saved Phrixus's sons and now I learn that he taught you, his sister-in-law, all you know."

"And Theonoe," I added, unwilling to see her deprived of the credit which was due. "Theonoe taught me all she knew."

"You are very loyal."

Somehow, it seemed very easy to say quite openly, "I loved her."

"You must tell me more about her, after I have performed my sacrifice to Ares."

Naturally, as a seer and priestess, I was well used to the time required for such rites, but I could not contain my impatience as I waited for Jason to complete his ceremony. I told myself that this was because I lacked sympathy with Ares, but even whilst I uttered this excuse I knew that it was untrue. The real reason for my impatience was because I wanted to continue my exciting interchange with Jason. Not only were the words different from the usual grumbles with which my relatives normally greeted my presence, but Jason's whole stance was different from the courtiers at the palace. Young I may have been, but I was not too young to realise that Jason's eyes flickered with more than the desire to be polite to his host's daughter.

Eventually, Jason was finished and we set off slowly back to the palace. How slowly may be calculated from the fact that it took us four times as long to return from the shrine as to reach it. My father, by apparent happy coincidence, was looking over his horses when we appeared and thus was able to intercept us before I could entirely conceal my joyous air. Since hospitality decreed that Aeetes escort Jason inside, my father was able to do little more than shoot a commanding glance in my direction. I chose to misunderstand his order entirely and removed myself to the women's quarters, where I spent some time examining myself in my hand-mirror. Why not? Jason had said that I was beautiful – it was natural that I wanted to reassure myself that this was so. Was my hair really more silken than that of the girls of Greece? Was my complexion finer? Was my body more graceful?

I had no means of comparison, but, as I twisted and turned and pirouetted, I could certainly see that my eyes were glittering with a light which had not been there before. Indeed, for all that we were enduring dull, wretched weather, I shone as if I had been bathed in radiance by Helios himself. I wanted to prance through all the corridors of the palace, sending light and warmth into all of its dark, dank corners. However, my sense of self-preservation restrained me from this wild impulse. It would clearly not be sensible to appear before my father until I had my feelings more tightly under control. Whilst Aeetes felt lust, rather than love, towards his women, I suspected that he would have little difficulty in correctly interpreting my unusual bloom. I had even less doubt that he would happily crush that bloom as quickly as it had appeared. It was much safer for me to retreat to my bed on the grounds of some unidentified illness. Apart from anything else, such a tactic would give me time to think.

XII

The next morning, I was surprised when my father made no effort to drag me off and question me. Indeed, he deliberately seemed to ignore the chance of intercepting me when he observed Jason approaching. For his part, Jason appeared relieved that Aeetes had not pressed him to go hunting that morning.

"I asked him to excuse me," he explained to me as we set off together. "I told him that it was my custom to sacrifice to Ares three mornings running."

"Did he believe you?"

"Yes. At least, I think he did. He even said that I ought to ask your help again." Jason smiled gently at me. "I am glad that he did. I should have sought you out anyway, but this way we need not worry if anyone observes us together. I have much I want to say to you, Lady Medea."

A small voice warned me that I ought to consider whatever my father was plotting. I ignored that warning. Jason's glance had sent shivers coursing through my body and all I wished to do was to discover what he wanted to say.

Several hours later, I had made the interesting discovery that Jason's lips were not just intended for talking. Some people might consider that my maidenly modesty ought to have been outraged by his daring, his boldness, his audacity. However, instead of slapping his face or shrinking away in disgust, I returned Jason's kisses with as much eagerness as he gave them. After all, whilst the physical sensation was a new one to me, kissing was hardly something that I had never witnessed before. Indeed, mere kissing was considered distinctly tame at the very masculine court of Colchis. Fortunately, Jason did not seem to think that the sort of rough fumblings which characterised Colchian feasts suitable for a princess. He restricted himself to stroking my hair and murmuring flattering comments about my wit, my beauty and my cleverness. Eventually, I roused myself from this rapturous delirium.

"Jason, what are we going to tell my father?"

"Do we need to tell him anything, my beautiful lady?"

"He's bound to notice that something's up. He won't be fobbed off with a pretence that we have done nothing other than perform chaste sacrifices to Ares all morning."

"What do you want to do? Has your father other plans for you?"

I frowned. "I don't know. He has said that it is time that I was married."

Jason seemed to realise that I did not entirely trust Aeetes, but he was too tactful to say so outright. "Has your father mentioned any names? I only ask because if he has no particular man in mind, perhaps he might not be as angry as you fear." He hesitated modestly. "I… well… I have achieved a number of adventures and I did restore his grandsons to their mother."

"That's half the problem. Aeetes doesn't think that you came here purely to restore Chalciope's children. He suspects that you're here for another reason."

Jason stopped tickling the back of my neck, apparently disturbed by this statement. "How can you be sure? It's perfectly natural for me to break my journey in Colchis."

"That's not what Aeetes thinks." I sighed. "And I am sure he is suspicious because he ordered me to find out what you're doing in Colchis."

Jason twisted round so that he could stare into my eyes. "Medea! I thought I could trust you."

I hastened to reassure him. "Of course you can, Jason. Why else do you think that I am telling you this information? I want you to understand that things are not as simple as you think." I sighed again. "In any case, even if you asked for my hand in marriage, he might refuse. You're a foreigner, for a start."

"Your sister married a stranger."

"Yes," I agreed gloomily.

Jason appeared affected by my sudden change in mood. He watched my face for several moments before asking urgently. "My dearest, was there something odd about Phrixus's death? The noble Chalciope dissolved into tears when I mentioned Phrixus and she must have had time to get over his death." As I hesitated, he went on. "The servants, too, seemed loath to speak of him. I gained the impression that all was not right."

"Did my sister say nothing at all about Phrixus?"

"Only that she grieved for him." Jason suddenly seemed concerned lest I thought that he was complaining about Chalciope. "Your sister was very grateful for the return of her sons, but she must be very upset about Phrixus – she did not even mention that I should encounter her beautiful sister at the palace."

Although I was tempted to recommence our flirting, my common sense told me that we had to decide how to deal with my father. Moreover, I was unsure if Jason appreciated how unsafe the situation might be. Nevertheless, it was hard to speak of my suspicions. Apart from anything else, might not Jason be repelled if he learned that I was sired by a callous poisoner?

"Do not look so sad, my honey," Jason coaxed. "Whilst I am at your side, I shall keep you safe. Just tell me what you fear and I shall protect you from it."

Giving a mental shrug, I did as he asked. "There is a rumour that Phrixus died at my father's hand. Now do you see why I fear telling Aeetes that you wish to marry me? He might kill you too."

Jason gave a small sigh. "I trust that, by the time Lord Aeetes grows to dislike me, we shall be far away in Greece."

"Greece?"

"Of course, my dove. Would you have me live out my days in a foreign land?" I must have stared rather vacantly at Jason for he went on patiently. "Phrixus could not leave Colchis, but there is no reason why I cannot go back to Greece. It is my home, and I shall receive great honour and renown when I return there."

"Oh."

Jason smiled kindly upon my confusion. "We have progressed very far in a few days, my beloved. It is not surprising that you had not yet thought that we shall live in Greece. But think of the benefits! Here you are constrained by your father and brother. In Iolcos, you will be welcomed and honoured as my bride. Here you unhappy. There I shall devote myself to making you happy. Here in Colchis you are kept apart from your sister. In Iolcos, I hope that you will be able to create your own family."

I blushed at this mention of children. Jason put his arm round my shoulders and pulled me towards him.

"Do I have your permission to ask your father to marry you?"

I nodded, suddenly unable to speak.

XIII

Jason and I agreed that he would approach my father that evening at the feast. To begin with, I argued that it would be best to ask Aeetes's permission in private, but Jason was unconvinced of this plan.

"If I speak to him on his own he may agree to begin with and then change his mind. It will be much harder for your father to withdraw his permission after he has given it publicly."

"But he may not give his permission at all if you address him in front of the very Colchians who might have formed my suitors if you had not appeared."

"That is precisely the point. You say that none of those nobles has yet spoken openly of their desire to marry you. If Aeetes turns me down, he will risk precipitating a series of demands for your hand in marriage."

My lack of conviction must have shown itself in my expression because Jason continued. "Don't forget, my dearest, that I understand men better than you do. Once I speak of marriage it will be obvious to everyone that Aeetes has been considering it. He can't reject me on the grounds that you are too young, therefore other men will approach him. If he accepts a man of Colchis he risks antagonising all the other Colchian aristocrats, who will resent seeing one of their number promoted above them in importance. However, if he accepts me, their hatred and resentment will be focussed upon me, rather than upon him."

"Perhaps you are correct, but what of Aeetes's hatred and resentment? He won't enjoy being out-manoeuvred publicly. Surely it would be safer to speak to him in private?"

Jason laughed confidently. "My sweet Medea, if you are

92

worried about my safety then you should welcome a public request. Aeetes won't poison me off in the midst of a feast. Everyone would know why he had done it. But he might just resort to a lethal cup of wine to celebrate our contract if I met him in secret and no-one knew what I'd done to arouse his ire."

This articulation of my hidden fears effectively ended my opposition to Jason's plan. Instead, I turned to more pleasant topics. Indeed, such is the natural buoyancy of the young in love that I spent some of the afternoon planning precisely what to wear at my betrothal dinner. The little slave-girl who attended to me grew tired helping me, and she stared in incomprehension when I suddenly winked back tears at the sight of myself standing proudly in rippling robes which traced the contours of my body beneath their lapping folds. I bit back an irritated exclamation. How was she to know that I was grieving for the fact that Theonoe could not share in my joy and would never learn how fine a man Jason was?

Unsurprisingly, I grew increasingly nervous as I waited for the time of the feast to approach. It was one thing to float away on happy dreams of marital bliss, but the fact remained that Aeetes was a distinctly wily man. I was, indeed, more than a little surprised that he had not intervened already. If he had trusted Apsyrtus's discretion more he would never have thrown Jason and me together as he had. I was busily fighting off a nightmare thought that perhaps my father had sent Apsyrtus to spy upon us when the door to my chamber crashed open. Aeetes stood on the threshold, observing me with sardonic interest.

"Well, my daughter, I doubt that such finery is intended for me."

"I do not want our visitor to return to Greece with tales of our lack of hospitality."

Aeetes laughed. "Perhaps you do not. More to the

point, have you discovered why our friend Jason has come to Colchis?"

Sensing that limpid innocence would have no effect other than to enrage my father unnecessarily, I thought rapidly. "I gather that Jason wants to speak to you about his plans."

"Does he, indeed? Or, perhaps I ought to say, does he, by Ares?"

On that somewhat sinister note, hinting as it did at a greater knowledge as to what we had been doing at the shrine than I should have liked, Aeetes left.

To outsiders, the feast must have appeared to be going extremely well. My father was in jovial form and kept pressing food and drink upon his guests. Jason, in particular, was invited to help himself to all the finest dishes and my father's steward hovered close by, ready to pour wine into the cups whenever Aeetes gave a brief nod. I watched this generosity with a certain amount of foreboding: Colchian wine is strong, but deceptively easy to drink. I very much hoped that Jason would not allow his wits to become fuddled out of a desire to placate his host's apparently munificent nature. In particular, I was concerned that Aeetes might seize control of the situation and make it impossible for Jason to talk of marriage. However, I was wrong. Jason had clearly been biding his time for a suitable opening and, just as I had started to despair, he spoke to my father in a clear, controlled voice.

"My Lord Aeetes, you know that I am a prince, the son of a king. You have also heard of my many great quests and how the gods have helped me on those adventures. Now I must tell you of another quest in which I wish to prevail."

Silence fell upon those surrounding Jason and my father. Aeetes gave Jason a brief nod, although the smile which flickered about his mouth reminded me unpleasantly of the tongue of the serpent which lurked in the grove. "Speak, O son of Aeson."

"I seek the hand of your daughter, the Lady Medea, in marriage."

Even although those dining at the lower ends of the long tables could not possibly have heard Jason's words, the frozen attitudes of those above them made them pause in their feasting. My father continued to watch Jason in a calculating manner.

"I am a prince, the son of a king," repeated Jason. "My birth makes me a suitable husband for your daughter, and my achievements show that I shall make a good husband."

"I cannot, precisely, see how driving off the Harpies prepares you for the joys of married life," observed Aeetes. "Nor, indeed, do I entirely follow why the ability to collect a band of young heroes is necessary to be a good husband. I trust that you do not think that you would need to gather such a band to recapture my daughter by force should she choose to run away from you?"

Jason was, unsurprisingly, somewhat taken aback by this cynical response to his attempt to set out his marital credentials. "I meant that I hope to be considered worthy of her hand," he replied in stilted tones.

"I'm not laughing at you, boy," responded Aeetes offensively. "I was merely trying to gauge the value of some of your qualities. After all, there is the question of a dowry to be considered."

The mention of a dowry ought to have made me relax. Surely it meant that my father was going to agree. However, I found myself becoming even more tense than when Jason first began to speak.

"The dowry, Lord Aeetes?" stammered Jason.

"Yes, don't you have that custom in Greece?" enquired my father, with the velvet smoothness which he normally adopted when he felt that he was out-manoeuvring somebody. "Odd. I thought that the Greeks prided themselves on being quite modern and far-thinking. Phrixus certainly seemed to think that they were." He snapped his fingers at his steward. "Broach the special wine which we laid down last year, and bring the first cup to Jason, son of Aeson."

As the steward padded off, I bit my lips in terrified anticipation of the outcome of Aeetes's command. It could hardly be coincidence that mention of Phrixus had led on to a request to fetch this strange special wine which my father apparently possessed. Clearly, the so-called wine was laced with poison, quite possibly the yew berries which had killed Phrixus. The question was, ought I to order the steward not to pour it, order Jason not to drink it, or to race round and dash the cup and amphora onto the ground, thus ensuring that the poison was scattered amongst the rushes which covered the floor? I tried desperately to catch Jason's eye as I quickly attempted to calculate the possibilities. Clearly the steward would ignore my orders in favour of my father's. If I ordered Jason not to drink the poisoned wine I would make him look foolish in front of the entire company. And even if I managed to dispose of this lethal drink, what was to stop Aeetes from poisoning Jason later? However, since I could not sit there and watch my father kill my lover in front of my eyes, I began to rise from my seat. Aeetes noticed the movement.

"Stay where you are, Medea. You shall share the amphora of wine with me and Jason when I am satisfied as to his answers. You, of all people, would not wish me to take lightly my responsibilities towards you."

Jason smiled in my direction, apparently pleased with this response. I, on the other hand, was not in the slightest bit reassured by my father's words. Instead, I detected a hidden threat in his promise that I should share the wine with Jason. True, Aeetes had said that he would also drink it, but what was to prevent him from watching us drain our cups and then changing his mind and toasting us with a different vintage? In fact, a quick-acting poison could have killed both of us before he was even called upon to invent an excuse for drinking something else. I stared hopelessly at Jason, willing him to understand my fears. He was a hero; he would do something. Or if he could not, surely he would give me some indication as to what I ought to do?

"The dowry, boy; what do you seek?" Aeetes took off the broad gold armlet, chased with patterns of running deer and ferocious wolves, which he wore every day. He waved it practically under Jason's nose. "Is it my gold that you seek?"

"No, Lord Aeetes. I do not seek glittering gauds like that, fine though they may be. I seek a different form of gold to accompany the Lady Medea on her journey to Iolcos. I ask for the Golden Fleece."

In the frozen silence which followed this request, Aeetes's face was like a mask: a warped mimicry of humanity, at once lifeless and menacing. Eventually, he hissed. "The Fleece?"

Jason paused momentarily, seemingly surprised by Aeetes's apparent ignorance. "Yes. There is a fleece which is made of gold. It is said that you have it here in Colchis." When Aeetes still did not speak, Jason added, "The gods themselves have spoken to me of it."

I winced inwardly, hoping that no-one else would think that Jason sounded blustering and rather uncertain of his ground. However, my father now intervened.

"Did my daughter tell you this tale? Is that why you wish to marry her?"

"No. The Lady Medea knows nothing of the Fleece, nor have I spoken to her of it. The Fleece is a man's business."

"You speak correctly. The Fleece is not for women. But you have not answered my question: who told you of the Fleece?"

Jason appeared to have regained his self-confidence now that my father was prepared to acknowledge the existence of the Fleece. "I learned of it through an oracle and, after consulting various priests and making the correct sacrifices, I set off to search for it. The Fleece is the ultimate goal of my many quests."

Aeetes smiled sourly. "Your oracle may have misinformed you."

"Are you claiming that the gods have spoken falsely? Do you deny that you possess the Fleece?"

"No, no. But you forget that the gods may speak to me, too. I, too, may receive oracles. And one of them told me of the visit of a stranger, a foreigner, who might one day seek the Fleece. Can you deny that you are a stranger to these shores, a foreigner from a far-off land?"

"I am Greek."

"And thus alien here."

Jason gave a brief nod of acknowledgement of this logical corollary.

"Do you not wish to learn the rest of the oracle?" enquired Aeetes mockingly. "After all, it sets out the fate of this bold outsider who comes to seek the Fleece."

"Doubtless, you will tell me it."

"Quite so," Aeetes agreed. "And since you have completed so many audacious deeds already in your quest to come to remove my property, you will not be daunted by the orders contained in the oracle. Indeed, you may think them distinctly tame and uninspiring. After all, where is the challenge in yoking two bulls, ploughing a field, and sowing some seed? Any farmer could do that, let alone a noble hero like you."

By this point, it must have been obvious to the entire

company that Aeetes was toying with Jason. However, Jason did not buckle. "Presumably there are some more details which you have not yet given me."

Aeetes nodded slowly. "How astute you are, Jason, son of Aeson. There are indeed a few minor points which I had passed over. But they will become clear as you undertake your task. Or do you wish to back out now and scurry back to Greece without my daughter?

"No. I am fated to seek the Fleece and, if I fail, then my fate was to fail."

"Very well, then. Let no man say that I did not give you the chance to change your mind. Come, let us seal the pact with a jug of wine. Steward, the amphora which Phrixus left!"

XIV

By the end of the feast, I was a mass of different emotions. First, I was conscious of the calculating glances which many of the men were throwing in my direction. They clearly were wondering what my role was in Jason's demand and whether I would become available for marriage to them should Jason fail in his task. Secondly, I was frightened that there was some noxious drug in the wine that my father insisted that Jason and I drink to toast my betrothal. Finally, I was longing for the feast to finish so that I might seek Jason out to talk with him. Although he was clearly suspicious that the tasks set him would not prove to be as straightforward as my father had claimed, he could have no idea of the danger which awaited him. Hence, when I eventually managed to slip away from the remaining men who wished to congratulate me on my good fortune, I was more than a little tense when I reached Jason. He kissed me chastely upon my hand.

"That went rather better than I had expected from your warnings, Medea."

Surprise at Jason's reaction and the fact that I still feared that 'Phrixus's wine' was actually poisoned wine made me speak in sharper tones than I had intended.

"Really? What makes you think that?"

Jason stiffened. "You told me that your father might be furious and reject my suit, but he seems quite content to let me marry you."

"But, Jason, you don't realise that he's got something dreadful planned for you. Those bulls were a gift to him from Hephaestus; they breathe fire and their hooves are made of bronze. They run wild in the temple grounds because no-one dare approach them."

It would be unfair to say that Jason preened himself,

but he certainly was not as concerned by this information as I might have expected.

"My dear child, I am not completely unused to such strange phenomena. After all, I managed to sail the *Argo* through the Clashing Rocks which could have crushed all of us out of existence."

I bit back a retort that the Rocks, while perhaps terrifying, could not run around or scorch flames. "The seed is no ordinary seed, either. Athena gave it to my father. When Cadmus sowed similar seed at Thebes, armed warriors sprung up from the soil. The same thing will happen here and you will be one man against many." I sighed heavily. "I can help you with these tasks, but it is all so unnecessary."

"What do you mean? Don't you want me to gain the Golden Fleece? Don't you realise that it is the purpose of my great quest? Can't you see that it is what led me here from Greece?"

"Of course I want you to succeed, but why didn't you tell me what you sought instead of announcing it to the entire hall? I could have led you to the grove where the Fleece lies hidden. And I could have sent the serpent which guards it to sleep. We could have left Colchis with the Fleece without my father ever knowing what you wanted, and without you having to undertake these dangerous tasks."

Jason's chin jutted out. "Don't be ridiculous, Medea. How could I gain glory if I just tamely removed the Fleece from its hiding-place? You're the daughter of a king; surely you understand the importance of renown. Don't you want my name talked of with breathless admiration? What sort of fame do you think I would gain if I skulked away like a sneak-thief?"

"I don't care. I think it's silly to run unnecessary risks." I tried not to cry. "You could be hurt or even die, Jason.

And even if you succeed, how can you be certain that my father will let you leave with the Fleece?"

"He gave his word."

"He's perfectly capable of inventing some little detail which he can claim that you did not fulfil. Then he'll refuse to give you the Fleece and you'll have risked your life for nothing." I shot Jason a sad smile. "My beloved, couldn't you have been satisfied with me and not asked for the Fleece?"

Jason scowled. "You don't understand, Medea. I was sent on a quest and I cannot abandon it. It is man's work and I must not retreat from it." He suddenly seemed to become aware that I was upset and stroked my hair. "Dear Medea, I know that you are frightened that I shall be hurt, but you would not wish me to turn tail in the face of danger. When we are in Greece you will want to be called the wife of a hero, not the wife of a coward."

"But if you fail, I shan't even be a widow, much less a wife."

"If you tell me all about the bulls and the seed then I shall know how to deal with them."

"Why can't you let me fetch the Fleece and we could be away in your ship before morning?"

Jason stared at me incredulously. "I don't think you understand what you are saying, Medea. I cannot accept that suggestion. I would rather die than crawl back to Greece, having stolen the Fleece like a snivelling slave."

"Then you probably will die," I snapped. "Even my best efforts may not save you from the creatures of the gods or my father's wrath."

"If you feel like that," retorted Jason, "then perhaps I should be better making my own efforts, rather than relying on the efforts of a woman whose love appears very changeable."

I stared at Jason, miserably conscious that my failure to

control my emotions had provoked a quarrel between us. We had been deliriously happy earlier; now the air crackled with our antagonism. "I'm sorry, Jason," I remarked eventually. "It is my love for you which makes me fear for you. Of course I shall help you to the best of my ability."

"And it is my love for you which makes me want to return to Greece a hero, with you sharing my glory by my side."

Jason readily agreed that I would prepare various magic potions to help him in his task. The actual preparation did not demand much time, but the unguents had to be left to cure for several days. Naturally, Jason fretted somewhat at this delay, but I was determined not to act hastily – laurel and marsh cinquefoil are notoriously tricky ingredients and it seemed foolish to risk Jason's death for the sake of the forty-eight hours which it would take to be certain that the ointments were ready. For most of that time I was ecstatically happy. Jason was kind and loving, constantly whispering reassurances about our future as he held me close to him. Again and again he told me how much he loved me; how he honoured me for my knowledge of the secret arts; how he respected me as he had respected no other woman before. As I lay snuggled against his broad chest, I could feel his heart throbbing and knew that mine was likewise out of control.

However, despite this pulsing joy, darker misgivings about the future sometimes surfaced. Put at their most basic, I had a superstitious dread that something would go wrong with the perfect love which seemed to exist between Jason and myself. At the time, I attributed these fears to the example of my father's life and his contempt for my mother. Moreover, those who made up my father's court seemed to hold women in low regard, whilst Apsyrtus viewed me with indifferent contempt. When I compared the men at Colchis with Jason, I was very well aware of my great good fortune. Jason said that he found my company exciting and stimulating; my father barely tolerated it. Jason actively praised my intelligence; most men feared or denied it. Jason respected me; my family reviled me. Therein lay the problem. The gods are capricious and whimsical. It might suit them to grant me the joy of Jason's love now, only to strike him – or me – down shortly afterwards. I might use every ounce of knowledge I possessed to protect Jason, but all the powers I had were nothing as to those of the gods.

I was very relieved that Jason had agreed to let me prepare sacred liniments to protect his body. After he rejected my suggestion that we seize the Fleece and flee, I had been afraid that he would spurn my magic salves, too. But another problem gnawed at my happiness: would Jason suffer on my behalf once we left the shores of Colchis? I had overheard mutterings in the palace about unwanted foreigners swanning in and marrying the princess. If the nobles of Colchis did not approve of Jason the Greek, how might the Greeks of Iolcos regard Medea of Colchis? Eventually, I came up with a solution which I lost little time in offering to Jason.

"My dearest, we love each other with such great love that it makes me so very happy. I want to do all I can to help you."

"Sweet Medea, I know that you do."

I smiled up at Jason, grateful for his trust. "Before you go to tackle the tasks which my father has set you, I should like us both to swear a joint oath."

My lover frowned, confused at my request. "An oath?"

"Let us swear to Zeus Horkios, the keeper of oaths, that in return for our marriage, I shall enable you to acquire the Golden Fleece."

Jason still seemed puzzled. "But why, Medea? I know

that you will help me."

"Jason, those bulls are fearsome and the armed warriors which will spring up from the ground will be truly terrifying. If you face them with the slightest doubt in your mind about my love for you, you will falter and then you will be killed." My voice trembled, despite my best efforts to sound calm and rational. "I cannot bear the idea of your going into battle without every protection which I can give you."

"But you've already prepared those ointments. You said that they will stop my skin from blistering when the bulls breathe fire."

I shrugged. "Without my ointments and potions you would have no chance at all. But spells and potions are not everything. You cannot let even one part of your mind be distracted as to whether I will lead you to the Fleece."

"Frankly, Medea, this idea of an oath is more likely to distract me. It makes me feel that you don't trust me."

I gave a cry of horror. "Jason, oh, my beloved, how could you think that?"

"What else do you expect? You want me to swear an oath that our love and the Fleece are two parts of a whole. It sounds like some sort of contract which a pair of traders would enact. Do you think that love is to be bought and sold like that?"

"I think of our love as being as golden and shimmering and delicate as the Fleece itself."

"Then why tarnish it by tying it up in a contract? What have I done to make you treat me like this?"

"You don't understand, Jason, it's not like that at all. This oath will show everyone – my father, those at Colchis who don't like the idea of our marriage, even the gods themselves – how much I trust you. Don't you see? I am demonstrating quite publicly my complete confidence that you will succeed in gaining the Fleece. After all, if you don't gain the Fleece, then the oath would mean that I could not marry you. Anyone who has seen us together will know that I love you." I stammered the next words out in a rather embarrassed manner. "Jason, have you not noticed the bloom on my cheeks, the sparkle in my eyes, the sheen on my lips? Can you not see how much I adore you? Everyone else can. Now let them see that I trust you, too."

Jason frowned thoughtfully. "I do not like this oath for you, Medea. If I fail, I will not be able to marry you and that will leave you unprotected. Your father will be able to carry out his plans."

Now it was my turn to sound perturbed. "Plans? What plans?"

A heavy sigh was the only response.

"Jason, please tell me. What have you learned?"

"I don't know whether I ought to tell you. Chalciope told me in confidence."

"Chalciope?"

"Yes. Apparently your father intended to marry you off to her eldest son. She only told me when I offered to bring the eldest boy – Argus – along to the palace with me. She was frightened to let him go. She thought that it might be an excuse to keep him near at hand until Aeetes decided what to do with him."

A long schooling in palace politics meant that I had no need to ask for an explanation of what fate my father might have in mind for Phrixus's child. Jason saw from my face that I had grasped the point.

"I hate to tell you such things about your father, Medea, but now do you see why I do not wish you to swear this oath?"

I gulped and my determination wavered. Then I forced myself to be resolute. "No, Jason, I shall swear it. You are risking your life; I must show faith in you. By swearing, I can prove to all Colchis that I trust you and that I am yours." I shrugged. "Doing so may sway my father's opinion or it may not. More importantly, just as you will be tested by the gods as you battle for the Fleece, might not this news be a test of me? If the gods do not think that I am worthy of you, they will let you die. My love will be an extra layer of protection for you, both now and at Iolcos."

"Iolcos?"

I flushed, hoping that I was not going to hurt Jason's feelings by referring to slights which he had suffered. "My father," I began awkwardly, "has sometimes called you a stranger and a foreigner."

Jason made no reply, but his mouth tautened.

"I think that he does so to provoke you to anger. Perhaps he seeks an excuse to send you away from the palace. I don't know. But… but the people in Iolcos may have similar views."

"My people," commented Jason rather haughtily, "understand how to make a guest from another land feel welcome. Moreover, we Greeks are very enlightened. We look to the skills and knowledge of the person involved, rather than merely comment upon their accent or strange garb."

Momentarily feeling relieved that going to live in Iolcos might not be as difficult as I had feared, I continued. "Nonetheless, some of your countrymen may not approve of the fact that you, their prince, have married a woman from a strange land. They may think that you ought to have chosen a woman of Iolcos instead. Our oath might help you to explain matters."

"What do you mean?"

I chose my words with care. "Lots of your people will rejoice that you have brought great acclaim to Iolcos by winning the Golden Fleece. They may be more prepared to welcome me if they realise that you regard me as part of the Fleece."

"That I won you both together, do you mean?"

"Yes," I agreed, certain that Jason's basic honesty would lead him to tell the people of Iolcos how I had helped him. When they knew that, they would be unlikely to try to reject me as a foreign interloper. Even if they did not applaud my aid to their prince, their own common-sense would show them that it would be foolish to drive me away – after all, that would lead to them losing both their prince and the Fleece, since Jason would refuse to let me go into exile alone.

XV

Our oath that our marriage would come into effect when Jason gained the Golden Fleece was sworn in front of the altar of Zeus. We were alone; Jason insisted upon that for my own safety. I did not care about the lack of excited onlookers, but his devotion brought swift tears to my eye. No-one had shown any interest in protecting me since Theonoe died and she, of all Colchis, deserved to see me kneel before Zeus with the man who swore to marry me. But Theonoe was dead and buried in a cold, cold grave where none could speak and none could see. I had poured libations on her grave that morning, but I knew that even if the sacrifices did bring her back to brief, flickering life, that moment of life would be in the underworld, not here in Colchis, not watching me. Thus our pledge went unwitnessed by man or woman, although the whispering of the ilexes and cypresses told me that the god had heard.

Some people might consider that I had betrayed my father by so readily siding with Jason – an unknown foreigner, an adventurer who had come to remove one of my father's greatest treasures. What, they might ask, did I know of Jason which made me choose him over the duty that I so clearly owed to my father? In many respects, that would be the wrong question. More to the point would be to ask why I should choose to side with Aeetes. He, after all, had done nothing to earn my trust. Everything that I had learned of him was bad. How could I honour a man who regarded the raping of slaves as natural? How could I admire a king who had ruthlessly destroyed a gentle old man for no better reason than that an imprecise oracle had spoken vaguely of the threat posed by a stranger from across the seas? Had Aeetes loved me, had he even tried to win my love when he brought me back into his life, I might have regretted my choice more. As it was, I was glad to help do Aeetes down. I knew that without the Fleece, my father would struggle to maintain regal status, but I did not care. In fact, I rejoiced to think that Phrixus would be so soon avenged and in so apposite a manner.

However, early on the morning of Jason's ordeal, I thought nothing of what might happen to Aeetes. Instead, my whole mind was focussed on Jason. I was all too conscious that, if my potions failed, the fire-breathing bulls would burn him alive, his skin blistering and his blood boiling and bursting out of his veins. It was all very well telling myself that the ointment worked against hearth-fires, but what would happen if the bulls' fiery breath burned with far greater heat? Would Jason be protected, or would he shrivel before my eyes? The fact that Jason strode forth confidently into the sanctuary where the bulls lived made me feel even worse. He clearly had no doubts; how would he feel when he realised that he had trusted me and I had failed him?

I rather think that I closed my eyes momentarily when I heard the first snorts of rage from one of the bulls. Certainly, the huge creature appeared in front of Jason in far less time that seemed possible. I stared at its shining coat, glistening over the rippling muscles underneath. Its horns shone in the rising sun and its eyes glinted malevolently as it caught sight of Jason. Dust rose as it pawed the dry ground with its hooves. I imagined Jason, caught on the ground, gored and trampled, his ribs snapping like sticks and his crisp curls matted with blood and dust. I felt dreadfully alone as I waited to watch Jason die.

Jason slid deftly to one side as the bull thundered past. Annoyed at having missed Jason, it snorted angrily and tried to draw up from its charge. As I prayed to Hecate the night-wanderer to protect Jason, the second bull appeared.

It approached at a slower pace, as if incredulous that any human would have dared to enter its enclosure. Then, as it came closer, it opened its mouth and bellowed. Flames belched forth and Jason lifted his shield as if to ward off the burning breath. In terror that my ointment had failed, I bit my lip so hard that blood ran down my chin. Then I realised that Jason had acted instinctively. If my magic salve had failed to quench the flames, then Jason would already be screaming in agony as the fire flickered round his legs. Instead, he levelled his spear and struck the bull's left foreleg. Now it was the turn of the animal to feel fear. It roared again, but this time in pain. Its comrade pricked up its ears, and, even at a distance, I could see how it readied itself for another charge. I forced myself not to call out and distract Jason, but I need not have worried. He was already grappling with the second bull, and its bulk prevented the first bull from being able to touch Jason. At one point, I thought that Jason was going to be thrown to the ground and trampled to death, but I realised that he was trying to entangle the leather harness round the creature's legs. The original bull was now bellowing in exasperation, but it still could not get close enough to harm Jason.

Slowly, steadily, Jason forced the leather harness round the second bull, before steering it in the direction of the stone plough. When he managed to latch the harness to the plough, the animal stopped struggling, as if it knew that it had been defeated. However, there was still the other bull to contend with, and its rolling eyes suggested that it was furiously angry. Again and again it charged at Jason, but he sidestepped round the plough, waiting for it to tire. Eventually, its proud head began to droop and its flanks heaved with exhaustion. Jason walked cautiously towards it, but although it tried, it could summon up no more than a feeble bellow.

It seemed to take forever for the field to be ploughed, but I knew that I could not relax whilst Jason was busy. There was little threat that the bulls would break free; the real danger lay in what would follow after the seed was sown. I watched every move Jason made as he ploughed long, straight furrows, hoping that his sword would prove to be as straight and true. Conquering the bulls had been the hardest part of his task, but if he forgot my instructions now he would still die.

At last, Jason led the bulls back to the side of the field and prepared for the third ordeal. Moving briskly along the furrows, he sowed the seed which my father had given him. By the time that he had reached the end of the rows, the first handfuls of seed which he had sown were beginning to swell in size. Retreating rapidly, he seized the first of several large stones which we had placed in strategic positions before daybreak. Even although I had once heard my father describe what would happen, I was shocked at how swiftly the field appeared to fill up with armed men who began to advance upon Jason in disciplined silence.

Jason lifted the rock and threw it into the midst of the ferocious warriors. The front soldier, who moments earlier had seemed intent on slaughtering Jason, assumed that he had been attacked from the rear. Twisting round, he hurled himself in savage fury on the man behind him. The neighbouring warriors were drawn into the fight and soon the terrifying silence had turned to uproar and shouting on all sides. Jason waited. So savage was the fight that there was little else for him to do. When the warriors had finished destroying each other, there was one exhausted warrior left for Jason to cut down. I watched with pride as Jason dealt the deadly blow. And in the midst of my relief and pride, I was glad that I had been able to serve my beloved. My spells had not failed him and my hands had ground the sharpest of edges onto his sword. Together, we had defeated my father's plan that Jason might die.

However, there was still another monstrous creature to be defeated. Jason seemed overawed when I told him what was entailed. I was not surprised. There was always the chance that my potion would not work and the hideous creature would not be lulled into somnolence. Jason was trusting his life to my knowledge of sorcery. Not unreasonably, he wanted to be certain that I knew what I was doing.

"How can we be sure… That is, how do you know all this, Medea?"

"I have studied the magic arts all my life. Constant observation and constant testing of my observations means that I continually learn."

"And it is your testing which means that you know that this serpent will fall asleep?"

I nodded, thinking that now was not the moment to express any doubts. "Yes. The recipe works. I could not have given thanks-offerings to the ram if the serpent had been awake." I gave a brief sigh. "We must sacrifice to the ram later when we are safely out of the grove."

"To the Fleece?"

"Yes, didn't I explain? When the ram was alive, it carried Phrixus away from his murderous stepmother. I am glad that it will be easier to perform the correct ceremonies in future."

"Indeed."

I smiled gratefully at Jason. "I knew that you would understand, my beloved."

"Then let us go to the grove immediately, before your father invents another task for me to undertake."

I was as eager as Jason to fetch the Fleece and for the same reason – I did not trust my father at all. Although he was not meant to have watched Jason's contests, I thought it highly likely that there were spies near the temple of Hephaestus, all primed to see whether Jason was gored, fried, or kicked to death. Since any hidden watchers would be reporting failure of first the bulls and then the warriors to rid Aeetes of his annoying guest, I suspected that my father would take action himself. Most likely, he would shortly be keeping a watchful eye on the grove where the Fleece lay hidden. My own strategy, had I been king, would have been to arrest Jason or kill him outright before he could come close to seizing the Fleece. However, Aeetes was peculiarly inclined to twisted casuistry; it was eminently probably that he would prefer the blood-guilt of Jason's death to fall upon the serpent, rather than himself, since that way he could claim that he had played no part in Jason's destruction. It seemed to me that the sooner we acquired the Fleece, the greater our chances of escaping alive with our booty.

We began to snake our way through the undergrowth, but we made slow progress. Jason's strong body, which I had so admired in the palace, was unsuited for weaving between prickly thorn-bushes, and the sword which I had lovingly sharpened kept snagging on twigs. My nerves began to play up.

"Can't you keep closer to me? We can't afford to waste time."

"There's no need to hurry."

"There is. My father may be laying a trap for us. The sooner we deal with the serpent the better."

I was tormented by an irrational fear that the hours spent dealing with the armed warriors might have dulled the effectiveness of my potion, but I could hardly tell Jason that. However, his frown warned me that I was not showing the courage which he, as a hero, would expect. Although I pulled myself together, I could not help repeating my plan to him.

"Remember, you have to wait for me to sprinkle the serpent with the potion. Only the person who made the potion can use it effectively."

When we reached the hollow, I was very frightened. Facing the serpent was always a terrifying ordeal, but on previous occasions only I had been involved. Now, Jason's fate also lay in my hands. If anything went wrong it would be entirely my fault. I could not help wondering whether it would be worse to perish with Jason, or to survive, knowing that Jason had died trying to protect me from a hideous monster. I swallowed, then forced myself to concentrate. Gently moving a thorny twig from my face, I studied the serpent. It was still as towering; still as evil; still as menacing. I froze as its eyes seemed to flicker in my direction. Could it see beyond me to Jason? I stepped forward to tackle it.

I suppose a hero would have felt exhilaration at dealing with such a monster. Certainly, Jason's tales suggested that the Argonauts positively relished facing strange beasts. I was no hero. I did not seek fame or renown. If we could have left Colchis without the Fleece I would have agreed without hesitation. Indeed, I had suggested it. But Jason said that he had to take the Fleece, and I was driven by the desire to protect Jason. So I walked forward, holding my branch in front of me and praying to Artemis to let me succeed. To my relief, Jason obeyed my instructions and kept well back in the bushes until the serpent lay collapsed upon the ground. Then he joined me. Looking with distaste at the creature's sinuous coils, he unhooked the Fleece from the branch on which it hung. He sagged momentarily under its weight.

"Glory, I never thought that it would be this heavy."

"It's all the gold on it," I commented, fighting down an insane desire to giggle at the explanation. I watched Jason staggering across the hollow centre of the copse and cursed myself for not realising in advance that it would be difficult to carry. "Go ahead to the *Argo*," I urged. "I'll keep watch over the serpent and then catch you up."

"Perhaps that might be best. You can sprinkle more of the potion over it if it wakes."

"Yes," I agreed, trying desperately to sound certain that my brew would have the desired effect. On the few times when I had come to sacrifice to Phrixus or the ram, I had been very careful to ensure that I did not outstay the protection afforded by the first dose. "Testing and observation," I muttered to myself. "Artemis protect me from having to test this new possibility."

I could hear Jason as he fought his way through the grove. He was a hero and, as such, might well curse the bushes for impeding his progress. But I was a girl and could see the benefits of silence. It was not just that Jason's voice might waken the serpent, but his words might help my father to plot his path. Huddled next to the serpent's slimy head, it was all too easy to imagine Jason emerging from the grove and walking straight into an ambush. I shivered, seeing Jason struck down before he even had the chance to draw his sword. Would my father tell me what had happened? Or would he destroy the body and leave me to wonder whether Jason had sailed back to Greece without me?

Thoughts of Greece reminded me that I had my own task to complete. I forced my gaze back down onto the foul creature by my side. Had its eyelids flickered? Was the beast about to awaken? I told myself that the eyelids had only seemed to move because of the rising and falling of the serpent's flanks as it breathed. But I found it hard to fight off my increasing terror. I could see every detail of the poisonous fangs in the creature's cavernous mouth, but I had never felt less like learning new knowledge. All I could think of was what would happen if those fangs drove themselves into my flesh. How long would I take to die? How agonising would the pain be? Weakly, I wished that Jason were there to help me keep my courage up, but that was ridiculous. The entire reason for Jason's visit to the grove was to remove the Fleece, and that goal could hardly be achieved if he had to remain to comfort a feeble, cowardly girl.

Eventually, I judged that Jason must have made his way out of the grove. I swiftly scattered some more of my potion upon the creature's upturned head, before retreating rapidly. It took considerable control not to empty the entire amount over it, but I wanted to have a final dose spare in case it were to follow me. It was better to risk the serpent awakening slightly earlier than to risk having to tackle it with no protection whatsoever. All the same, I hoped that, if it awoke, the second dose would keep it sufficiently drowsy so that it would not perceive that the purpose for its solitary vigil had been removed.

I rapidly followed Jason's trail – it was easy to see where he had been because there were scattered twigs and leaves upon the ground. I was surprised to notice that he had made a diversion from the main path, but blessed the broken foliage which showed me where to follow him. Moments later, I heard swearing as Jason cursed the thorny bushes for snagging the Fleece. Forgetting my own strictures about the need for silence, I called out in a low voice.

"Jason? My love, are you there?"

"Medea?"

I had no time to wonder why my lover sounded surprised. I burst through the final set of bushes, my heart flooding with joy.

"You waited for me! My sweetheart, you are so brave."

"I didn't want to go on to the ship without knowing

that you were safe. I know that that wasn't our plan, but how could I leave you?"

He gave me a crushing hug, and then we set off out of the grove and across the barren field of rocks.

XVI

The journey to the *Argo* was uneventful, although it was accompanied on my part by physical and mental exhaustion. The ordeal in the grove had drained me so much that all I wanted to do was curl up in some dark corner and sleep and sleep. However, I knew that I had to keep going until we reached the ship and were able to sail away from Colchis and away from my father. Moreover, I was deeply apprehensive as to what we would discover when we reached the harbour, since my father was perfectly capable of killing the crew and burning the boat. When we finally trudged along the dusty track which led to the main harbour, I could not hide my relief when I saw a ship riding safely at anchor where Jason had said the *Argo* would be. Everything looked so friendly, so normal. I could have cried from sheer reaction. The sight of the helmsman chatting to a passer-by brought further reassurance. Surely the men must be safe or the helmsman would not look so relaxed. However, when the passer-by turned round and stared at us, I stopped feeling so sanguine: it was Apsyrtus.

"What is your brother doing here?" asked Jason, his voice sharp with concern. "How did he know to come here? Did you tell him anything?"

I shook my head. "Of course not! I wouldn't have trusted him with our secrets. Perhaps he's just interested in the ship – you told me that he wanted to look over it."

"Why the blazes need he choose now?"

"We must pretend that there's nothing strange going on."

"Don't you think that he might possibly notice that I'm carrying a huge, golden sheepskin?"

"Yes, but we've got to buy as much time as possible. If

we look guilty, he may shout for help. If we try to appear normal, he'll be confused and that may give us just enough time to get on board before he summons aid."

"But the Fleece?"

I cast around for a decent excuse to be carrying off my brother's birth-right. "Tell him… tell him that Chalciope wants to see it. Tell him that we're fetching it for a ceremony of sacrifice to Phrixus. Tell him that Aeetes asked us to convey it to her."

By this point, we had reached the Argo. The helmsman's eyes widened at the sight of the Fleece, but he prudently did not comment upon it.

"Young Apsyrtus here wanted to see the *Argo*, Jason."

Jason gave a false smile. "We're always delighted to see you, Prince Apsyrtus. Why don't you come on board and see how the oars are arranged to give us extra speed?"

I was rather appalled at this suggestion. It was all very well abducting Apsyrtus, but Jason did not seem to have considered how we would then return him to Colchis from Iolcos. I certainly did not want my brother living with us, but we could hardly abandon him on a remote island, a possible catch for slave-dealers.

My brother glared at Jason. "What are you doing with the Fleece? It is my father's, and it will be mine when I am king."

"Your father is sending it to your sister Chalciope."

"I don't believe you. You said that you wanted it as a dowry for Medea. You can't be taking it to one sister whilst also taking it as the price for marrying the other. Or do you now claim that you aren't going to marry Medea? Do you favour Chalciope instead?"

"I am going to marry Medea."

Apsyrtus snorted contemptuously. "Perhaps you are, but I know that my father has no intention of giving the Fleece to you as dowry or as any other type of gift. What's more he *can't* give it to you. It belongs to the king of Colchis. Any king who gave it away would be giving away the source of his power. Do you think that my father would do that, even to get rid of her?"

Jason nobly refrained from losing his temper at this insult to his bride. He placed the Fleece carefully on the hot, dusty earth and again smiled at Apsyrtus. "I am very happy for you to accompany us on our trip to Chalciope. You can watch her perform sacrifices to the Fleece in Phrixus's name and then you can accompany the Fleece back to your father's palace. In fact, your presence would make the ceremony more powerful. Naturally, my fellow heroes will be present, but you are a prince."

Jason sounded so convincing that Apsyrtus's confidence faltered momentarily. Then a black scowl descended across his face.

"You're a liar and she's a traitor. My father will kill you both."

Apsyrtus had scarcely finished speaking when Jason grabbed him. The helmsman gave a shrill whistle and moved in front of the struggling pair, so that nothing could be seen from the quayside. Two sailors appeared almost instantaneously and assisted Jason in dragging Apsyrtus up the gang-plank. Another two heaved the Fleece on board, while the rest methodically prepared to cast off. Just in time, I leapt on to the gang-plank before an over-eager sailor could remove it. The helmsman stared at me with unconcealed interest.

"Are you coming with us then?"

"Of course. I am going to marry Jason."

"Oh. I see. Maybe you'd best be going below then."

Wishing that the sailor had sounded more enthusiastic, I bolstered my morale by reminding myself that Jason had been very wise to observe secrecy in relation to the crew. Admittedly, our betrothal had been announced publicly at the palace, but perhaps it was best for the crew not to have been gossiping all round the port. The less that people talked about Jason and me, the less likelihood that anyone would suspect that I might run away with him.

The press of sailors scurrying about raising the sails prevented me from moving from my position by the side rails for some time. When I finally went down to the rowing deck to seek Jason, I found him cuffing Apsyrtus round the head.

"You can watch the Fleece to your heart's content now, you little brat. And your chances of being released will depend entirely on how you behave whilst you do so."

My brother caught sight of me. "Medea, tell this oaf to let me go."

I bit my lip. Apsyrtus had spent most of his short life mocking and deriding me, but he was my brother, linked indissolubly to me by blood.

"Jason," I began tentatively, "don't hit him, please."

"The cheeky little beggar called me names and tried to bite me."

I turned to Apsyrtus. "I know you must be angry, Apsyrtus, but we shall let you go back to my father, I promise. There's no point annoying Jason when you're on his vessel."

Apsyrtus glared at me. "That's easy for you to say: you're not losing the Fleece; you're not losing the symbol of your kingship. No, you're running away with some rotten adventurer."

Jason gave a hearty laugh. "You call me an adventurer, but don't forget that you enjoyed hearing about my adventures. If you hadn't wanted to learn how to be a hero you wouldn't have come to the *Argo* today to talk to my crew. Why don't you treat this as an adventure until you go back home?"

Absyrtus shot Jason a look of ineffable contempt. "Do you think that I am a child of seven to talk to me like that? This is not an adventure. This is theft; theft of my father's property and of mine. Would you stand back and do nothing about such theft?"

I had never respected my brother before that moment. Previously, I had regarded him as a petulant, unpleasant small boy, but I suddenly began to believe that perhaps he did possess some of the elements of kingship. However, I did not have the chance to react to his words, for a sailor appeared, demanding Jason's presence urgently. My lover bound my brother's hands behind his back, before dragging him up onto the deck beside him. Even in the short time since the boat had been launched, we had travelled a surprising distance. I was taken aback to see the shore merging into the horizon – Colchis was now a hazy blur, not my homeland. Naturally, Jason was not disturbed by such thoughts. He scanned the sea with an experienced eye, before turning to the helmsman.

"What's up, Ancaios? Is it that boat over there?"

"Aye. I watched her set sail from the harbour. I've no doubt she's pursuing us."

One look at Apsyrtus's triumphant face convinced me that he had no doubt either. Jason frowned thoughtfully.

"Can we outsail her?"

Ancaios shrugged his shoulders. "We've a start on her, but she's a racing vessel and the sailors will know the winds and the waters better than we can."

Jason muttered something before turning to me. "You're a sorceress, Medea. Can't you cast a spell to change the wind or something?"

I grimaced, conscious that I was letting down Jason the first time he asked for my help. "I'm sorry. I don't know what to do. Magical powers work differently on sea than on land. In any case, even if I could think of something, we would probably lose the wind too."

"Best to get our rowers in position in case the wind does fail," suggested Ancaios, generously ignoring my incapacity to achieve anything useful. He glanced at the sky, which had turned an ominous orangey-red. "Or, indeed, in case the wind gets too strong. If a tempest blows up, we'll have to lower our sails before they are ripped to tatters."

It struck me that the pursuing vessel was perceptibly nearer than it had been a few moments ago but, aware that I knew nothing about seamanship, I remained silent. However, to judge from Ancaios's expression, my suspicions were correct. He watched in silence before at last summoning a sailor with orders for the rowers to add their power to our attempt to outflee what must be my father's ship.

Although the *Argo* seemed to make a sudden surge forward when the white oars began to beat the glassy waves, it made no difference to the distance between the two vessels. If anything, the other drew even closer. There came an abrupt shout from Apsyrtus.

"My father's catching up with you. I bet you wish you hadn't taken the Fleece now."

Since this was precisely what I was trying not to think, I was grateful for Jason's curt command that Apsyrtus be quiet. "It could be any ship," he added. "You have no certainty that your father is on it."

Apsyrtus took this rebuke in silence, glowering at Jason with resentment and bitter hatred. Time passed. Jason paced backwards and forwards, while I wondered if the rhythm of the rowers was beginning to slow. Why else could I now pick out the colours of the ship behind us, discern distinct figures on it, and even recognise the painted prow? Apsyrtus continued to crane his neck towards the pursuing boat, as if in a despairing attempt to reach closer towards his own territory. Suddenly, he gave a gleeful crow of delight.

"It *is* my father. See, there is King Aeetes, standing on the prow. Ah, Jason, now you will learn how a king deals with his enemies. When you feel the lash upon your naked back and you see your blood flow down your legs and onto your feet, will you regret what you have done? When your limbs are torn… Ugh."

Whatever threat Apsyrtus had intended to utter died in his throat as Jason hit him so hard that he crashed back onto the side of the boat. Since I knew that Apsyrtus's hands were tied, I bent to help him upright, only to stare in horror at his limp body and the head that lay at a strange angle.

"J… J… Jason," I stammered. "Something terrible's happened. I think…" I gulped. "I think that you've killed him."

XVII

It was an accident – at least, to begin with Jason always swore to me that it was. In was only later in his drunken maunderings that he used to claim that he had always intended to punish the brat for daring to challenge him. Even now, I don't really know which tale to believe.

What happened next, I admit, is distinctly unpleasant. But to this day, I cannot see an alternative. My father's ship was overhauling us; was now within hailing distance; would soon have us at his mercy. I looked to Jason for guidance, but his lip trembled and his hand shook. Gods! That hand should have seized his sword in the joy of the fight and the throbbing desire to protect me. But instead it quivered, just as Jason's voice quivered when he gasped something about throwing the Fleece overboard. I rejected this suggestion, equivalent as it was to abject surrender.

Moreover, I knew my father. I knew his fierce pride and his spiteful, savage anger. For taking me, Jason would die. For taking the Fleece, Jason would die after hours of vengeful cruelty. The Fleece was my father's property and I was his property. Aeetes allowed no thieves to steal even the seeds which fell from his uncut wheat. When I was seven, a man was brought before Aeetes, accused of pilfering a few bunches of grapes. His terror was pitiable and his grovelling whimperings of contrition could hardly be heard through his fear-haunted weeping. My father had him tied to a stake and flogged to death. That was the first time that I saw a man's ribs exposed whilst he was still alive. A spot of blood landed on Aeetes's hand. He licked it off, before remarking unemotionally. "You stole my grapes; now I drink your blood-red wine." Those grapes were Aeetes's property, just as I was and the Fleece was. But Apsyrtus was his adored only son. And Apsyrtus lay dead on the deck of our ship.

No matter how shocked I was to see my brother stretched out limp and broken at my feet, I knew that Jason's safety lay in my hands. Now was not the time for chicken-hearted hopes of mercy – my father did not know what mercy was. Now was the time for action. As I seized Apsyrtus's body, I noticed that even in death he had a mocking sneer on his face as if he was about to tell me once more that I was a mere girl and that he was the prince, the ruler-to-be, and my master. This ghostly memory helped steady me for my task. With savage, searching fingers I grasped his slim arm by the humerus and hacked at his shoulder-blade with Jason's sword. My knowledge of sacrifices came in useful here. Instead of mindlessly yanking at Apsyrtus's arm, I swiftly found the socket and slipped the joints apart. Rapidly turning to the other arm, my fingers bit into Apsyrtus's young flesh as I cleaved Jason's sword for a second time. When the two limbs lay bloodily together, side by side, I turned to Jason.

"Throw them overboard. My father will stop to pick them up."

Green with nausea, Jason spurned my request. "Touch these repulsive objects? Have you forgotten that he was your brother?"

"No. But there is no other way to save us. Can you not hear my father's curses? He will show us no pity; he will never believe that you did not intend to kill his son."

With that, I hurled Apsyrtus's limp limbs far from the boat. Not stopping to watch them tossed like a child's plaything by the gaily lapping waves, I directed my attention to the lower limbs. Nails dug deep as the torso fought to defeat this latest assault. But Apsyrtus could no longer resist me and soon two legs were floating on the waves beneath. Then I hacked off his smug, sneering head and held it up to my father by its long locks.

"Here is your son; your perfect son; your son who killed my mother; the boy who outranked all and made my presence hateful to you."

I could hear a harsh screaming, like that of an eagle who returns to her nest to find the prize nestling vanished and gone. Holding the gory head still higher so that Apsyrtus could hear his father's execrations, I cast a final benediction of tears upon the waves before releasing the relict to drop into the all-consuming waves. The torso followed shortly after and we were free to sail onwards. Only the clotting blood on the deck was a reminder of where my brother had lain.

PART TWO: IOLCOS

XVIII

Just as my father execrated me, so too has the judgement
of the world. People say that Medea the murderess began
her career with her own brother. But it is not true. I
butchered the body, but I did not kill. If Jason had done
what I did, people would have recognised his initiative and
quick-thinking. They would have had no difficulty in
understanding that his actions had saved us from being left
as corpses floating on the surface of the sea. But a woman
who shows such masculine traits as initiative is regarded as
dangerous, callous and uncontrolled. How callous I really
was can be judged by the fact that I spent the immediate
aftermath of our escape vomiting up my soul over the side
of the *Argo*. Ironically, Jason was disgusted at my physical
reaction; heroes, seemingly, did not display such weakness,
only a woman would let herself go in the way in which I
had. Moreover, I apparently made matters worse by getting
in the way of the crew – as if any woman who is helplessly
retching green bile into the waves is capable of making
coherent judgements as to who needs to move where in
order to raise or lower sails.

The crew seemed ready enough to forgive me, but they
were disinclined to talk to me. I was disappointed, but
could understand their hesitancy in speaking to a woman
who was not related to them. Such conversations as I
overheard were restricted to fighting, and I found myself
flinching away from talk of bloodshed and violent death.
In any case, I only really wanted to speak to Jason, to be
with him at every moment, to gaze upon his strong face
and to listen to his sweet voice. However, even although I
was escaping to start a new life in a new country with a
man who loved me, I did not neglect what was owed to
Apsyrtus's spirit. It would have been hypocritical to say

that I grieved for him, but I was shocked and appalled at his end. The little boy who had so eagerly boasted of his hunting prowess had gone forever and I knew that I shared as much responsibility for his end as did Jason. I made several libations to his shade on the journey and planned a more formal sacrifice once we arrived at Iolcos.

That arrival loomed more and more in my thoughts. Jason had swiftly got over his upset at my treatment of Apsyrtus's corpse and returned to his loving words and caresses. In particular, he was happy to tell me about Iolcos and Greece. It was clear that Jason was immensely proud of his race and, to me, the Greeks did indeed sound a paragon among peoples. They did not descend to petty gossip or spite, but instead concentrated on important matters; they were not hidebound or reactionary, but eager to engage with new thinking; and finally – and to my mind – most importantly, they were concerned with the calibre of a person's intellect and what ideas he had to offer, rather than focussing narrowly upon his identity and background. Little wonder that when we finally sailed into the harbour at Iolcos I peered around eagerly at this fabled land.

What I first saw slightly disappointed me. Jason had talked of a rich and important city, but the harbour seemed no bigger than that back home in Colchis. In fact, if anything, it appeared to be somewhat smaller. However, I was not in a mood to carp and instead I contented myself by listening to the foreign, babbling tongues and observing the exotic appearance of the town. The men dressed in a similar fashion to Jason, but here and there I could see a few women threading their way through the bustling crowd. These looked very different from the ordinary women of Colchis, who did not wear such bright colours, such clinging fabrics or so much make-up. It was only months later that I learned that these glittering birds were prostitutes out to entice sailors to pour gold into their avaricious talons.

I turned to Jason with a mixture of eagerness and trepidation at having to meet so many new, foreign people.

"Will we go straight to the palace to meet your uncle? Will you warn me exactly what to say to him?"

Jason eyed the crowd thoughtfully. "I think it might be better if I seek him out alone to begin with and then introduce you to him."

I tried not to sound nervous. "I hope that he won't be angry that you married me at Colchis, rather than waiting until we reached Iolcos."

"What do you mean?"

"My father wouldn't have been pleased if Apsyrtus had wed a girl without his knowledge."

"Not a problem which will face either of them now."

I tried to explain more clearly. "I don't want Pelias to dislike me, because it will make matters difficult for you if he does."

"I'll not tell him that I've married you, then," Jason suggested. "I'll tell him that you helped me with the Fleece. That'll put him in a good mood towards you and we can approach the subject of marriage later."

I blushed and cursed myself for blushing. "But, Jason, if you do that, people will think…"

Jason's mind appeared to be on the lowering of the *Argo*'s main sail, which had snagged on the mast. "What? What will they think?"

"I've spent days on board ship with no other woman present. If you don't say that we are married, people will assume that I am not worthy of respect."

"A harlot, do you mean? Mmm. I suppose that they might. Tricky. I'll think about it."

"But, Jason…"

Jason turned an irritated face towards me. "I've told you that I'll think about it." His expression softened. "You must trust me, my sweetheart. Don't forget, my uncle stole the throne from my father. Do you think that I would risk telling him about you until I have ensured that you will be quite safe? I could not bear to expose you to danger."

I rubbed my head against his shoulder. "Forgive me, Jason. I did not realise that you were so concerned."

Jason smiled down at me. "And you must forgive me, too, my beloved. The knowledge that your safety and happiness lies in my hands is a consideration which bears heavily upon me. I face further challenges before I can sit upon the throne of Iolcos, but I did not bring you from Colchis to put you in harm's way." He stroked my hair. "Don't worry, Medea. I shall defeat Pelias and win the townsmen over. I know the ways of my countrymen and I can talk them round."

Jason continued to repeat his belief that he could win the people of Iolcos over to his side, both in terms of his right to the throne and in his choice of bride. I desperately wished to help Jason, but he rejected my offer.

"No, Medea, you have done enough already. I cannot ask more of you."

"But I am your wife, Jason."

"Not so loud, my dear. Remember that we must not let slip anything which might forewarn Pelias."

I sighed and followed Jason submissively as he brought me down the gang-plank. I had looked forward to this day – the day on which I would come ashore as a blushing bride, full of my brave new husband, full of plans to help him recover his rightful throne and ready to help him govern his kingdom. I was still full of plans, but rather than stepping off the boat with my head held high and my jewels flashing in the clear light, I scuttled onshore, my head and body swathed in unflattering folds of cloth. It certainly was not the entry to my new country which I had intended, but I trusted Jason's arguments – after all, he knew more about the likely reactions of the people of Iolcos than I did. A beautiful young woman who walked with the air of a princess might well excite suspicion, but a dowdy object who avoided meeting the gaze of any idle passer-by would not attract much interest.

Although I had accepted Jason's advice to disguise my appearance, I nearly threw all caution to the winds soon after. We journeyed through the usual cramped streets which surround every harbour until we reached a small, rather dingy house. Jason apologised for its exterior.

"I'm sorry to have to ask you to stay here until it is safe to bring you to the palace, but at least no-one will think of looking for you in this area."

"Who lives here?"

"An old woman who used to work at the palace and her daughters."

"An ex-slave?"

Jason's chin jutted out. "Yes. As it happens she was. Surely you aren't going to complain about that? Wasn't your nurse Theonoe a slave?"

I felt sudden tears wet my eyes. Jason and I had disagreed on the subject of Theonoe when he had found me crying five nights out of Colchis. Assuming that I was weeping for Apsyrtus or my father, he had been distinctly taken aback when I had informed him that I was grieving for the fact that I could no longer take offerings directly to Theonoe's grave. I explained that blood or wine was more likely to soak through the heavy earth to reach Theonoe's shade if such a sacrifice was performed in a location steeped in her presence. But Jason dismissed my fears, pointing out that I could sacrifice anywhere. I had not known how to convince Jason and, when he grew irritated by my attempts to do so, I had eventually given up, wondering if I was betraying Theonoe by doing so.

Jason's heavy knocking on the door broke through my thoughts. When there was no answer he knocked again. Finally, we heard stumbling footsteps and the sound of a latch being drawn back. The door slowly opened and a heavy-eyed woman stared out.

"Oh, it's you is it, Jason? Back after your travels and hungry?" She yawned. "You know we rest at this time – why didn't you wait until night?"

Jason frowned at her. "Hush, Gorgo. This is Medea. I want you to show her to your best room and allow her to rest. She is not to be disturbed in any way, do you understand? Not in any way at all."

Gorgo's eyes flickered over me in a peculiarly knowing manner which made me want to slap her face. "And where has Medea come from? She's not dressed as one of us."

"No," agreed Jason uncommunicatively. "She is not one of you and she is to be treated with respect. I want the place kept absolutely quiet whilst she is here – and no gossiping about her presence, either."

"You know I don't gossip," replied Gorgo, with a hint of a whine in her voice. "You of all people ought to know that I never talk about what I know."

"And that is why I've brought Medea here where she can wait in safety for me. I shall reward you well, Gorgo, for keeping the place quiet – don't let those girls of yours chatter or receive any visitors."

It struck me that Gorgo's eyes gleamed avariciously at the mention of a reward, but she led me off meekly enough. Leaving me for the moment to wash my face and hands, she returned to talk to Jason. When I rejoined them, Jason was looking rather sulky, whilst Gorgo now clinked as she moved. The explanation of this musical accompaniment was soon forthcoming.

"I've given Gorgo plenty of money to look after you, Medea, so you must ask for anything you want."

"All I want is you, Jason. Come and see me soon."

Jason kissed me softly. "You know that I may not be able to do so. Be patient, my dove."

Now began six days of intense worry and frustration which required all my patience to survive. I knew that Jason was unsure whom to trust, but waiting and waiting for news and never hearing anything was very hard. Every day I tried to push away images of Jason being captured, Jason being tortured, Jason being condemned to death by his uncle. And still I heard nothing.

Meanwhile, Gorgo's curiosity was running rampant. I saw little of her three daughters, but she seemed to have appointed herself as my guardian – perhaps even my jailor. She yawned her way through most of the day, but during the evening she would not leave me alone. There were questions as to where I had come from, questions as to what I wore, and questions as to Jason. Those were the hardest to fend off, accompanied as they were with insinuating glances and secret smiles. Naturally, I realised that she must have taken me for Jason's lover, but I found it intensely difficult not to burst out with the fact that I was, in truth, Jason's wife. However, I kept reminding myself that Jason had asked me not to reveal any information. Even if he – as a man – had not realised how uncomfortable the situation would be for me, it was up to me – as Jason's wife – not to give away anything which might make his situation dangerous. All the same, I was only human and my good intentions were not quite unbreachable in the face of Gorgo's constant pestering. After she had fingered my clothes and speculated what they had cost and what they might sell for here in Iolcos, she finally asked me the question which I was trying desperately not to frame in my own mind, lest it come true in reality.

"What will you do if Jason doesn't come back?"

"Do go away."

"Very hoity-toity, aren't you? First you won't talk about clothes and now you won't talk about your man. Or isn't he your man?"

"Go away. I'm not talking about Jason with you."

Gorgo cackled. "Maybe not. But there might be other things you have to talk about if he doesn't come back."

"What do you mean?"

Gorgo ran her eyes over me – something which I found curiously repulsive. "You might need to talk about how to earn your keep. You don't look like you're used to working, a decorative piece like you."

I was insulted. As far as I was concerned, my role as a seer back at Colchis had been very serious work. "Women don't need to spend their lives slaving over their weaving or fetching water-jars from the fountain."

"Indeed, no," agreed Gorgo, with another cackle. "But how would you earn the cost of that embroidery on the hem of your robe or those pretty bits of amber in your ears? Very decorative, they are. You'd find it hard to earn the money that Jason must have spent buying them for you. "

I did not understand why Gorgo was sneering at me, but her tone was clearly insulting. I promptly lost what little hold I had left over my temper. "Jason didn't buy them for me and I could quite easily earn enough money to buy two or three more pairs."

Gorgo's eyebrows rose. "Really? You rate yourself very highly, my fine lady."

"Naturally. I am a priestess."

Perhaps I had hoped for a gasp of shock and instant contrition. Instead, I received laughter. "What? A little fortune-teller? Do you cast the bones, my pretty? Poor Jason!"

Drawing myself up to my full height, I glared at Gorgo.

"I am a full prophetess, skilled in the ways of sorcery. I advise you not to mock my powers. No-one in Colchis dared do so."

Gorgo sniggered. It is humiliating to admit it, but she did. "Colchis? Who cares about some backward place like Colchis? This is Greece."

Iolcos was indeed Greece. And with Gorgo's mocking words, I began to fear that this wondrous new land was not quite as open and welcoming to outsiders as Jason had declared it to be. Was Jason the one who was mistaken? Or had I somehow gone beyond my allotted position and brought this hostility against myself? But Jason had said that people were judged for their quality of mind, not their origin. I tried to reassure myself that the problem lay with Gorgo. She certainly lacked sophistication and I rather doubted that she had the intellectual equipment or outlook necessary for the sort of priestly studies which I had undertaken. I glared at Gorgo, but she was still sniggering over the outlandish idea that women could have important roles. Finally she stopped laughing and got up to leave the room. As she departed, she threw a barbed remark back over her shoulder.

"Don't forget, Medea, you're no longer in Colchis. You're in Greece. And in Greece, women stick to women's tasks and don't pretend to be men."

XIX

Gorgo's comments upset me more than I cared to show. It would have been easy to retort that I was a princess of Colchis and that she ought to show me proper respect, but Jason had begged me not to reveal my true identity. Moreover, I suspected that Gorgo would either dismiss my story as an invented tale or sneer that princesses from backward lands were not the same as Greek princesses. As it was, I felt sullied by her presence. Even to hear her speak of Colchis or Jason was like watching a slug deposit a trail of slime over the delicate petals of a cyclamen. The more I defended myself or Colchis, the more destructive slime Gorgo would spread.

Thrusting away the lingering sound of Gorgo's cackling, I wrenched open the window of my room and gratefully drew in air which did not taste of the old woman's heavy perfume. I glanced down at the tiny courtyard below, wondering for how much longer I would be cooped up in this wretched place. Gorgo had interpreted Jason's instructions as meaning that I could not even seek the sun in the courtyard, despite its high walls which shut out spying passers-by. Resentfully, I noticed that the daughters of the house appeared to be allowed this privilege, since Praxinoe and Arsinoe were sitting on an old stone bench, happily gossiping when they ought to have been fetching water. I ignored their shrill voices, concentrating on the lizards, whose irregular swift darts measured strange dances on the stones. I, a princess of Colchis and the wife of Jason of Iolcos, had been brought so low that I envied those lizards their freedom to dart in the sun.

Suddenly I caught the sound of my own name. I froze. Even the lizards stopped their play and froze, hunched and motionless, as if they too wished to hear what was being said. Arsinoe was waving her arms, heavy with silver bracelets.

"But, Praxinoe, I don't understand. Who *is* this woman that Jason's brought?"

Praxinoe opened her mouth to speak, but Arsinoe was not finished. "Gorgo says that she claims to be a priestess, a necromancer."

"Gorgo was probably teasing you. She knows that you'll believe anything."

Arsinoe pouted angrily. "Don't be stupid. Why should she try to trick me?"

Praxinoe idly coiled her thick hair round her fingers and admired the effect for a moment, before yawning. "Gorgo's probably bored with this enforced holiday."

"She's getting paid enough."

"Yes, but she always wants more. If you ask me, if she weren't afraid of losing Jason's custom, she'd have done a little discreet entertaining, guest or no guest."

"You mean we would have," grumbled Arsinoe.

"Jealous because Jason's not casting admiring glances in your direction?"

"I can't imagine what he sees in Medea. She's not even good-looking."

Praxinoe stroked her plump arms complacently. "Be fair, she's pretty enough, if you like them thin and bony, with flashing eyes and scornful looks."

"Well, I don't like her and I don't understand why Jason does."

"Maybe she told him all that stuff about prophecy and he believed her." Praxinoe giggled. "Maybe he thinks that she's some sort of a goddess come down to earth. Never mind, Arsinoe, she's not a goddess or even a priestess; she's just some woman from Colchis. Jason'll soon get tired of her."

I retreated from the window and sank down onto the bed in shock. Jason had placed me in a bordello. There could be no other explanation for it. And I had been so bound up worrying about his safety that I had missed all the warning signs. Gorgo was an ex-slave, who pursued no obvious trade. No flower-garlands or vegetables were sold from her house. Nevertheless, she seemed to have plenty of money to spend on jewellery and perfume, and her supposed daughters were equally well turned-out. She had assumed that I was Jason's mistress and had clearly thought that there was only one way in which a woman could earn large sums of money. Finally, Gorgo had shown no surprise at Jason's arrival at her house, only at the time of his arrival. That, added to Arsinoe's complaints, made it obvious that he used to frequent Gorgo's dwelling – presumably to seek out Arsinoe's charms. He had probably slept with Arsinoe before he set off to Colchis.

"A princess of Colchis is not weak," I told myself fiercely. "The daughter of a king does not weep. A priestess does not show fear."

Despite these consoling words, I found that my fingers were twisting and untwisting of their own accord. Naturally, I knew that Jason must have had sexual adventures before he married me – life at my father's court had taught me that fact of life. Nevertheless, it had never occurred to me that I should come face-to-face with his cast-off mistresses, much less live in their houses. A worm of fear ran through my head that perhaps Jason had not cast off Arsinoe. Perhaps her ill-formed features and cow-like eyes were more to Jason's taste than my own. Urging myself to be loyal, I reminded myself that Jason had only spoken to Gorgo, not to Arsinoe. And if he had not visited me, nor had he sought out Arsinoe. Moreover, he had given specific orders to Gorgo not to bring anyone into the house. Surely that was an attempt to protect me? Surely?

Two days later, Jason appeared. He seemed somewhat surprised by the hesitant manner in which I returned his kiss.

"What's all this, Medea? I thought that you'd be happier to see me."

"I am happy," I whispered, feeling a traitor for the thoughts which had kept crowding into my head at night.

He laughed. "Did you think that Pelias would kill me? Silly child. Pack up your things quickly – I'm taking you up to the palace."

"The palace?"

"Yes, my delight. I want to present you to Pelias." He inspected me carefully. "Hmm. You've been fretting. Never mind. I'm sure my uncle will soon see how beautiful you are."

Despite my happiness at this praise, I could not help asking with some bitterness, "You don't think that I'll be too thin and bony for his taste?"

A swift expression of comprehension crossed his face. "Been quarrelling with the girls? Really, Medea, I'd have thought that you'd have had more sense. You know that I love you, so why have silly arguments which could have left you with nowhere to wait for me?"

"I didn't quarrel with them, Jason. I don't quarrel with prostitutes."

Jason looked at me with distaste. "I'm shocked that you can use such a word."

"And I'm shocked that you left me in a bordello."

By this point, I was weeping, but Jason ignored my tears.

"How can you ruin our reunion like this, Medea? I have been counting the hours until I could see you again and you spoil it by talking of things that no decent Greek woman would mention. In any case, I fail to see why you make such accusations." He laughed sarcastically. "I don't imagine you are going to tell me that you have been entertaining men here whilst I was absent trying to regain my throne."

"Of course not, but Arsinoe and the other two aren't Gorgo's daughters. They call her Mother in my presence, but Gorgo when I'm not there."

"If you're not there, how can you know what they call her?"

"I overheard them talking – and that talk made it obvious what this place is."

Jason drew back from me rather haughtily. "I am very disappointed that you have spied on your hostesses. I should have thought that your royal blood would have prevented you from such a lapse. Moreover, if you had resisted the temptation to eavesdrop you would not have been led to such low suspicions." He sighed and tried to speak more gently. "Really, Medea, you need to consider things more carefully before you accuse me of not looking after you properly. Where else could I have placed you? Normally, you would have been welcomed to the palace, but you know that I feared what Pelias might do to you. I could not ask the Argonauts to hide you because it would have destroyed your reputation if anyone had discovered you in the house of a man with whom you had already undertaken a long sea-voyage. Finally, if I had asked a nobleman from court to keep you safe, his slaves might have chattered and betrayed your presence." He sighed again. "I did not expect reproaches for trying to protect you. However, if you no longer trust me, I shall not ask you to accompany me to the palace."

XX

Of course I accompanied Jason to the palace. What alternative did I have? Colchis was no longer a practical proposition – not that Jason offered to put me on a ship home. As for remaining with Gorgo, I had no desire to follow her sneaking hints as to how I could earn my living. The only possibility was to go with Jason. After all, he was my husband. And a wife ought to trust her husband. If I stalked off now, how could I ever be sure that I had done the correct thing? The possibility that I had done Jason a grave injustice would haunt me for the rest of my life. In any case, I was still in love with him. I wanted to believe him. I wanted to trust him. His arguments were entirely plausible. If Pelias was as cunning as Jason claimed, I might not have been safe at the palace or in the house of some nobleman. And it was certainly the case that if I had stayed in the home of an unmarried man my reputation – or worse – would have been ruined. I shuddered at the thought. So I followed Jason.

As we swept through the streets, Jason ignored me. I could see from the set of his shoulders that he was still angry and annoyed. I could not decide if this meant that he loved me and was hurt by my apparent lack of trust. The alternative – that he was irritated by my questioning his actions – was rather harder to face, since it suggested things about my husband which I did not wish to contemplate. However, as we neared the palace, Jason slowed down and addressed me.

"Medea, please let yourself be guided by me until you are more familiar with life in Iolcos. I want all the citizens to be proud of their new princess. I want them to talk of your beauty, your charm and your love for me. I do not want them to gossip about thoughtless remarks uttered from anger or fear. You are used to a court environment; you must know how everything nobles do is poured over for indications of who is in favour and who is not. Do you think that I wish to see my citizens discussing you in that way?"

Suddenly, he caught hold of me and stared into my eyes as he whispered fervently. "Gods, Medea, don't you know how the very thought of you gives me a reason to live? That I adore you? That your body sends me on fire, and that your eyes could charm the moon from the sky for me? If it had not been for you, I should have renounced my claim to Iolcos and sailed far away. But I have spent these long days fighting for my ancestral rights because I want you to adorn a throne. I was wracked by doubt as to whether I could defeat my uncle's evil wiles and I was bitterly unhappy at being separated from you. But what else could I do? I have made it impossible for you to return to Colchis, so I must be able to offer you a throne in return for your sacrifice."

I stared at Jason, taken aback, but reassured by his fervour, which spoke of anguish similar to that which I had suffered when we had been apart.

Jason continued, as if impelled by a strange force to spill out his inner thoughts. "My delight, my dove, let us swear to support each other and not give way to foolish doubts. I want us to be together forever, not to quarrel over silly little things. Never doubt me again, my dearest, I beg of you. I cannot bear it."

"Jason," I breathed, as I lifted up my head to receive his kiss, "Jason, I love you."

By the time that we reached the palace, Jason had done his best to warn me what to expect. He had described the various important nobles, including what they looked like and whether they were trustworthy. He had even made a joke that I might be able to discuss sorcery with Kynaxilides, the resident seer of Iolcos. "He's easy to recognise, because he's blind."

"Seers often are," I agreed. "It helps them sense the gods' presence in other ways." Thinking that perhaps I ought to reveal something of my art to Jason as a practical demonstration of my trust in him, I tried to explain what I meant. "The gods don't often speak directly to men, and a blind seer cannot see any omens. But the gods send more signs than just flying birds and twisted entrails. Phrixus taught me to sense their presence in other ways."

"What do you mean?"

"Apollo's presence can come coursing through the still air; it can be sensed in the sudden rustling of an olive tree or the piping of a cicada. An unexpected noise in the middle of the shimmering heat shows that the god is there, watching, observing, speaking."

A quick shiver ran through Jason's body. "Don't, Medea. I don't like it when you do that."

"Do what?"

"Go all dreamy and distant as if you were actually listening out for the gods to speak to you. You even closed your eyes then as if you were as blind as Kynaxilides."

I shook myself. "Did I? I'm sorry, Jason. I thought that I was quite wide awake." I smiled apologetically. "I'll certainly have to be when I encounter Pelias."

Whilst I had fully intended to be on my guard when I met the man who had stolen Jason's throne, I was thrown off balance by the display which greeted my eyes when I was ushered ceremoniously into the great hall. Jason had warned me that he had presented the Fleece to Pelias. I was unhappy about his action, even although I recognised that he must have had little choice. However, what I had not expected was to see the Fleece stretched out on a table in front of Pelias, his sword lying on top of it, for all the world as if he had seized it himself. To make matters worse, Pelias had just replaced his goblet of wine next to the Fleece. Judging from the thud which had resounded as he set the goblet down, drops of wine would soon splash onto the Fleece, damaging its brilliant glory. I halted, distressed at the lack of respect shown. This was the remains of a noble animal, a creature beloved by the gods and the saviour of a good and honourable man. Surely it ought to be treated with greater reverence?

"Don't be afraid," hissed Jason. "You mustn't let Pelias see that you are afraid."

Thinking that it was more important that I did not let Pelias realise that I was blazing with anger, I stepped forward in Jason's wake.

"My lord, this is the Princess Medea."

Pelias bowed. "Enchanted."

"Greetings, O noble Pelias," I replied. Jason and I had agreed upon this form of address since it avoided the danger of calling him king and thus appearing to accept his usurpation of Jason's throne.

"So you are going to marry my nephew, are you?"

I inclined my head.

"Then I must make you known to my daughters. You will doubtless have much in common. And where have you been staying?"

"Jason brought me from Colchis."

"Colchis," mused Pelias. "I never visited Colchis, but I have heard tales of it."

I kept a set smile on my face, guessing that Pelias did not mean to be complimentary.

"You breed werewolves in Colchis, don't you? What's it like being in a man's company and never being quite sure whether he is who you think he is?" He grunted. "Must be odd living that sort of life. We Greeks don't face that sort of problem."

"Doubtless you have others to compensate."

Pelias roared with laughter at this response. "Aha, Jason, your little Colchian princess has spirit. Are you sure that you can cope with her?"

"Medea and I are of one mind, sir."

"Indeed? Whose mind – hers or yours?"

Naturally, I could not be seen to respond to that quip or it would appear that it was indeed my mind which dominated proceedings. I waited for Jason to respond, but he restricted himself to glaring at Pelias and changing the subject. I did not know whether to admire his restraint or to wish that he had spoken up for me. However, since the purpose of this meeting was to re-establish Jason amongst the nobles of Iolcos, I realised that my husband was correct to avoid unnecessary controversy. Nonetheless, I found it hard not to cry out in protest when I saw Pelias wipe his greasy fingers upon the Fleece.

"A pretty trinket, this," he commented. "Perhaps you have now proved your manhood after all." He belched loudly, before continuing. "And at least you're not such a whining namby-pamby as you were before you set off, complaining about your right to the throne and doing nothing to prove that you were worthy of it. Lord, boy, as if Iolcos needed another weak-kneed ruler after the last one."

Jason remarked in a stilted manner that he failed to understand Pelias's remarks.

Pelias waved his hand dismissively. "I mean your father, Jason. Loxias strike me dead if it isn't the case that Aeson was a weakling who bleated on about the rule of law and how the kingdom was his by right. Pah! He soon learned that a kingdom is there to be run by a *man*." He snapped his fingers at the nearest page, commanding him to fill up his golden goblet. "I've done you a disservice, boy. I assumed you'd be cast in the same mould. Your father would have pissed his tunic even to hear of the serpent which you defeated."

I darted a swift look at Jason, wondering what he had said about my help. Clearly, it would be gratifying to receive praise for my aid, but I could see that Jason's uncle was not the type to respect a man who relied upon a mere woman to achieve his goals. And since I had no intention of undermining Jason's new-found honour, I maintained a resolute silence.

Pelias waved his goblet in Jason's direction. "Come, nephew, let us drink to your success. And I acknowledge here in front of the assembled aristocracy of Iolcos that you will be king after me."

I frowned momentarily. I had understood Jason to say that Pelias was going to resign the kingdom to Jason almost immediately. This new proposal was suspicious. It was all too easy to imagine what Pelias really intended – not a gradual and gracious reassignment of power, but time for a devious usurper to plot further against my husband. Not for nothing had I observed my father outwitting men who thought that they had won his agreement to their plans. Pelias was not to be trusted.

Although I was impatient to be alone with Jason, the rest of the feast had to be endured. Pelias and his men drank heartily and, while they clearly considered themselves to be distinctly superior to the barbarians of Colchis, I could perceive few differences between their actions and the behaviour of the men at my father's court. Indeed, Pelias's sneers about the rule of law left me wondering whether Jason's own high standards had left him with an unusually generous view of his fellow Greeks. I knew that my husband respected intellectual qualities and careful enquiry, but I saw little sign of it amongst the company that night. I confess I was disappointed. I had hoped for stimulating discussion and exciting ideas, but the conversation revolved round hunting and notable feats of arms. Still, I reminded myself, this was a feast to celebrate brave actions; perhaps Greeks reserved their more cerebral moments for the daytime. Meanwhile, I should do well to keep a wary eye on what was handed to me and Jason. It might not be subtle to poison Jason off on the very evening that he presented his bride to Pelias, but it would have the merit of speedily resolving the question as to who was to be king.

XXI

My fears that Pelias might strike Jason down during the feast proved to be unjustified. However, when the meal finally dragged to a close, I was faced with another difficulty: I was married to Jason, a marriage acknowledged by both of us in the presence of Zeus, but Pelias believed that we were merely betrothed. I hungered to be fully reunited with Jason, but custom made that impossible. Jason could not even give me the caresses which I longed for; a restrained kiss upon my hand was all the physical touch which he allowed himself that night. Then he was gone and I was shown into my bedchamber by a gawping servant-girl. Her accent was thick and I could barely understand her words. However, she indicated that there were clothes for me and that I was to call her if I needed anything. I stared rather sadly at my lonely bed, wondering what would happen in the morning. I did not trust Pelias and I wanted to warn Jason about possible dangers. In fact, my court upbringing made me suspect that Pelias might send a killer to strike during the night. Having placed various glass containers by the door, where anyone entering would knock them over, I sank down onto the bed, resolved to stay awake for as long as I could.

The next morning, I was woken by the sharp smash of glass. Gabbling a prayer to Artemis, I sat upright, hoping that the noise would have frightened off any assassin. However, the maidservant entered, apologising and clearly fearful that she was going to be abused for her clumsiness. I attempted to hide my embarrassment and waved a gracious hand, hoping that such generosity would not lower me in her eyes. I need not have worried; her face showed her relief and she made it clear that she felt honoured to serve me. I let her run on, thinking that I might acquire some useful information, even if her barbarous Greek was a torment to hear.

Eventually, I realised that she was trying to tell me that I was to meet the king's daughters that morning. I had no objection to an audience with Jason's cousins. Indeed, after the hideous days in Gorgo's establishment, it would be a relief to have noblewomen to converse with. However, I felt that it would be much easier if only I knew precisely what Jason wanted me to tell them. Naturally, I knew that he wished me to pretend to be only betrothed, but how far could I speak of my life in Colchis? Jason's killing of Apsyrtus must be concealed, but could I mention how he had rescued my – previously unknown – nephews? I was aware that it might undermine Jason to explain how my potions had preserved him when tackling the fire-breathing bulls, but could I talk more generally of my role as a priestess?

I indicated to the slave-girl that I wished to speak to Jason, but her look of disbelieving shock told me that there was little chance that she would carry such a message to him. I recalled something that my father had said about the customs of the Greeks: 'a woman does not meet her husband until her wedding day, unless, of course, he belongs to her immediate family and she has met him before at a funeral'. Since my father had threatened to pack me off to some up-country chieftain as a pawn in a negotiation over territory, the concept of marriage to a stranger was not new to me. All the same, I was used to greater freedom to mix amongst the nobles at Aeetes's court and I judged that it would be hard to accustom myself to restrictions upon my movements – particularly since the existence of Gorgo's house made these restrictions seem somewhat hypocritical. Nevertheless, I was determined to do what Jason expected of me and, with eyes meekly downcast to disguise my frustration, I allowed the slave-girl to explain to me – a princess – the modes of behaviour in Iolcos. Then, once I was dressed, she led me to the palace.

Pelias's daughters were all older than I, but they seemed very unsophisticated. They had but two topics of conversation: fashion and children. Why they thought that their dreary garb was worthy of discussion was a mystery to me, used as I was to the glittering raiment judged suitable for nobility at Colchis. As for children, I prayed to Hera and Eileithyia, goddess of childbirth, that the offspring which I should bear to Jason would have more wit and intelligence than the uninspiring progeny which the air of Iolcos brought forth. However, my main concern at this point was not any putative children, but whether Jason would live to ascend to the throne of Iolcos. I was all too aware of how difficult it would be to ascertain the truth of what Pelias was really planning. I could not speak to Jason to repeat my warnings and I knew that he was much less likely to suspect Pelias than I was – Jason, after all, was a hero who mocked danger, and he also shared ties of blood with Pelias. I was not hampered by such considerations; on the other hand, I was hindered by the fact that I knew nobody at court, thus had no useful sources of gossip. Pelias's daughters seemed unpromising waters in which to fish for news of their father's intentions towards Jason, but it was my duty to tackle even the least likely sources of information.

The slave-girl's reaction to my unmaidenly act of speaking a man's name had served to warn me not to talk about Jason openly. However, whilst I was apparently studiously engaged in returning aimless responses to the princesses' careful conversation, I was in reality worrying over how best to raise the topic of Jason's future. If I shocked Alcestis and her sisters, I would gain no useful information – I might merely alert Pelias to my suspicious as to his probity. Ultimately, I decided, with considerable trepidation, not to question them about the kingship on the first day. It was too risky and it was clear that I was going to meet the sisters again.

Naturally, such was my concern for my husband, that once I parted from the princesses, I instantly castigated myself for missing a golden opportunity. It was all very well reminding myself that I had concealed my thoughts and beliefs for years at Colchis in order to survive in a hostile world – then I had only myself to consider. Now there was Jason as well. He had told me that, had it not been for the need to ensure my safety, he would have challenged Pelias to a duel to the death immediately he had arrived at the palace. If Jason could restrain himself from the behaviour natural to a hero in order to save me, surely I could have gone against my natural character of concealment and disguise in order to protect him?

Unsurprisingly, with this sort of guilt weighing me down, I was delighted to rejoin the princesses the next morning, even if the preliminary topics of conversation were honey and the difficulties of obtaining saffron for dying clothes. My observations on the flights of bees were greeted with such looks of incomprehension that my voice tailed off before I could even broach the – to me – fascinating question of how bees seemed to navigate through their territories. Hoping that Pelopia's murmur that I had misunderstood what she had said to Pisidice would be accepted as an excuse for my bizarre remarks, I schooled myself to listen with apparent interest to Alcestis's complaints as to the truly shocking way in which slaves wore through even the lowest grade of tunics.

Although I was desperate to gain some useful information for Jason, and although a thought kept pulsing through my head that Jason might already be lying, a still and lifeless corpse, in some storeroom of the palace, I maintained the meaningless chit-chat for what felt like hours. However, by the time that honey-cakes were brought in, I realised that the day had not been entirely wasted. I did not see how I could use the information, but it was obvious that the sisters had different characters. Alcestis was a worrier, whilst Hippothoe was a sharp-tongued shrew who had thrown more than a few remarks in my direction regarding my foreign upbringing. Since she was the closest in age to me, I wondered whether her malignant attitude was dictated by jealousy of my slim form and the arch of my eyebrows – hers were clearly plucked and must, in the natural state, have been thick and straight. However, Pisidice revealed another possible reason for her malice: the plans which Pelias might have had for Hippothoe.

"Father once said that he might marry Hippothoe off to Jason," she blurted out.

"Ssh," hissed Pelopia. "You'll embarrass Medea." She turned to me with what was intended to be a winning smile. "You must excuse Pisidice; she sometimes gets things wrong. Father never said anything of the sort."

I had already observed that Pisidice, whilst elegantly dressed and pretty in a plump, moon-faced manner, was decidedly slow-witted. Alcestis did her best to include her in the conversation, whilst Pelopia seemed to think that her sister was better kept occupied with embroidery-work, which, if the sample in her hands was anything to go by, she did exquisitely. Unfortunately for Pelopia, Pisidice was not to be hushed.

"Father did say so. He did. You weren't there. He said Hippothoe was the youngest so she didn't count as much. He said she'd do for Jason. He wanted to keep Alcestis to make a better bargain."

This information appalled me. Obviously, Pelias had

perceived Jason as a possible threat and had intended to neutralise him by binding him with ties closer even than those of nephew and uncle. I knew that my Jason was too upright a man to think of murdering his way to the throne, no matter how much Pelias might deserve it after his treatment of Aeson. A duel was one thing, but murder – no! Pelias, however, must have feared the justifiable wrath of his nephew and calculated that even a genuinely treacherous man might halt at the thought of slaughtering his own father-in-law. True, Pisidice's information appeared to date from the time before Jason had set sail to find the Fleece, but that did not make matters any safer for him. Quite the opposite – his success and my presence clearly made matters much worse.

I could see only two possible outcomes. Either Pelias would allow Jason to marry me, in which case Jason would become even more of a menace to the usurper of his father's throne, or Pelias would order Jason to break off his betrothal to me and marry shrewish Hippothoe. Since Jason would then be forced to reveal that I was already his wife, Pelias's full rage would be turned upon us both. Our deceit would be apparent for all to see and any who might have been inclined to side with Jason against the usurper, would change their mind and hail Pelias as the true regent of Iolcos.

"You seem very quiet, Medea," murmured Hippothoe with insincere concern.

"Don't worry," urged Alcestis. "Our father will soon sort things out."

I realised that Alcestis meant to be reassuring, but her words sent a sharp stab through me. I had little doubt that Pelias would soon sort things out – the question was, how?

XXII

Although I had fully expected Pelias to take action almost immediately, days went by and nothing happened. I met Jason at brief intervals, during which there was always another woman present, and, more importantly, one of Pelias's followers. I was confident that I could have managed to convey some information to Jason without the princesses understanding what I was up to, but there was little chance of fooling Brachos or Philippos. I confined myself to sending meaningful glances, but it was difficult to see whether Jason had taken my warnings or not. Certainly, on the few times that I attempted to speak to him in Colchian, or to make a disguised reference to events which we had shared, I was rewarded with a blank look of incomprehension.

Despite the fact that my contact with Jason was so limited, I busied myself in other ways. Spending time with Pelias's daughters was often an agony of dullness, but I hoped to gain some intimation of their father's plans from some careless word dropped from their lips. This hope remained unfulfilled. They had no understanding of court politics, unless their ignorance was a clever plan to avoid revealing Pelias's intentions to me. Ever-suspicious, I spent some time testing this possibility. Finally, I was inclined to acquit them of trickery after Alcestis apologetically explained that their father did not believe that questions of government were suitable interests for women. It was all too easy to imagine Pelias telling Alcestis and her sisters not to worry their pretty heads with man's work. After all, it was a phrase which my father had used to his concubines if they ever strayed outside the role allotted to them.

I was forced to admit grudgingly that Pelias might find it difficult to conceive of Pisidice aiding him in any way other than as a trophy to be sold to the highest bidder who wanted a pretty face and an empty head. Nevertheless, I found my hackles rising at the weak way in which the women of Iolcos collaborated in their own exclusion and isolation. Much though I had grown to dislike Hippothoe, I was prepared to acknowledge that she, at least, could have been trained to be more than a fetching display of the latest fabrics.

Whilst I was disappointed that the princesses of Iolcos took no interest in any aspects of government, I was not entirely surprised. However, it came as a considerable shock to me to discover that nor did they claim any meaningful role in sacred rites. Careful soundings revealed that they feared necromancers and hardly dared to carry out anything more than a basic libation. Whether that was through fear of the unknown or fear of angering the gods by their incompetence, I was unable to decide. Apparently, they did walk in some of the annual processions to the major temples, but Alcestis admitted that she felt nervous with everyone's eyes upon her and that she only undertook such tasks as a burdensome duty. I found it difficult to understand her dread. I had been accustomed not just to walk proudly at the head of public processions, but to conduct entire ceremonies. It was natural behaviour for a princess and, whatever else my father had done, he had never chosen to offend the gods by sending a low-status substitute to carry out important sacrifices. However, I reluctantly realised that there was no point discussing my art – or the correct role of a princess – with Pelias's daughters.

Moreover, the princesses were horrified at the impropriety of my wish to consult Kynaxilides the seer regarding a sacrifice in thanksgiving for my and Jason's safe arrival. In their mind, Kynaxilides was that fearsome, threatening beast – a man and, still worse, a man who was unrelated to them. In a moment of surging anger, I nearly retorted that Kynaxilides was blind and, as such, unlikely to be so overcome by my beauty that he would desire to rape me. I fought down the temptation. It would not help Jason if Hippothoe twisted my words to suggest that I wished to sleep with a blind seer rather than with my rightful husband. Instead, I turned the conversation to the momentous question of whether Amaryllis, the wife of Pelias's royal steward, was correct to have chosen the blue and white stripes, or if that was too daring, given her figure.

Days continued to slip by. For all the women's talk of stripes and stoles, of colours and costumes, no-one seemed eager to talk of my wedding to Jason. Indeed, the main topic of conversation became the rumour that Pelias intended to send out an expedition to track down the real source of amber, that bronze-gold warm jewel which holds the sun in its heart, even in the depths of winter. Such talk chilled me as effectively as the kiss of snow itself. It was abundantly clear that a man of character, courage and experience would be required to lead any exploration of this nature. Who else would be chosen other than my brave Jason? How convenient it would be for Pelias if he could remain as regent whilst Jason was lured away from his rightful role as lord of Iolcos. I had heard enough gossip to surmise that this was how Pelias had deflected Jason's anger when he had arrived to claim his father's throne. Presumably, Pelias had hoped that Jason would die on the journey to Colchis or would be devoured by one of the many monsters which we keep there. Well, Pelias had misjudged then and, I sincerely trusted, he would misjudge matters now.

But the difficulty remained. I had to speak to Jason properly. However, it was almost impossible to gain access to him for more than a few minutes and, when I did so, he appeared to resent my urgings to carry out the ceremony. Naturally, I was proud of his increasing popularity and his importance, but I felt more and more cut off and ineffectual. If only we had announced on the evening of my arrival at court that Jason and I were joined in marriage, I should not have been kept from his side by the customs regulating Greek females.

Again and again, I was tempted to exclaim that we were man and wife, but I knew that too much time had passed. To have hidden the glad news during the journey and in the first few days at Iolcos would have been understandable, if unflattering to Pelias, but not to speak of it once Jason had introduced me to his uncle the king was ludicrous. No-one would understand why we had not spoken out before – the only credible explanation would be that we were making it up. In fact, I even reached such a pass that I started to wonder whether Jason intended to renounce our supposed betrothal. Part of me wanted to put the matter to the test, but I shrank from the humiliation that would await me if my own husband were to repudiate me. I also did not want to be disloyal – Jason must have some sort of plan which he was carrying out. If I spoke up too soon I would destroy everything through my lack of trust. And, above all, I feared Pelias's vengeance upon my husband if I revealed the true state of affairs. While Pelias still contemplated marrying Jason off to Hippothoe, Jason was safe – even if I was not. But if I revealed that Jason was married, then Pelias would strike. That is what my father would have done, and I saw no reason to believe that Pelias was any less ruthless than Aeetes.

It would have been easier to bear this constant fear and suspicion if I had been granted the freedom which I had enjoyed at Colchis. Alcestis, Pelias's eldest daughter, seemed to view what little I had told her of my previous life with abhorrence. She could not see that what she regarded as the licentious laxity only to be expected of barbarians was, in fact, a tribute to my father's authority. No Colchian would have dared to lay a hand upon Aeetes's daughter and, as I grew older, their awe for my powers was such that many of them feared me in my own right. But as anxiety over the delay in organising my wedding grew, I was denied what had been my solace in times past. Here at Iolcos I had no chance to commune with the gods at sunrise. I could no longer weave bryony and rue into chaplets and watch the thin flame flare up as I cast the twining circles upon the sacred altar, all the while chanting the hidden words of the rite. Even the opportunities to pour libations or make ritual observations of birds in swooping flight were restricted to the few precious minutes which I could snatch from the people who constantly surrounded me, chattering about trivial incidents in their trivial lives. There was no liberty; no opportunity; no independence of thought. I felt suffocated and suppressed. And, as I fought not to be smothered by the banality of my new existence, my one true companion was fear – fear for Jason, and fear that my powers would die if I did not exercise them.

The moon had waxed and waned twice before a change came to my situation. And when it did, I was relieved that I had not shared my disloyal thoughts with anyone. By this point I had discover an isolated walk which ran beside the south side of the palace. The women-folk tended to avoid it, shunning the fierce light beating down from the sun. However, I welcomed Helios's rays. Not only did that shimmering glare guarantee me solitude, but I drew strength from the piercing, crystalline purity which surrounded me. When I perceived even the quartz on the ground glittering as if with internal life, how could I doubt that the gods were willing me to continue my struggle in Jason's cause? I raised my arms in a soundless invocation to the great giver of life and listened for an indication that my prayers had been heard. I was expecting a breath of wind in a breathless landscape, or a sudden, flickering call from a cicada. But I had never heard so strong a response as the heavy rustle which came from the leaves behind me. I turned instantly, wondering what creature the immortals had sent as a messenger. The light was in my eyes and, when I perceived the human form standing in front of me, bathed in dripping gold, my heart raced. A god himself was there.

Just as I was recalling the stories of mortals who had been struck down for observing an immortal in the flesh, the presence in front of me spoke.

"Medea, my dove, thanks be to Zeus that I have finally managed to find you on your own."

The shadow of a kite, flying high above us, swooped across me and the bird's thin keening cut through the clear air. But I had eyes and ears only for Jason.

"My dearest beloved! You have come at last!"

Jason grasped me in his strong arms and stared deep into my eyes. "My love, my reason for life, it has taken stratagems more cunning than those necessary to win the Fleece to be able to gain the prize of your company."

"I have longed for you, too. And I have feared for you."

"Feared for me? What do you mean? Did you think that I no longer wished to be with you?"

Although what I had really referred to was my very great fears that Pelias was plotting against my husband, I was foolish enough to admit that I had started to doubt whether Jason truly cared for me. Although he tried to disguise it, Jason was clearly hurt.

"How could you not trust me? I thought that I could rely in you."

I hastily tried to patch up the situation. "Jason, husband, I do trust you and you can rely upon me. I was frightened that Pelias intended to send you far away to the north, where the men with heads in their bodies keep the secret of the source of amber."

Unfortunately, this explanation did not serve to placate Jason. "Am I so weak that I would fear to tackle such a challenge? Have I not defeated the Harpies and faced fire-breathing bulls without quailing? Would you have me reject such a quest, one worthy of my status?"

"If I could come with you, I would embrace all challenges," I responded sturdily. "But I want to see you restored to your true position as king of Iolcos."

Jason gave a short laugh. "Women are always attracted by the baubles of position. But let us discuss your lack of trust no longer. I came here with the intention of deciding the exact point at which we should insist upon holding our marriage-ceremony."

Eager to reassure my beloved that I was not motivated by baubles or trappings, I hastened to state that, as far as I was concerned, our solitary pledge before the eyes of Zeus was everything which any woman could wish. "The voice of your love, Jason, is the jewel which I wear to celebrate our union. I need nothing more, certainly not the sort of costly ceremony which would normally be performed for someone of your status."

Jason smiled. "That is sweet of you, Medea, but don't forget that no-one knows that we are married. Think how shocked they would be if they observed us together now!"

I essayed a hopeful smile in response. "What matters is what we two know to be true. Oh, Jason, do you not realise that the vow you swore is all the reassurance I need?"

"I do, but we must be practical. I have heard that Pelias would like me to be married to his youngest daughter."

I caught my breath in horror. So it was true – and not just an idea which dated to before Jason's attempt to win the Fleece. "Pisidice said so," I murmured in alarm. "Jason, you must be very careful."

"Pisidice?" he repeated. "Medea, have you been talking about us to Pelias's daughters? Don't you see how dangerous that is?"

"I do," I protested. "And Pisidice said it unexpectedly. I didn't ask any of them outright."

Jason frowned. "But you have been trying to discover things?"

Perhaps I ought not to have grown cross at this point. Perhaps I should have reminded myself of all the times at Colchis when I had resolutely restrained from defending myself. But I could visualise only too clearly the fate which Pelias probably intended for Jason. Imagining the grave which would hold my husband's rotting corpse unless we could outwit Pelias, I retorted angrily. "Don't you understand? I have been separated from you. Every evening I have lain in bed wondering whether you were going to survive the night, and every morning I have woken wondering whether I should have to prepare your body for burial. Of course I tried to find out what was going on. But you ought to trust me, too, Jason. Do you really think that, fearing for your life as I have been, I would ask any careless question which would expose you to danger?"

The grunt of disapproval which greeted this statement was hardly reassuring. "And if you knew what I have gone through, Medea, kept apart from you, tearing myself in two with agony and misery, would you continue to doubt me?"

I attempted to protest that I did not doubt Jason, but

he overrode me. "You must remember, Medea, that you are a woman and, as such, unskilled in matters of state. You must not attempt to interfere." Then, noticing the tears glinting in my eyes, he tried to console me. "Come, my dear, I know that you meant it for the best. But, in future, leave these things to me. After all, I understand these people – I am one of them."

It did occur to me that Jason had been brought up far away from Pelias's reach, but it seemed pointless to waste what little time we had on irritable squabbles. "What do you suggest?"

"What we arrange now, we must stick to," responded my lover decisively. "I am constantly spied upon and I do not know when I shall next be able to reach you alone." He sighed. "And now that you have probably alerted Pelias to your suspicions, it is imperative that we act quickly."

Unconsciously, I issued a small squeak of protest. Jason ran his hand over mine briefly.

"I know that you didn't mean to harm me, but it does make things harder."

"I shall do whatever you want."

"Good. Well, my plan is this. Alcestis worries about her father's health. She asked me whether he seemed to have aged since I went to Colchis."

"And has he?" I enquired. Pelias seemed perfectly fit to me, but I had no mode of comparison.

Jason wrinkled his brow thoughtfully. "I agreed with Alcestis. He walks more slowly and his hair is greyer. His breath is often foul, too. That is not a good sign."

I raised my eyebrows in some surprise at this observation. I had noticed the same phenomenon and had attributed it to the sour wine which Iolcos produced. However, my surprise was caused not by my differing diagnosis but because Jason was showing knowledge of medical matters. Naturally, I had picked up a good deal of information from Phrixus as he taught me about the various uses of herbs, but this was a new side to my husband and one which impressed me.

Jason seemed not to notice my reaction. "Alcestis has heard some rather wild tales as to what sorcerers can achieve. She believes that it is possible to rejuvenate the old."

An image of Theonoe, her life floating down to Hades on short, gasping breaths, came before me. My eyes filled with tears. If I only I had possessed such skills, I could have saved her, sending the bright blood racing round her body again, restoring her to health and my love.

Jason's voice broke into my thoughts. "For goodness sake, Medea, you aren't still weeping for that old slave-woman? I thought you said she died months ago. Haven't you got over her death yet? Men who fight risk death every time they go into battle, but we learn to put things in their rightful place."

"Wouldn't you grieve for me if I died?"

"Of course I would, but you would be my wife."

Feeling guilty at not defending my feelings for Theonoe more effectively, I allowed myself one snarling complaint. "Even if I could make Pelias young again, why would I want to? He'd be even more of a threat to you than he is now."

Jason laughed. "Dear Medea, you don't think that I really want to help my uncle, do you? No, no; Alcestis has presented me with a very useful weak point in Pelias's defence and I intend to make full use of it."

I have to confess that I stared rather vacantly at my husband. "What?"

"Have you said anything to Alcestis about sorcery?"

"A little," I admitted cautiously, hoping that Jason would not be annoyed at my indiscretion.

"What exactly did you say?"

"Only some remarks about augury. I stopped immediately I realised that she and her sisters were taken aback."

"But you haven't denied having any powers?"

I shook my head.

"Good. Now listen. Pelopia has already been stuffed full of tales about how Colchis is a land of mantics, witches and seers. She's passed on the more lurid of these to Alcestis, who is currently half-way to believing that every other family in Colchis harbours a creature of supernatural powers."

"Why hasn't she spoken to me to find out the truth?" I demanded, reasonably enough.

"My dear cousins rather suspect that you may be a werewolf."

"That's ludicrous."

"No, not ludicrous – useful. Once they learn that you are only a witch, their main reaction will be one of enormous relief that you won't come and tear their throats out in the middle of the night."

"And?" I prompted, sure that Jason was not motivated by the desire to spare his cousins anxiety.

"And then they'll be all too ready to fall in with your suggestions as to how to help their dear father become young again."

"I don't understand."

Jason sighed impatiently. "Think, Medea! If you were a rather gullible woman who saw a witch turning an old ram into a lamb, wouldn't you believe the witch when she said that she could do the same thing to a man?"

"But I told you, I can't do that – whether to a sheep or a man. Only the immortals have that sort of power. And I'm a priestess, not a witch."

"If you can produce an ointment which defends its wearer from fire, then surely you can conjure up images."

I suddenly realised what Jason wanted. "You mean, you want me to pretend that the ram is rejuvenated? You don't want me to actually do it?"

"Exactly. Kill the adult sheep, boil up its limbs, and then magic up a brisk, leaping lamb to take its place. That'll fool Alcestis nicely."

It wasn't exactly the sort of task which I was used to, but I thought that I could probably manage it. I said so, rather hesitantly. Jason seemed irritated by my uncertainty.

"Honestly, I'd have thought that someone trained by Phrixus could manage that sort of simple sleight of hand – or wasn't he as good as you claim?"

I thrust away my anger at the lack of respect shown to the dead seer and focussed on the challenge which Jason had proposed.

"I'd need to experiment and I don't know where to find the ingredients I would need."

"Alcestis will fetch you anything you want." There was a trace of a sneer in Jason's voice. "For some reason my dear cousin loves Pelias and would do anything to preserve him. She will, but not quite in the way in which she intended. Cooked meat lasts longer than fresh."

I shuddered. "Jason, it's a terrible death."

"Don't you think that Pelias deserves to die for what he did to my father and to me?"

"Yes, but this method is cruel. The princesses will bear a burden of guilt for the rest of their lives. If I killed someone I loved – even by mistake – I would never stop torturing myself for what I'd done. They're your cousins – they share a blood-tie with you. Surely you can't want them to suffer like that?"

Jason shrugged his shoulders. "Pelias is threatening us and our lives. How else are we to prevent him? Do you want to see my headless corpse upon the palace steps?"

"No! No! But surely we could kill Pelias ourselves? I

could easily prepare poison and slip it in his food."

"Hardly," retorted Jason. "Do you think that Pelias is going to let a known witch anywhere near his table?"

"He doesn't know about my powers."

"You've told my cousins; they'll have told Pelias."

I was becoming fogged as to what the princesses did or did not know. Jason continued. "In any case, Pelias has a food-taster and even if you did manage to kill Pelias, the people of Iolcos would never let you live to enjoy your triumph. They'd rise up and slaughter you – and me."

I was aghast at the thought of Jason being torn apart by an angry mob, but I was still appalled at the solution which he had proposed to our troubles.

"Surely we can think of something less cruel? I don't like the princesses, and I hate Pelias for what he's done to you, but it's so horrible to imagine their joy at restoring their father turn to grief and guilt. I can't do it."

"Don't you understand? We've no time to come up with alternatives, especially now that you've let Alcestis see that you don't trust her father." Jason ran his hands through his hair. "It's practically impossible for me to get away from court to plot and plan with you. I have to appear normal when I'm keeping Pelias company and I can't appear normal if I'm trying to work out how to depose him. I've been trying to buy time by pretending to go along with his schemes to stay as regent for the next year." He sighed. "Medea, you know how much I respect your intelligence. I had rather hoped…" His voice trailed off.

"What do you mean?"

He sighed again, more heavily. "I had hoped that you might have come up with a solution, but I suppose that it was too much to ask of you. I'm sorry, Medea, I oughtn't to have relied so much upon you. I ought to have agreed to go on the amber expedition – that way, at least I'd have got you out of this mess, even if it meant that I should never be able to reclaim my rightful throne."

At the plaintive note in Jason's voice I was overcome with guilt. I was Jason's wife, and a wife should help her husband. It was dreadful to think of Jason placing all his trust in me and for me then to let him down. I had achieved nothing during the many days at Iolcos. Indeed, I had been selfish enough to imagine that Jason was enjoying the life at court – the exciting hunting parties, the great feasts and, above all, the adulation of those who heard his tales of adventure. In reality, Jason had been living a lie to deceive Pelias. My misjudgement made it all the more essential that I help him now. How else could I save Jason from a shameful death?

XXIII

Jason must have sensed my fear and reluctance, because he was very loving in the short time that remained. As he left, he made me promise to practise conjuring up images. I agreed unwillingly and was rewarded by seeing the strain melt from my husband's face, to be replaced with the sunny vitality which had so charmed me in his first days at Colchis.

"Swear it, my dearest, and seal our compact with a kiss."

I swore.

Jason had persuaded me to display my powers to Alcestis on the following day. This request displayed a flattering level of trust in my ability, but I wished that I had been granted more time – not just to practise my deception, but also time in which to think of an alternative method of dealing with Pelias. However, Jason had made it clear that we had no time; Pelias intended to announce Jason's betrothal to Hippothoe once Kynaxilides had pronounced the omens to be favourable. I was tempted to slip something into the seer's food to make him ill and unavailable, but I rejected this solution. It was too close to my father's – admittedly more ruthless – treatment of Phrixus. I had no desire to have Kynaxilides's death upon my conscience if he reacted unexpectedly to my potions. So I fell in with Jason's plans and asked Alcestis for the necessary herbs. She gave orders for the palace storerooms to be ransacked at once and even offered to accompany me outside the grounds of the palace should I need to search for any ingredients in the fields. Such devotion made feel physically sick and, on the pretext of needing absolute silence, I was able to search for fly agaric on my own.

Before dawn the next morning, Alcestis was ready to accompany me. She had commanded an old ram to be brought to an olive grove which abutted the palace and I could hear its bleating as we picked our way through the rocks, trying not to trip over the gnarled olive roots. Alcestis had been warned not to talk, but her eagerness was palpable in every light step which she took. For my part, I should have dearly liked Jason's support, but it was obviously unsafe to have him accompany us. Not only might it have raised suspicions that Jason was not happy about marrying Hippothoe, but his presence might have cast doubt upon the miraculous rejuvenation of the ram and revealed it for what it was – a trick.

Alcestis's orders had been carried out to perfection. A cauldron half-filled with water was waiting above an unlit fire. I motioned Alcestis to draw back to the edge of the grove and, murmuring a prayer to Athene, goddess of wisdom, I lit the fire and cast the first portion of herbs into the water. As I waited for the bubbles from the water to add their moisture to the clammy dawn, I attempted to convince myself that Jason and I could still draw back; that I could treat this as an ordinary sacrifice. After all, ever since I had seen the lack of respect which Pelias showed towards the Fleece, I had been praying for an opportunity to make a sacrifice to apologise for his treatment of the Fleece. I did not think that it was imagination which made me notice that the Fleece was losing its sheen in the sordid surroundings of Pelias's court. Even if no-one else cared, the Fleece was dear to me because it was all that was left of the ram which saved Phrixus.

Perhaps it was the thought of the Fleece which made me conscious of the fretted tuggings and pullings of the sacrificial victim at the end of the rope. It wasn't used to being tied up alone in an olive-grove, away from the rest of the flock. At Colchis I had carried out a great many sacrifices and I was used to wielding the knife with the bold stroke which the gods demand. But, somehow, this old ram was different. Looking back, I wonder whether my pity for the ram then was what led to things going very wrong later. Did I misplace my stock of sympathy? Would I have been better to keep it for humans? However, whatever the after-effects of my compassion, at the moment of the killing I could not bear to leave the poor creature afraid. I petted his head, stroking him softly and murmuring words of reassurance which he cannot possibly have understood.

"Don't be frightened. You are going to join another great and good ram; a saviour among rams. He will look after you. You need have no fear. I remain here to watch over you as you go to the saviour of Phrixus."

With that, I slit his throat. There was a brief gurgling noise, then his legs gave way and he collapsed upon the dusty ground. Remembering that I was meant to be there to fool Alcestis, I blessed the dawn for hiding my tears and attempted to pull myself together.

The butchery of the ram was foul – not in terms of the physical actions, thought they were hardly pleasant – but foul because I had reassured him that he would be safe. Indeed, as I spoke the appropriate incantations, I found myself soundlessly praying that I could, indeed, restore the old creature to his former youthful glory. But I knew that this could not be. Once past Acheron, no soul returns, whether dead before their time or not. I could not bring the ram back to life any more than I could Phrixus or Theonoe. And my duty was not to grieve for an old ram, but to ensure the safety of my husband. So I turned my attention back to my rites. I loosened my hair, leaving it to stream out behind me. Then I raised my flaming torch of burning pitch and began to circle round and round the cauldron, praying aloud to the gods.

"O triple Hecate, wanderer of night, inhabitant of the crossroads, O Persephone, queen of the dead, O Hades, ruler of the shades below the ground, I call upon you to observe Aurora rising in the West. Just as she sends dawn to bring Helios's light upon the world, dispelling sooty Night, so too does my torch represent the rays of life. See how Helios strikes the trees and ground, how he kisses the watercourses and pools, how he rejuvenates the world. So too, O Dictynna, shall you restore life to this ram and send him back as brisk and lively as he was in the days of his youth. Here is the sloughed skin of an adder, which hides in caverns. Here is the wing of a bat and the feathers of an owl, those secret creatures which flit unseen through dark night. Come, O Lady, come aid me, come on the shiver of a breeze and bring life with your breath."

As I chanted, a fine miasma arose from the cauldron. Then a wraith of thicker mist spiralled upwards, twisting and writhing, before the creamy-white vapour began to coalesce. Even although I knew that it was a mirage, I wondered momentarily whether the immortals had taken pity upon the helpless victim and returned him to the world which had betrayed him. Then common-sense took over. A man beloved of the gods may live on in the Isles of the Blest, but an animal survives his death only in memory.

Alcestis must have been watching with rapt attention because, at the very point when the vapour seemed to become solid, she moved forward to see what I was doing.

"No!" I ordered hastily, remembering Jason's instructions. "You are mortal. If you come closer, your presence will contaminate and destroy my power. You must wait."

Then, when I could no longer see her, I stretched inside the folds of my dress and drew out the lamb which was hidden within. I gently undid the cloth which had prevented it from bleating, before caressing it and placing it on the ground near the cauldron. It was frightened and bleated, a wild wailing which carried above the bubbling of the cauldron.

"You may come forward now," I called, as I threw in more herbs to stop the white vapour.

Alcestis approached, her eyes shining as she saw the lamb. "It is magic, Medea; quite outstanding magic. Your skill must come from Apollo himself."

I gave a modest smile. "I have studied for many years."

"My father will be restored to his youth and happiness. He will no longer suffer the aches and pains of old age. He will see well again and be able to throw his hunting-spear with all the cunning of old."

"There will be no more pains," I agreed, with a leaden heart. What I said was true – after the first sharp stab of betrayal, Pelias would feel nothing again.

"When, Medea? When can we carry out this miraculous transformation?"

I nearly blurted out that we had to ask Jason, but fortunately – or unfortunately – remembered in time that to mention my husband would lead to Alcestis's immediate suspicion. "Let it be tomorrow," I ordered. "You must not tell him what you are going to do. Tell him that you wish him to perform a special sacrifice for his health and the happiness of Iolcos."

Alcestis nodded earnestly. "I shall do so. The occasion is appropriate for my brother will return shortly."

"Your brother?"

"Yes. Acastus has been travelling, but we heard word that his ship is due to arrive soon. How wonderful it will be for him to find his father restored to youth and health."

I bit my lip. Pelias's son had been of some concern to me when I had learned of his existence, since it seemed to me axiomatic that Pelias would not wish to hand over control of Iolcos to anyone other than Acastus. However, when I had learned that Acastus was conveniently away, I had dismissed him from my mind as not being an immediate threat. Now, it appeared that he was far more of a danger than I had previously assumed. Perhaps he was the reason behind Jason's sudden urgency – it would be like my beloved to try to protect me from any worry and not to tell me of Acastus's arrival.

"I hope that you will like Acastus," continued Alcestis. "It cannot have been easy for you to move from Colchis. Perhaps Acastus's tales of travel will entertain you more than we princesses can. We have led a more sheltered life than you."

This humble speech left me feeling even more guilty than before. Alcestis must have sensed my unhappiness, but, instead of censuring me for my foreign outlook, she seemed to blame herself for not having had the wider experiences which I had. It suddenly struck me that, if I had known of her attitude earlier, it might have been possible to arrange things differently. Perhaps I could have persuaded her to help me to win Pelias's acceptance of a marriage between Jason and myself. Then reality took over again; there was no chance that Pelias would have listened to the pleadings of one woman for another. It was clear that he despised his daughters' brains and I could not imagine that he would be softened by any arguments which were based upon ideals of love. No, I would be better sticking to Jason's plans, rather than listening to the feeble weakness of my own heart. Jason himself had pointed out that he knew these people and I did not. Just as I had known how to win the Fleece in my own homeland, Jason was a better judge than I in his. I had to trust him and his plans.

XXIV

I spent much of the rest of the day on the isolated walk near the palace, hoping that Jason would seek me out there. However, there was no sign of him. The women had their midday snack apart from the men, but I ignored the rattle of platters being carried from the kitchens, thinking that this was the ideal time for Jason to speak to me without interruption. In any case, I was in no mood to touch food or to chat with Alcestis, knowing how I was about to betray her. Fortunately, she must have assumed that I was drained by my early-morning activities, for she made no effort to find me as she had done on previous occasions when I had tried to sneak off on my own.

Jason was present at the evening meal and I attempted to attract his attention by careful grimaces. He gave me one direct look and then studiously avoided meeting my eye. I thought that he had understood my desperate need to talk to him, but he made no move in my direction at the end of the meal, nor did he appear on the terrace. I waited and waited, fretting at the delay. Then I realised that he must have feared compromising me should anyone chance upon us walking together in the dark, so I returned to my room. I stayed awake most of the night, an oil lamp sending its soft gleam of invitation through my window. True, the window was too small to admit the entry of a boy, let alone a grown hero like my husband, but the aperture was more than large enough to allow a prolonged conversation. But Jason never came.

By the time that there was a slight lessening in the black night, I felt haggard and uncertain. All night I had argued with myself as to what I should do. Duty and love dictated that I carry out Jason's plan unaltered. He had placed himself unreservedly in my hands at Colchis; surely it was my turn to repay his trust by following his instructions? I dressed drearily, wishing that instinct would not tell me so strongly that what my husband had proposed was wrong. Noise from bedrooms nearby suggested that the princesses, Jason's cousins, were getting up in anticipation of the miraculous cure of their father. The thought of their faces, reflecting the bright hope which Alcestis's had shown the previous dawn, spurred me into action. Grabbing the red bag in which my ingredients were held, I sped out of the palace and into the grounds. An owl screeched on my left and, praying to Hecate to protect my deeds from harming others, I forced myself to walk purposefully to the olive grove. There, a dim figure loomed out of the morning mist. My heart jumped. Pelias would question me and never believe the tale which had been spun to his eldest daughter. I could almost have welcomed his likely response were it not for the fact that Jason would suffer alongside me.

"Medea, my sweet, you are here."

My fickle heart lurched again, this time in surprise.

"Jason?"

"Whom else would you expect? I have come to provide support to you."

"J… J… Jason," I stammered. "I can't do it. I can't."

My husband's tone seemed to grow stern. "What do you mean? Were you incapable of conjuring up a mirage yesterday?"

I longed to be able to lie, but I thought it unworthy of our love to deceive Jason. "No. I carried out your plan exactly. But…" again my voice faltered.

"But what?"

"It is too cruel to Alcestis. She thinks that Pelias will live. It will break her heart to feel that she murdered him."

I distinctly heard Jason snort. "You are too fanciful, Medea. Do you think that there is such a great love between Alcestis and her father that she will never forget what happens today?"

I attempted to argue the point. "I know that Pelias despises her, but that does not stop her loving him. If we are to kill Pelias to save our own skins then we ought to do it openly and accept responsibility, not crush another in our path."

"It's rather late to put forward these quibbles. After all, you indicated to me last night that all was well."

"I didn't! I was begging you to talk to me."

"Oh, is that what you meant by those strange grimaces? I'm sorry, I assumed that everything was under control. Truly, Medea, it's far too late to change anything, particularly now that Acastus is due to arrive today."

"Today?"

"Yes. Pelias told me last night. Once Acastus arrives, there is nothing that can be done to save our marriage."

I must have emitted a squeak of protest because Jason's voice softened and he caressed my head, running his hand softly over my hair and cupping my chin. "My sweetheart, my dove, my true one, don't you understand? When Acastus is installed in the palace, Pelias will either kill me outright or attempt to neutralise me by an immediate wedding to Hippothoe. It breaks my heart to tell you this, but Pelias envisages rounding off the feast to welcome Acastus home with the marriage rites between Hippothoe and me." He paused reluctantly. "Apparently, he thinks it most suitable for Acastus to preside over his sister's wedding."

I bit my lip in despair, as Jason continued.

"My beloved, what alternatives have we? I could refuse to marry Hippothoe, but Pelias would order my death for the insult to his daughter. Naturally, I would fight, but how can I defeat Pelias and all his men? And when I had been cut down in the fight, what would happen to you? I am not prepared to risk the appalling brutality which Pelias would inflict upon you after my death. Your safety compels me to act."

"Couldn't we leave Iolcos now, this minute?"

"My sweet child, we would never make it out of port. No, my dearest, you must be brave and work with me to defeat Pelias."

There was a pause and then Jason resorted to his final argument. "Surely you do not love Alcestis more than you love me?"

I denied this with vigour and my husband responded with the logical conclusion. "Then, my sweetest love, you must carry out our plan. It will be quick, and then we shall both be safe. If you hesitate, we shall both suffer Pelias's vengeance – and I know from my father's fate quite how cruel Pelias can be."

Naturally, in retrospect, I can see exactly how Jason manipulated me. Each time he spoke of the danger to me he knew that I would imagine him suffering some unparalleled savagery. And since I was desperately, madly in love with him, I did not approach the matter with the level of detached logic which I ought to have used. Thus Pelias died. Not, to be fair, that I cared much for his fate – he was, by his own admission, a usurper who had driven Jason's father from his rightful place as king of Iolcos. Nevertheless, I was distinctly unhappy about using his daughters to cut him down. Jason later sneered at these scruples as typical feminine weakness, but even to this day I wish I had let my 'feminine weakness' override a heartless plan. Guilt is a terrible burden, and there must have been something else which we could have done which did not leave Alcestis to bear such a grief.

Even now I can see that procession in the grey dawn, Alcestis leading, radiant in her belief that her father was to be saved from the slow degeneration of old age, whilst Pelias accompanied her, clearly unaware of his fate. Apollo only knows what powers of persuasion Alcestis had used upon her sisters to attend and, perhaps more importantly, not to tell Pelias what they intended to do. Jason had foreseen that Pelias might doubt the fantastical tale of the rejuvenated ram and had ordered me to warn Alcestis that the magic would not work if she told her father in advance of the miracle which awaited him. All Pelias knew was that his daughters wished him to accompany them to a sacrifice to celebrate Acastus's return.

As they approached the bubbling cauldron, Pelias looked somewhat taken aback to see me presiding over the ceremony. Alcestis must have sensed his doubt because she ran her hand down his arm, as if soothing a frightened animal. A vision of the tethered ram occurred to me and, inspecting Pelias in the half-light, I realised that he was, indeed, old and tired. I thrust away the question as to whether that made my actions less or more reprehensible and concentrated on the task in hand. I could not delay matters: the king was bound to demand to see the sacrificial victim and there was none present. The tender eagerness in Alcestis's eyes almost prevented me from speaking, but I suddenly thought of one small thing which I could do to make her life easier. I nodded to Hippothoe and announced in as awe-inspiring a voice as I could conjure up, considering that I was shaking like an aspen in a storm, that the youngest must carry out the sacrifice.

Hippothoe blanched, but took the sharp dagger from my hand automatically. I nodded again and she struck like a practised warrior, the keen blade slipping between Pelias's ribs to stab through into the caverns of the heart. Just like the old ram on the previous morning, his legs gave way and he lay on the ground. Unable to speak, I gestured towards the cauldron and, with unseemly fervour, the women hacked off Pelias's limbs and flung them into the cauldron. His torso and head soon followed, the eyes staring sightlessly out upon his daughters at their strange play. The water in the cauldron was bubbling nicely and Pelias's legs kicked in a grim mockery of life. I dashed to one side where I was promptly sick, heaving my guts up until green bile was all that dribbled down my chin.

When my retching subsided somewhat I was aware of a shrill keening in the background. I forced myself to listen to the hateful words.

"Why doesn't he arise from the cauldron? Father, oh Father, what has happened? Father, speak to me. Father."

Then Hippothoe rounded upon me. "What have you done, Medea? Why has our father not come back to life?"

Alcestis turned her face, streaming with tears, upon mine and added her silent plea.

I couldn't face them. I couldn't tell them the truth that it was a heartless plot; that it was Pelias or us; that I had fooled them to preserve our own lives. Instead I stammered out something about having made a mistake with the ingredients. Indeed, hearing the wailing anguish which arose from Pisidice and Pelopia, I prayed to Helios, my grandfather, to undo the havoc which I had wrought. But it was the wrong time of day – Helios had not yet fought down black Night – and no help came.

"Make him come back," pleaded Pisidice. "I want Father back."

I tried to make some further excuse, but was stalled by the sight of Jason striding towards us, confident in his victory.

"Pelias will never return to you. You may as well pour water upon the fire unless you want to cook his limbs as well as butcher them."

At that point, I was overcome with retching again and missed the lordly manner in which Jason put the fire out with the very water which was stained red with Pelias's blood. When I looked up, I saw a collection of pallid limbs, drained of the scarlet blood which had given him life. Pelopia appeared nearly as pale as the remnants of her dead father, but she turned upon me savagely.

"You vicious, treacherous liar! You planned this, didn't you, Medea? We welcomed you and this is how you repay our welcome. Barbarian!"

Alcestis now intervened. She was clearly frightened, but impelled to understand the disaster which had just destroyed her world.

"Why, Jason? Why?" She gestured disdainfully in my general direction. "I could understand why that foreign woman might wish to harm us, but why you? You are our cousin. You shared blood-ties with us and our father."

"Not much blood about Pelias now," grunted Jason. I winced, thinking that he could not realise how brutal he sounded. However, he was not finished. "Why should I have spared you? You point out that Pelias was my uncle, but did you ever stop to tell him that he drove my father into exile and caused me to be abandoned? Did you ever try to persuade Pelias to return what is rightfully mine? Of course not; you were too busy enjoying being princesses at court and hoping that your father would discover some fool ready to marry you because you were the king's daughters. You are all equally guilty. When have you shown me the respect which is my due? Have you acclaimed me as a hero? Have you treated me as a king? No, and now you taste my punishment."

Despite my predicament, I could not fail to admire Alcestis's dignified response. "And you shall taste the punishment which the people of Iolcos will mete out upon you."

"Yes," spat Hippothoe. "You will suffer and so will your foreign whore. The sooner you flee, the better your chance of escaping."

Jason laughed with what sounded like genuine amusement. "Your cousinly concern touches me – do you fear that I shall be torn apart limb from limb like Pelias here?" He stirred the remains with his foot. "No, you are mistaken. I shall be installing myself in the palace, whilst you'll be left preparing this meat for burial." He turned to me. "Come, Medea, we must return to the palace to inform the people of the accident which has befallen their leader. They will be shocked and grieved to learn that Pelias's daughters have assassinated him."

XXV

Although Jason's remark about assassination struck me as in singularly poor taste under the circumstances, my main concerns were the grief of the princesses and the possible reaction of the Iolchians.

"Do you think that the people will attack you?" I asked Jason, rather fearfully.

"I doubt it. They're a calculating lot and I can't see them risking their lives for a corpse. Now, if there were another convincing candidate, there might be a bit of difficulty, but I'm Pelias's nephew. Why shouldn't I become king?"

"What about Acastus?"

Jason stared at me in surprise. "What about him?"

"Surely he's a real threat to you. Shouldn't we make sure that his ship is intercepted? If he's greeted with news of his father's death when he lands, he'll be bound to try to whip up antagonism against you."

"I would if I thought that he was anywhere near Iolcos."

"But you said he was arriving today."

"He's not."

"But you *said* he was."

"I thought he was and then I learned that he wasn't."

I couldn't accept this. "How? You told me this morning that Acastus was coming. No-one else was in the grove apart from us and the princesses. So who could have told you that Acastus was no longer due to arrive today?"

"Don't make such a fuss, Medea, when I'm trying to concentrate on how best to ensure a swift handover of power with no problems."

I was not to be put off. "Did you lie to me?"

"Honestly, Medea, don't exaggerate. I was trying to

persuade you to do what was best for us both."

My aggrieved silence must have convinced Jason that he needed to explain further. He tried to sound patient. "It is true that Pelias told me that he hoped that Acastus would return shortly. He regretted having spoken immediately he had let slip the information, so I assumed that the happy event was due to occur soon. It was vital that we did not leave things too late. Moreover, I knew how badly you would feel later when you realised that you had let me down the first time I asked you to help me." He grasped my hand and stared into my eyes. "Think how our relationship would have suffered if that had happened. I could not have borne it, Medea." He sighed. "I may have made a mistake, my dove, but you are so important to me. I was trying to act in your own best interests."

I wished so much for the comfort of Jason's arms after the days when we had been kept apart, but my conscience prompted me to speak of the princesses. "Alcestis and her sisters will grieve bitterly. I wish that we had not tricked them."

Jason sighed again, this time impatiently. "I cannot imagine why you are so upset over Pelias's fate; look what you did to your own brother."

"That was different; that was necessity – and I didn't kill him."

"Well, you didn't kill Pelias either, Hippothoe did."

I struggled to articulate my instinctive sympathy with the women's anguish. I knew from Theonoe's death how a sense of culpability could attack and overwhelm one, but I realised that Jason would not understand any reference to a dead slave. "Please, Jason, don't call them assassins to their face. Their guilt will be terrible enough to bear without being constantly condemned by the one who undermined them."

"I don't believe that their love for their father was so

very strong that they will collapse under the strain. They were eager enough to dismember Pelias's corpse when decent women would have been revolted by the thought. However, if they distract you too much, I can easily expel them from Iolcos."

I was silent. It was clear that I could not protest too much upon the princesses' behalf or they would suffer even more. Try as I might, I could not altogether banish the disloyal thought that Jason, just like the people of Iolcos, was also calculating.

Whilst I might have had significant doubts about our joint course of action, Jason clearly had none. Naturally, I knew that it was vital to present a bold front when reporting the news of Pelias's death to his court, since any suggestion of uncertainty would be rewarded with swift vengeance. Nevertheless, Jason's swagger was not assumed. He was relishing the chance to pay back several old scores and – judging from the expression which I surprised crossing Brachos's face – there must have been several men that morning who wondered what awaited them. Jason made no announcements as to his intentions, but ordered a grand feast that evening.

"See to it, Brachos," he ordered, with the air of one who had ruled successfully for many years. After a few more trivial comments, my husband the king turned to me. "Medea, my sweet, I wish you to sit at my right hand during this feast. It is important that my people see that I am a king with important foreign connections. I hope that this is not too much to ask."

Since Jason had seen me gracing my father's court, I automatically supposed that his apparent concern for any maidenly diffidence was assumed for the occasion. Indeed, I should have been furious to have been denied the chance to support my husband on his first appearance as king.

Entering into the spirit of things, I bowed my head low and replied in subdued tones. "Your will is mine, my lord."

Jason seemed please with my ready understanding of matters. Then his eyes flickered over my robes with a tinge of dissatisfaction. "You need something more suitable to wear."

Since most of my clothes were, by now, probably gracing the shoulders of one of my father's mistresses, I was fully in agreement as to my parlous state. Jason's solution, however, worried me. "Hippothoe's about your build. Take what you want from her."

I opened my mouth to protest as to the unwisdom of this action when Jason let his gaze drifted over the court. "Iacchus, your wife used to attend to my mother, the queen, did she not?"

"That is so, sire."

"Then let her wait upon my wife, Medea. She will need to find robes fit for her status tonight."

Iacchus's consent was swift, perhaps because he had no concept of the difficulty of weaving robes fit for a queen in less than a day. He was soon at my side, bowing low and begging me to follow him. I did not like to be separated from Jason, but I fully understood the importance of making a fine spectacle that evening. Moreover, I was deeply relieved that Jason had so publicly acknowledged our relationship. I had feared that, somehow, in the midst of Jason's success he might be brought low and forced to deny me. So, although I was still worried about the tactlessness of raiding Hippothoe's clothes-chest for the finest of her robes, my heart was dancing at the thought that, finally, Jason and I were recognised as husband and wife.

Iacchus left me in the hands of the slave-girl who looked after me, begging that I would forgive him for going to seek his wife. I watched his departure with amusement. Naturally, he would be eager to explain to Arachne the circumstances which demanded her sudden attendance. I was wandering backwards and forward, idly wondering what Arachne would be like, when the door banged behind me. I turned round to find not a complaisant elderly woman, but Hippothoe, raging in anger and ready, by the look of her, to tear the veins out of my throat and drink the blood spurting from them.

"There you are, you harlot. You should be ashamed to show yourself here! But let me tell you this, you may steal my father's life and steal his kingdom, but you needn't think that you will steal the clothes off his daughters' backs."

I was irritated by this melodramatic statement. "I am so glad to see that embroidered fabrics are of greater importance to you than who is the ruler of Iolcos."

This measured statement clearly impressed the slave-girl, who was gawping at both of us, but Hippothoe's eyes looked as if they would explode under the pressure of her anger.

"You… you bitch, you strumpet, you whore! You come here and use magic to kill people and then you laugh. By Zeus, when Acastus returns, you and that bastard Jason won't laugh for long."

"And when should I expect this fate?"

"You think that I would tell you that? I suppose you're hoping to kill Acastus, too. Well, I've got a better suggestion for you. If you're so desirous of wiping out the men in my family, why don't you start with that treacherous trail of slime, your dear Jason?"

With that, she left tempestuously.

Later that evening, I tried to warn Jason that Hippothoe was a dangerous enemy and that she had spoken of Acastus's return. Jason, who seemed to exude self-confidence that night, was uninterested in warnings.

"Pah, ignore her. She'd like to cast a curse upon you, but you're a witch and she isn't." He gesticulated towards the crowd. "Do these men look like rebels to you? No, they know that they can't bring Pelias back, so they'll accept what's happened." He gave a sardonic laugh. "She must have been very fond of that piece of glittering gossamer that you're wearing to show her hand quite so obviously. If she'd had any sense, she'd have kept her mouth shut and tried to win me over to her father's plan of marrying me off to her."

This repetition of the idea that my own marriage to Jason might have been lightly set aside to suit the whims of state hurt me, but I argued that Jason had phrased things tactlessly. After all, I was sitting by his side, acknowledged by all as his wife and the queen of Iolcos. And if I spent much of the triumphal feast trying to console myself that Jason really did view me as his wife, the events which followed it made it very clear that I was his spouse. For the first time, we were able to sleep together. We lay, joined as one, in Pelias's bed, the bed in which Jason had been conceived, and the bed in which our own son, Mermerus, was conceived that very night.

XXVI

The days which followed were dreamy, warm days, shot through with the taste of honey and the scent of wild flowers floating on an almost imperceptible breeze. It should have been perfect, but I knew that it was not. I struggled for understanding, but I felt drugged and incapable of catching the infinitesimal hints by which I normally attained knowledge. Was the honey too sweet, the flowers too cloying? Probably, but at the time, all I could sense was that our joy was threatened.

Jason brushed away my fears and, since I could provide no actual evidence by which to convince him, I could sympathise with his ill-concealed suspicion that I was merely suffering from some female malady. It was certainly the case that I had begun to feel queasy each morning and that hardly enhanced my chances of interpreting the flight of larks. What even the least observant at court had no difficulty in interpreting was the hatred which Jason's cousins felt for him. True, it varied. Pisidice cowered away from him; Hippothoe glared and mouthed curses; whilst Pelopia and Alcestis preserved a frosty dignity on all occasions. Jason was displeased with them and spread the story which I had begged him not to tell – that they had killed Pelias. Whilst this was strictly true, the good people of Iolcos seemed to find it hard to match their former princesses' demeanour with one of guilt.

Jason pointed out to me several times that I had been wrong to persuade him to keep quiet about their actions, but – quite apart from any considerations of unkindness – I was convinced that I had been correct. The women had been utterly distraught in the days following Pelias's death and funeral. To have claimed at that moment that they had struck Pelias down would have failed utterly and led to unhelpful questions as to who, actually, had stabbed him. My own invention, that Pelias had been overcome by a vision of Artemis, was much better. Not only did it plausibly explain both death and grief, it was also eminently flattering to the dead man and Iolcos. The citizens, who now belonged to a land worthy of the attentions of a powerful immortal, were far too busy preening themselves to wonder at the convenience of Pelias's death for Jason.

For his part, Jason dismissed the idea that Acastus any longer presented a threat. Four moons had passed and still Pelias's son had not appeared. As far as the new king was concerned, Acastus would never return. Indeed, he was happy to share this view with any who asked, including the boy's sisters. Looking back, I wonder whether his barely-concealed pleasure in predicting that Acastus's bones were mouldering on a desolate shore was one of the things which made me nervous. After all, Acastus was well-known to the people of Iolcos; he had grown up there and for years they had regarded him as their future king. Declaring that Acastus was dead was unlikely to help Jason gain popularity. And, increasingly, it became clear that Jason did need to establish himself. His assumption that people would be happy to see Aeson's son restored to his rightful place had not proved to be correct. Moreover, Jason's method of conducting himself towards those who were lower in status grated – particularly with men who were significantly older than he was and who had been accustomed to, at least outward, respect from Pelias.

Brachos was the first to feel his displeasure. Not only was he demoted from his position as steward to the king, but Jason insisted that he handed over the golden armlets and rings which had been gifts from Pelias. I learned too late to stop Jason from publicly presenting these treasures to his new steward, a wizened little man with an oleaginous smile. Cleon was ready to do whatever Jason asked, and even more ready to receive his reward. Brachos must have loathed watching Cleon flaunting the symbols of his new power – not least because everyone else at court could observe his humiliation. I could not help comparing how my father had demoted people. Mostly, they were sent off to farm their lands, laden with gold and honour. A few he had quietly killed. It was ruthless, but effective.

Thoughts of my father reminded me how he had always preserved a network of relationships which produced a harvest of information. Jason lacked such links. He had not grown up in Iolcos and his father was long dead – as were most of his father's friends. I doubted whether many men would bother to warn Jason if dissent began to build. I knew that I ought to help my husband and I tried to talk to the nobles at court. I even tried to talk to the slaves. But each time I was greeted with the same frozen faces and the same expressionless voices. Then one night, some six months after Jason had ascended the throne, I overheard a conversation between an important noble called Melesias and the seer Kynaxilides.

"I know she talks to you, Kynaxilides. Does she tell you of her husband's plans?"

"No, she speaks of sacrifices and the ways of the gods."

"And they are strange enough to fathom," grunted Melesias. "If it is true that Acastus is dead, why didn't Jason marry Alcestis? It would be much harder to dispute his claim to the throne if he had done so."

"Perhaps he wanted a wife who could commune with the immortals."

Melesias gave a harsh laugh. "What does he need a priestess for? He's got you."

"It reflects well upon a man to have a priestess as his consort," responded Kynaxilides mildly. "There is a certain lustre which attaches itself to any who understand the ways of the gods."

"And Jason certainly likes glory."

Kynaxilides ignored this spiteful remark. "Moreover, Jason may not trust me. Seers have been known to misinterpret the signs. And even if Jason believes that I am honest, he may fear that I will interpret what I want to see, rather than what is there."

Melesias ignored this suggestion. "If he didn't like Alcestis, there are three others to choose from."

"Perhaps he isn't sure that Acastus has died."

"You mean the princesses would expect Jason to stand aside if Acastus did return? You might be correct – Medea certainly won't request that of him."

"And the princesses do not like him."

"Liking has no place within a royal match."

"True, Melesias, but they may have more knowledge about how their father died than we do."

"What do you mean?"

"I am blind, but I can hear how they speak. There is fear in their voices and there is hate in his. He has always hated them."

"But they are mere women."

"And a woman can inflict hurt without using a knife – particularly where a man's pride is involved. Jason wants a wife who worships him as a hero, not one who glowers at him in silent hatred. Our princesses never praised his courage even before their father's death; they certainly would not do so now."

Melesias sounded convinced by Kynaxilides's disparaging assessment. "Jason certainly enjoys telling tales about his voyages, although we've heard them all several times before."

"All heroes seek honour, just as a seer seeks truth."

I shrank back into the shadows, overcome with a strange sense of betrayal. Kynaxilides had been careful in what he had said, but I realised that he was an enemy of my husband. I cursed myself for naivety in assuming that I could depend upon him. Just because Phrixus had been the only person other than Theonoe whom I could trust at Colchis, that did not mean that all seers were as gentle and kind as he had been. But I had never seen any sign of anger with the new regime when I talked to Kynaxilides. Indeed, he had been kind when I had told of my pregnancy. I blushed in the darkness, grateful that Kynaxilides had preserved that secret. Then I pulled myself together. Why was I worrying about whether Kynaxilides liked me or not? He was not Phrixus and my duty was to my husband. That duty was clear. I ought to tell Jason that Melesias and Kynaxilides were plotting against him. Then Jason would drive them out of Iolcos and we would be safe.

I still do not know what I ought to have done. But at the time, the child growing within me made me sluggish and indecisive. Part of me argued that I ought to protect Jason, while another part insisted that I had overheard grumbles, rather than a plot. Nor could I dismiss the possibility that Jason might take harsh revenge upon Kynaxilides and bring down the wrath of the gods upon himself. Perhaps I would have told Jason had I not been presented with another, better excuse to warn him that he was growing unpopular.

Alcestis's visit was as surprising as it was unexpected. Hippothoe still spat hatred at me whenever we had the misfortune to meet, while the others tended to pretend that I was not there. For Alcestis to seek me out was utterly unpredictable. After some stilted discussion about each other's health, Alcestis almost visibly gathered up her courage and launched into what she had to say.

"I have no desire to help your husband, but I care for the people of Iolcos. You are an outsider, but I was born here and have never lived anywhere else. I know these people and I know that they are unhappy."

She paused, as if waiting for an outburst on my part, but I was thinking of the cherry-trees in blossom in Colchis and the cherry-tree which I had planted to shade Theonoe's grave.

"Aeson was not a good king. Your husband thinks that he was, since Aeson was his father. It is right to honour and respect one's father, but a king is a father to all his people, not just one boy. And, just as it would be wrong to neglect a child and allow him to grow up without caring what became of him, so it is wrong to regard a kingdom as a plaything. My cousin does not know how Aeson ruled, but I do and our subjects do."

I noted with interest how Alcestis could not bring herself to say Jason's name. Then a wave of nausea struck and, in the attempt to avoid Alcestis noticing that something was wrong, I asked the first question which occurred to me. "What did Aeson do?"

Alcestis blushed, but forced herself to continue. "He was not content with his marriage." Her blush grew deeper. "There are some women who do not care for such ties, but they are found in the lower end of the city, near the docks.

"Like Arsinoe," I found myself thinking.

"However, Aeson tried to corrupt some of the wives of our leading noblemen."

Recollections of my father's court suggested to me that some of them probably did not need much corrupting, but I was aware that such a remark would cause Alcestis to close up – nor would it enhance Jason's reputation if she were to spread it.

"Such behaviour made Aeson very unpopular," commented Alcestis primly. "Moreover, he spent money wildly and then created new taxes to pay for his amusements."

I allowed myself a sarcastic aside that this must have roused still greater anger against Aeson. Alcestis nodded.

"My father said that it took years to build up trade again. That was why he was so keen to trace the route by which amber reaches our islands."

"So that he could channel it through Iolcos?" I enquired, immediately seeing the possibility which such a monopoly could bring in terms of both trade and taxes. "Clever."

Alcestis seemed momentarily gratified at such appreciation of Pelias's skill, before her eyes filled with tears again – either with memory of his loss or from fear that her brother, too, was lost.

"What did you want to tell me about Jason?" I asked rather awkwardly.

"Men here remember his father and they talk. They see that your husband enjoys celebrating feasts; they know that he has raised a new toll on ships entering the harbour and they fear for the future." She gestured with her hand. "Iolcos is like the sea on a summer's day when the gusting west wind is gathering out of sight; it lies apparently calm, but is boiling beneath the surface, ready to hurl forth all its fury in a sudden storm. Medea, all is not right in Iolcos."

Alcestis's use of my name softened the bristling anger which drove through my body. "Why do you tell me this?" I asked curiously. "You owe us nothing."

"I owe you vengeance. But it is not you who have caused me to speak out. You may have killed my father and demoted us to the status of humble petitioners at your husband's table, but I am still Pelias's daughter and I still care for Iolcos. If there is a rebellion, people will be killed, and women and children will left to sit beside the fire, weeping their hurt out before the gods."

She got up to depart. "You must tell your husband that he is not ruling well. There is your child to consider. Do you want him brought up in exile as your husband was?"

Stunned at this unexpected knowledge on Alcestis's part, I ushered her to the door, before resuming my seat to ponder what she had told me. The information about Aeson I dismissed as impossible to prove and unimportant even if it were true. There were probably few people in positions of power who remembered his reign, while those who did would be highly unlikely to risk their lives to rectify an historical wrong. Much more serious was Alcestis's warning about discontent at Jason's own actions. Thanking Hera that at least I did not have to worry about Jason attempting to bed various unidentified noblewomen, I bit my lip thoughtfully. It was a source of regret to me that Jason did not discuss decisions of state openly in my presence. However, he had been so taken aback at the suggestion that I might have anything to offer that I had realised, without any possibility of misinterpretation, that this was yet another activity in which Greek females were not allowed to engage – even if they had the capacity to understand the questions at stake.

I swore under my breath. I was not experienced in the politics of raising tax, since it was not something on which my father had often openly expounded. Nonetheless, it was abundantly clear to me that if taxes were raised so high that ships preferred to trade elsewhere, then Iolcos would lose, rather than raise, money. A ship, after all, can easily move to a new base.

I prowled backwards and forwards restlessly, scowling at the floor in frustration. The question remained, had Alcestis had spoken accurately? She had never before demonstrated such interest in the mechanics of good governance and I could not dismiss the possibility that someone had put her up to speaking to me. However, was that not, in itself, significant? Anyone who cared enough to suggest that Iolcos might face a rebellion in the near future must be someone who was aware of discontent. Alternatively, if Alcestis's claims were utterly false and the people of Iolcos were ready to accept Jason's rule, then surely the very fact that someone had been prepared to risk his neck cobbling together such lies suggested that there was, indeed, great unhappiness amongst some circles.

I continued to stalk to and fro, wishing that I did not feel so isolated from the ordinary people. At Colchis I could have conducted some special sacrifice at the harbour and used the opportunity to listen to the rumours and talk which swirl around any port. But, by now, I had spent enough time at Iolcos to realise that mixing with the people who lived by the harbour would be greeted with appalled and disgusted horror. Jason had pointed out several times that, since I was a stranger, it was all the more important that I observed Greek customs fully or he would suffer condemnation for having brought a foreign-born woman into the royal family. If there was already displeasure at his rule, I could scarcely add to it by behaving like one of the women whom Aeson used to bed. I groped for a solution, but could think of none, other than to try to warn my husband again about the likelihood of discontent fomenting a challenge to his rule.

XXVII

I had still not found a method of persuading Jason to take more precautions when the news which Jason had dismissed as an impossibility came true. Acastus was not dead; his bones were not turned over by boars searching for truffles in the rich earth of the northern forests, nor did his skeleton sway and float amongst Poseidon's caverns. Acastus stood before us, young and proud and true. Somehow Jason, the hero of my blood and progenitor of the young life growing within me, appeared to merge into the grey shadows when Acastus presented himself in Pelias's great hall.

"I scorn to lurk in hiding," he proclaimed, his haughty stance drawing all eyes upon him. "I returned expecting to greet my father, the noble Pelias, but instead I am told that he died mysteriously, that my sisters weep every day at his tomb, and that you, Jason, have installed yourself upon his throne. What say you?"

I willed Jason to reply with dignity and tact, but when I saw my lord grow red and cross I feared for the outcome.

"You, my cousin, have been away a very long while, chasing stories which slaves use to quiet their eager nurslings. The tale of the road to the isles of amber is one of diaphanous wisps and wraiths. You must have been imbibing those tales long after you ought to have reached maturity if you throw wild accusations in my direction."

"I throw accusations, Jason, but they are not wild."

"Indeed? Then why do you speak of my cousins, the princesses?"

Knowing that Jason intended to say that Hippothoe had cut down her father, I winced. Such a course would only serve to distress the women and anger their brother and any supporters at court.

"I speak of them because you have betrayed them and their father. You have set a tale afloat that my sisters killed my father. What nonsense! Who had anything to gain other than you – you and that foreign creature who now rules as our queen? Who immediately installed himself upon Pelias's throne? You did. Who demoted the princesses in status? You – or your consort – did. Who ignored my claims? You did."

Jason interrupted this list of accusations angrily. "And where were you, cousin? Were you here, ready to help with the task of ruling Iolcos? Were you present to succour your sisters in their grief? No, you were gadding about on some never-ending excursion into foreign waters. Naturally, I became king – much to the relief of the people of Iolcos. And, whilst you are keen to promote yourself as Pelias's heir, the gods will strike you dead if you deny that Pelias stole the kingdom from my father. Aeson was the true king of Iolcos and I am Aeson's son. Iolcos is mine."

"Iolcos is made up of more than one man, cousin," remarked Acastus dryly. "If you ask them, you will find that the people of Iolcos disliked your father, and dislike and despise you. If I had discovered Iolcos in good heart, with trade flourishing and the people happy, I should have buried my differences with you for the sake of the city. But since I find the people fraught with sorrows and ships sailing far from our land, I wish to bury something else – my sword in your black heart."

By now, the light was too poor to trace Jason's reaction on his countenance, but I felt him quiver next to me. I cautiously slipped my hand over his, wishing to remind him that it would be foolish to react too openly. He grasped it tightly, much as a warrior grasps his weapon before he strikes.

"Well now, cousin Acastus," he retorted, "you seem more than a trifle put out. Surely you must realise that events wait for no man? Just because you were busy playing with one-eyed monsters and giant birds there was no reason for the rest of the world not to pursue its own business. And, as I say, we have been busy here in Iolcos. You should listen to the true purveyors of news, not maimed and crippled slaves who claim to interpret the wisdom of the gods."

I gasped, wondering how my husband had learned that Kynaxilides was an enemy. Jason rose in his seat, pride apparent in every aspect of his bearing. "And now that you have finally graced us with your presence, cousin, I can announce the news which I have long wished to give to the people of Iolcos. I know that you will rejoice with them to learn that before two moons have passed Iolcos will have a new heir – the boy whom my wife Medea is carrying within her."

Acastus cast an unemotional, searching glance over me, as if seeking confirmation of Jason's claim. Perhaps my embarrassed blush convinced him; perhaps it was the sight of my swelling belly which, by now, was obvious beneath the fabrics heavy with gold and silver embroidery.

"A child, I grant you, but not necessarily a boy and certainly not one which has yet come to term. And, even if your consort does breed a male child, that does not entitle you to my father's throne."

"*My* father's."

"No, Jason. Aeson ruled for months; Pelias for years. And do not argue that people of Iolcos have suffered for years, waiting for your return and the chance to depose Pelias. Had they felt like that, they would have risen up against Pelias whilst you were still a child."

Jason sensibly ignored the trap of arguing that Pelias had been so despotic that no-one had dared to challenge him. Instead he laughed contemptuously. "To follow your argument, why has there been no attempt to overthrow me? Because the people know that I am the rightful king and the one best for these unsettled times. I make foreign alliances. I gain honour which redounds to the glory of Iolcos. My reputation serves to enhance the reputation of Iolcos. I brought the Golden Fleece – you bring an empty ship. You are as empty as the spurious assertions you mouth with such windy assurance."

As the dispute raged, I was aware of the frozen silence throughout the hall. This was not merely a quarrel between two cousins, but an open debate as two rival candidates set out their claims to be king. It was not my pregnant state which caused my stomach to heave with spasms of nausea, but the fear that Acastus's silken courtesy was making more impression upon the nobles than my husband's logic. Jason had been eager enough to keep reminding me that I was a stranger to Iolcos and that every mistake I made would be doubly-criticised because of my foreign birth. If only he could see that he was in a similar position. Acastus had been the heir apparent, growing up amongst many of the men present that evening and regarded as one of them. But Jason had been raised abroad, far apart from the noble youths of Iolcos who ought to have comprised his playmates and companions. He had returned for long enough to declare his claim to the throne, before setting off on an exotic foreign adventure. True, he had succeeded, but he had returned with a foreign woman in tow. It was only too easy to see what the noblemen of Iolcos must think: foreign-bred, foreign-wed. Would they really celebrate at the thought of a half-Colchian princeling to rule over them in the future? Or would they regard the homecoming of their own prince Acastus as a welcome return to normality: one of themselves, born and reared in Iolcos, and ready to marry one of their own?

By the time that the evening had drawn to a close,

Jason had made a number of mistakes. His anger had driven him to drink too much which, in turn, made him bluster and utter threats which he could not hope to put into practice. By contrast, Acastus had remained in command of himself and had argued each point with an icy detachment which was as impressive as it was chilling. No-one else said anything, but I sensed that the sympathy of the audience lay with Acastus. When we retired to bed, I tried desperately to alert Jason to the dangers which he faced, but my bold husband merely laughed off my warnings as the false presentiments which affect pregnant women. As I lay nestled within the protection of his strong arms I desperately hoped that Jason was correct.

Acastus struck two days later. Looking back, I can never understand why he bothered to warn Jason of his intentions, unless it was that he wanted to be seen to have acted in a heroic manner. Whatever Acastus's reasoning, Jason had failed to make any preparations and the first that he knew of his rival's support was when a detachment of nobles appeared, led by Melesias.

"You must leave Iolcos immediately. You are no longer king."

Jason stared at him in disbelief.

"Don't be ridiculous. Do you really mean to tell me that you want that mealy-mouthed stripling on the throne of Iolcos in preference to me, a proven hero?"

"The Fleece does not give you the right to rule," stated Melesias implacably. "In particular, it does not give you the right to rule badly. You have been on the throne for seven months. Yet what have you achieved? There is anger amongst the traders, but you are uninterested in their woes. The harbour is empty, but you do not care. And you have humiliated men for no reason other than that they were loyal to their king."

"Precisely," interrupted Jason. "Why should I keep

Brachos or the others when I knew that they hated me?"

"Did you give Brachos a chance? And what belief could we have in your judgment when you adopted a creature like Cleon, who is only interested in whatever he can gain for himself."

"But loyal. Cleon is very loyal. You'll discover that when he brings soldiers to cut you down."

Melesias laughed. "So loyal that when we told him what was happening he fled north as if he were pursued by Ares himself."

"Rebellion brings death and destruction in its wake. You will all suffer for this. You are fools, driven by a desire for glory which you can never achieve. You envy my glory, which is why you are trying to pull me down."

I was watching from the side and, although I deplored Jason's choice of words, his physical presence – like a lion stretching itself, fully conscious of its glorious muscular strength – was such that I wondered if the delegation would give way. But they were not to be cowed.

"This is not rebellion," responded Melesias flatly. "This is restitution."

The door opened again. For a moment I wondered if Cleon had returned with troops to save his master. Instead, Acastus strode in.

"I warned you, Jason, that I would not stand by to watch my father's work destroyed."

"I am the king."

"How can you be, when every important nobleman in Iolcos is against you? Look at them. Do they want you to remain?"

Jason looked, and I looked. I could see no signs of mercy upon the set faces. If Acastus were to draw his sword and run us through, there was nothing which we could do to prevent him. I shivered. What had my unborn child done to deserve such a fate?

Acastus spoke again. "Were you not my cousin, I should kill you. It would be a just punishment for the unhappiness which you have brought upon my sisters. But you are kin and, whatever you may have done, I do not dishonour the gods by slaying my kinsmen." He nodded scornfully in my direction. "Take your Colchian witch with you – I hope she proves as treacherous to you as she has been to my family here."

PART THREE: CORINTH

XXVIII

Thus it was that we scurried onto a ship sailing towards mainland Greece: Jason, myself and a slave-girl who had been one of five who had waited upon me in the short interlude in which I had been queen of Iolcos. I was reminded of the last time when Jason and I had set sail together. Then we had been leaving to seek a new future in Iolcos, accompanied by Jason's comrades and the Fleece, proof of his heroic status. Now, we were fleeing Iolcos, seeking refuge wherever it might offer, accompanied by a lone slave, who seemed more inclined to hurl her guts out over the prow of the vessel than to help care for her heavily-pregnant mistress. Still, as I looked round, summing up the losses which we had incurred – no homeland, no comrades, no Fleece – there was one comfort. At least we did not face the hideous torment of my brother's death, his body torn to pieces and scattered upon the angry waves.

The ship on which we had set sail was Corinthian. Her captain was a great talker and proud of his home city.

"Yes, we did a lot of trade with Iolcos until the new taxes came in," he told us one evening as the stars were beginning to glimmer and flicker, shining a way across the wine-dark sea for those who knew how to follow their secret paths. "Of course, once word got round that the place was charging tolls on practically everything you could think of, from wool to the right of a boat to stay in harbour whilst it loaded up with goods, most of us avoided Iolcos and went to easier places." He spat over the side thoughtfully. "You were lucky. I only dropped anchor on the calculation that the good people of Iolcos must be so desperate for trading-vessels that I could mark up my goods enough to pay for the preposterous new taxes." He glanced at us. "I've never carried a king fleeing into exile before. Still, sir, if the gods are with you, you'll soon be able to return. Maybe I'll have the honour of carrying you to Iolcos, as well as from it."

I bristled at his familiarity, but Jason seemed not to care. Nor did he apparently care that Acastus had paid out good gold to our captain to convey us to the mainland. Indeed, when I had complained at the insult, Jason had merely laughed and advised me to be thankful that we had not had to waste our own money. He had even laughed at my fears that Alcestis had somehow managed to put a curse on us.

"Just because my cousin warned you not to risk having our child grow up in exile doesn't mean that she is behind this temporary set-back. In any case, even if he is born in exile, is that so bad a thing? Am I a failure?"

I looked at my husband, conscious that adversity made me love him all the more, since it would be unutterably disloyal to stop supporting him when he needed me most. "Of course not, my dearest. You have defeated monsters and travelled where no man has travelled before."

Jason seemed to grow visibly more confident at such words. "Yes, when I tell the king of Corinth that he entertains the man who drove off the Harpies, the warrior who sailed between the pillars of Heracles, and the hero who won the Golden Fleece, he will realise that he is not dealing with any ordinary traveller."

Just as I was thinking rather selfishly that I had helped Jason win the Fleece and that it was now abandoned in a foreign land where none would honour it as the saviour of Phrixus, Jason looked sadly towards me. "If only, Medea, I could tell the Corinthian king of your skill and courage. But I know my fellow-countrymen. He would be awestruck – but also suspicious. It is better if we do not mention your courage and resolve; I do not want him to regard you as a dangerous outsider."

Perhaps I sounded wistful when I agreed, for Jason smiled one of the smiles which made his whole face light up. "My dove, what is important is not what some strangers learn about you. What is important is that I know and honour your ability. When we are more established at Corinth it may be that we can tell a few select people of your powers – the gods know how much I should like to boast of your prowess, but I have your safety and the safety of our child to consider, as well as my own wishes."

It was evening when we arrived in Corinth. The flaming sun was dying behind the headland, but all was bathed in its final blood-red kiss. Even the buildings appeared a fiery coral as our vessel tied up at the harbour. Jason stepped off the boat with the appearance of one who is very much in command, whilst I was seized with an ill-timed attack of nausea. The slave-girl Terpsichore waved her hands around uselessly until the spasm passed and then the three of us set off towards the town; Jason in front, I following behind and Terpsichore making up the rear, clutching three heavy baskets. Jason had no contacts in Corinth and the ship-captain had advised him against approaching the king without warning, so we ended up spending the night in a rather run-down house which catered for those away from home. Jason apologised for its lack of amenities, but by that point I was so glad to lie down somewhere which did not shake and shiver or plough up and down that I no longer cared that I was hardly living up to my status as Aeetes's daughter and Jason's wife.

The next day, Jason set out early and returned very late, murmuring placatory noises in my ear, whilst I tried not to annoy him by repeating the terrors which had plagued my mind all through the long hours when we had been apart.

For ten days, this sequence of events repeated itself. On the eleventh, Jason returned early in triumph.

"Creon has agreed to our living in Corinth," he announced. "I knew that he would see sense when he realised who I was. We shall soon be able to move from this squalid hovel." He gestured dismissively at the worm-eaten door and the general air of dilapidation. "It's about time that we had somewhere better suited to our status."

"I wish he had seen you before today," I murmured. "Then we would have known the good news earlier."

"What? Oh, yes. Quite. Well, you know what king's courts are like – busy places. It takes time to find the right people to introduce you."

I might have paid more attention to this somewhat artless speech had I not been so relieved that I would not bring my child into the world on board ship. The uncertainty of our position had left me fearing that we would spend the rest of our lives sailing from one land to another in a hopeless search for somewhere to live.

Jason's voice cut into my thoughts. "It would have been easier if we had had the Fleece to bargain with. It's unfortunate that you couldn't have brought it with you."

I nodded silently, although I wondered whether I could have borne to give it – and the memories which it contained – up for a second time. Then common sense reasserted itself. Obviously, if the only way in which I could have won a place for my unborn child was to sacrifice the Fleece, I should have had to have done so, no matter what my personal inclinations were. After all, was there really any difference between handing it over to Pelias and to Creon, except that it would have been more accessible in Corinth than it was in Iolcos? Indeed, the Fleece was now more inaccessible to me than in its original place in the grove at Colchis. I hoped that Acastus would show it more honour than Pelias had done.

Once we had moved into more suitable accommodation, Jason spent a great deal of time at the palace improving his contacts, while I calculated and recalculated the probable date of my confinement. As the day of my delivery grew closer, Terpsichore seemed to grow more attentive. I was grateful for her help and all too conscious that I was cut off from the support of any relatives. When the birth-pangs struck, I could not believe the pain involved. I called upon Hera and Eileithyia. As the first shafts of stabbing torment relaxed, I thought that the gods had taken pity upon me. Perhaps childbirth was not as hard as old women claimed. Perhaps I was one of the lucky ones. Then the pain returned, striking more rapidly, more violently.

Terpsichore did her best by trying to bathe my head with cool water and to feed me wine steeped in herbs, but what good was water against the spasms which sliced through my body like a sharp lance through skin and muscle? I called upon Theonoe, but how could she help me from beyond the grave? I begged the gods to cut loose the thing inside me. Was I to be destroyed by the very creature which I had nurtured for nine months? How could any woman endure this unendurable pain; this treacherous assault from inside her own womb? I begged Terpsichore for syrup of poppies, but she did not know how to prepare the mixture and shook her head hopelessly at my request. The sweat was gouting in streams from my body and I could smell the sour odour of fear – whether from myself or the slave-girl I do not know. She would not open the minute window, claiming that it was unhealthy, and it was only when I swore at her that she obeyed my order. The dank atmosphere retreated somewhat, but again and again I was racked with slashing, piercing torture; pain so great that I could not have imagined it had I tried. Then, when I thought that I had already died, there was one thrusting agony worse than all those which had come before. I arched upwards, then collapsed back, certain that my body had been split in two.

I lay there, faintly aware of a nebulous resentment. Eventually, this resentment resolved into a complaint that Terpsichore had not cleaned my body properly for burial, but had left it lying in a pool of clammy sweat which would soon attract the flies. Whether I spoke out loud or not was unclear, but she suddenly loomed over me, thrusting a pink, mewling blob towards me with the gesture of one who conveys an indescribable favour. I closed my eyes swiftly to blot out the sight. Was being dead not enough punishment for having stolen the Fleece and killed Pelias, without having monstrous illusions imposed upon me as well?

As the pain receded into more manageable proportions, so too did some of my senses return. It crossed my mind that the blob which had been thrust in my face might be a baby and I gesticulated faintly that I wished to see it again. Terpsichore obliged and this time I saw a tiny face, wizened like a monkey and as full of intelligence. I held out my hands and it wailed in protest.

"He's hungry," explained the slave-girl, noticing my hurt at this rejection. "He wants something to eat."

"He?" I repeated softly, knowing that Jason had predicted a boy. "Is it a boy?"

"A fine boy, my lady. Your husband will be pleased."

My face contracted at that remark. Jason would be delighted, but I could not help thinking of my own mother and the comments which she must have endured after my birth on her failure to produce a male child. I suddenly wished very much for her presence and for that of Theonoe. How proud Theonoe would have been to see the puckered, wailing face of my first-born, and how much I

216

had wished for her help during the birth-agony.

I was very grateful that Terpsichore had cleaned up the baby and the room by the time that Jason returned. She had even managed to scavenge some lavender to make the room pleasantly-scented. I lay back in the bed, my son nestled at my breast and awaited Jason's reaction.

"Medea, is it true? Do I have a son?"

I nodded and held him out to his father. The child raised a low, protesting wail, but Jason seemed pleased. "Aha! He is already practising a war-cry. Well, little Mermerus, I hope that you will grow up to be as strong and brave as your father." He turned his attention to me. "You look tired, Medea. I hope that you did not find the birth too hard."

Conscious that I had not been as brave as I should have liked, I avoided the question. "We have our son."

"We do indeed," chortled Jason with delight. "And I trust that he will soon have little brothers to join him, eh, Medea?"

I smiled weakly. Nothing would induce me to go through that agony for a second time. Fortunately, Jason did not seem to expect a reply. He kissed me briefly, touched his son and bounded out of the room.

It took me some days to recover my energies, but I was consoled by the presence of my son, who grew more beautiful every day. His eyes gazed into mine and he emitted tiny gurgles of pleasure when I spoke to him or gently ran my fingers down his spine. His coppery shock of hair thickened, his body filled out and his skin was no longer wrinkled. Jason listened patiently to my recital of these triumphs, but he was also busy with his own attempts to secure our future and I saw little of him during this time. I felt vaguely guilty that I did not notice his absence more, but with the fascinating bundle nestling in my arms it was hard to concentrate on anything else taking place around me. Even when we moved into a bigger house and Jason decided to provide me with my own room in which I could nurse Mermerus during the night, my main reaction was one of relief that I could croon loving words to my darling boy without worrying about disturbing Jason.

However, in the midst of this pleasure, I became aware of Terpsichore's behaviour. To begin with, she seemed full of excited anticipation. This, with the selfishness of a new mother, I attributed to the arrival of my delightful boy, but Terpsichore then moved from excitement to a fit of extreme sullenness. She roused herself to attend to Mermerus, but displayed a sulky disinclination to do anything for me at all. Eventually, I forced myself to tackle her on the subject. Each tactful question was greeted with a grunt or a silent shake of the head. Finally, I grew cross.

"For goodness sake, Terpsichore, what is wrong with you? I'm fed up with you constantly being in the sullens. You're behaving like a spoilt child."

"Spoilt, am I? How would you behave if you were promised what you had dreamt of and then had it snatched away from you?"

I glanced down at Mermerus's contented face as he suckled at my breast and shivered. I thought that I would die if I were to lose him. My voice grew more gentle. "But, Terpsichore, what have you lost?"

"Just my freedom. I don't suppose you'd care what that means to me, my lady, you being free and not knowing what it's like to be forced to obey another's will."

"Terpsichore!"

"Report my insolence to my master. If he beats me so hard that I die that'd end everything." She snorted sarcastically. "If I were to try to make away with myself that would be a crime – a slave doesn't even possess her own body."

I stared at her aghast. "But, Terpsichore, I never promised to free you."

"The master did. He said to us five slaves that he needed one of us to come with him to look after you on the voyage. He said that he'd free whoever came. Well, it was a bit of a risk, but I don't want to spend the rest of my days saying yes, master, no, master and taking whatever comes to me. So I agreed to go. I didn't expect to be freed straight off; I knew that you'd need someone with you until you had birthed. But you've got everything you want – a husband and a fine son. Why do you deny me what I want?"

"I haven't."

"The master says you won't let me go."

I struggled to understand this claim. "I did not even know that there was a possibility that you might be freed. I have told Jason that I am grateful for your help. Perhaps he interpreted it as meaning that I wanted you to remain as my slave. I promise you, Terpsichore, that I have not refused to free you."

"I don't want your promises. I don't trust promises any more – *he* promised me my freedom." After that defiant speech, Terpsichore burst into ugly tears which set Mermerus off. It was impossible to think in the midst of this communal wailing and it was some time before I calmed down first my son and then the slave-girl.

That night I was eager for Jason's return. I paced backwards and forwards, wondering for the first time what he did all day. On some occasions he had made remarks about hunting expeditions, but surely that could not happen every day? When he did finally put in an appearance, it was apparent that he was tired. I wished that I had chosen a better time to speak to him, but when I offered to leave the matter until the next day, he insisted on hearing what was worrying me.

"No, no, if it is so important, we'd better deal with it now." He smiled wearily. "I shouldn't like you to think that I don't listen to you."

I attempted to explain my unhappiness that Terpsichore had been brought to Corinth on the understanding that she would be freed.

"Oh, nonsense, Medea. She's only a slave; don't listen to her."

I thought of my poor Theonoe, badly treated by my father because she was 'only a slave'. "It doesn't matter whether Terpsichore is a slave-girl or a princess; did you tell her that she would be freed if she came to Corinth with us?"

"No."

I was somewhat taken aback at this bald statement. It felt extremely disloyal to disbelieve Jason, but it seemed incredible that Terpsichore could have invented her story. I probed more deeply. "Did you say anything to Terpsichore about her freedom?"

Jason dragged his tunic off and scratched his chest. "Yes. But I didn't promise to give her it immediately we arrived at Corinth."

"What did you say, precisely?"

"I wasn't precise at all. It was hardly a legal contract witnessed by the gods."

"But you gave her the impression…"

"That's her fault, stupid girl. If she chose to come here on some wild belief that she would be immediately rewarded with her freedom then she rates herself and the dangers of coming to Corinth far too highly."

I suddenly lost my temper. "Jason, how could you? You deliberately let that poor girl think that she would be freed and now she's trapped miles away from any of the people she grew up with. It's cruel and unkind."

220

Jason yawned. "As I said, she's only a slave."

"You made a promise to her which you had no intention of keeping. You *lied* to her."

"Do grow up, Medea. She's a slave; what I said to her doesn't count. And where would you have been if I hadn't brought her along? Would you have liked to have given birth with no-one to help you? How else was I supposed to provide you with a nurse – you should be thankful that I thought of your needs whilst I was being driven from my kingdom."

For once the argument that Jason had done this for my sake had no effect. "If you lied to her for my sake, then you can also free her for my sake."

"I shan't."

"Then I shall."

Jason raised his eyebrows. "You're a woman, Medea. You don't own Terpsichore; I do."

XXIX

When I saw Terpsichore's face the next morning, I realised that there was no need to break the news to her that Jason had refused my pleas to free her. The livid bruise on her cheekbone showed all too clearly what the views of Terpsichore's master were on the subject of slaves who whined to their mistresses about unfair treatment. I swallowed convulsively. There was nothing I could say to console her. Terpsichore was equally silent and kept her eyes on the ground as she attended to my and Mermerus's wants.

Throughout the day I worried over my actions. If only I had left things until daytime. If only I had handled things more tactfully. Then Terpsichore would not have suffered. Why had I rushed into complaints when I had seen that Jason was tired? Why hadn't I stopped to consider how exhausted he must be with the strain of trying to begin a new life? Had I become so bound up with Mermerus that I no longer had time to consider Jason's feelings? Was that why Jason had lost his temper and acted so out of character?

As I stared moodily out of the window, wondering how to resolve an impossible situation, my thoughts turned to my own family in Colchis. Was I really in a position to criticise Jason's actions? My brother had happily chastised any slaves who dared to look at him in the wrong way, let alone complain about him, whilst my father would have done much worse than merely beat Terpsichore. Both of them had had the advantage of being brought up by their own fathers, whilst Jason had been abandoned when he was not much older than my own darling Mermerus. I clutched my son convulsively. The thought of my baby, crying for me whilst I was held captive miles away from him, bit into me like a sword-thrust. Never; I would never abandon Mermerus. I would never leave him to be brought up by strangers, calling for me in pain or want. I would never let him be taken from my arms.

Although Mermerus's delighted coos soothed me somewhat, I was not entirely distracted by him. Somehow I had to try to persuade Jason that Terpsichore had thoughts and feelings, too. However, since that seemed likely to be a long task, I could at least devote myself to fashioning a salve to soothe some of the pain of her bruised face. I was relieved to have something practical to address and I was still more relieved to discover that my skill was returning to me.

It had been a very considerable shock to me to find, early in my pregnancy, that my magic arts had deserted me. Utter terror had threatened to overwhelm me when I first realised that my spells and potions no longer worked. However, I had forced myself to consider the problem as rationally as I could. Eventually, I had persuaded myself that my skill was linked to Artemis and that the process of growing a child interfered with the fruits of Artemis's knowledge. I had kept repeating this logical explanation throughout my pregnancy, firmly thrusting away the hideous fear that my deception of Pelias's daughters had led to the gods revoking my art. Now even so simple a test as a soothing ointment seemed a vitally-important indicator of my future.

When I summoned Terpsichore, she was reluctant to anoint herself, but I finally coaxed her into doing so. Perhaps my concern persuaded her that I meant no harm; perhaps she feared my temper. Whatever the reason, the unguent worked sufficiently well for her to ask for more in case the pain returned during the night. My eyes met hers briefly and I realised that she, as well as I, was hoping that the hunting-trip which Jason had mentioned that morning would resolve into one of several days' duration. She dreaded further pain and humiliation, whilst I dreaded the idea of my wonderful husband behaving in exactly the kind of degrading manner which I had seen so many men display.

Jason did not return that night, although I lay half-awake, with one ear open to catch an early warning of his presence. He did, however, reappear the following afternoon, full of stilted, offended dignity. He flung a bag of gold upon the table.

"There, don't say that I don't try to look after my family."

I was hurt by this accusation. "I have never made such a comment."

My husband gave a bitter laugh. "Well, I thought that I'd stay away to give you time to think what you'd do if I weren't here. Who'd ensure that you had food and clothing?"

The implication that Jason needed to buy my love when he knew that I adored him upset me dreadfully. However, I forced myself to appear calm. Terpsichore would hardly be helped by another argument. Furthermore, I had, indeed, used the time for some careful thinking, although Jason might not have been flattered if he had known my conclusions. I was sure that Jason was naturally good and kind – his love for me surely proved that. So his ill-treatment of a helpless slave-girl must have sprung from his upbringing, which had done nothing to foster gentleness or compassion. Jason appeared to be immensely proud of the superior training which Chiron had provided, but I did not see that growing up wild amongst a pack of young boys compensated for a mother's love and reassurance. The entire emphasis of Jason's childhood, as far as I could judge, had been on competition – whether competitive sport, competitive fighting or competitive singing. Presumably, there had even been competitive deceit. So, just as Terpsichore was trapped by her unfortunate birth, I feared that Jason was probably trapped by his early life.

Moreover, I was well aware that the masculine world of a king's court similarly emphasised the attributes of bravery and competition. I could see that the question of keeping a promise was one of principle, but I rather doubted whether men who were always vying to be the best would consider that a promise made to the lowest in society was quite as valuable as one made to the most exalted in rank. Perhaps an even stronger source of Jason's apparent injustice was the fact that he lacked an established position at Corinth. I had seen enough of the jockeying for position amongst the younger noblemen at my father's court to realise that Jason must be under considerable scrutiny at the moment. It was easy to see how such a strain might have led him to behave in an ignoble manner.

Looking back, I cannot quite believe that I was naïve enough to think that I could slowly bring Jason to change attitudes which had been drummed into him from babyhood. But I was full of the glow of new motherhood and still very much in love with my bold, fine husband. It is, of course, possible that I was subconsciously aware that I had no-one else to turn to – Colchis was forever cut off from me and I was hardly likely to be welcome at Iolcos. However, I honestly think that at this point I wanted to help Jason to become as perfect as I had previously thought him. Hence I tried to be as loving as possible towards him, thinking that such actions would help to lessen the strain which he was undeniably suffering as he attempted to establish himself. The unintended consequence of this would have been clear to a more experienced wife – Jason, naturally, assumed that I was afraid of being abandoned by him and started to trade on this perceived weakness.

To begin with, I did not notice that Jason was no longer treating me with the scrupulous respect which he had originally shown to me. Admittedly, part of the reason for my oversight was that I had fallen pregnant again and – just as before – my rational faculties were not enhanced by nausea and weakness. Even more distracting was Terpsichore's sudden illness. Jason was surprised by my concern for a mere slave, pointing out that she was probably pretending to be ill in the hope that I would let her off her work.

Although Terpsichore's sullenness had not endeared her to me, I felt pity for the girl as I looked at her pale, wan face. It was all very well Jason telling me that I was too soft, but Terpsichore was a fellow-being, even if she were a slave. Her pallor suggested loss of blood, and I found a few rags which she had used to staunch nose-bleeds. I gave her nourishing brews and, even when Jason was present, I insisted upon her resting. It was ridiculous for someone who was so weak to attempt to sweep the floors and grind up grain for flour. She seemed grateful for my aid. But within days, I was laying out her body for burial. I followed her to the grave, tiny Mermerus clutched in my arms, praying that Terpsichore might find her freedom wherever she now was.

Terpsichore's death shocked me badly. She was not related by ties of blood, but she had been part of our household and I was dreadfully aware that any of us could be snatched away as suddenly as Terpsichore had been. As I tried to push away visions of dying in labour to leave Mermerus growing up without a mother, I unconsciously looked to Jason to provide some strength and reassurance. Unfortunately, Jason seemed much more occupied in his expanding group of cronies than with the home-life which I was trying to provide for him. He began to make it clear in a variety of indefinable ways that I was no longer as pleasing to him as I had been previously. I was conscious that my body was swelling unattractively, but Jason also began to make rather barbed remarks about how I seemed incapable of keeping the house properly.

"This place does not reflect well upon me. Why don't you take more pride in giving me a comfortable home?"

As I looked round the room which I had struggled to clean that day, my patience snapped. "Why can't you provide me with a slave? I've asked and asked you to get one."

"We don't have enough money to waste at the moment."

My eyes travelled to Jason's new cloak, draped casually over a stool. Jason followed my glance and flushed. "You know I have to present a decent appearance at court. It's bad enough being in exile, but I'm damned if I'm going to have anyone pity me for being poor as well." As I began to speak he added, "Anyway, all of my friends have wives who can manage a household. Why can't you?"

"Because I'm worn out with nausea. Because Mermerus requires constant attention. Because I was trained to interpret the signs of the gods, not to be a domestic drudge."

"There are plenty of priests in Corinth – they hardly need your skills here. You're just lazy, Medea. Lazy and proud."

Jason marked the seventh month of my pregnancy with a new slave to replace Terpsichore, but I found it hard to sound suitably grateful, particularly since Jason kept telling me what a sacrifice it had been to him to find the purchase-price. Pelagia's presence certainly made an enormous difference to my life, but I could not help reflecting rather bitterly that Jason would not have needed to devote so much thought as to why I was a failure domestically had he acquired her months earlier. Moreover, although Pelagia's aid meant that the house was impeccably neat and tidy, there was no change in Jason's attitude. He boasted about his increasing connections with the king's circle, but it seemed to me that the more time he spent at court, the more dissatisfied he grew with me.

In particular, Jason commented more and more on the fact that I was not Greek. When we were in Colchis, he had seemed enchanted by my origins – but what was exotic and fascinating in Colchis was foreign and embarrassing in Corinth. Whereas I had been his 'little dove' in Colchis, now I became his 'little barbarian'. It was meant affectionately – or, at least, I thought so at first, and I tried to treat it as a playful joke, even although I disliked it. Then he said it in front of some Corinthians while we were attending a festival in honour of Artemis. I saw the reaction on their faces and, when we got home, I asked him to stop. He seemed aggrieved.

"Why?"

"It makes me feel uncomfortable and the Corinthians think that you mean it. I don't like it."

"Don't like this, don't like that," he jeered. "Maybe I do mean it. A Greek woman wouldn't complain all the time like you do."

"A Greek woman wouldn't be called names in front of her peers," I pointed out, reasonably enough. "Her father would intervene to protect her."

"Yours won't. And your brother can't. Your only defender is me, so you should do what you're told."

Stung by the cruelty of his reply, I grubbed around for an insult to hurl back at him. "It pleases you to call me a barbarian, but you can't even speak your own language perfectly."

Jason turned dangerously purple. I knew that he prided himself upon the purity of his diction. "How dare you insult me?"

"I'm not. I'm sticking to facts. You use strange phrases."

Jason interrupted before I could bolster my case with examples. "A fat lot you know about it. Any strange phrases arise from the fact that I was educated by a centaur."

"And *I* was educated by the son of Helios. Do you think that the offspring of a god gabbles barbaric Greek?"

Put in a position whereby he would either insult the gods or admit to the justice of my case, Jason did neither. Instead, he sulked and complained about how appallingly rude I was.

In retrospect, I realise that I could have been more tactful, but, in reality, when Jason complained about my rudeness, his concern was not for what I had said – especially since he had said much worse of me. What he really objected to was the fact that I had dared to defend myself.

XXX

I grew increasingly unhappy as Jason's behaviour towards me changed. I could not understand why he no longer seemed to enjoy what he had relished at Colchis. Then he had honoured me for my knowledge of prophecy, now he made contemptuous asides whenever I mentioned Phrixus or Theonoe. Then he praised me for possessing spirit and independence, now he criticised every aspect of my behaviour which did not fit in to some Greek ideal of the perfect woman. He did not even bother to explain why he was absent for long periods of time. Nonetheless, I tried to be loyal to him and to support him where I could. I suppose I hoped that, once Jason was properly established, his obvious despondency would lessen and we could return to the love which we had shared in Colchis and Iolcos. However, my attempts to sustain him were not always met with much gratitude. It was only after another ghastly confinement, during which I had endured worst torments than the first time, that Jason seemed to feel any pride in me.

"Two sons!" he purred, as he gazed down upon little Pheres nestling in my arms. "Ah, Medea, you know your duty. No girls yet, thank goodness."

I was so relieved that Jason had greeted Pheres's arrival with pleasure that I ignored the manner in which he had phrased it. At the back of my mind I resented the thought that girls were to be deplored and regretted – after all, had I not been a girl? Nevertheless, I thrust my resentment away and told myself that Jason had expressed himself badly. What was important was that Jason was happy. Now we would be a proper united family, just as Jason had planned when we were in Colchis. True, we were no longer living in royal estate, but we were together and we were safe. To judge from Jason's accounts, he was respected by the king and I had my two perfect boys. It should have been enough.

It should have been, but it wasn't. To begin with, Jason seemed to think that tiny babies required no attention whatsoever.

"Why are you always busy with the children?" he grumbled. "Why can't Pelagia look after them? What do you think I bought her for?"

I stared at him incredulously. How could I possibly turn Mermerus and Pheres over to Pelagia? They were my beautiful boys. I wanted to do everything for them – to nurse them, to smell their sweet skin, to stroke their downy hair.

"But I'm their mother. I should look after them."

"How can they possibly notice who looks after them? It doesn't matter whether it's you or Pelagia as long as someone does it."

I was reminded again of the fact that Jason had had no mother – no wonder he could not understand the bond between a woman and her children. Well, my sons would have a mother's love. They would not grow up unaware of the soft caresses of a mother's lips. They would learn the gentle art of love from me, just as they would learn bravery from Jason.

Jason was uninterested in my plans to give his sons a better upbringing than he had had. "You may be their mother, but I'm your husband."

Then the drinking began. Or perhaps Jason had been drinking too much already but I had been too exhausted and sick to notice before. Whatever the truth, it soon became very clear to me that Jason grew resentful and aggressive when he drank to excess. And with that aggression came condemnation of me. It wasn't just remarks about my appearance or my foreign nature; Jason seemed to hold the entire female sex in contempt. I found myself growing increasingly annoyed every time Jason made sententious declarations concerning the true purpose of women. He began to claim that women were unimportant, since all they could do was give birth. A man, on the other hand, was brave and honourable, because he fought courageously in wars. It took all my restraint not to point out that Jason had never taken part in a proper battle and that, the only time he had fought armed warriors, he had done so with my help and advice. But restraint only appeared to enrage Jason.

"I can't see why you're so quiet and demure now, Medea. You've never been in the past."

"I don't understand you."

"Would you call hacking your brother to bits demure?"

"I hated it. I hated it. But it was a crisis. It was the only way in which I could save us from my father."

Jason snorted. "Just as well Aeetes didn't appear. I suppose you'd have killed him, too, just as my dear, gentle cousins killed their father and dismembered him."

"But…"

"It's all your fault we got thrown out of Iolcos. I should still be ruling there, but your idiocy got me expelled."

The unfairness of this accusation compelled me into defensive speech. "I did exactly what you asked of me."

"You can't have carried out the plan properly or I'd still be on the throne."

"That's illogical."

"What do you know about logic? You're a woman. You're all the same – you hide viciousness behind a mask of loving sweetness. You're vicious and my cousins are vicious."

By this point I was nearly in tears. "But that's not true,

Jason. Your cousins killed Pelias because they loved him. They thought that they would rejuvenate him. That's why I begged you to think of another plan. You know that I said that it was too cruel. I can't bear to think of how unhappy they were."

"Then don't think about them. In fact, if you'd spent less time worrying about them and more time worrying about me, I'd still be ruling in Iolcos. It's your fault that I'm not." He paced up and down the small room. "I am a king. I am a hero. Creon will be glad that he gave me hospitality when I return to Iolcos and resume my rightful position."

Although I had every sympathy with Jason's desire to return to Iolcos, I was sure that he was being unrealistic. However friendly Creon was towards my husband, there was no chance that he would lend him the necessary ships and men to mount an invasion. Even if Acastus were to die of natural causes, I could see no way in which Jason would be welcomed back. He had been tried as a king and had failed; rather than accept Jason's restoration, the nobles would elect one of themselves to rule. I attempted to explain this to Jason, but he lost his temper and accused me of not supporting him.

"You don't believe in me. You don't want me to succeed."

"I do, Jason. I am your wife and I want to help you. If I thought that there was a chance of success, I would support an expedition to Iolcos. But I don't think that you will ever recover your throne. Your life is now in Corinth."

"How can you possibly understand what I feel? I am an exile."

Despite myself, my voice quivered. "I cannot return to my homeland, either."

Jason made a dismissive gesture. "Colchis. Pah, what's Colchis compared to Iolcos? In any case, I was a *king* at

Iolcos. Here I am nothing."

"You aren't nothing. You are a husband and a father. Please, Jason, can't you try to be happy with me and your two fine sons?"

"Sons? What are sons when I have lost my kingdom?"

The first time that Jason dismissed his children in such a manner, I was incredulous. Naturally, as their mother, I was more than a little biased in my judgement that no finer boys had ever lived, but Jason was their father – how could he possibly be indifferent to them? However, by the time that Pheres was two it became apart that Jason's sole interest in his sons was that they proved his manhood to his drinking-cronies at court. In all other respects he was completely detached – he showed no interest in playing with them, he never brought them presents, he never wanted to learn from me what they had been doing. Indeed, he seemed to have only two responses to any comment which I made about them. The first was that, as a woman, I naturally found them interesting, since my brain wasn't fitted for anything else. The second was that they would have to be sent away when they were older because I pampered them until they were only fit to be girls. Since I hated the thought of being parted from my precious boys for even half a day, I found it difficult to disguise how much it hurt me to contemplate them being sent off to endure the sort of education which had 'made a man' of Jason. To avoid having to hear such threats, I often tried to ignore conversational openings which would have naturally led on to what the boys had been doing. However, this tactic was generally doomed to failure. Either I was accused of being sullen and rude for not wanting to talk to my husband, or an unnatural mother for not being ready to speak of my sons.

I slowly gave up hope that Jason would learn to love

his children, but my hope that Jason would gain an established position at the Corinthian court became stronger and stronger. To begin with, my hopes had been driven by love for my husband – I wanted him to be accepted and honoured by other brave men. After we had been in Corinth for nearly four years I had another, more selfish, motivation.

As in all royal societies, Creon had his favourites at court, and these favourites changed over time. After our arrival, Jason was soon accepted by Creon, mostly on the grounds of my husband's quest for the Golden Fleece. In the first few months everyone wanted to hear Jason's story from his own lips and he gained great popularity and fame. Then the novelty began to wear off and the nobles returned to their usual preoccupations. True, Jason could hunt and feast as well as any of them, but he was no longer the cynosure of all eyes. He bitterly resented this change in his status and I was enormously relieved when, after a year, Creon began paying him more attention again. However, Creon was a careful ruler and he seemed inclined to rotate his favours. Perhaps he felt that no-one would consider rebelling against him if all believed that they had a chance of being raised to particular honour by the king. Or perhaps he was conscious that Jason was not a Corinthian and that it would not do to honour him too much above the nobles of Corinth.

Whatever the cause, I doubt whether Creon ever considered how Jason's wife and family might be affected by these manoeuvres. When Jason was confident that Creon honoured him, he would return home, boasting about his influence with the king. When another nobleman appeared to have gained greater authority, Jason became tense and angry. I suppose I should have realised quite how much Jason's pride was hurt at being so dependent upon Creon, and how much Jason must have loathed wondering if all his honour and newly-gained wealth would evaporate on the king's whim. All I knew was that it was at these times – particularly if he had also been drinking too much – that Jason would turn upon me.

"You undermine me," he snarled one night. "If you behaved like a proper Greek woman I shouldn't have to endure remarks about my foreign wife."

I could not think of a tactful response, but Jason had not finished. "Why did you have to attend the spring festival?"

"I needed to make sacrifices to the gods."

"You could do that in the courtyard. You didn't need to attend a festival."

"But other women did."

"Some, maybe, but they were escorted by their husbands."

I shrugged. "You had promised to come with me. You didn't appear."

"I was busy."

"Perhaps, but we had agreed that I would make a sacrifice to the gods. That's why I accepted Philesia's offer to accompany her to the shrine."

My explanation of our neighbour's generosity did not seem to convince my husband. "I've told you before not to leave the house. If you go out you are seen by other men. It is not decorous."

I looked at Jason thoughtfully. "Are you worried about decorum, or the fact that your friends might see me and realise that I'm foreign?"

Jason's sudden flush convinced me that my suspicions were correct. "I am your husband and you must do as I tell you. You ought to stay in the house. You have no need to go outside – Pelagia does the shopping and fetches water."

"Does that apply to your sons as well?" I demanded bitterly. "Do they look foreign too? Are they to be shut up just in case they bring shame on you?"

"Stop exaggerating, Medea. All that's happened is that I've pointed out to you how you ought to behave. Surely you don't want people to comment unfavourably upon you?"

"I am not afraid of what people think. I am a king's daughter, not a slave like Terpsichore to be beaten and humiliated."

Instead of being ashamed by this reminder, as I had hoped, Jason was amused. "Ares take me, are you still moaning about my having tricked that little cow, Terpsichore? You didn't know half of it."

I froze, wanting to know more, but determined not to give Jason the satisfaction of seeing me ask for information.

"You're so unobservant that you might not have noticed that I beat her because she'd complained about me. But did she also tell you that I slept with her to teach her not to whine in future?"

"You mean you forced yourself upon her against her will?"

"Yes, I raped the little bitch." He laughed at the memory. "Call yourself a witch, Medea, you didn't even notice that she was up the duff and had to get an abortion."

I stared into the blackness, immeasurably disgusted and ashamed that I had ever loved this repulsive brute.

"I nearly laughed myself sick when you started protesting about your principles and how I ought not to cheat slave-girls. Pah! It's not principles you were worrying about; you're just jealous if I look at another woman."

XXXI

I had thought Jason perfect. Even when I had begun to see
his flaws I had still wanted to help him become perfect.
Now I was forced to acknowledge what should have been
obvious earlier. Jason was anything but perfect. He was
flawed – dreadfully flawed – and all my efforts would do
little change him. A man who could boast about what he
had done to Terpsichore was worthy of no respect at all.
Perhaps enforcing his will over that poor girl had been
Jason's method of compensating for his loss of power and
status at Iolcos. However, even if that were the case, I was
glad that he had been driven into exile. If he had abused
his position of authority over Terpsichore, the gods alone
knew how Jason would have behaved if he had ruled a
kingdom for long.

For some time I waited to see whether Jason would
attempt to win me round or to apologise, but he behaved
as if nothing had happened. Perhaps he regarded his
dreadful actions as natural – or perhaps he had been too
drunk to remember the next day precisely what he had
said. For my part, I tried to blot out my hurt and despair
with what little normality was left to me – my boys.

Since they had been born within a year of each other,
my sons were similar in terms of height, although
Mermerus was heavier and darker in colouring. However,
my boys had completely different personalities. As befitted
the elder, Mermerus was confident in his own estimation
of himself as the real head of our little family. His brother
Pheres was less secure and much more inclined to seek
reassurance on my lap. I often wondered guiltily whether
the strains which I had endured during his pregnancy had
marked Pheres in other unseen ways, but he was basically a
happy little boy with enough assurance to stick up for

himself when Mermerus teased him. For his part, Mermerus could easily have abused his greater strength to maltreat his baby brother, but my eldest was as kind as he was handsome and as clever as he was kind. Both boys adored each other and I often found them flopped down together in a patch of shade when they had grown tired of chasing each other in and out the house.

Mermerus was the more talkative of the pair and loved to tell me what he had been doing, smiling all over his face as he did so. Pheres had bursts of sudden noise, but was quite content to share my physical presence in silent contemplation of some unknown conundrum. Naturally, as any proud mother, I tried to discover my sons' interests. Mermerus was fascinated by birds winging past the house – even before he could talk he had murmured throaty sounds of pleasure whenever he saw them. Was this the first signs of budding prophetic ability? Or would he become an inventor, someone who could learn to harness the power of flight? Pheres did not show the same intense interest in the natural world as Mermerus but, as he became older, Pheres loved to explore wherever he could. Sometimes Mermerus would accompany him on these expeditions, but Pheres was equally content on his own – perhaps because he was telling himself all sorts of exciting tales as he peered behind stalks and dived into bushes.

Had it not been for Jason, I think that we three would have been idyllically happy. Unfortunately, Jason always loomed in the background, like a menacing storm-cloud. When Mermerus was five, Jason acquired quarters near the palace, which meant that he was away much of the time, but it amused him to return unexpectedly and to see our reaction. I could generally send the boys out for a walk with Pelagia or – since Jason generally appeared at night – could, with reason, claim that they were asleep. Nevertheless, he sometimes demanded their presence so that he could sneer at what weaklings I had bred. He singled out Pheres in particular for his attention, but there was one evening when he turned upon Mermerus. Pheres was already in bed when Jason appeared, muttering maledictions against people who did not pay due honour to a proven hero.

"Klearchos is the only decent one amongst them," he declared, before noticing his elder son. "Take yourself off, Pheres. When you're a hero, I'll talk to you."

Mermerus looked confused, but politely corrected his father. "I'm called Mermerus."

"Don't speak to me like that. You're called whatever I choose to call you. I'm your father and if I chose to call you a slave then you'd be one. Be thankful I only called you the name of your snivelling brother."

I made a sign to Mermerus to leave the room. Jason must have seen me, because he swore. "Damn you, Medea, how dare you undermine my authority?"

"You can shout at me all you like, but I shall not let you threaten my son."

Jason slammed his hand on the table. " 'My son, my son,' that's all you ever say. I suppose you wish you could have reproduced without me since I'm so unimportant to you."

"You used to say that Greeks respected justice. Is it just to threaten a little boy?"

"He's not Greek. He doesn't count. And what I said is true. If I choose to disown him and you, you might both very well end up as slaves. How would you look after miserable Mermerus and pathetic Pheres then?"

I told myself that he did not mean it. I told myself that his threats were just a method of enforcing obedience, exactly like my father's threats to marry me off to a neighbouring barbarian king had been. I told myself all that, but my fears remained and this time they applied to my sons. I might be prepared to take risks with my own safety, but how could I ignore anything which threatened my boys? I never wanted Jason to come near my sons again. I never wanted to see Jason again. Separation was the obvious solution, but I doubted whether it would be simple to achieve. The few years which I had spent in Corinth had taught me more than the flaws in my husband's character – they had also taught me the lowly position a woman endures in the Greek world. Now I was about to learn how difficult it was to be escape the snare of an unhappy marriage.

Greek females are expected to endure isolation from the world or lose their good name, and Jason had taken full advantage of this custom to cut me off from all outside influences. I did not meet his male friends, I was not introduced to the women at the palace and any suggestion that I might attend court functions was greeted with scandalised horror. Nevertheless, I had slowly built up acquaintances with women who lived nearby, many of whom had got into the habit of asking me for salves to heal scalds or potions to take away headaches and fevers. It was obvious to me that I could expand my dealings into an actual trade which would have kept my family free from want. However, when I cautiously broached the idea to three of my most assiduous seekers of medicines, my interlocutors were, with one accord, quite appalled.

"Medea, you can't leave your husband!" exclaimed Melpomene, a honey-cake held motionless, half-way to her mouth.

"No matter what he's done," Hygeia agreed. "You'd bring the most terrible shame on your father."

"He lives far away and would not learn of it," I retorted sombrely.

"But you would be shunned," urged Philesia, the eldest

of my visitors. "My husband wouldn't let me talk to you."

"And think how your sweet boys would suffer," protested Melpomene. "No-one would want to speak to them. You couldn't let them grow up under that sort of shadow. They would be shunned as well."

"And," pointed out Hygeia, somewhat more practically, "Jason would take them. So you wouldn't benefit."

Philesia attempted to console me. "Maybe things are done rather differently in Colchis, but you must believe us when we say that you would be utterly cast off if you took such a step here in Corinth. The only way in which a woman leaves her husband is if he divorces her for barrenness – and that hardly applies in your case."

Conscious as I was of a swelling under my dress, the product of one of Jason's unwanted couplings, I scowled. "Why should it depend upon the man?"

"It does," responded Philesia. "It always has done, and I don't suppose that it will ever change."

"Don't you have a male relative who could act for you?" demanded Hygeia. "He could demand that Jason returns your dowry – that might make Jason realise that he's got to be a bit nicer to you. Men hate losing money."

"Especially when they always regard a dowry as belonging to them," stated Melpomene with a nod.

I did not intend to inform the trio of the precise circumstances as to why my dowry of the Golden Fleece was no longer available, but I indicated that their suggested solution was impossible. "I don't suppose it would have helped even if someone could act for me; Jason just says that I have to do what he tells me."

"That's men for you," agreed Hygeia. "The best thing is to let him think that you are obeying him and do precisely what you intended all along."

"Or," laughed Melpomene, as she waved a pair of

pretty gold bangles at the others, "persuade him that he came up with the idea in the first place."

When the women left that afternoon, I was in despair. They did not know quite how bad the situation had become with Jason but, even if they had, their advice would have remained the same: smile pleasantly and win him round. They did not seem to recognise any principles of justice or fairness. Just because a man had brute force on his side, did that make him a better judge of right or wrong? Did it even make him a better hero? Jason swaggered round Corinth, posing as the noble abductor of the Golden Fleece, but it was a mere woman who had gained it for him.

XXXII

I saw little of Jason for some months. Corinth was passing through a time of uncertainty and he claimed that he was needed by the king. Mentally I scoffed at this explanation, but my neighbours told me that my husband was gaining a reputation as an eloquent speaker and a wise adviser.

"Jason's doing well for himself," Hygeia informed me one afternoon. "My husband says that he spoke so well that even Kleophon was impressed, and Kleophon distrusts anyone who can't trace their ancestors back through five generations of Corinthian nobles."

"Who's Kleophon?" asked Mermerus, who was lingering at the doorway.

"A very powerful general, Mermerus. You should be proud of your father – maybe you'll grow up to be as important as he is."

"I would rather die than be like my father," snapped Mermerus and rushed out into the courtyard.

I made some apology for Mermerus's rudeness, but Hygeia seemed surprised.

"I didn't realise he had a temper."

"He doesn't."

Through the window came the sound of my boy shouting at Pheres that he wasn't going to play at soldiers, that he hated soldiers and he loathed heroes. Hygeia laughed. "All mothers think their first-born is perfect."

"Mermerus *is* perfect. And he adores Pheres, and Pheres adores him."

"Of course, Medea."

That night I remembered the eloquent speeches which Jason had used to make to me. What a fool I had been to trust him. At Colchis, I'd believed his praise of my skills; at

Iolcos I'd let him talk me into his plan to kill Pelias. And every time he had shown his inherent cruelty at Corinth, I'd believed his ready excuses: he had been tired, he was worrying about our future, he didn't really mean to shout at me. Even although I had believed the excuses less and less, I had still gone along with them, partly because it was the easiest thing to do and partly because, if they had been true, I could never have forgiven myself for destroying a relationship which could have been perfect. But now I had no interest in Jason's eloquence. Let him spend his time making fools of the Corinthians – I didn't care what happened to them. But I did care about my sons, and Mermerus's outburst showed me how much damage Jason was doing to my children.

At that point, Jason entered, smelling of alcohol and with a gleam in his eyes which I had learned to associate with a savage desire to hurt me.

"Is this how you waste your time when I'm not here? Why don't you stop sitting around and do something useful – surely you could do some weaving?"

I shrugged uncommunicatively.

"Damn you, listen to me. My arm's hurting again – it's all prickly and hot. Give me something to make it better." He thrust his arm in my face, pointing to a swelling over the wrist. "The last salve you made didn't help at all. I thought you were supposed to know about this sort of stuff – or was that just some of your barbarian boasting? I want something to fix it properly before I go hunting again."

My thoughts ran to hemlock – that would cure Jason's pains forever. Something must have shown upon my expression, for Jason thrust his head down towards my face, glaring as he did so.

"A salve, my gracious and good lady, a salve. You don't suppose that I'd drink anything which you made me." He guffawed, trying to make light of his fears. "You're so ignorant that you might poison me by mistake."

"I don't think so," I replied gnomically. Jason was too stupid to understand that I meant that if I were to poison him I should do so deliberately. Instead, he chortled at my apparent submissiveness.

"Learned to do your lord and master's will at last, have you? Zeus, Medea, that almost makes up for being forced to look at your glum face." He laughed again, as I had known he would. Jason always liked to pretend that his worst insults were jokes. "I've got a good idea. If you're so miserable, why don't you put an end to your sorrows? You killed your brother, so what's to stop you killing yourself?" He smiled unpleasantly. "Are you worried what would happen to your sons? Maybe you're right to be. Maybe I'd throw them out altogether. Maybe I'd let them starve. Or I could recover some of the cost of their keep by selling them to a slave-merchant. There's one who comes in regularly from Colchis. Do you like the idea of your father buying your boys?"

I ignored his words and gazed at his wrist with detached interest. "I can certainly give you a salve, but it won't do much. You will continue to suffer from swelling and prickly, stabbing pains."

Jason looked annoyed, but also slightly apprehensive. For all his sneers at my ability, he knew that I had considerable understanding of a number of matters which were shrouded in darkness to him.

"What makes you so sure of yourself?"

"I've seen such swellings before on a comrade of my father. He wouldn't listen to my advice, so they continued to afflict him."

"What was your advice?"

I shrugged. "I told him to drink less. The pain was always much worse after he had been sampling the wines of Colchis to excess."

Jason stared at me in disbelief. "Are you accusing me of being a sottish lout, like some barbarian in Colchis? By the gods, Medea, I'll teach you to speak to me like that." He grabbed me by my hair, pulling me closer to him. "You better do as you're told, Medea. You're meant to be my wife."

I suppose I should have cowered or flung myself at his feet, begging for his forgiveness and promising never to transgress again. I did neither. Instead, I snatched up the knife which I had been using to chop herbs. "If you hit me, I shall thrust this into your black heart."

"Damn you, you bitch, don't you dare do anything of the kind." He let go of me, breathing hard. "By Hades, I miscalculated when I married you."

"Then why did you?"

"For someone who prides herself on her ability to interpret a lot of damn-fool birds, you are remarkably dense. What do you think drew me to you – your beauty? Your wit? Your intelligence? Of course not, you silly cow. I married you to get the Fleece." He rolled his eyes upwards. "And what a lot of rubbish I had to listen to from you, maundering on about that stupid story about Phrixus and how important the Fleece was to you."

My face flamed with humiliation, but my beloved husband was not finished. "You were so easy to fool. You thought that I asked for the Fleece in public so that I could force Aeetes into letting me marry you. But I did it to make you help me." He snorted. "I knew that you might come out with some feeble argument that we could flee to Corinth without the Fleece, since our love was enough. But once all Colchis knew that you were betrothed, you'd have never risked the shame of being rejected and left without a lover. So you had to help me win the Fleece."

"And once you had the Fleece, why didn't you

abandon me at the water's edge, or in Corinth?"

"I thought about it, but decided to play safe." He smirked. "After all, we had a contract, didn't we? And you came in handy at Corinth to get rid of Pelias – or so I thought."

"I see. How very heroic of you."

Jason shrugged. "All very well for you to sneer; your plan of killing Pelias didn't exactly work out. If I hadn't married you, I'd still be on my throne."

"It wasn't my plan. It was yours, all yours, just as killing Apsyrtus was your deed."

"Regretting that you don't have someone to protect you? Zeus, I wish I'd left you at Gorgo's. You'd have soon learned how to please a man.

"So it was a bordello."

"Of course it was. I visited it regularly before I left Corinth. Arsinoe was a right little goer – much more fun in bed than you. You ought to be grateful that I didn't abandon you there and marry one of Pelias's daughters as he wanted." He grunted angrily. "Pity I hadn't, but they were a damned cold bunch and they'd never have helped me against Acastus. I checked that before I decided to acknowledge you again."

I ignored this latter point. "You would have rewarded me for winning the Fleece for you by condemning me to a life of prostitution?"

"Exactly; how swift you are to understand these things. And bear in mind, Medea, that I could still do so. The Corinthians wouldn't care; they think that you are a barbarian. And your sons wouldn't care, either – I'd soon sort them out."

I suppose that it was a trifle cowardly of me to be afraid of Jason, even although I still held my knife in my hand. But since we had come to Corinth, Jason's gluttonous eating and drinking had made him put on considerable amounts of weight. As I watched his eyes, glittering like a rat's and with about as much humanity in them, I was very conscious that Jason was twice as heavy as I was. Moreover, Mermerus and Pheres lay asleep in the next room, and Jason was between me and the door.

"Afraid that I'm going to use you as a woman should be used?" he jeered. "Don't worry; there are plenty more exciting opportunities available to me and none of those women go on about themselves as you do."

With that he stormed off, slamming the door so violently that the whole house seemed to shake as if struck by Poseidon the Earth-Shaker.

XXXIII

That evening I began bleeding. Gouts of scarlet stained my thighs and dripped onto the floor, running along the cracks between the flagstones. Pelagia ran to fetch rags and, as she tried to mop up the vinous stains, I suddenly remembered the blood-soaked rags which Terpsichore had attempted to hide from me. Poor girl, she must have feared that I would realise what was happening to her, but why would I have suspected that she was having a miscarriage when the only man in the house was my own husband? I had loved and trusted Jason; it had never occurred to me to think that he could not be depended to keep his lust under control. But Jason had killed Terpsichore as surely as if he had cut her down in battle.

I clasped a fresh rag, wondering afresh at the irony that, when I had buried Terpsichore, I had consoled myself that at least I did not have to feel responsible for her death, as I had for Theonoe and Pelias. How wrong I had been. If I had not complained about Jason's failure to honour his promise to Terpsichore, he would not have raped her. Was I about to die in a similar way to her?

I seemed to bleed for hours and the pain grew worse and worse. It felt as if someone was scraping my insides with a sharp knife, wrenching my body apart thin slice by thin slice. Finally, there was a stab of excruciating pain and I felt a heavier lump of blood slither out of me. I must have fainted, because when I came round Pelagia was mopping my dank hair back from my brow and staring anxiously at me. It was only when I blinked that she smiled with nervous relief.

"I thought that you had gone, my lady."

It seemed to take my brain an enormously long time to work out what she meant. I wanted to warn her not to be too confident, but I could not form the words and I relapsed back into a stupor, only occasionally surfacing to reach conscious thought.

I am certain that the one thing which stopped me from floating off across the Styx that night was the thought of my boys. At one point Mermerus came in, disturbed by the commotion. Pelagia tried to shoo him away, but he evaded her and approached the bed where I lay, weak with the loss of blood.

"Mama!"

I was too weak to smile, but a tear trickled down my face.

Mermerus tried to reassure me. "Don't cry, Mama. I'm here. Nothing will happen to you whilst I am here to protect you."

My darling boy did not understand why this made me cry all the more, but he stretched out his hand and gently touched my face. I made a great effort and held back the tears. Mermerus gazed into my eyes and seem to be comforted. I drifted off again. When I came to again, my first thought was that it was daylight. Then I became aware of Mermerus, curled up next to me, his head resting upon my arm. This time I managed a smile.

"My boy!"

Mermerus rubbed his head against mine and kissed me. "Mama, you are better!"

Naturally, I did not recover as swiftly as Mermerus assumed I had. Not only had I the physical effects of the miscarriage to deal with, I also had to prepare the tiny body for burial. Pelagia had offered to carry out this sad task, but I was determined that my daughter would have some care from me. I reluctantly realised that I was not yet capable of leaving the house, but I wanted it to be my hands which bathed her perfect, miniature form and my hands which wrapped her in her tiny shroud. It was my hands, too, which placed the offering to Charon upon her eyes and tucked a tiny rope of beads into her hands to give her something to play with in the afterlife. Then, with a kiss upon her brow, I handed over my child to be given to the gods.

Although I knew that it was the shock of Jason's treatment of me which had triggered my miscarriage, I still felt culpable. Had I not wished for my powers back? Had I not hoped that my pregnancy would soon be over so that I could practise my arts? It was perfectly possible that the gods might have answered my wishes in a manner which I had not considered. I tried not to dwell on this fear. Instead, I searched for the energy to plan for our future, but it was hard to care about anything whilst I grieved for my lost little one. Part of me recognised that she was better dead than being brought up in a land where her sex condemned her at birth to a lifetime of sneers and obloquy, a culture in which her sole purpose was to bear boys and be obedient to first her father and then her husband. She now lay shrouded in her grave – was that so much worse a fate than to spend her years shrouded away from the world, lest any hint of individuality or independence bring the taint of immodesty upon her family?

Jason continued to torment me for some time afterwards. He learned of my miscarriage and pretended to show sympathy, all the while laughing at me.

"How dreadful you must feel to have lost a child. You must worry that you made a mistake and didn't look after it properly – I suppose it's easy to make mistakes when you've only born two children. Now Klearchos says that his wife lost their sixth child, but went on to have twin boys to make up for it shortly afterwards. He was very relieved because she stopped thinking that she had failed him."

"I do not feel a failure."

"Indeed? I suppose barbarians regard the family as less important than we Greeks do." He shrugged. "They must do. After all, just consider what you did to your own brother. First you killed him and then you cut him up like a butcher cleaving a sheep."

"You killed him."

"No-one in Corinth thinks I did. The rumour seems to have spread that you did the killing. They all think that you are twisted and sick. Perhaps we should try to redeem your reputation. Shall we see if you can have twins, like Klearchos's wife?"

Jason would not have made that comment had he been aware that I was taking careful precautions to ensure that I did not fall pregnant again. It was not merely a matter that I desperately needed to retain whatever protection from Jason which my magical arts could bring. I was also utterly repulsed by the idea that I might breed a child which resembled him. I knew only too well that such a boy would be cruel, arrogant and deceitful. It would mock suffering and delight in hurting people. I had no desire to bring such a creature into the world. Instead, every day I thanked the gods for having sent me Mermerus and Pheres – always loving and kind, always so pleased to see me, always bringing me so much joy. They were so completely antithetical to Jason that I sometimes wondered whether they really could be his progeny. However, unless a god had visited me in the guise of Jason, they could have no other father. It was better to marvel at the gods' generosity than to question why they had granted me such boons.

It was for the sake of my darling boys that I attempted to fall in with the attitudes which guided Corinthian society. Naturally, I thought that it was quite ludicrous that I, a trained seer, could not attend most sacrifices, much less conduct rituals openly. Nevertheless, I reminded myself that Mermerus and Pheres would suffer if I protested, so I made no comment on the strange state of affairs that a mediocre augur was rated as the highest prophet in Corinth. Nor did I point out that the skills of the king's herbalist, spoken of with such awe, were feeble in the extreme. I was a foreign woman; clearly I could not know more than the sophisticated male Corinthians. Instead of demonstrating my own knowledge or sharing wisdom with other respected mantics, I forced myself to lead the life of an exemplary Corinthian woman. My hair was always covered; I was always decorously dressed; I had no interest in how the state was governed or opinions on any new laws. I was shallow; I was limited; I was bored to screaming-point. But the women who frequented me to seek out my nostrums complimented me on how well I was adjusting to life in Corinth. I think they genuinely meant it. They did not see that I felt patronised by such praise nor did they suspect that my compliance was only outward. Inwardly, I was still Medea of Colchis; Medea who had been trained by first Theonoe and then Phrixus; Medea who was a princess in her own right.

Fortunately, Jason grew bored of visiting me so frequently. Philesia, who had clearly hoped for a rapprochement, consoled me with the thought that he might yet return for good. Hygeia pointed out that I should be thankful that Jason's mother was not alive.

"Not only would she constantly say that you had ruined her son's life, she would insist on taking control of your children."

Philesia nodded gloomily. "That's probably why Jason hasn't taken them away from you already. They're still too young to live in a purely masculine environment."

My mask of complaisant wife dropped somewhat. "No-one is going to take my boys away from me," I hissed angrily.

Melpomene was too busy giggling to pay attention to my response. "I wouldn't say that Jason lives in a purely masculine environment."

Philesia frowned at her, but I motioned Melpomene to continue. I wondered if she was about to confirm certain suspicions which I already had.

"My slave told me that Jason's got the loveliest girl up there in his quarters. He's quite bewitched by her."

"Or by her dowry," I remarked acidly.

Three pairs of eyes swivelled round to stare at me.

"She's not a Corinthian," protested Hygeia.

"No Corinthian girl would live like that with a man."

"Jason bought her from a trader from Thrace," Melpomene explained. "You'll probably get a new kitchen-slave when he's bored with her."

I yawned in an attempt to pretend that I regarded these revelations as quite normal behaviour. "Probably saves money in the long-run. Mistresses are more expensive than slaves."

Philesia sounded relieved. "Oh, you knew about Xanthe. We were never sure whether you did. Yes, they say she's terribly expensive – how else could she afford all those clothes?"

"And her jewellery," commented Melpomene enviously. "She has gold diadems, and gold bracelets, and pearls looped round her neck."

I dimly recalled a tall woman walking through a crowd in the market-place. I had noticed her, not for her glittering array of cascading wealth, but for her air of freedom and independence. I had envied it and wondered whether she was a member of the royal family, since I had observed no other rich freewoman who seemed to send out such a sense of purpose and assurance. Jason's mistress seemed to be granted all the liberties which a mere wife was forbidden.

XXXIV

Later that evening, when I had kissed my innocent sons and put them to bed, I mulled over the news which I had been brought. No wonder Jason always claimed that there was no money to pay for any luxuries for the children. No wonder I had become increasingly reliant upon what I earned by bartering my potions and salves. Naturally, Jason would find a better use for his money than supporting the family which he had brought into the world. I despised him even more, although, recollecting some of my father's companions, I was hardly surprised. However, the hypocrisy of Jason's comments revolted me. He insisted that for a Greek woman to show even the slightest independence of thought would bring great shame upon her family, whilst for her to have an affair would stain her family for generations. On the other hand, my husband, who was so stridently authoritarian in his outlook on female modesty, was happy to flaunt his sexual conquests so openly that even well-behaved, obedient Greek wives like Philesia could gossip over them.

I had been well aware that my mother had not had an easy marriage, but Jason had implied that women in Greece were respected and honoured by their menfolk. He had even alluded to the recognition which was given to those of ability, whether male or female. What a fool I had been to believe him. I had even less freedom of action than I had at Colchis and there were only two ways in which a woman could gain respect at Corinth: if she were a citizen, she was honoured if no-one talked about her in public, while if she were a non-citizen, her value came if she was so fabulously sensual that men drooled their family wealth into her lap.

It might have been easier to bear if Jason had ever

loved me. But drink had revealed the truth when he spewed out his hatred and loathing of me. Jason did not love me and he never had loved me, either at Iolcos or Colchis. For my part, I had loved him – or, at least, I had loved the person he had pretended to be. But Jason had deliberately destroyed my love for him and, what is more, had enjoyed doing so. Little wonder that I abhorred and despised him.

The next time Jason graced us with his presence, I forced myself to speak calmly to him.

"It clear that you are no longer happy living with us. Would it not be better if you were to move entirely to your quarters? You would be nearer to your friends and to the king there."

"Trying to throw me out, Medea? Why might that be? Have you found someone who doesn't mind a barbarian in his bed?"

I waved away this insult as irrelevant, but Jason was not finished.

"Perhaps it's because you are a barbarian which makes you incapable of understanding oaths. Of course, in Colchis you probably don't care about sticking to promises made in the sight of the gods." He spat on the ground. "Or, more likely, you're so busy stuffing yourselves up with silly tales of being descended from the sun that you don't think that basic matters like honour apply to you."

"Your meaning is unclear, Jason, but, however much you may sneer at me, you, of all people, ought to know that I revere the divine ones."

Jason muttered something uncomplimentary about soothsayers under his breath, before grinning unpleasantly at me. "But you're not Greek. A Greek would realise the importance of the oath you swore to me. Didn't you swear that you would marry me if I got the Fleece?"

"No."

"How strange! I quite thought that the two were linked."

I struggled to reign in my anger. "They were indeed. You swore that you would marry me if I helped you to win the Fleece."

"And now you want to change your mind. How fickle barbarians are!"

"Don't be ridiculous, Jason. I gave you the Fleece."

"And I gave you marriage, so what have you got to complain about, you silly bitch?"

It suddenly occurred to me that Jason was deliberately trying to provoke me into losing my temper. Did he hope that I would strike him and thus give him the perfect excuse to cut me down with his sword? Jason was certainly a coward – presumably he would find it much easier to justify killing his wife if he could claim that she had gone mad and run amok. I was determined not to fall into his trap; I had fallen into quite enough already.

"You are undignified, Jason."

A sprite of fury danced in my husband's eyes. "You, a woman, dare to criticise me? By Zeus you need to learn your place." He laughed coarsely. "Of course, what your real problem is that you're pining for a man inside you."

I gazed at Jason in disbelief. "Do you really think that the only thing which matters to a woman is whether she has someone in her bed?"

"Obviously. Look at you. A good dose of sex would sort you out. But you're so ugly at the moment that no-one could bear to sleep with you."

On that uplifting note, Jason strode off, apparently convinced that he had proved his point.

In the face of Jason's vicious hostility, I could not understand why he would not let me leave him. I knew perfectly well that he was not motivated by a desire to honour the oath which we had sworn together before

Zeus. Nor did I think that he feared disapproval from Creon or any of the noblemen at court. It was easy for a Greek man to dissolve his marriage, and I suspected that Corinthians might not regard the ties binding a man of Iolcos with a woman of Colchis as being as strong as those which linked a Corinthian man and woman. So why did Jason insist that I remain? Was it because he enjoyed tormenting me? Did his control over me compensate for his lack of power at Corinth? Or was his pride hurt by the thought that any woman dared to suggest that marriage to him was hateful and loathsome?

Certainly, Jason appeared to be motivated by a completely irrational hatred of the female sex as a whole. Clearly, he loathed any abilities which I possessed, but he seemed equally contemptuous of all other women. Was it because he had lacked a mother's love whilst growing up, or was it because he was an arrogant bully? I did not know and I no longer cared. All I could see was that I was trapped and my boys were trapped. If Jason chose to interpret my oath as still applying, even although he was so blatantly uninterested in a genuine marriage, honour compelled me to remain in Corinth with him. Jason might lie and cheat and deceive, but I was not Jason. I could not break my sworn word or smash a contract witnessed by the gods. I left that to Greeks to do.

XXXV

Months went by. I was aware that most of Corinth must know that Jason had left his strange, foreign wife and was entertaining a string of increasingly exotic – and expensive – mistresses. I endured the mockery which showed half-veiled in the eyes of those who had never approved of my existence. I endured it for my sons' sake, but my hatred of the Corinthians grew. They might look at me with distaste, but they could not begin to fathom how much I detested them. The nobles at court might join Jason in muttering maledictions upon me, but they could never guess that it was my foreign upbringing which gave me both the power to strike Jason dead and the restraint not to.

Perhaps my restraint was purely superstitious. Looking back, I wonder whether we would have been fared better if I had cast yew berries into Jason's wine. However, at the time, I kept repeating to myself that every time I had used my powers for some black end, someone who was innocent had suffered. Theonoe had begged me not to ask her to reveal the secret of the grove; I had forced her to speak out and she had died. Phrixus had warned me never to use my magic arts for harm, but I had ignored him and he had died too. Most obvious of all was what had happened to Pelias. Had Jason tackled him man to man, my husband would have behaved like a hero; but he skulked behind my skill and Pelias's daughters were left in intolerable grief over their murderous assault. With three such clear examples of how a major invocation of my talents might go dreadfully awry, was it any wonder that I feared to punish Jason as he deserved, particularly since my boys were the most obvious target for any divine revenge? I hated Jason; I loathed him; I execrated his very name. But I adored my boys, my darling, gorgeous boys. They were my very existence, my joy, my happiness, my all. How could I risk them for the sake of someone so vile and despicable as my husband?

For all that Jason did not wish to live with me, he was still happy to make use of my magic arts. The only difference was that, whereas in Iolcos he had used my skill to rid himself of Pelias, now he sought to acquire cures for men at court. He must have guessed that it was safe to do so, knowing that I would not harm the innocent, even to damage his own reputation. Naturally, Jason was not motivated by an altruistic desire to help people; I assumed that he wished to ingratiate himself with the powerful – and some of those who cautiously entered my little house were very high up indeed. However, it also crossed my mind that perhaps Jason hoped that I might fall for one of my visitors; then he would be able to spurn me on the grounds of shameless adultery.

If that was Jason's plan he was singularly mistaken. I had no desire for another man in my life. Why should I seek out hurt and wretchedness? Perhaps some rare men could bring love and companionship to their wives, but the stakes were far too high for me to take that sort of risk. In any case, I already had love and companionship from my boys. Mermerus talked to me constantly and made me laugh. Pheres was less vocal but extremely affectionate. He would happily sit glued next to me for hours, while even Mermerus, older and more conscious of the expectations placed upon a Greek boy, snuggled confidingly in my arms when he thought that no-one would notice. How could I reject that sort of love for the spurious and transient love which was all a man would bring to me?

Even although Jason's purpose in coming to visit me was to seek my aid for his friends, he could not resist taunting me whilst he was there. He repeatedly reminded me of my inferior status as a woman and missed no opportunity to comment upon my barbarian origin. Generally, he also reminisced with contempt about Colchis and complained that I had ruined his chances of staying on the throne of Iolcos. Sometimes, however, he would strike a new note. On such evenings he boasted as to how much he had drunk that day, or bragged about how many women he had bedded. He appeared to think that that such achievements made him more attractive – indeed, practically irresistible.

"That must be the reason why you've not yet tried your wiles on anyone whom I've brought here," he declared smugly one evening, when he was waiting for an important guest to be escorted to me. "You're still pining for me."

I maintained a firm silence, not wishing to discuss a concept as repellent as it was untrue. Unfortunately, Jason had been helping himself liberally to wine and was in the mood to torment me.

"You see, you don't deny it. You're like all women; you're desperate to have a man in your bed. And you know that I'm the best, so you're desperate to have me."

Thinking that it was precisely because of Jason that I was desperate *not* to have a man in my bed, I contented myself by saying that Jason was wrong.

"Sulky again tonight, Medea? Are you bleeding? Gods, women are disgusting."

"Then why do you sleep with them?"

"See, I told you that you were jealous!" He belched and dragged his hand across his mouth. "I've half a mind to take you on the couch before Aegeus comes. Then you'd have to admit that you enjoyed having me."

"I'm not one of your bought mistresses," I snapped. "I don't have to pretend to enjoy any aspect of your company."

"Sour-faced, lying bitch. Aegeus would suit you down to the ground – he's impotent." Jason gave forth another long belch, which triumph appeared to please him immensely. "Imagine being king of Athens and not able to wench properly. What a life; he might as well be a eunuch – or a woman."

Naturally, when the illustrious visitor arrived, his face carefully shrouded from view, Jason did not display such a lack of respect. Nor did he refer to him by name. All the same, I think that I should have guessed that this particular seeker of knowledge was the most important who had ever crossed my threshold, both from his air of command and Jason's fawning obsequiousness.

Jason was swiftly, albeit courteously, banished outside. Then Aegeus began to explain his predicament. Armed with the useful information as to who was really sitting opposite me, I ignored talk of a large reward which was available should I be able to help him. Money would certainly be convenient, although if Aegeus gave it to Jason I should see little of it. But there were other possibilities which this man represented. I found it hard to hide my eagerness. Even although I had aided some important Corinthians, I knew that they would never attempt to stand up for me if I were to complain of how I was treated by my husband. Jason was too well-established for any individual Corinthian to risk unpopularity by protesting at the treatment of a barbarian woman who had killed her own brother. But Aegeus was not Corinthian. Moreover, he occupied a position of great power in his own country. Was there a chance that I could use his particular circumstances to improve my own?

"You are generous, my lord. However, I do not seek gold or silver. Money is less important to me than the opportunity to practise my skills. There are many whom I have helped who have offered little more than grapes or eggs."

This true, but artless, statement appeared to impress

Aegeus. "Indeed? It is not many who would act in such a way."

"I was set the example in my youth. The noble Phrixus taught me that the accurate interpretation of an oracle was what mattered, not gold promised for an interpretation which the seeker wished to hear."

"Phrixus? He was a renowned seer."

I bowed my head. "That is so."

"What else did he teach you?"

"Augury; divination; oneiromancy; how to address the gods through sacrifices; the interpretation of portents."

"And your knowledge of salves and herbs? I have heard that you know much of these arts."

"I began studying the correct use of plants at the age when knowledge blooms."

Aegeus regarded me thoughtfully. "Many claim that they have these skills, but few can prove it. Whom have you helped here in Corinth?"

Hoping that I was about to make the answer he sought, I frowned. "You must understand, my lord, that many consult me without telling me their names. But even if I do know the person whom I treat, it is not right that I should speak of their troubles. They speak to me in confidence, sure that I shall not gossip to their wives – or their enemies."

"But surely you can at least describe some of the problems which you have tackled."

I shrugged, as if uninterested. "All the problems which you would expect, from warts to interpreting the flight of birds or supplicating the gods for the birth of a healthy son."

"And do you provide poisons as well as cures?"

I stood up. "If you seek to do harm, I advise you to consult someone else."

He waved me back down. "No, no, I merely wondered

how extensive your actions were."

Slowly, and with considerable hesitation, my noble visitor explained his problem. A friend desperately wanted a son, but none had been born to him. The oracle at Delphi had said that he could be helped, but did not provide the necessary details as to how this longed-for child would be conceived.

I listened carefully to this halting speech, before folding my arms abruptly. "My lord, I cannot help you if you do not speak the truth!"

"I have done."

"You may have many friends who are childless, but the person on whose behalf you have sought me out is yourself."

Aegeus gazed at me in obvious stupefaction.

"The Pythia has her ways and I have mine," I added gnomically, thinking that Aegeus would be furious with Jason if he knew what my ways had been that evening. "Now, if you want me to treat you – for I can treat such problems – you must be open with me."

My display of apparent omniscience must have convinced the Athenian, because he promptly spilled out a number of embarrassing details which no man could wish to describe to anyone, far less a woman. Perhaps my foreignness helped him to forget that I was female. It hardly mattered. What was important was that I knew exactly how to cure Aegeus – and what I could exact in return.

After I had reassured Aegeus, the king was eager to offer me a reward – money, gold, precious jewels. "I must reciprocate your help," he pleaded. "At A-, in my country we repay gifts with gifts. You have promised to help me, so I must help you."

"There is something which I would rate far more highly than jewels, but which would cost you much less."

"Tell me; I wish to thank you."

"The right to practise my skill," I replied softly. "The customs of your country are those of a good and generous people. I wish that I could reside there and use my arts to interpret the will of the gods."

Aegeus's eyes flickered over me in calculation. He must have been wondering how far-reaching my knowledge was and how the Athenians would react to their king bringing home a strange, foreign priestess to cast spells amongst them.

"My country is indeed a great one, but I do not know what your homeland is, O Medea."

"I am the daughter of Aeetes, son of Helios, and the king of Colchis."

The stillness of the figure in front of me suggested that my noble guest was impressed by my bloodline, not least because my ancestral link to the gods was closer than Aegeus's.

"Why do you want to come to my land?"

"You have not yet told me where it is," I pointed out. "But if all of its noblemen are as honourable as you, then it must be a place where knowledge is rewarded."

Flattery can be very effective. Aegeus promptly revealed that he was an Athenian, although he retained enough caution not to state his name.

"Ah! That explains your open attitude to my sorcery. Here, in Corinth, the men are frightened of such wisdom. They do not understand it and seek to keep it hidden away out of sight."

"We Athenians are bold in more than just the battle-line," commented Aegeus, clearly glad to be able to sound brave about anything after the emasculating experience of discussing his impotence. "We do not deny that things exist just because we cannot explain them."

"A truly sagacious approach," I agreed, wondering how

much longer we would have to keep complimenting each other. I gave him a little hint to hurry up. "In such an atmosphere I should be able to achieve even greater results than what I have promised to do for you."

"Would your husband wish to accompany you?" asked Aegeus doubtfully.

I shook my head, relieved that the king obviously did not want to have to provide house-room to a famous hero who might cast him in the shade. "No, Jason is very busy here in Corinth. He has many comrades and many plans for the future."

Aegeus must have heard rumours about our relationship because he did not press the point. "In that case, I would be happy to welcome you to Athens, so long as the king of Corinth does not object to your leaving his realm."

I cast a timid glance in his direction. "My lord, I would be very grateful if you could swear an oath to provide me with sanctuary at Athens."

"Why?"

"Your king may not be as welcoming as you are, but if you can tell him that you swore that you would help me then he could not complain at your generosity."

Aegeus laughed. "I don't think that the king will object to anything I do. Still, if it will relieve your mind, I am quite prepared to swear by the almighty gods that I will provide you with sanctuary at Athens in return for your help in giving me a child."

"And I may bring various goods with me, and, perhaps, my slaves?"

"Subject to the same proviso that if Creon objects, you will have to return." He laughed. "Don't worry about your chattels, though. I'm sure I can replace all of those at Athens."

"Not quite all, my lord."

XXXVI

I could not wait to be rid of Aegeus, although I had to maintain the polite fiction that I was enjoying talking to him. He must have been amused that I did not demand his name, but was satisfied with a curiously-wrought brooch as proof of his identity. For my part, I had no place for amusement; I was too busy going over and over the agreement. Aegeus had sworn to give me sanctuary. He had sworn that he would accept my goods and slaves. True, my boys were free-born, but if calling them slaves would get them safely away from Jason, then I was quite prepared to lie about their status. Pelagia would back me up if offered her freedom in return. In fact, given that she liked the children and disliked Jason, she might well lie on my behalf without any expectation of a reward.

Once we were safely in Athens under the protection of the king I could soon make enough money to keep us. The sole danger lay in escaping from Corinth. Aegeus had made it clear that his oath did not extend to spiriting me away from Corinth, nor would he prevent me from being sent back to Corinth if Creon demanded it. However, I calculated that Creon would be unlikely to demand my return, since he would not wish to offend as important an ally as the king of Athens. Why would Creon insult his guest by suggesting that he had done something wrong in allowing a foreign woman and her two irrelevant, unimportant children to come and live in Athens?

I kept looking for flaws in my plan. It was true that Jason might object just to interfere with my hopes. However, I reminded myself that, while Jason was growing in importance, he was nothing like as important as Aegeus. Nor could Jason be sure that I had flown to Athens. Admittedly, he had escorted Aegeus to my house, which might make him suspect that I had fled with the king. On the other hand, I was fairly sure that he would be incredulous at the idea of someone actually choosing to help me. I knew to my own cost that Jason was so vain that he could not conceive that the qualities which he despised might be admired by another.

My family's future now rested on whether I could conceive a plan which would enable us to flee Corinth unnoticed. There were two danger-points: how to get beyond the city-walls, and how to leave Corinthian territory. The first was easier to resolve. I could leave at dawn to pick herbs whilst Pelagia could later take the boys out of another gate. What was strange about them playing in the meadows and then slowly drifting towards wherever I was waiting? However, the children could not be expected to walk the whole distance to Athens and I doubted whether we could carry enough provisions between us to feed us on the journey. I was also fearful of the risk of bandits who haunted the roads inland. What chance would two women and two children have against a group of determined men? The seas would be safer, but years at Corinth led me to wonder whether a Corinthian ship would take us on board without the express authority of a male relative. I could have cried in frustration. Finally, after all these years, I had the opportunity to escape from Jason and his constant mockery and contempt. I could flee his biting hatred and unceasing cruelty. I should have been revelling in a blissful sense of freedom. But I was still a caged bird because I could not fathom how to get my boys safely from Corinth to Athens.

The next morning, Mermerus noticed that I was sad. "What's wrong, Mama? Are you tired?"

"A little; don't worry."

Mermerus frowned. "I'll look after you."

I tried not to cry. "I'm your mother; I ought to look after you."

"And I'm a young warrior." Mermerus rubbed his head against mine. "Warriors protect their womenfolk."

"I don't want you ever to have to fight, my darling."

Pheres had been only half-listening to this conversation. "I met Father when he came here last night. He says that I need to be much tougher. He says that I ought to be sent away. Does he really mean it?"

I stiffened. When I had lain awake through the long night desperately trying to concoct a means of escape, I had started to wonder whether I would be better not to take the risk. Aegeus's promise would still apply in a few years time and had I not always planned to flee when Jason could no longer prevent my sons from leaving? After all, it was that prospect which I had repeatedly held out to myself when there was no miraculous Athenian alternative in view. Every time that I had wondered whether I could continue the life which I led, I had reminded myself that one day my sons and I would be free. Was it safe to risk that freedom by trying to snatch it too hastily? Pheres's comments gave me the answer. There would be no freedom for Pheres if he were taken from me. Even if Jason did not destroy my son's body, he would poison his mind.

"Your father makes silly comments at times, Pheres. Ignore what he says."

"I told you Mama would know," commented Mermerus. "Priestesses know everything."

I kissed him and his little brother. "Not everything, my darlings, but I know that I adore you both."

Although I decided that Jason had probably indulged in tormenting Pheres because he was bored waiting for Aegeus to finish his consultation with me, I still did not trust my husband. I knew that Jason had no interest in the children and would not wish to be bothered with their presence, but I also thought that he was perfectly capable of demanding that Pheres be sent off to act as a page to one of his cronies. That I was determined to avoid. Pheres was far too sensitive to be exposed to the brutish thuggery of drunken men. It would damage him irreparably, whilst the thought of my little boy frightened, alone, and crying for his mother was almost enough to make me grab my jar of hemlock and set out to find Jason that instant. However, I made no such move. After all, I had had despicable insults heaped upon me for years and I had endured them. Indeed, I had endured them although I was a princess while Jason could not even retain his own kingdom – a kingdom, moreover, which was not as powerful or rich as Colchis. Every time I had considered punishing Jason, I had concluded that the safety of my boys was much more important than my own personal vengeance for his mockery. It still was. Revenge might offer itself later.

I was very conscious that Aegeus would not remain for much longer in Corinth. Whilst the king had sworn that he would provide me with sanctuary at Athens, I did not wish to delay matters so long that he might repudiate his agreement with me – I had had enough experience of how Jason dealt with oaths to be distrustful of any such promises, whether sworn in front of the gods or not. Thus it was imperative that I made a plan for our escape. I knew that no man in Corinth would help me, but – unlike men – I did not regard women as a negligible force, incapable of any action.

Many of my female neighbours not only ran their households efficiently and well, they also helped conduct the affairs of the farms or fields which lay in their family's possession. Might I not, therefore, be able to arrange the loan of a horse and cart to journey to Athens? The more I considered the question, the more it seemed to me that perhaps one of the women whom I had aided might be prepared to help me – after all, women understand the concept of reciprocity just as much as men do, even if what they swap is sympathy and honey, rather than swords and stallions.

Nevertheless, although I hoped for feminine solidarity, I realised that I might well be asked why Jason could not arrange the loan of horseflesh for me. Therefore I was faced with a critical question: did I approach someone who was sufficiently irresponsible that it would not occur to her that my husband might have a role to play in such an arrangement? Or did I seek out a woman who had a realistic view of how vile men might be and might thus be prepared to aid another woman trying to escape from a trap? The latter alternative appeared unlikely in the extreme – most of the gossip which my female neighbours swapped tended to be trivial and revealed an unfailing belief in the superiority of the male sex. That left me with the daunting prospect of risking my boys' future by trusting that some flibbertigibbet would not chatter about the strange fact that I had asked to borrow a horse to go on a herb-picking expedition.

I was trying to screw up my courage to approach flighty, silly Melpomene when what seemed to be a miraculous intervention by the gods occurred: sensible, careful Philesia appeared at my house, diffidently requesting a love philtre. Since there is only one reason why a woman seeks an aphrodisiac, it did not take me long to gain her confidence.

"Georgos has a mistress," she wept. "I thought he truly loved me. My mother always warned me that men have their ways, but Georgos was so kind that I thought he cared for me. But he was kind because he was indifferent."

"Not completely indifferent," I suggested. "After all,

you have born him sons."

"That's all he cares about. He is proud of them, but he isn't proud that I bred them. I don't think he even recognises the role I had in bearing them."

I sniffed contemptuously. "If men had to give birth, they wouldn't brag so much about fighting. Some men live their entire life without taking part in a campaign, whereas every woman risks her life each time she is pregnant."

"Georgos hasn't been in battle," admitted Philesia, before adding loyally, "of course, that's because Creon is a good king and has sound relations with other states. He's even entertaining the king of Athens at the moment and hopes to make an alliance with him. At least, that's what Georgos says."

Keen to avoid seeming interested in the subject of Aegeus, I returned to Philesia's woes. "I'd rather fight three times in the battle-line than give birth to one child. You've got three sons and two daughters. That makes you the equivalent of a hardened veteran of fifteen conflicts."

Philesia attempted to pull herself together. "It's very good of you to say so, Medea, but Georgos doesn't see it like that."

Although I knew that I ought to be concentrating upon my own problems, I could not help but feel incensed upon Philesia's part. "How does he see it, then?"

She blushed. "He says that I am old and wrinkled. He wants something young and pretty."

"And I suppose he would think it equally justifiable if you objected to a warrior's battle-scars and demanded a younger, more handsome husband? Bah! Men make me sick!"

Philesia looked rather shocked by this exercise in logic. "But that's different, Medea."

"Is it?" I demanded. "How?"

"Well, because… Well, it is."

"It is because men say that it is. They expect to have pretty, obedient playthings and justify their wants by saying that they are men and they fight. But women face just as many dangers – try counting up how many women you know who have died in childbirth. Our lives are just as dangerous as men's lives. In fact, we are more likely to die young. So we ought to be the ones who demand what we want, not men."

"I just want Georgos back."

I glanced at Philesia sadly. I could give her a few potions which might help make her feel, and thus look, more attractive, but there was nothing which I could brew which would destroy the memory of the bitter betrayal which her husband had dealt her.

XXXVII

After Philesia's unexpected revelations, it was easy for me to induce her to help me. She was so desperately unhappy herself that she had no real interest in why I suddenly needed access to a horse and cart. At one point, she roused herself sufficiently to seek reassurance that I was not planning to kill Jason and flee Corinth. Such a request gave me an enlightening insight as to what my neighbours really thought of both me and my marriage. However, since I could confirm that meting out justice to Jason was not my immediate intention, she readily agreed to provide what I wanted and, equally importantly, not to talk about it.

I found it almost impossible to contain my relief. My boys would be safe. Finally, we should be free from Jason's constant taunts and insults, his simmering hatred, his brooding malevolence. We could emerge from the crepuscular world in which we resided, where our thoughts and characters were shuttered and hidden from sight. We would be bathed in sunlight, revelling in the warmth of freedom, basking in the kiss of Helios. My boys would be granted a true life, not one hedged around by threats and constant fear. The taste of freedom is a glorious thing, far greater than any aphrodisiac. And freedom tastes even more ambrosial when you have spent years longing for liberation.

I did not tell my boys. They were too young to be burdened with such hopes. I had tasted abject misery too many times to risk inflicting the same despair upon them. Far better for them not to know that they were about to escape incarceration than for them to pray for release and find the fetters locked tight about their wrists once more. We could celebrate when we reached Athens. All the same, I could not help hugging and kissing them again and again that evening. Mermerus wanted to know why.

"Just because I love you so much," I whispered.

"Then why are you crying?" he demanded, as he brushed a tear from his hair. "Love is a good thing."

"It is," I agreed, trying to make a joke. "But you are such perfect boys that I have to cry sometimes to let the gods know how much I care for you."

Was it a silly thing to have said? Of course, what I meant was 'I have to cry because the thought of not having you fills me with the haunting terror of black nightmares. I have to cry because I am begging the gods to grant you to me for another day, another passing of the moon, another year. I have to cry because my fears are my attempt to propitiate the holy ones.' But how could I say that to a little boy? How could I tell my son that I sometimes wept over him whilst he slept because I dreaded the thought of losing him so much that I could have sworn that I suffered physical hurt? He was too young to know of the fears which stalked the air around him. So I didn't tell him the truth. And afterwards I wondered if the gods had not known the truth. Perhaps they thought that I rejoiced too much in my wonderful, splendid sons. Perhaps they wanted to punish me for such vaunting pride. Who can tell the ways of the divine ones? Maybe there was something written into my boys' blood which meant that, even whilst they were growing, they were already condemned by fate. All I know is how often I tried to appease the gods, and how often I formulated soundless prayers to beg that my sons be spared from harm.

XXXVIII

I didn't think that I could hate Jason more than I already did. I knew his untrustworthy nature, his crudity, his vicious cruelty. I had discovered the complacency and self-regarding bombast which lurked just beneath the smooth exterior which he adopted when he deemed it worthwhile. I had suffered from his lies, his boasting and, above all, his smug assumption that, as a Greek man, he was far superior to me, a barbarian woman. I had endured all that and more. I had even come to realise that, consciously or unconsciously, his hatred and contempt were bound up in his recognition of his own inadequacy. He derided barbarians because he hated to be reminded of the terror he had felt when forced to confront Aeetes's monstrous creations. He despised women because it was easy to sneer at their courage and sneering made him feel stronger and braver. And he scorned and spurned me because I knew the truth. To all Corinth he could pose as a great hero, but I knew how he had really won the Fleece. Thus he hated me – after all, I could have exposed him at any moment. His new, noble friends would have sniggered themselves sick if they had learned how much he had owed to me.

No wonder Jason wished to force me to acknowledge that he was my superior in every way. If he compelled me to accept his own assessment of my character, intelligence and ability then I would never dare to speak against him. I should be like Pelagia – his slave, offering unquestioning, unhesitating obedience. But, whilst that might have been very convenient for Jason, it was not what he had offered me when we exchanged our vows before Zeus. He had offered a partnership based upon mutual respect and trust. I had given him both; I had never threatened to expose the reality of how the Fleece was won. Indeed, I had considered it quite natural that I should help my husband. Jason, however, had not responded in kind. My skills made him feel inadequate, thus he decided that I was at fault. Even although he had been glad to benefit from my powers, he derided me for possessing them. He had tried to bring me low so that he could climb upon my broken body and pretend that he was a hero atop a monument. But I had not yet fallen and so he hated me all the more.

I knew all this and I thought that I could not execrate my husband more than I already did. Then came the announcement.

Jason swaggered in, looking even more pleased with himself than usual.

"You won't be seeing much of me in future, Medea. In fact, this is that last time that I shall bother to visit you."

I could scarcely believe him. Was this another trick to torture me with false hope? Or had Creon finally grown bored with Jason's presence and ordered him off on some quest suitable to his supposed status as a hero?

"You don't look very interested," complained my husband. "Don't you want to know why I'll be too busy to waste time talking to an uneducated, barbarian witch?"

"Since your actions are rarely marked by logic or your comments distinguished by truth, I don't suppose that anything you say will enlighten me noticeably."

"Sarcastic little bitch, aren't you? Typical woman. When they can't think of a decent argument they just sneer at a man. Mind you, the reason that you don't understand things is because you are stupid. But even you can't be so stupid that you'll fail to understand my news. I'm going to marry Glauce."

I attempted to remain calm, although the name struck quivering terror in my heart. "Indeed? Which Glauce might that be? Some trull from the docks or an unfortunate slave in your clutches?"

Jason guffawed. "You are ignorant, aren't you? Glauce's Creon's daughter. He's agreed to betroth her to me and we shall be married within a few days. I've got the chance to forget the past and start again. I shall be King of Corinth when Creon dies – you could never give me that."

"Indeed?" I repeated. "And how do you intend to explain away the fact that you are already married?"

"Zeus and the immortal gods! You don't really think that I'm your husband, do you?"

"I rather think that Zeus believes that we are – or don't you remember your oath?"

"Pah! A few words muttered to keep an untamed foreign girl in order don't count for anything. I never meant them and Zeus knows it."

"You're a liar. Your oath was quite definite and you told all Iolcos that we were married." Jason attempted to wave this away dismissively, but I was unfinished. "More to the point, when I wanted to leave you, you sneered at me for not understanding that sworn oaths must be kept. You said that foreigners didn't appreciate honour. If I was expected to keep to our oath, even when I wished to dissolve our marriage because you were no longer biding by the terms of our agreement, why should you be treated differently?"

Jason eyed me contemptuously. "Gods, but you are stupid, Medea. You are a woman. What I say to you doesn't count."

"But I am expected to be tied by what I say to you?"

"Of course! I'm your master, after all. Do you still not realise how inferior women are to men? Women can't think properly and so they must obey a man." He smirked arrogantly. "If you were really honest with yourself, you would realise that your unhappiness is caused by the idea of another woman sleeping with me. You can't bear to think that you are old and unattractive to men."

"I am only unhappy when I think that I remained here in this city of festering liars in order to adhere to a worthless oath."

Jason groaned. "Ares help me, can't you get it into your stupid, foreign head that different rules apply to men and to women. What have you got to complain about, anyway? I took you out of a backward hole and brought you to Greece. I've exposed you to concepts of justice. You've seen what it is to live by the rule of law, rather than to observe the caprices of an uneducated king. I've even enabled you to gain a reputation amongst the women for being clever with herbs and potions. None of that would have happened if you had been stuck in barbarian wasteland like Colchis – no-one would have heard of you, but I have won you fame."

"What have I to complain about?" I repeated bitterly. "At Colchis I already had a reputation for wisdom. Men were not ashamed to admit that I outranked them in terms of understanding of portents and sorcery. So you have not enhanced my reputation; here at Corinth your priests' grasp of prophecy and the magic arts is so limited that none can even imagine the profundity of Colchian knowledge. As for notions of Greek justice, they are certainly new to me. At Colchis a man who broke his sworn oath was despised as a dishonourable outcast. Here, a liar and oath-breaker appears to think that he will be rewarded by the very gods by whom he falsely swore."

Jason yawned, feigning indifference. I ignored his yawn.

"As for my wider reputation, the fame you have won for me is, in reality, infamy. You have let the Corinthians believe that I killed my brother. You have told them that I murdered Pelias. You have sheltered behind the obloquy which you have heaped upon me. You killed Apsyrtus; you planned Pelias's murder; and you caused poor

Terpsichore's death."

"Ah! I knew it! You're jealous because I took that slave to bed! All women care about is their sex life. They are perfectly loving and sweet to their husbands whilst they are being bedded, but immediately a man grows tired of his wife's demands, she turns into a sour, angry harridan. And that, dear Medea, describes you perfectly. If I slept with you, you'd stop complaining."

I rejected this claim disdainfully. "Sex is irrelevant to this matter. In fact, the thought of sleeping with you is so utterly repugnant that I cannot contemplate it without feeling actively sick. No, Jason, as a self-confessed Greek who lives by the rule of law, you ought to be able to understand that my anger is based on the fact that you have broken a contract. Our agreement was clear: I would supply the Fleece as my dowry and, in return, you would marry me. Did I break our contract when you lost my dowry? No! But you insisted on enforcing that contract when you were no longer living with me, even although anyone could see that you had broken our contract twice over. You appealed to my sense of honour. You demanded that I remain married to you. You refused to let me leave Corinth. That is why I object. It is nothing to do with sex. You lied to me; you made use of me; you are a cowardly blackguard."

Colour mounted on Jason's cheeks. "Damn you, I'll make you pay for that."

"Yes," I responded, contempt dripping over every syllable, "remaining married to you would be punishment. But it's probably too late to ask Creon to let you off your promises to him. Why does he want to marry the girl to you, anyway? Is she cross-eyed and hump-backed? Does he believe that any husband is better for the poor thing than for her to continue to live at home?"

"She's pretty enough," Jason retorted. "You may

pretend to despise my charms, but Glauce is very eager to be linked to a hero. And it certainly will help me to be married to the king's daughter – I can look forward to an assured old age even if I don't inherit power when Creon dies." He laughed. "Princesses are useful things at times, eh, Medea? It'd have been a lot harder to acquire the Fleece if you hadn't fallen for my sun-tanned arms and my good looks."

"As well as your lying tongue and your false promises."

Jason shrugged. "Perhaps it will teach you to curb your tongue if I tell you that you helped me to win the Princess Glauce as my bride." He glanced at me with cruel satisfaction. "Aegeus was delighted with whatever you said to him, and that made him much more inclined to agree to an alliance with Creon. Creon's been trying to get one for years so he was, naturally, only too happy to reward the man who had introduced Aegeus to a wise woman."

"I don't suppose you troubled to point out that the wise woman was your wife?"

"Of course not. I said she was a mad old crone who had come from foreign parts. I may have even suggested that she was a slave." Jason loomed menacingly over me. "You wouldn't like me to swear that you were my slave, would you, Medea?"

"Would you have to swear that before the gods as well?"

Jason brushed this minor detail aside. "Anyway, I haven't come to let you whine and complain – I've told you what's happening and no amount of begging from you will change my mind."

My stomach contracted, but I strove to appear unperturbed. "What have you come about?"

"The children."

XXXIX

Jason soon made his intentions clear.

"I've thought for a long time that you are bringing my sons up badly, Medea, but until now I have not been able to offer them a settled home. So I've left them with you, even although it has been a matter of great reluctance to abandon them to your unnatural callousness and cruelty."

"Unnatural?" I exclaimed, in a voice which sounded too shrill. "Look at the times when you addressed them by the wrong names! Or does being so drunk that you can't tell your own children apart not make you an unnatural father?"

"Sons belong to their father. They must obey his orders."

"You make them sound like your slaves."

"And if I deny their paternity that fate might await them. After all, they would be barbarians in a Greek land."

I knew perfectly well that Jason was saying such things to torment me, to pay me back for my contemptuous reference to his lies and deceit. Nevertheless, I could not expel the fear from my mind that Jason might be able to put his threats into practice. What I had seen so far of Jason's much-vaunted Greek justice and rule of law did not reassure me that women and children would have any role to play in arriving at decisions. If Jason, as a man, swore his sons' bloodline away, I doubted whether any court – let alone one overseen by Creon – would listen to me. However, I knew that it would be fatal to let Jason see that I was afraid.

"A trifle excessive to enslave your own children," I commented. "It might give rise to suspicions that you were something of an unnatural parent."

"Do you object to me not liking your precious brood?"

Jason jibed. "Why in Hades should I like your spawn?"

"Then why do you suggest that they live with you?"

"It annoys you for a start – unless I am correct and you are as unnatural a mother as you were a sister." Jason guffawed. "I can just imagine you trying to flee from Corinth and hacking your whining brats to bits and strewing the limbs upon the sea in the hope of delaying me. Well, I've news for you, Medea. I shouldn't bother to stop to collect their bodies, especially not if doing so would prevent me from capturing you and hacking you to death." He laughed again. "So you should be grateful to me for taking them off your hands. Now you won't be tempted to kill them as part of some lunatic attempt to sail back to Colchis."

Terrified that Philesia had somehow let slip my plans, I forced myself to respond convincingly. "How can I return to Colchis? Don't you realise that when you killed Apsyrtus you cut me off from my homeland forever?"

"And your stupid attack of conscience over Pelias means that I'm cut off from mine forever," retorted Jason. "However, I shan't deny that I shall take great delight in thinking about you stuck here wondering about what's happening to those brats, particularly since no-one will listen to your complaints. After all, what sensible, rational man would not immediately see the benefits of your precious offspring being brought up at court as half-brothers to the princes which Glauce and I shall breed?"

Ignoring the fact that any sensible, rational woman would immediately identify with the agony which coursed through me at the thought of losing my boys, I attempted to find an argument which might convince Jason. "I don't suppose that Glauce would agree with you. Apart from anything else, she won't want much older male offspring living in the palace whilst her own sons – if she has any – grow up."

"Are you afraid that your milk-and-water pair would kill off any heirs?" demanded Jason incredulously. Then he laughed. "No. I suppose what you fear is that Glauce's sons would murder their feeble half-brothers. Well, your specimens wouldn't be much loss and, even if they were to become as combative as you are, I'm sure they would be cut down pretty swiftly. But they're as weak as women." He guffawed again. "Maybe they can find a role under my new offspring – perhaps as eunuchs. That would solve the situation perfectly. After all, you seem to think that men ought to behave like women, so we could start the experiment by emasculating your own sons."

"You will soon get bored having to look after them," I warned.

"What makes you think that I intend to look after them?" queried Jason. "I shan't waste any time over them at all."

"Then why do you want them?"

"Revenge, Medea, revenge. Look at all the years you've spent preening yourself on your supposed cleverness and looking down your long, foreign nose at me. I'll remove those brats if I have to drag them screaming and yelling from your arms. In fact, it will give me even greater pleasure to take them if they do whimper and howl; you will hate it all the more and I shall have repaid you for the times when you've sneered at me and flaunted your ridiculous claims to be a superb seer. You'll grovel at my feet, but you will have brought your punishment upon yourself."

On this note of virulent hatred, Jason stalked off, warning me that he had placed a guard on the house.

I have to admit that for some time I gave way to my emotions. I had known that it was dangerous to trust to hope, but we had been within days of tasting freedom. I cursed myself for not having fled immediately Aegeus had offered sanctuary, but, even as I did so, I realised that the practical difficulties of reaching Athens could not have been overcome without some level of planning. Moreover, Philesia's help would not have been available until she had learned the truth about Georgos.

All the same, however much I tried to convince myself that I could not have fled sooner, I still felt utterly responsible for the calamity which threatened us. Jason's comments as to my arrogance I dismissed. Whenever I had spoken of my skills it had been when he had encouraged me to do so, most particularly when he was busily trying to worm his way into my confidence at Colchis. If he had chosen to pretend to admire women with interest in matters beyond domestic chores, then it was hardly a sign of overweening hubris that I had revealed my knowledge. If he resented the fact that a woman might possess skills and understanding which he lacked, it merely revealed his own inadequacy – whether of character, or intelligence, or both. But it was my fault that I had not pushed Philesia into making the transport available more swiftly. Why had I taken pity on her when she cried that she could not visit the farm that day because she had been so happy there with Georgos? Why had I not forced her to go despite her tears? Why had I accepted her promise to do so five days later? If I had been more ruthless we could have been already on the road to Athens – and freedom.

Eventually, I roused myself to check whether Jason's final threat was true; was there really a guard watching the house to see that I did not sneak off with the children? Dragging a veil over my face so that no-one could see that I had been weeping, I set off slowly to the fountain. Fetching water was one of Pelagia's tasks, but it was a good excuse to leave the house for a few minutes. Sure enough, there was a thick-set, swarthy man lingering on the corner of the street, watching the passers-by. I suppose that Jason might have observed him and thought that it would be amusing to pretend that he was there to spy on me, but I feared that it was much more likely that Jason's story was true. My husband, like so many men, objected to petty affronts to his pride, although he enjoyed insulting those who could not strike back. This scheme was exactly like Jason: it was twisted and cruel, but would require no effort from him. He would never have bothered to revenge himself upon me in this way if he expected to have to live in close proximity to his own children; he must have assumed that he could lose Mermerus and Pheres in the bowels of the palace, whilst still inflicting great pain upon me.

That evening, I tried to think of a solution. Ought I to try and bluff my way past the watcher in the shadows? Should I send the children on ahead with Pelagia and attempt to leave later? Would that precipitate the very disaster which I feared? I even momentarily considered allowing the boys to go to live at the palace in the hope that Jason would become wearied of their presence and allow them to leave. However, I soon dismissed that idea. The memory of Pheres's white, pinched face as he told me that his father wanted him to be sent away strengthened my resolve that, whatever it took, my boys would never be abandoned to Jason's care.

XL

Since any appeal to Jason's better nature would only lead to more heartless treatment, I was forced to consider who might help me. Aegeus had made it abundantly clear that he had no wish to be embroiled in any arguments between the Corinthians and me. It was highly unlikely that he would support any plea that my sons be granted to my care, not Jason's. Perhaps that was natural. Perhaps a man would automatically side with another man, just as I would tend to assume that a woman who had cared for her children from the day that they were born was the best person to continue to nurture them. I wondered briefly whether Aegeus would be swayed by the fact that Jason had openly spoken of his contempt for his sons, but it seemed a frail argument to which to trust my boys' future. Jason would twist his words and claim that he had merely derided their upbringing, not the product of his loins.

However, there was one man who might just side with me – not because he had any sympathy with a mother's outlook, but because he was a realist. I had little doubt that Creon would be just as swift as I had been to realise the dangers inherent in raising the sons of two different mothers together. Whereas I feared that keeping Mermerus and Pheres at the palace would be tantamount to asking for them to be murdered when their putative half-brothers grew up, presumably Creon would fear that my sweet boys might kill his grandsons. Naturally, I knew that my sons were not cruel and calculating, but Creon was a man well-versed in the arts of politics. He would be a fool if he did not consider the likelihood that Jason's older boys might perceive the chance of taking control of Corinth at the expense of their younger, weaker siblings. Hence, the following day, I approached Creon himself.

As I walked through the streets, I was conscious of disapproving looks from the men whom I passed. It was so long since I had walked freely through Corinth that I lost my way several times. When I reached the palace the guards refused to let me in. I tried every gate, but the result was the same. It was only when I thought of the slaves' entrance that I had any success. Instead of a pair of armed soldiers, there was a sleepy old man sitting on a stool. He attempted to protest, but I overrode his plaints and strode in through the narrow entrance. Memories of my father's palace taught me to look for the cleaner, wider corridors and, sure enough, before long I was in the main section of the palace.

I knew that I might still be stopped by guards, and my fears were borne out when I reached the throne-room. The soldiers were polite enough, but adamant that I could not be admitted. I refused to move. After an hour, an advisor appeared and the soldiers whispered to him urgently.

"Who are you and why are you here?" he demanded.

"I am a prophetess and I must speak to your king."

"Why?"

"It concerns the princess. I can say no more to you."

The advisor kept questioning me, but I refused to say anything further. Eventually, he bid the guards open the double-doors and he re-entered the throne-room. I continued to wait, noticing how every passing man stared at me incredulously, as if I were a fabulous monster from another world. Women seemed to be singularly invisible at court, apart from one young creature who drifted past, casting a contemptuous glance in my direction. I inspected her thoughtfully, sure that she must be the princess, Glauce. As Jason had said, she was pretty enough, although most of her attractiveness was created by her rich clothes and fine jewels. Her face certainly revealed no intelligence or strength of character, something which must have increased her suitability in Jason's eyes. However, I was uninterested in Creon's daughter; my concerns revolved entirely round the fate of my sons.

Eventually, I was ushered into the king's presence. He seemed angry when I revealed my identity as Jason's wife and he had no sympathy with my predicament.

"Why should I interfere? Sons belong with their father."

"Sometimes, but Jason will have other sons with Princess Glauce. Would it not be better for them to grow up without being overshadowed by older half-brothers?"

Creon ignored this point, much to my dismay, since it was the argument most likely to convince him. "You should be happy that Jason acknowledges your children as his. There are not many men who would be as generous as he."

Realising that Jason could not have told Creon the truth, I tried not to bristle with fury. "Jason and I were married in Colchis. Our children are his legitimate sons, just as I am his wife, married in the sight of Zeus."

"Colchis?" repeated Creon. "Why would a Greek hero want to marry some woman from an outlandish place such as Colchis? No, no, be thankful that Jason has stuck by you all these years and don't complain that he has finally decided to settle down with a wife."

"A hero?" I repeated. "Perhaps you are correct. Perhaps we are very outlandish in Colchis. But at Colchis, heroes actually carry out their deeds. Of course, as you say, Jason is a *Greek* hero. Maybe that explains why he let me give him a potion to protect him from the bulls which breathed fire; maybe that is the reason why he could not discover for himself the way in which to defeat the warriors which sprang up from the dragon's teeth; maybe that is why he cowered in the grove whilst I sent the fearsome dragon to sleep. Jason isn't a hero; he is a coward who skulks behind women's skirts when there is danger and then boasts of his courage when there are none to challenge him. You will do your daughter no good if you marry her off to him. He doesn't even love her; what he wants is the royal status she will bring him. He boasts that he will rule Corinth after you die."

"You barbarians are all the same – no ability to consider things rationally and logically. Why can't you accept that Jason no longer wishes to be involved with you?"

"As for that, my lord, for many years I have not wished to be involved with him – in fact, ever since I discovered his true nature."

"Then why didn't you leave him years ago? I shouldn't have stopped you from leaving Corinth."

"He insisted that we must abide by the oath which we swore before Zeus." I paused, wondering whether it was worth further humbling myself in front of Creon, before deciding that anything was worthwhile trying if it might keep my boys safe. "Corinth is a trading nation. You understand business here. What would you make of a man who agreed a deal, demanded that the other party kept to the letter of the agreement even when the conditions had been broken, and then, when it suited him, tried to sneak out of the deal?"

"Is that what you are accusing Jason of doing?"

"Yes. We had a contract. He enforced it when I grew unhappy. He insisted that, even although we were to all effect living apart, I was his wife. But now that he sees a comfortable old age as your daughter's husband, he denies that there was any oath and demands my sons, whom he despises and hates."

"Jason warned me that you were jealous. He underestimated quite how vicious you were. No wonder he wants to take his sons away from you."

"Vicious?" I repeated. "Jealous? No, Creon, my problems lie not with jealousy, but because I believed the oaths which that man swore. I believed all the lies he told me. I believed that he was an honourable hero. But he is not. And I have proof of how he lies and cheats. He will have told you that he introduced Aegeus to a wise woman. He will not have told you that that wise woman was I, no more than he will have told you that I am Medea, princess of Colchis, daughter of Aeetes and granddaughter of Helios."

Creon stared at me in amazement and then, just as I was hoping that I might have finally struck home, he threw back his head and roared with laughter.

"He told me that he had taken Aegeus to a madwoman and I see that he spoke the truth! Granddaughter of Helios, indeed. Well, your silly talk amuses me, but I shall not have my son-in-law insulted. You will leave Corinth tomorrow and never return."

"But I can prove that it is true," I cried desperately. "How else would I know that Aegeus was impotent?"

Creon suddenly stopped laughing. "If you're going to throw that sort of remark around, all the more reason to see you banished. Immortal gods, do you think that I'm going to risk Athens's wrath by allowing some crazed barbarian to mock their king?"

I tried to protest that I was not mocking Aegeus; that all I wanted to do was to prove that I had told the truth and that Jason was the liar. However, it was in vain. Creon had clearly made his mind up. He had not believed my tales of marriage, but, far more conclusively than my complaints about the female realm, my knowledge of the male world had condemned me. It was far too dangerous to let me remain in Corinth, ready to expose both Jason's cowardice and the intimate details of the health of the king of Athens. I had hoped to defeat Jason by resorting to politics, but I had lived outside Colchis and its court for too long and had thus made a disastrous calculation. Creon was uninterested in any possible threat to his grandsons from Jason's children – perhaps because he had already decided to poison them off. His main concern was to avoid destroying a promising alliance, and he would risk his daughter's happiness – as well as destroy me – in the process of preserving it.

XLI

That evening, Jason turned up, practically shaking with rage. "So, you foreign witch, not content with insulting me you must mock the royal family and its most illustrious ally. Will nothing stop your hatred of me?"

Although, in retrospect, I might as well have told Jason that only his death would achieve that, I had caught sight of an armed guard out on the street. There was no point in precipitating violence by hasty words. So I played for time. "What do you mean?"

"Creon complained to me about your insolence. How dared you, a mere woman, demand to speak to the king? How dared you appear at the palace uninvited and alone? Don't you know what you must have looked like?" He snorted angrily. "I always suspected your morals, and now I know the truth – you're no better than some streetwalker, flaunting her wares."

"I went alone because I have no male relative to protect me."

"Not even your precious brats?" sneered Jason. "Pah! You don't understand the conventions of decent society. You've never tried to fit in."

"I have. I have swallowed any number of hurts in order to conform to Corinthian ideas of what is correct."

"Corinthian," repeated Jason. "That's the point, isn't it? You think that the ideas are Corinthian; you don't understand that they are what every civilised society respects." He shrugged arrogantly. "Why should you, when you come from a backward, barbarian hole like Colchis? Still, you'll be going back there tomorrow, you and your foreign spawn."

I fought down my shock. It was essential that I did not remind Jason of my desperate need for my sons, since that might encourage him to take them away that very night. However, it was equally vital that I find out whether Jason meant what it sounded like he meant. Perhaps Creon had changed his mind and seen the benefits of Mermerus and Pheres accompanying me. "The king has issued his decree," I agreed neutrally.

"Are you going to Colchis?"

"I suppose so. Iolcos won't have me back."

"Don't be so certain," grunted Jason. "The Iolchians might be delighted to welcome you back. Then they could deal with you just as you dealt with Pelias. They could boil up your sons at the same time. Or perhaps they might do that first to make you suffer more."

I tried to contain a shudder, but Jason noticed it. "Don't you like the idea?" He pretended to think. "I know what to do. I'll keep your brats here after all, until I learn that you've reached a place of safety."

Bile rose up in my throat. I was a fool to have even hoped for a moment that Jason would let Mermerus and Pheres escape. I should have known that he had no intention of granting anything that I wanted. He had only hinted at the chance of letting the boys leave for the pleasure of rescinding his permission. There was no point in trusting anything he said – he would say first one thing, then another, for the sheer joy of hurting me.

"Of course," added Jason, with an air of great generosity, "if you obey me, I might possibly take pity upon you and send them on later. But that would only happen once I knew where you'd gone."

Despite my searing disappointment, Jason's plan was quite obvious to me. He wanted to keep the boys as hostages for my good behaviour, whilst at the same time tormenting me with hopes that I might be granted them. I doubted very much that I should ever be allowed to see my innocent children again once I had left Corinth, and if

Jason knew that I was living at Athens, he would do everything possible to harm me there. Such knowledge would certainly encourage him to veto any invitation from the King of Athens requesting that my sons come on a visit to strengthen ties between the two courts. However, since Jason clearly expected me to be destroyed by his swift changes of mind, I was determined to show little of what I felt. Moreover, I had a plan of my own.

"Doubtless you know what is best."

Jason looked distinctly surprised at this outbreak of reason on my part. "I do. I'm a man and you're a woman. I've told you what will happen."

"Yes," I sighed. "I have thought about what you said last night and I realise that you are correct. We women are too inclined to be ruled by our passions and emotions. We cannot bear to think of another woman proving to be more attractive than we are; nor do we always see that the dictates of diplomacy must come before personal pleasure."

"Are you trying to get me to change my mind?" demanded Jason suspiciously.

"No. I have come to see the truth too late."

Jason guffawed. "You *are* trying to change my mind. Zeus take me, Medea, I've no desire to bed you again. I never wanted to sleep with you in the first place, so I'm hardly likely to turn down Glauce, who's younger, prettier, and comes with a kingdom attached. Can't you see the benefits she offers me?"

"And does she truly love you?"

To judge by his features, Jason was revolted by such a sentimental thought. "How in Hades would I know? She'll do what's asked of her. Love doesn't come into it – and nor do you."

"I know," I agreed humbly. "All the same, I should like to send the princess a gift to make it clear that I bear no ill-will."

"Don't be a fool; you'll need all the money you can get, now that I'm no longer supporting you. And I don't suppose Glauce would want anything of yours; she'll get much finer gifts from the nobles at court who will be trying to ingratiate themselves with Creon."

"Ah, but she will like the provenance of this one. It was my grandfather's."

"The problem with you, Medea, is that your claims are too far-fetched. If you'd said that the Sun was your grandfather six or eight times off then people might believe you. But you overdo everything. You say you're a priestess, not a mumbling witch, and you claim to be the granddaughter of a god, rather than Aeetes's byblow."

"I don't suppose that Glauce will mind, not when she sees how beautiful the robe is."

Jason yawned. "Don't think that I'm going to take it tonight – I've got other fish to fry. And you won't be allowed anywhere near the palace, either tonight or tomorrow."

"Couldn't you send a guard to collect it?"

"The only guard who'll be coming here is to see that you leave Corinthian soil. Send your wretched brats with it, if you're so keen on giving away your patrimony."

I spent much of the rest of the day in preparation. First, I begged Philesia to make sure that the ox and cart would be ready early the following morning. Then I had to prepare the robe which I was to send to Glauce. Finally, I had to warn Mermerus and Pheres exactly what to do.

"Glauce is going to marry your father tomorrow and we must give her a gift."

"Why?"

"It is customary, Pheres. We must not seem to lack manners. It may be that Glauce will say something about becoming your stepmother. If she does, do not appear surprised. Tell her that you hope that you will be able to serve her well."

Mermerus was listening intently. "Has Father said that we are to live with him?"

I hated lying to my boy, but I had no choice. "He is unsure, so do not be frightened by anything he says. He does not love you as I do." I fought to get my voice under control. "The most important part is this: once you have given the robe to the princess, you must leave immediately. Do not let anyone stop you, not even your father. Make any excuse you like, but you *must* leave."

"Do we come back here, Mama?"

"No, Mermerus, you are to go to Philesia's farm."

"The one where Pheres got stung by a wasp?"

"Yes. Do you remember the way?"

Both boys nodded solemnly. I swallowed hard. "You mustn't be frightened. Wait for me there."

"Are we going to escape with you?"

"Don't think about escape, Pheres. You must concentrate entirely upon being polite to the princess and then leaving swiftly, without anything to suggest that you are trying to flee."

"Don't worry, Mama, I'll look after Pheres."

XLII

The next morning, I was up early. I concocted a spurious errand to keep Pelagia away all day because, although I believed that she sympathised with me, I was not prepared to entrust my boys' future to anyone other than myself. Once she was gone, I devoted myself to Mermerus and Pheres. I had no idea when the guard might come for me and I did not want to rush my farewells to my sons. Now that they were older, my boys needed no woman to dress them, but that morning they let me garb them in sturdy sandals and their finest tunics. Perhaps they knew that I needed to touch their soft skin, to bury my head in their golden hair, to kiss their sweet lips. I picked out their favourite toys and put them in a bag, carefully buried under our food and what little money and jewels I possessed. I knew that a ball and some stuffed animals could be of no use on our journey, but my sons loved them. Therefore their playthings came with me.

I had been determined to show no grief in front of Jason's henchman, but when the time came to say goodbye, I wept as if this truly was the last time that I should see Mermerus or Pheres. Only the fact that I was upsetting them made me give them one last hug and a brief command to go to the palace, before turning resolutely away along the road out of the city.

For some time the guard did not address me. Eventually, once we were well out into the countryside, he spoke. "Were the little lads going up to the palace, then?"

"Yes, they should be there now."

"Going to watch the wedding?"

"Yes."

"Wish I was there, too," he grumbled. "There'll be a great feast with lots of wine."

"I'm afraid that I can't offer you any."

"That's all right, lady. You'll need to keep everything for your journey. Err... where is it that you're going?"

"Anywhere that isn't Corinth."

"Ah," he remarked bucolically. "Don't you like it, then?"

"I never want to see it again."

There was a pause whilst the guard ruminated upon my response. "Do you know your way?" he finally asked.

I nodded. "I keep following this road."

"That's right," he agreed encouragingly. "Err... I can come a bit further with you if you want."

Since it was palpably obvious that my custodian was worried that his fellow-soldiers would have drunk the palace dry before he returned, I felt secure in stating that I would manage without his assistance.

Eagerness warred with duty. "If you're quite sure…?"

"Quite sure."

"Then I'll be off. Good journey, lady."

"Thank you."

Although I believed that my ingenuous guard was already racing back to the city, I stayed on the road which led northwards for some time. Only when I was sure that I was not being followed did I retrace my steps until I reached another, smaller track which led in the general direction of Philesia's farm. I was terrified that I might take a wrong turning by mistake and, as the sun mounted the sky, I worried incessantly that my boys might have already reached the farm and be wondering where I was. I thrust to the back of my mind a worse image – one of them intercepted by Jason or Creon, of them unable to flee, of them crying for me.

At last, I saw the farm in front of me, apparently deserted. I approached it with great caution. There seemed to be no-one there. I stayed still, listening intently. Only the keening of a kite could be heard as it flew high above, its shrill, eerie note echoing across the azure sky. The stones made tiny clicking noises as I crept towards the barn. If anyone was there, they would be alerted to my presence. I slipped inside, waiting for my eyes to accustom themselves to the darkness. A low grunting scared me momentarily, before I remembered the ox. Sure enough, a shaft of light breaking through a crack in the wall revealed the cart and the patient animal standing in its stall. Philesia had kept her promise. Closer inspection showed that she had even placed a bag of food and a few spare clothes inside the cart, along with two goatskins of water. I blessed her generosity. Whilst the food and water might have been a kind contribution to my supposed picnic, the garments could only mean that she had realised that I intended to escape. Whether she also had guessed that I planned to flee with my boys was less clear, but she had been both brave and thoughtful in the midst of her own grief.

Now came the wait. Even in this parched, apparently uninhabited, landscape there could be hidden eyes and ears, and I was frightened of drawing attention to the farm. If Georgos suddenly appeared he would recognise me. Even if he believed that Jason had let me leave with the boys, I doubted very much whether he would allow me to drive off in his cart, however much I might protest that Philesia had given me permission. So I waited in the cool darkness of the barn, listening to the rats rustling and scuttling; waiting and waiting and waiting.

The stones crunched. I sat bolt upright. Had I imagined it? No. The stones crunched again. I edged forward nervously. The sunlight outside was so bright that I was momentarily unable to discern anything other than the harsh blaze of Helios. Then I picked out two small figures, one of them stumbling with weariness. I dashed outside the barn. Mermerus saw me and raced towards me, Pheres following him, all traces of tiredness dropping from him as he shot forwards.

"Mama, oh Mama!"

"My boys, my boys."

Pheres said nothing, but he buried his head in my chest.

I have never experienced such a moment of ecstatic happiness as that moment, and I shall never do so again. I had my sons, my glorious, beautiful, loving sons. My family – and I – was whole again.

"Come, we must get the ox-cart out of the barn and set off."

"We are really, truly escaping at last?"

"Yes, Pheres, we are. I hope that everyone will be too busy at the palace to worry about where you are, but we must keep alert."

Mermerus went inside and began to coax the ox into the shafts. Even at that moment, my heart swelled with pride at his competence. Pheres was clinging to my hand, but when he saw the ox emerging, he offered to assist. "Help me hold it when I stop," requested Mermerus, before suddenly staring out towards the horizon. His voice changed. "Mama, I can see horsemen." He tried to sound brave. "I'll protect you and Pheres, Mama."

"No, Mermerus. You must run away. Pheres, go with your brother. Try to reach the woods and wait until it is dark. Then go to Athens and tell King Aegeus that I sent you. Give him this bag and tell him there are potions in it. He will look after you."

"But what about you, Mama?"

"Go, Mermerus. Please. I love you both. I want you to go. Please."

Mermerus must have seen from my face that there was no time to be lost because he grabbed the bag in one hand

and his little brother's hand in the other. I stayed where I was. If Creon wanted a victim, he could have me.

The kite still flew high above, but now its keening was for us and the sun's harsh glare only served to put my sons in danger. Perhaps I had prayed to the wrong gods. I should have prayed to Hecate, inhabitant of crepuscular dark, controller of hidden forces. With her aid might we have been able to sneak through the horsemen unnoticed? I sent a fervent plea to whichever gods were listening to save my boys. Let me suffer, but let them be saved.

I had scarcely uttered this prayer when the leading horseman rode up to the farm and jumped off his mount.

"You! I should have guessed that you didn't mean to go quietly, having recognised your true place as a woman. You malevolent, scheming, cowardly bitch, do you know what you've done?"

In the hope of buying time for Mermerus and Pheres, I shook my head. "What's happened?"

Jason spat on the ground in his rage. I wondered whether he was about to run me through with his sword then and there, but the arrival of more horsemen seemed to stop him. "You've killed the princess. Once she'd been given your robe by your repulsive offspring, she immediately took it out of its wrappings, ignoring my gift of amber earrings. She held it next to her body, charmed by its beauty. She even weaved backwards and forwards in front of a mirror, admiring how the robe glittered when the light caught it."

"I am glad that it caused her pleasure."

"Pleasure?" Jason stuttered. "Only a sick, filthy barbarian would talk about pleasure. Don't you understand what your gift did? First of all, she complained that it clung round her, like an ivy round the trunk of an oak tree. Then she screamed that a burning sensation was spreading over her skin. She clawed at your cursed robe, but it seemed to have become glued to her body. Creon heard her wailing and rushed in. He tried to tear the robe from her, but the poison on it became smeared upon him. I heard him exclaim that a cut on his hand was stinging like salt rubbed too close to a wound. He tried to pull away, but his old skin seemed to melt before my eyes. Blood and flesh became mixed as one. It was like one of those infernal apparitions you conjured up with Pelias."

"Ah, you acknowledge my powers now, do you?

"I acknowledge them, all right. So does Corinth." He scowled petulantly, "Some of the nobles thought that *I* was responsible. Do they really think that I would destroy the girl who was going to bring me so much honour and status?"

"And whom you loved so much that you raced to her rescue when she was in danger."

Jason stared at me in surprise, apparently unaware of my ironic tone. "Don't be stupid, Medea. I wasn't going risk my life pulling that thing off her any more than I'd intended to wait in the grove at Colchis for you. That only happened because I hoped to lose you by following a minor track. I fully expected the serpent to wake up and deal with you whilst I got away from Colchis with the Fleece." He glared at me as if this failure of his plan was my fault. "Instead of which the Fleece snagged on a branch and I got stuck. It would have been much better if the serpent had caught you; then none of this would have happened. What was on the robe, anyway?"

"A mixture of toad's venom, naphtha and the poison of a castor-oil plant."

"By Zeus, I'd like to smear you with it. But I've got a better plan. You must hand over one of your children to compensate me for the loss of Glauce. And I mean hand over – you will lead him by the hand and give him to me." Jason smiled wolfishly. "It will help to reassure him."

"And what do you intend to do with him?"

"I shall look after him as he deserves, I swear."

Jason must have thought me a fool. I certainly no longer trusted his word, and the way in which his sword-hand unconsciously reached for the hilt of his blade was sign enough for me. Jason would kill our child in front of us and then, as likely as not, taunt me for having sent him to his death.

Just as I was praying that Jason would carry on talking and give the boys more time to flee, a commotion from behind the barn drained my heart of all hope. Three stocky men appeared, dragging my sons along with them.

"What is it?" demanded Jason curtly.

"We found these two trying to hide. We wondered whether they were the pair you were looking for."

"Well, well, well," drawled their father. "Mermerus and Pheres, two woodcock in a bag." He glanced at me, flaunting triumph gleaming in his eyes. "So, Medea, which one shall I take? Will you choose, or shall I? Or shall we ask them which loves you more?"

I found my voice. "Why don't you let me compensate you for Glauce?"

"What, conjure up a princess and a kingdom for me? No, Medea, this time I'll settle for revenge. I'll take Pheres back with me. Or shall it be Mermerus?"

"It is unkind to separate them. Take me instead."

"No. I shall have Pheres. He won't have a stepmother, but I'm sure he won't be upset for too long."

If Jason had chosen my darling Mermerus I might have taken the despairing risk that his sword-arm lied, that he did not intend to slaughter Mermerus straight off. But I could not abandon Pheres to Jason. It wasn't that I loved Mermerus less, but he was older and stronger and better able to withstand Jason's twisted whims. However, Jason hated Pheres and I knew that it would destroy my younger son to be trapped with Jason for years. Indeed, even if he did not kill him there and then, I greatly feared that Jason would not let Pheres live to grow up and join me and Mermerus in Athens. Neglect and misery could kill him as surely as deliberate murder.

"You must allow us to say goodbye."

"Be quick about it."

"Let us go inside," I pleaded. "We cannot escape."

Jason glanced round at his men complacently. "No, you're trapped now."

XLIII

I did not want Mermerus to know was happening, so I killed him first. He would have guessed if he had seen Pheres unaccountably fall asleep. And because I knew that Pheres would grieve so badly for his adored big brother, I killed him too.

XLIV

My first-born did not flee from me in terror. He curled in confidingly when I said that I wanted to cradle him, to place my arms around his body, to tell him how much I loved him. He was not afraid. He did not die alone or abandoned. He did not see the Eumenides approaching, grim Death upon their faces. His sole entreaty was that the gods might keep the three of us together. Then he gave a choking grunt and was gone. He died hearing my voice repeat over and over again that his mama adored him. So too with my defenceless Pheres. Better for him to die in my arms than to be slaughtered upon the dusty ground or turned into a humiliated, tortured slave.

Then the rattle of the barn-door recalled me to where I was. Jason strode in, closely followed by his men. If I had not been so grief-stricken, I could have laughed at his desire for protection from an unarmed woman.

"You have overstayed your time, Medea."

I remained where I stood, uninterested in responding. Jason sneered. "I suppose you're plotting something new against me. Well, I shan't touch anything which you've touched."

"Do you swear that?"

"By all the gods on Olympus."

"Your men have heard you," I replied, before stepping aside to reveal my sons' bodies.

"What have you done?"

"You will never mock them again."

"But they were mine! It is not up to you to decide what to do with them."

"I gave birth to them."

"I was their father."

"A fine father – one who jeered at them constantly,

who sought to separate them from each other."

"You have done this because I took another woman to my bed. The female sex is repulsive in its desire for vengeance."

"Not as repulsive as a father who threatens to call his sons slaves."

"You made them servile."

"They were kind and loving."

"Womanly! You made my sons into women."

"They are no longer your sons."

"Give me their bodies."

"Never! You will never touch them."

"You cannot stop me."

"I can and the gods can. You swore not to touch anything which I have touched. If you place your hand upon my sons, you will be revealed to your men as an oath-breaker."

"Curse you, Medea, how dare you bargain with me?"

"I am not bargaining; I am telling you what will happen – that is one of your favourite phrases, is it not? I shall take my dead sons with me and set up a shrine in their honour. You would not allow them to be together in life; they shall lie entwined in death for all time. Now leave me."

With that, I picked up first Mermerus and then Pheres and carried them out into the sunshine's final caress. There, I laid them to rest gently in the ox-cart and covered them with the robe from my hair. I mounted into the cart and urged the ox forward. I drove in absolute silence past the ranks of Jason's men, the sun glinting on their weapons. No-one moved or spoke. Were it not for the heat, they might have been mistaken for statues carved from gelid, emotionless ice. The silence hurt and the sun was blinding, but it was tears, not the sun, which blinded my eyes. My boys were dead. I rode with corpses towards Athens and freedom.

PART FOUR: ATHENS

XLV

Later, the Corinthians said that I escaped in a chariot drawn by dragons – a typical Corinthian exaggeration. Did it never occur to them that, if I could summon up such a mode of transport, I should not have done so immediately my boys joined me at the farm? Either they lacked the capacity for logical thought which Jason had claimed was innate to all Greeks or they were afraid to admit the truth. The reality was that I drove the cart out of the farmyard and onto the dust track without any of Jason's guards trying to stop me. They were afraid to. They saw the bodies and knew that I was polluted with the miasma of blood-guilt. They dared not touch lest they, too, be tainted with that same miasma. Jason did nothing either. Perhaps he also feared pollution, or perhaps he was too shocked to act. I did not know and I did not care.

So I travelled along the road to Athens. I buried my sons, having wrapped them in robes which I had hoped to wear in freedom. I placed fresh herbs and their childhood toys around them. I kissed their sweet lips for a last time, and then another time, cradling their limp corpses as I wept wracking sobs, my body arching cataleptically with grief. Then I raised a shrine over them – my sons, buried forever in the ground, never to be touched again by my hands, never to be kissed. Never again would Mermerus run to greet me; never would Pheres clamber up to lie in my arms; never would I cradle my boys again.

For fourteen days after I entombed my boys I could not weep. It frightened me that I could not. Men looked at me and said that I did not care. They did not see my fear and shock. Instead, they said that I was callous and heartless. But they did not change their minds when I did begin to cry. They did not notice that sores opened up on my cheekbones through my constant weeping for my glorious sons. Or, if they did, they attributed it to barbarian practices of ostentatious mourning, claiming that I scraped my cheeks with my finger-nails. But I did not need to resort to such actions when I lived every day with the raw, wailing pain of my boys' deaths. My heart yearned and throbbed, my mind reeled and tore. How could my boys be dead? My boys, my wonderful, adored boys. My boys were dead – and I was their killer.

I drove myself halfway to Hades retracing what I had done and what I failed to do. If only I had tried to flee earlier; if only I hadn't decided that we needed the ox-cart; if only we had met elsewhere. 'If only, if only' went round and round my head in an unceasing threnody until I could have screamed curses just to hear another set of words. But there were no other words to hear. Every action I had taken, every speech I had made leered before me as a mistake which had led inexorably to my boys' death. If only I hadn't tried to defend myself against Jason; if only I hadn't miscalculated Creon's reaction; if only I hadn't helped Aegeus. If I had been the cowed, obedient Greek wife that Jason so clearly wanted, would my boys be lying stiff and lifeless in a hollow tomb among the hostile rocks?

Then I began to question the motives for my actions. My plan for killing Glauce had, I thought, been based on pure practicality. If there had been nothing in place to distract Creon when my boys tried to slip away, the king would have sent out search parties to track them down. After all, having issued so clear an edict that they were to remain with Jason, it would have looked as if Creon could not keep control in his own kingdom if he ignored their flight. My answer to this difficulty had been to slay Glauce and to leave Jason enmeshed in her fatal embrace. No-one would care about two children in the ensuing tumult, and my sons would be at liberty to flee.

It had seemed plausible at the time – so plausible that I had followed it. But afterwards, alone without my sons, I tormented myself that the plan went wrong because I had been too eager to hurt Glauce and the Corinthians, that I had put my desire for revenge above my children's safety. Why else had I made the disastrous assumption that Jason would rush to Glauce's aid? I knew that he was a coward. Why had I not foreseen that Jason would be left alive to track down his sons, fanning out a net to catch them like a huntsman chasing the russet deer? I could not deny that I had wished to punish Jason and Glauce for mocking me. I had deeply resented the pale, haughty creature who had wafted past me at the palace, with only a contemptuous stare for me as I waited to beg for my sons to be restored to my care. Moreover, I had wanted to see Creon writhe with anguish for his insults to me. I had loathed and despised the Corinthians for their derision of Colchis. So had I allowed myself to be driven by a lust for vengeance rather than my love for my children?

Was I also selfish? Should I have spared Mermerus? I had thought that I could only save Pheres from Jason by killing him. But was I wrong to sacrifice Mermerus? Ought I to have given him the chance of life, instead of judging that it was better that both die together in love, rather than for one to grow up haunted by his brother's death? Indeed, was I wrong to assume that Pheres would die at Jason's hand? Should I have taken the risk that Pheres would have been allowed to live – perhaps neglected and abused, but still alive? Was it an egotistical grief at being separated which had prompted my actions, rather than a selfless desire to spare my children the terrible grief of parting?

Still worse was the spectre which visited by night to accuse me of sacrificing my beloved children through jealousy that Jason had left me for another's loins. I told myself that Jason had slept with a fine selection of women before his reputation as a hero had brought the king's daughter into his orbit, but still I questioned again and again whether my resentment of Jason's treatment of me, and my hatred of his constant mockery, had led me to destroy that which was most dear to me. If that was my real motivation, then my guilt was truly terrible and my actions were for nothing – Jason's response to their bodies clearly indicated that he would not grieve for Mermerus and Pheres as I did. Even if he regretted their deaths, he would not regret his actions since he would not see the connection between the two.

I even began to worry whether my beloved boys knew how very dear they were to me. Had Mermerus known that I adored him? I could not bear the thought that my darling boy did not understand how desperately I loved him, but it was true that Pheres demanded attention in a way in which Mermerus had not. I found myself talking to Mermerus, pleading with him that, because I had instinctively protected Pheres, he was not any less loved. But it was too late to tell him, just as it was too late to tell Pheres that I was devoted to him. And so I wept. I wept every day – deep, uncontrollable sobbing. I could never tell when it would strike and it worried me if it had not struck, but I wept. It would have upset my boys had they lived, but each lay in his brother's arms, too sound asleep to be woken, even by their mother's wailing pleas for the gods to relent and send her sons back to be kissed and adored once more.

XLVI

It was at this point that Aegeus sought me out. I had been some days in Athens, but I took no interest in my surroundings. Why should I care to observe the gnarled boles of the olive trunks when I could no longer feel the flow of my sons' hair between my fingers? What interest had I in the city's buildings when I had no-one for whom to build a home? Why should I devote myself to the shrines on the Acropolis when my mind saw only my sons' grave? My sole purpose now was to tend that low mound and to see that, in death, my children received the love which they could no longer gain in life. Who else would perform the sacred rituals if I did not? Who else would remember and weep for them if I, too, joined them in the grave?

Nonetheless, in the midst of my numb anguish, I had to deal with Aegeus. I had promised to cure his childlessness in return for safe haven at Athens – just because I no longer cared whether I found sanctuary did not mean that I did not owe him my half of the bargain. However, his visits lacerated me. Even to hear the word 'child' – I never spoke it, but he seemed to drag it into every sentence – made me wrench in stabbing pain. Nor could I truthfully console with him over his affliction. Aegeus' childlessness was nothing as to mine. He had no sons; I had killed my sons.

My days passed in grief. I did not notice the colour or texture of my clothes. Instead, I remember that my boys were alive when my robe was woven; my boy was smiling when I wore this wrap; my boy nestled into me and played with the tassle on this girdle. I no longer even recognised myself when I drifted past mirrors in the palace. I had not been a shrivelled, grey ghost when my boys were alive; who was this fraudulent shade which had taken my place to be tossed and buffeted by the faintest flickering of the wind?

If daytime served as a scourge of memory then dusk mimicked my sons' endless night. Whatever my motivation, whether good or bad, I could not deny that my desire to flee Corinth had brought my children to their death. However, the realm of dreams was the worst torment of all. I would see my beloved boys, happy and contented, playing together or snuggling into my arms, chattering away. I would reach to touch them, to feel their sleek hair, their smooth flesh. Then I would waken, to find that my bed was bare and empty, abandoned of life.

After a while, I tried to conjure up their images. I sought herbs and wayside plants by night and brewed concoctions by the light of the new moon. But the sinuous, shifting mists revealed not my boys as they had lived, joyous and vibrant, but my sons lying dead upon the ground, unmistakeably lifeless, without animation or spark. I tried again, this time in full, scorching light, with eagles and the haggard falcon soaring overhead. Still the mists refused to display my sons as they were. Even when I entreated and begged Helios to help me, what was portrayed was my boys beyond all doubt dead. Then, as if to punish me for my temerity, my dreams and my waking moments were filled with images of my sons lying dead in my arms, or of their cadavers jolted by the movements of the ox-cart into a grim mockery of life, or of my boys curled up dead in their grave. Dead, always dead. I strove to remember happier visions, but they were chased away by apparitions of corpses. It was as if I had lost the capacity to remember them as they were when alive. No prayers or sacrifices helped. My greed to see their images had killed my memories, just as my greed to escape Corinth had killed my sons.

Time must have passed, although I was unaware of it. If I had stopped to consider it, I suppose that I would have been grateful to Aegeus for allowing me to live at Athens. Had I been thrust into exile I should have had less time to talk to my boys in my head. But I did not think about Aegeus, nor did I notice the whispered conversations at court which seemed to falter if I floated past. I lived mechanically, inhabiting a grey world of my own, circumscribed by my grief.

Then the inevitable happened. Aegeus decided that if I could cure his childlessness then I would make him a suitable wife. I fell pregnant. I gave birth. I looked at the child with no feeling. And as it grew, I had no feeling. It was named Medes. I think that Aegeus meant it as a compliment to me, but such a name suggested that it was mine. It was not. *My* children were dead.

It might have been easier if I had used abortifacients to kill it in the womb, but I had made a pact with Aegeus and, unlike Jason, I stuck to my pacts. And, to be fair to Aegeus, he stuck to his pact too, although it was easier for him because he actively wanted a child and rejoiced in the thing which I had produced. But I found it destructively hard not to resent it – even hate it – as a replacement of my golden boys.

Naturally, Medes needed nourishment, but each time I fed him his pap I saw not his wizened, swarthy face greedily sucking from my body, but my real children dying in my arms. Four or five times a day I watched my beautiful sons die at my hands. I could not stop myself, but then, I did not try. To have driven away any image of them would have been a betrayal of them, an attempt to expunge their very existence. Small wonder, then, that the child grew up a strange, sullen little thing, closed and reserved, with no tendency to laugh. Perhaps even at that age he was conscious that I watched him, compared him, and found him wanting. Perhaps I was only too ready to regard him as less accomplished, less handsome, and less skilled than his dead brothers, but I truly believe that he lacked every grace and joy which my golden boys had borne. However, there was one way in which Medes did help me. As he grew, my compulsive comparisons between him and my sons brought happier images back to me. No longer did I always see death: sometimes I was granted the sight of my sons at play; of Mermerus bringing joy to my heart with his laughter; of Pheres trusting and happy. So I was grateful to that extent, and Aegeus was proud of his son. But we had no more children. One was a fulfilment of a pact, two would have been betrayal.

Betrayal was a constant theme in my heart. I recollected times in Corinth when I had admired other children – thinking that one had a charming smile or another an adorable laugh. Might the gods have interpreted such admiration as meaning that I was not content with my own sons, that I wanted a replacement? Did they not understand that any pleasure I had derived from other children was an expression of how much I loved my own? If I saw a boy who looked like Mermerus or Pheres then I wanted them to be loved just as my own sons were. It meant that I could not bear my boys to be unloved, not that I did not love them.

Similarly, I worried that I had been so wrapped up in my love for my children that the gods thought that I was complacent. It is at moments of greatest good fortune that there is the greatest need to acknowledge that happiness is completely dependent upon the gods' good will. There are many tales of proud mothers destroying their children by a too-ready vaunting of their offspring's prowess and good looks.

However, to blame the gods was false. The sole responsibility lay with me. If I were exceedingly fortunate, the divine ones would make my sons' time in Hades as painless as could be, but they would do no more. Had I not begged and beseeched Helios to save my sons, his great-grandsons? But no help had come. Instead, Jason's cronies had dragged my boys out of the scrub like a pair of runaway slaves. The gods cared nothing for me or my sons, whatever my parentage might be.

XLVII

Time passed. Men say that I haunted the court; that I did not keep to a woman's place; that Aegeus was too dependent upon my advice. As usual, men were wrong. My sole interest in diplomacy was to learn that Jason was dead. My sole interest in Athenian politics was to preserve the sanctity of my sons' tomb and to ensure that no-one dared build near the shrine. If Aegeus asked for guidance I gave it, in a totally disinterested fashion. Athens was not my home; I had no reason to faction-form or seek the advancement of one family or another.

Months passed. News came that Jason was dead, struck by the prow of the Argo as he lay in a drunken stupor. He had spent that evening as he spent so many others, bewailing his ill-fortune and his lost heroic youth, wondering why he had not been better treated by Fate. I spat on the ground at the news. The messenger who brought it thought that I did so to avert the evil tidings. He was wrong. I spat from hatred and loathing. I spat as I ought to have spat upon Jason whilst he was alive. But it was too late. My family lay dead and Jason's death could no longer set us free.

Aegeus became curiously perturbed, apparently fearing that the news of my heroic suitor's demise might rekindle my youthful ardour. He need not have wasted his time. If my boys had still been alive, I would have happily danced upon Jason's grave. But my boys were dead, so I did not. However, Aegeus kept returning to the subject of my supposed feelings for Jason until one night I could bear it no longer and told him so. He responded angrily.

"That means you still love him."

"I do not."

"You do. How can you still care for him after all this

time?"

"If I truly loved someone, I could grieve for them until the end of time."

"Especially if they were a hero? Especially if men tell tales of their adventures and women pray to have so brave a lover?"

It was cruel of me, but I laughed. I simply could not believe that Aegeus was jealous of a bloated drunk. "You were at Corinth. Were you really so impressed by Jason? Did you admire his sycophantic flattery and his nauseous self-regard?"

"No." There was a pause, before Aegeus added sulkily, "But everyone spoke of his adventures."

I shrugged. "Talk. That was all Jason ever did achieve."

Aegeus glanced round about him, visibly taking comfort from his surroundings. "You are correct. Jason was never a *ruler*."

My comment had been intended to indicate contempt for Jason, rather than praise of Aegeus. Nonetheless, Aegeus had a point. He was a king and he had kept his throne. Admittedly, the Athenians were so quarrelsome that it was relatively easy for Aegeus to ensure that no man came close to rivalling him. All the same, there had been challenges – challenges which Jason would have handled with far less tact than Aegeus.

Aegeus seemed to sense something of what I was thinking. He stretched out his hand towards me. "Come, Medea, you are a fine wife, has it not occurred to you that we should breed more sons? When I had no heir, my squabbling noblemen imagined themselves ruling Athens. The birth of Medes stopped that speculation, but something might happen to him. My throne will be still more secure if there are other fine boys to succeed me. Would you not like more?"

The Athenian king might have been tactful towards his

nobles, but the crass stupidity of that question hurt me more than a blow. I never talked of my golden boys to Aegeus, but only a blind man could have failed to notice how much time I spent praying by their tomb. How could anyone assume that I would betray them by spawning substitutes?

I suppose, in retrospect, Aegeus may have been trying to be kind. He may have even thought that my speech indicated growing love and respect on my part. In a way, I did respect him. I had grown up the daughter of a king and I could recognise good governance when I saw it. Aegeus ruled Athens well, and stability had brought trade and some wealth to a desiccated, infertile land. But if I respected Aegeus, I did not love him, nor did I seek to do so. How could I, if that meant replacing my splendid sons? In any case, I had not married for love. My reasons for wedlock were simple. I killed my golden boys. I sold my body to remain nearer to theirs.

So I rejected Aegeus's offer. I pretended that I did not notice his desire for my company. He slept with me, but no child grew in my womb. I remained barren and I was glad. But I was forced to be more aware of my surroundings and I observed how some of the nobles talked. One called Anarchos tried to make trouble. He whispered about foreigners who ensnared the king. He suggested that it was odd that Aegeus was seen emerging from my room, but that no children emerged from my loins. He even hinted that Medes was not Aegeus's son and that I intended to put my own foreign-sired brat on the throne.

It would have been easy to poison Anarchos, but that would have led to further unwelcome rumour. Nor had I any desire to kill his wife, even although striking her down in childbirth would have been a peculiarly appropriate revenge. Instead, I resorted to pestilence. Neighbours noticed how Anarchos's olive-trees withered and died, but not their own. His well seemed to be full of green scum, whilst theirs continued to provide sweet water. It was his wheat which grew rust-coloured as blight struck. His neighbours noticed all this and drew their own conclusions. Since Anarchos was clearly cursed, no-one wanted to speak to him. He was even shunned at one of the rural festivals and he dared not visit any in Athens itself. Everyone agreed that Aegeus acted most generously in lending Anarchos the money he needed to visit Delphi in order to free himself of whatever curse the gods had sent upon him. And when Anarchos returned five moons later, he was too busy trying to rebuild his ruined farm to have time for evil-minded gossip.

I do not know whether Aegeus realised what Anarchos had been saying or what action I had taken. However, he grew more distant from me at around this time. He still discussed the governing of Athens with me – perhaps because he knew that I, alone of his confidants, would not talk about his ideas to anyone else. Nonetheless, he made no attempt to repeat his seduction of me. Nor did he again express his desire to have more sons. By this point, the Athenians had learned that an oracle had foretold the birth of the king's longed-for son. Perhaps their awe regarding Medes's birth helped to make Aegeus less cautious about the need for more potential heirs.

For my part, I was not actively cruel towards Medes. I might shrink from his touch and the sounds of a child running might cause me to flinch as if felled by a blow, but memories of my own childhood showed me the dangers of a child growing up in an atmosphere of rejection and contempt. I could not provide Medes with love myself, nor had I any intention of betraying my sons by doing so, but I bought a slave-woman who doted upon him. I found him a good tutor. I told him that his father was proud of him. On the few times when Medes asked if I was, I merely replied that it was not correct for a mother to express pride. And that, certainly, was the truth. Perhaps if I had never articulated – even to myself – how wonderful my glorious boys were the gods might have spared me them.

XLVIII

Years passed. Life was not as secure in Athens. Aegeus no longer listened to my advice but surrounded himself with young men whose youth made him feel less old. He began to make mistakes in his diplomatic manoeuvres. There was a war with Crete and King Minos insisted on harsh peace terms. Since his long ships could strike across the seas almost without warning, Aegeus was forced to accept what Minos demanded, but the nobles were alarmed. Then ambassadors came from Corinth. Aegeus was relieved that the Corinthians still wished to be allies, but the Corinthian king had noticed Aegeus's diminished status and took advantage of the situation to drive a hard bargain. The news leaked out and more than just the nobles began to mutter.

The Corinthian ambassadors harmed me, too. They made no reference to my past, but their very presence reminded onlookers that Athens's queen had fled Corinth as a murderess. It was one thing to provide refuge graciously at a time of good-fortune, but now that the city was struggling, the people forgot that I had never sought Aegeus's hand. Instead, secret whispers hissed through the dark streets, murmuring that I had snared the king; that I wanted to rule a great city; that Aegeus's mistakes were the result of my interference, not an old man's loss of cunning. And as the talk spread, so too did the question as to whether Athens's current difficulties were attributable to my physical presence in the city's midst.

One night, Aegeus came to me.

"Medea, I do not like the things I hear. My advisors tell me that the city is full of rumours and suspicion. The people talk of the wrath of the gods and how it does not always strike immediately. They say that our violet-crowned city no longer smells sweet to the gods. They say that losing the war with Crete is only a beginning and that there is much worse to come." He paused. "I do not wish to ask you this, but I must. Are you free of pollution?"

I shrugged. There was no point pretending that I did not understand his words. "I carried out all the correct ritual ceremonies of purification before I reached Athens. If I had not done so, my sacrifices at my sons' tomb would have been in vain."

"Why won't the people believe that? Why don't they realise that the gods would have putrefied the sacrifices if you were unfit to touch them?" He sighed. "Things are much harder now than they used to be."

I felt sorry for Aegeus at that moment. He looked worn-out and old. If he had not been a king he would be spending most of his time by the fireside with his cronies, bragging about the glorious deeds of his youth, rather than dealing with delegations and war. I hesitated momentarily, before saying as gently as I could, "Can't Medes carry out some of your unimportant duties? I know he's far too inexperienced to talk to envoys, but he must know how to give ritual offerings to the gods."

"It would be inappropriate."

I watched Aegeus leave, wondering what he meant by that last remark. Perhaps the implication that he was no longer strong enough to carry out all of the many tasks of ruling a city made him feel Death stalking his tracks. Perhaps he felt that the Athenians would shudder at the thought of my offspring Medes officiating at an altar. Perhaps he even thought that himself – he certainly seemed to be spending less time with his son than he had before the rumours began to spread. As for myself, although I knew that I had been ritually purified, I was certainly not cleansed of guilt. I was as guilty as the day on which I crossed Athens's borders, and I would stay guilty until my last breath sighed its escape from my body.

XLIX

As a priestess, it would have been natural if I had turned to the birds to predict Aegeus's future. After all, Phrixus had trained me well in the signs of the eagle and the whirling movements of hawks. However, in Corinth I had lost my former ability. Sometimes I was able to interpret the signs correctly, but at other times I made mistakes and confused what I saw with what I hoped to see. I lost confidence and began to set myself tests, of which only I could be the judge. They confirmed the erratic nature of my interpretations and I knew that my skill was no longer reliable. I do not know if Artemis abandoned me on the night I slept with Jason or whether my ability was destroyed by the years I spent cooped up in Corinth, unable to track the wheeling eagles across the wide sweep of the sky. Whatever the cause, the result was the same. I could no longer trust any prediction I made. Perhaps that was why I knew how emasculated Aegeus felt as he sensed his own ability waver and wane.

Naturally, I had never told Aegeus – or anyone else – of what I had lost. If Athenians enjoyed frightening themselves about what their witch-queen could achieve, why should I reveal that I was weakened and more vulnerable? Regarding my current concern, I turned to more earthly powers of visual observation to see how the nobles behaved and whether I was correct that Aegeus was starting to shun his son. As for Medes, if he had noticed anything unusual, he must have been confused by the strange change in his circumstances – first his father began to neglect him and then his mother sought out his company.

Medes had reached that curious stage where at one moment he was a young man and the next he reverted to being still a youth. I found it strangely unnerving. I had never really considered how my own sons would have changed when they arrived at the cusp of manhood. Would a moment have transformed generous, joy-bearing Mermerus from being my adored child to an identical palimpsest of Jason as a young man? Had he all along been fated to grow up into a boorish, drunken oaf, all his youthful promise corroded and blackened? Would sensitive, loving Pheres have followed? I abhorred the picture, yet could not push it away until one day a stranger arrived at court.

He was taller than the other young men, lissom of limb and confident of manner. If he was not a nobleman's son, then he had unquestionably been brought up by someone of rank. I observed him and realised that my splendid Mermerus would have grown up to be such a youth. But my Mermerus would have been more handsome and more gentle. I turned my head aside to hide my grief. My Mermerus was fifteen years in the grave – longer than he had lived – and my Mermerus would never return to me. Nor would little Pheres, no less loved and grieved for every morning when the sun rose and every evening when the sun set. So it was with a sense of shocked outrage that I recognised the sword which this youth wore on his baldric. How had this stranger acquired a sword which Aegeus claimed he had dedicated to the gods years ago?

Odd pieces of gossip which I had ignored when I first arrived in Athens suddenly returned to me: there had been talk of a princess of Troezen, Aethra by name. I had not cared that she was deemed beautiful and that rumour claimed that Aegeus had visited her. Aegeus was a man; naturally he would go whoring around. But there had never been any mention of Aegeus having a son by this Aethra.

Then Aegeus himself appeared, full of courteous welcome for a visitor.

"Greetings, stranger. My men tell me that you have come from afar and have encountered dangers along the way."

"That is so, sire."

"Ah well, Athens will not object to your slaughtering bandits upon her territory. And it is no bad thing for a young man to prove himself. What do you call yourself?"

"Theseus, sire."

I stared at the unknown, wondering whether his mode of addressing Aegeus concealed a hint of his origins. 'Sire' might be more than a polite honorific; it might be literally true. Did I discern a copy of Aegeus around his eyes, could I trace Aegeus's contours about his chin? I wanted to be wrong, I prayed to Hera that I might be wrong, but I could not spurn the evidence of my own eyes. This youth had sprung from Aegeus's loins as clearly as the wax impression drops from the agate seal-stone. I was overwhelmed with anger so great that I thought that a wave of hornets had invaded the throne-room. Then I realised that it was the sound of fury coursing through my head. I had spent years grieving for my sons in the full knowledge that I should never see them this side of Acheron – and probably not even afterwards. And now Aegeus, who already had a kingdom, an admiring populace and a son, had suddenly been granted an additional son for whom he had never even grieved.

Ever since I had fled from Corinth I had worn a blue glass phial on a necklace around my neck. I found it a comfort to know that I could leave this world whenever I chose, but I had always resolved to remain in the upper world where I could ensure that proper sacrifices were performed at my sons' tomb. Now I took the phial and, almost without thinking, I poured the contents into a goblet of wine and handed it to the unknown.

"Drink this, Theseus, and be welcome."

Theseus bowed low towards me, causing his sword to come into Aegeus' view. Then he lifted his hand to drain the chalice. Aegeus must have seen something stamped upon my face because he knocked the goblet out of his son's hand. "No! Don't touch it!"

The boy handled things surprisingly well. He bowed to his father. "I am grateful for your warning, sire, but my mother, Aethra, always said that you would treat me well."

"Aethra? By Zeus, I had almost given up waiting for her to send you. Are you truly Aethra's child?"

"Indeed, Father. Do you not recognise your own sword?"

I left them to their fawning reunion. Being men, both of them apparently saw no difficulty in ignoring Aegeus's utter neglect of the previous fifteen or sixteen years. It was enough that they were father and son.

What followed was very unjust. I could accept Aegeus's pronunciation of banishment against me, even although I had acted almost unthinkingly. However, to blame Medes for my actions was excessively unfair. Unless Aegeus was quite blind he could hardly have failed to observe that I had never been devoted to Medes, so why would I have risked my position on Medes's behalf? Or perhaps Aegeus had no understanding of what maternal love might encompass. Such words may sound odd coming from me, a killer who, by her own admission, had not even tried to form a bond with Medes. Nevertheless, I *had* adored my children and I knew that Medes had never been granted one hundredth of what my golden boys had received. Furthermore, although I was of little use to Medes, Aegeus's own behaviour struck me as callous and unkind – Aegeus had hoped for a son to appear, but he had never even warned Medes that there might be another sibling lurking in the vicinity of Troezen. No-one had warned me of the existence of Chalciope, but I had not been raised as an adored only child. Medes had. Hence when Medes appeared at my chamber, bewildered and confused, to explain that he was being expelled from Athens on the grounds of having plotted against his half-brother, I found it hard not to feel pity for him. I did not love him – I never could – but I pay my debts.

I had one bitter, brief confrontation with Aegeus when he accused me of seeking to rule through Medes. "You've always wanted to rule, haven't you, Medea?"

"And you are afraid of not ruling. You are afraid of the Athenians. You hear them say that you are too old and you know it's true. You fear that they'll drive you out. If you were young and vigorous you would challenge them. But you're old and afraid, so you've driven your own son out in favour of a youth you know nothing about."

"I know Theseus's parentage – and I know Medes's parentage."

"Insult me as much as you like. It doesn't hide the truth. You have sacrificed your son in the hope of distracting your critics."

"Don't talk to me of sacrifices. That's what you wanted Medes to start on, wasn't it? A few sacrifices before the gods – and then a swift sacrifice of me."

"You fool. That idea was motivated by pity, not a plot."

"Pity? What do you know of pity?"

"Enough to pity an old, sick man who is too tired to rule."

"But not enough to spare your own children. Your blood is poisoned, and Medes bears that poisoned blood. You killed your sons, Medea. I do not intend to let Medes kill me."

L

Since Aegeus had ordered that Medes and I leave Athens by sunset, there was very little time. I left Medes in his chambers, helplessly trying to select what he would need for a lifetime in exile. I was rather more accustomed to fleeing from a city, so I concentrated not on what I could take, but on what I could not take. I had left Corinth carrying the bodies of my sons. Now they lay in Athenian earth; held tight by Athenian soil. And since I was to be banished forever from Athenian land, this was the closest that I would be to their bodies for the rest of eternity. So I left my rings and my diadems, my vials and my potions, my silks and my gauzes. I abandoned them all for another few moments next to my dead boys.

The priestess who guarded the path to their shrine recognised me immediately. As she stepped to one side to give me greater privacy, I saw her eyes widen as she took in the retinue of armed guards which accompanied me. I rarely came in state to my sons' grave and there was a curious tension about the men which must have revealed that all was not well. Nor was it usual for my escort to fan out, clearly ready to prevent any hopeless attempt to evade their clutches. I did not care. There would soon be wild rumours spreading throughout Attica – what did it matter what anyone thought tonight?

I had only the smallest of sacrifices to offer – a jug of wine hastily snatched up as I left the palace. However, I poured it out with all the ceremony which I could command. Tugging out my golden earrings, I thrust them into the fire which flickered and fought against the sable night. Then, after reciting prayers of intercession to the gods, I spoke directly to my dead children.

"My golden boys, my splendid sons, only you know

how much I grieve for you, only you know how much I love you. This is where I laid you to rest, and this is where I raised a shrine to you. I asked the gentle earth to rest kindly on you and it has done so. This place is sanctified by your presence and the gods know that you sleep here. They have been generous; they have allowed me to visit you here so very often. But now the time has come when I am no longer allowed to visit you. I have been ordered to leave Athens. And so I must leave you forever. I can never speak at your grave again. I can never wrap my arms around your tomb again. You will never hear my voice whispering through the heavy coverings of your endless rest."

I paused, wondering whether I had imagined a tremor in the earth. Was Mermerus still trying to comfort me from beyond the grave? Was Pheres trying to reach out for me? I shook myself. I was not here to seek comfort, but to try to explain.

"My presence has been forbidden and I must go into exile. But even although I cannot take you with me, I shall still grieve for you every day, just as I have done since the day you died. No mother could have had such glorious boys; no mother could grieve more than I do."

I heard a rattling of weapons behind me. The guards were growing impatient but there was still so much to say.

"Even if I had a lifetime to tell you how much I loved you it would still not be enough. So do not think that my departure means that I no longer weep for you. Oh my boys, I wanted to save you; I wanted you to live; I wanted so desperately much to set you free. I miss you so desperately. And now I shall lose touch with even your grave. Mermerus, Pheres, your mama loves you. Never forget that; mama loves you."

I was still murmuring all the pet names I had ever called them when the guard touched my wrist. I protested, but he was inexorable. I retreated, begging the gods to take care of the grave. As I left the sacred enclosure, I caught sight of the priestess. I sent a final plea through the night to her. "Honour them; remember them; keep their memory alive." Then, as the guards placed me on a horse and we began to jolt down the track away from the sanctuary, I cried out once into the Stygian gloom – not a ritual ululation, but a howl of unendurable grief that now I had lost everything.

Epilogue

So we returned to Colchis. There was no other place where Medes might gain a welcome and I no longer cared what Aeetes might do to me – I had not done so since my sons died. As it was, Aeetes greeted me with guarded hostility.

"Well, my daughter, you now know what it is like to lose a child."

My hands twitched. "That is so."

"Do you bring me a grandson to replace Apsyrtus?"

"No child can replace a dead one."

"Then if he cannot replace Apsyrtus, perhaps I ought to kill him to exact repayment."

"You would do better to kill me."

"But you have skills in sorcery, Medea."

"I sometimes wish I had not."

Aeetes made no response to that, but began to bargain with me. He had been deposed by his brother Perses years earlier and he knew that only supernatural powers could help to restore him to his throne. "Your son can also help me; he is strong and well-trained in arms."

"What about Chalciope's sons?" I asked cautiously. I had been somewhat surprised to learn that she was living with my father, and I was unsure what had happened to her children.

"They're in Greece," responded Aeetes abruptly, "they're half-Greek, after all."

"And you had their Greek father killed," I retorted, remembering gentle Phrixus and how he had suffered at Aeetes's hands.

"Which is why I prefer his sons on the other side of the sea." He shrugged. "I was wrong about that oracle. I thought the stranger who would deprive me of my throne was Phrixus. It was Jason. I wish I had slain him on the spot."

I found it hard not to agree, but if Jason had died in Colchis, I would never have had my sons.

"Fleece, son, throne – and daughter – all lost because of Jason." Aeetes glared at me, "I could kill you now with great pleasure. Your blood, after all, would make a suitable sacrifice to my son."

I bowed my head in agreement.

"I would kill you even if that meant that I never regained my throne." There was a long pause as Aeetes seemed to dream vengeful thoughts. "However, the news slowly trickled back from Greece that it was Jason who murdered Apsyrtus. Chalciope persuaded me that it would be wrong to kill you if you ever returned. I have sworn not to. So you are safe, my treacherous daughter."

It seemed unlike the Aeetes of old to be revealing his intentions in this way. I briefly wondered whether he had calculated that I might kill him and put Medes on the throne of Colchis if I felt threatened. "That was generous of Chalciope," I murmured, waiting for my father's next move.

Aeetes suddenly rose to his feet and stalked out of the room. On the threshold, he turned. "She said that I owed her a life."

He strode off, leaving me to ponder Chalciope's remark. Why had she asked for me to be spared when I could be blamed for so much? And why had she not plotted to kill Aeetes to avenge her husband? Had she not loved Phrixus enough? Was she too weak, despite her four sons? Or was she simply weary of killing?

I was weary of killing, too.

I had no real interest in whether Aeetes or his brother Perses ruled Colchis, but if Aeetes owed Chalciope a life for Phrixus's death, what did I owe Aeetes for Apsyrtus's?

Moreover, I wished to pay what I owed to Medes. So when Aeetes asked me to concoct the necessary poisons to destroy Perses I did so. Aeetes was grateful, and would have named Medes as his successor. However, Medes wanted to carve out a greater territory of his own – perhaps he had more of Aegeus in him than he thought. So Aegeus's son left towards the lands east of Colchis, whilst I resumed my nomadic wanderings until I reached a shrine on the borders of Athenian territory.

I know that I can never return to Athens, but I have come as close as possible. My offerings are smaller than I could make in Colchis, but I am closer to my sons. My words would not reach across the sea from Colchis, but perhaps they hear my voice whispering through the night to them. Perhaps my libations of blood-red wine may reach them by hidden ways through the earth. Perhaps.

I know that the world traduces me, but I am so very tired now that I wonder whether what the world thinks matters any more. Sometimes, when I am particularly weary, I even wonder whether I threw myself into the arms of calumny and detestation upon a false calculation. Mermerus was growing up. Might I have gazed into his eyes one day and seen, not the amber eyes of love, but Jason's eyes – contemptuous, arrogant and cruel? Then I remind myself that Mermerus made me laugh, that he brought me so much joy. He died at my hands, but he died my perfect son, my gorgeous, gorgeous boy. Nor can I believe that sensitive, vulnerable Pheres could ever have grown into a boor and a lout. The sole miscalculation which matters is that I attempted to keep my sworn bargain even when Jason broke his. Had I escaped earlier I could have given my adored sons the love which I promised them – not just one golden summer in Athens for my golden boys, but love for all time until I died.

The hardest part of exile is to be cut off from my sons'

tomb. If I thought that the gods would listen, I might pray to be allowed to return to tend the site. I fear that it is uncared for now – grass must straggle across it, while herbs riot in flower and mice plunder the seed of summer. Lizards will freeze motionless beneath the sun, taking cover from the tortoises which lumber and spell out the thoughts of the gods. Even the circling eagles, the very sentinels of Zeus himself, may no longer know that beneath that low mound sleep two perfect boys, cut off before they could prove to the world their generosity and love.

But why should the gods pity me? My plight would be pitiful if I were pitiable. I am not. I am culpable. I destroyed my perfect family. I was the killer of my innocents. And my punishment is that no-one believes that I adored them. So every day I torment myself with questions. Did they know that I worshipped them beyond the regions of the Styx and back? Did I fail to see the truth too late? Did I act too late? Would I have acted differently if my daughter had lived? Was I totally at fault?

Was I?

finis

22879358R00201

Printed in Great Britain
by Amazon